The
RED HAND ADVENTURES

PRAISE
for the
RED HAND ADVENTURES

"O'Neill has an eye for detail, atmosphere, and action...this is a rousing period piece."
—*Publishers Weekly*

"Whether intended for a YA or adult audience, this is a book the entire family can enjoy reading...The book reads like a Boy's Own adventure and is filled with action involving bandits, pirates and rebels, reminding the reader of such grand entertainments as Rudyard Kipling's *Kim*, Michael Chabon's *Gentlemen of the Road* and John Milius' *The Wind and the Lion*...Four Stars."
—*Kenneth Salikof for IndieReader*

"Debut author O'Neill incorporates a great deal of cultural and historical context in his story...and will make the readers feel as though they have traveled back in time and fallen into that world. An exciting, exotic tale...The cliffhanger ending all but demands that readers jump to the next installment of the series."
—*Kirkus Reviews*

"Block out the next few hours, because you won't want to put this book down!"
—*Kevin Max, Founder and Editor, 1859 Oregon's Magazine*

MORE PRAISE
for the
RED HAND ADVENTURES

Selected for School and Library Battle of the Books Contests
around the country
(Rebels of the Kasbah)

Selected for the National Battle of the Books Contest
(Rebels of the Kasbah)

Selected as a *Publisher's Weekly* indie select book
(Rebels of the Kasbah)

Silver Medal Winner for the Mom's Choice Award
(Rebels of the Kasbah)

Bronze Medal Winner for Best Book Series—Fiction
in the Moonbeam Children's Book Awards
(Red Hand Adventures)

Gold Medal Winner of the Independent
Book Publisher's Living Now Award
(Wrath of the Caid)

— WORD ON THE STREET —

For **Rebels of the Kasbah**

KCamp (Denver, CO USA): Great to have for *Battle of the Books*.

Eva Jones (Age: 11 Grade: 5): *Rebels of the Kasbah* is an amazing novel. It is spun together with foreign elements, gore, trickery, and leadership. One excellent aspect is the personality you get from each character. The description he gives is impeccable—it feels like you're standing right there in the scene. I don't know how Joe O'Neill did it, but he did!

Xander ForeverBookish (Top Middle Reader Book Review Blog rated it 5 of 5 stars): AMAZING! You NEED to read this!

Books on the Edge (Middle Reader Review): It reminds one of the classics like *Treasure Island, Oliver Twist*, and *Aladdin* while written in a language suitable for young readers of today. Yup it's one of those books that you hope your son or daughter would read and find heroes among its pages....and who couldn't use a well written hero or two?

Reviewed by Kenneth Salikof for IndieReader: ...reads like a Boy's Own adventure and is filled with bandits, pirates and rebels, reminding the reader of such grand entertainments as Rudyard Kipling's *Kim*, Michael Chabon's *Gentlemen of the Road* and John Milius' *The Wind and the Lion*.

Dr. Jean Lowery, CEO *Battle of the Books*: "When I sat down to begin reading *Rebels of the Kasbah*, I couldn't turn the pages fast enough until I reached the last page and said—NOOOOO, I need to know what happens next! "

Franny: I could feel the sand stinging my face, this story is so descriptive, and so creatively told by the author. *Rebels* was heartwarming, exciting and inspiring. I can hardly wait for the sequel!

Heather P (M.Ed.-Reading & Language Arts-Former Classroom Teacher-Book Lover!): Hands down a great book for middle school readers, all the way to adults!

This Kid Reviews Books (Top Middle Reader Review Blog): O'Neill writes a captivating story that kept me on the edge of my seat! I couldn't put down! The characters are believable and...have a unique personality.

— WORD ON THE STREET —

For **Wrath of the Caid**

Margaret rated it 4 of 5 stars on Good Reads: The kids at Remann Hall Book Club truly love this series. They no sooner finish one book, than they want the next one. I love the maps, the sense of adventure in far-away places, and the longing the stories create for the reader to know more.

Marie rated it 5 of 5 stars on Good Reads: I was so excited to finally read this book! It picked up right where *Rebels of the Kasbah* left off and just amazed me again. I liked the fast-paced action of this story and how it takes you all over the world and back again! There were some good humorous parts that made me laugh, some scary scenarios that made my heart race, and an ending that once again makes me NEED the next book! I highly recommend *Wrath of the Caid* to any adventurous young reader.

I Be Readin: Can we get up and cheer for this one? This novel reminds me of the famous series written by J. K. Rowling. No...there are no wizards or broomsticks, but the battle of good versus evil continues in O'Neill's writing and you can't help but get caught up in this story, and would totally adapt to big screen.

For **Legends of the Rif**

Kumara rated it 4 of 5 stars on Good Reads: "It is exciting from start to finish reminding me a lot of the *Boys Own* adventure story's I read when I was a lot younger. ...it's impossible not to cheer on the good guys as the bad guys get their comeuppance in these scenes. Each time this happened it left a smile on my face as we have been through a lot with these characters over three books."

C. Anderson- (Middle School Teacher, Portland OR): As a teacher, I recognize how this series is a major draw for reluctant readers...my favorite element of this installment is the increasing sense of morality discussed in the book through narration, character dialogue and character action. Thank you Joe O'Neill for this adventure!

Black Ship

PUBLISHING

Adventure Novels with a Shot of Wry

EX LIBRIS

The
RED HAND ADVENTURES

BOOK III

Legends of the Rif

JOE O'NEILL

Legends of the Rif

COPYRIGHT © 2014 BY JOE O'NEILL
Art Direction by Kristin Myrdahl
Graphic Design by Anna Fonnier
Composition by Margaret Copeland/Terragrafix
Illustrated by Lamont Russ
India and Ceylon Maps by Allison Kim
Wanted Poster by Josh Espinosa
Edited by Sara Addicott
Copyedited by Bedelia Walton
www.redhandadventures.com

Black Ship

PUBLISHING

ISBN 978-0-9851969-8-1

For Mahinda and Yolande Athulathmudali
who have shown me the wonders of their Ceylon.

SPECIAL THANKS

I'd like to thank all the people at Perseus/PGW/Legato for their
support and belief in the Red Hand Adventures. It's a pleasure to work
with so many people who are relentlessly passionate
about the written word.

And, of course, I am grateful for the talented people on our Red Hand
Team who make all of this possible. You know who you are, thank you!

Last, but not least, a bow to Lamont Russ, who labored endlessly to create
the outstanding character illustrations for the Red Hand Adventures.

I hope you enjoy Legends of the Rif.

— Joe O'Neill

TABLE OF CONTENTS

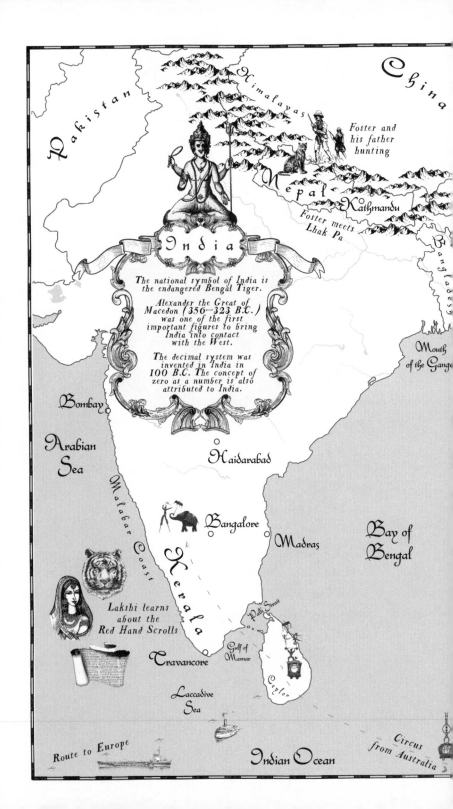

Pakistan

Himalayas

China

Foster and
his father
hunting

Nepal · Kathmandu

Foster meets
Lhak Pa

Bangladesh

Mouth
of the Ganges

India

The national symbol of India is
the endangered Bengal Tiger.

Alexander the Great of
Macedon (356–323 B.C.)
was one of the first
important figures to bring
India into contact
with the West.

The decimal system was
invented in India in
100 B.C. The concept of
zero as a number is also
attributed to India.

Bombay

Arabian
Sea

Malabar Coast

Haidarabad

Bangalore

Madras

Bay of
Bengal

Kerala

Lakshi learns
about the
Red Hand Scrolls

Travancore

Palk Strait

Gulf of
Mannar

Ceylon

Laccadive
Sea

Route to Europe

Indian Ocean

Circus
from Australia

Please note: We strongly suggest first reading *Rebels of the Kasbah* and then *Wrath of the Caid* before reading *Legends of the Rif* because the Red Hand Adventures books are meant to be read in chronological order. Each book has several plot points, character introductions, and events that can be fully understood and enjoyed only by having read the entire series in order.

CHARACTERS RETURNING FROM *REBELS OF THE KASBAH* AND *WRATH OF THE CAID*

Tariq (tah-reek): An orphan; kidnapped and sold to Caid Ali Tamzali to race in deadly camel races

Fez: A friend of Tariq's; fellow slave to the tyrant Caid Ali Tamzali

Aseem (ah-seem): A friend to Fez and Tariq; fellow slave to Caid Ali Tamzali

Margaret Owen: An English girl; kidnapped and sold to Caid Ali Tamzali

Aji (ah-jee): Tariq's best friend on the streets of Tangier; killed by a street thug named Mohammad

Sanaa (sah-nah): A beautiful Moroccan assassin; part of the resistance, instrumental in prison escape

Malik (ma-leek): A respected tribal leader; part of the resistance

Zijuan (zee-wan): A gifted Chinese woman and sage martial artist; rescued Tariq from streets of Tangier

Jawad (juh-wad): A slave and camel jockey; betrayed Tariq, Fez, and Aseem

Charles Owen: A decorated colonel in the British army; kidnapped by pirate crew; father to Margaret and David

Louise Owen: A devoted wife to Charles; mother to Margaret and David

Captain Basil: An Algerian pirate captain; kidnapped Charles Owen

Lieutenant Dreyfuss: A corrupt lieutenant in the British navy; tried to kill Charles Owen

Caid Ali Tamzali: An evil warlord; feared ruler of the Rif Mountains

Note: For definition in this series, a Caid (k+aid) is a warlord in Morocco who answers only to the Sultan, the sovereign ruler of Morocco. He controls his own territory, but pays taxes and owes all allegiance to the Sultan. However, a more common definition of a Caid is a Muslim or Berber chieftain, who may be a tribal chief, judge, or senior officer.

The Black Mamba: The most ruthless assassin in Morocco; a loyal servant to Caid Ali Tamzali

Melbourne Jack: An Aboriginal adventurer trained by Foster Crowe in Australia; searching for the diary of Alexander the Great

Foster Crowe: A master of the Red Hand. He runs a circus that travels across the world which is actually a training ground for agents of the Red Hand.

Amanda: A teenage girl; takes care of young Melbourne Jack in the circus

Cortez/Sharif Al Montaro: A notorious bounty hunter; hunts Charles Owen and Captain Basil

Matthew Hatrider: An army friend of Charles Owen's; offers to help Louise find Charles

Alice Fitzgerald: A new friend of Margaret's from Ireland

Henri (ahn-ree): A revolutionary and anarchist; rebel to the French government and loyal to Napoleon Bonaparte

Timin: A former betting parlor boss, imprisoned and left homeless; friend of street boys

Sister Anne: Head of St. Catherine's School in the south of France

The French Students: Sophie, Etienne and Inez; roommates of Margaret's at St. Catherine's

CHARACTERS INTRODUCED IN
LEGENDS OF THE RIF

Raja the Seer: Fortune teller in Foster Crowe's circus

Roy Ferguson: An untrustworthy admiral in the British Royal Navy

Lionel Hedgecock: President of the Far Indian Trading Company

Tuareg: A well-known and respected band of nomadic people

Moussa Ag Arshaman: Renowned leader of the Tuareg people

Abdul Maheida: A sergeant in the Caid's army

Wu-Chiang: A suspicious character hiding in the jungles of Ceylon

Azmiya (az-mee-uh): A girl in Chaouen living with an evil uncle

PREVIOUSLY IN THE
RED HAND ADVENTURES

Morocco. 1912. In Book I, *Rebels of the Kasbah*, Tariq, Fez, and Aseem are three young boys kidnapped and sold into the Kasbah of Caid of Ali Tamzali to race in deadly camel races. Along with Margaret, an English girl who was also kidnapped and sold into the harem of Caid Ali Tamzali, they plan a daring escape with the help of an undercover assassin named Sanaa, who was notified to help Tariq by his guardian—the venerable sage Zijuan.

Following their successful escape, the kids join a resistance tribe in the Rif Mountains led by an honorable leader named Malik. After gaining valuable information on the kasbah's vulnerabilities, Malik and his warriors stage a daring attack on Caid Ali Tamzali and his kasbah.

Meanwhile, Margaret's father, Charles, is kidnapped by a pirate named Captain Basil and joins forces with him when he learns a corrupt British Lieutenant named Dreyfuss is attacking helpless African fishing boats and villages.

In Book II, *Wrath of the Caid*, the Caid unleashes a man named The Black Mamba to find and kill, Tariq, Aseem, and Fez, and destroy the resistance tribe. Margaret is sent to live in England, as it's no longer safe for her in Morocco. In England, she gets in a bit of trouble and is quickly sent to Saint Catherine's boarding school outside of Marseilles, France where she befriends some French school girls. Lieutenant Dreyfuss sends a spy by the name of Sharif Al Montaro to capture Captain Basil and Charles Owen. Tariq, separated from his friends, meets an Aborigine named Melbourne Jack who begins to explain the secrets of the Red Hand and the exploits of his mentor—Foster Crowe.

Legends of the Rif

CHAPTER
— *I* —

SO IT BEGINS

S hiva the wolf walked on the mountain trail just prior to sunrise. The weather was cold and her paws felt stiff against the hard rock. She could see her breath in the air and quickened to a light jog to warm her body. It was best hunting early in the morning, when it was dark, as that is when the critters came out to feed and drink. She'd had some luck lately on this particular ridge, killing three rabbits and four squirrels in just two days. She had four cubs to feed and hunting was a constant chore. She had hoped to get something bigger today, perhaps a small deer, so she could rest for a couple of days.

Her cubs were nestled in her den, fast asleep, and understood to stay hidden until their mother returned to guard them.

As she walked along the mountain path, she thought she saw a deer off in the distance. She would have to be very careful, as a deer could out-run her and she might only get one chance for a kill in a surprise sneak attack. She would have to position herself perfectly.

Lowering her back, she slowed her gait to see if it was a deer and, if so, if there was an advantage she could gain.

That's when it happened.

She'd been so busy surveying the horizon that she neglected to look at the ground in front of her. There was a steel trap covered with twigs to hide its presence. She'd seen similar traps in the past and had always managed to negotiate and avoid them.

Not this time.

Her right hind leg stepped right on the trap spring, causing it to snap shut right on the leg.

Letting out a loud "yelp," she jumped up, causing the trap to come off the ground.

It was chained in place!

She continued to yelp and cry and tried to pull her leg out, which dug in the teeth of the trap deeper into her skin.

After the initial shock, the pain was excruciating. Blood dripped from her leg where the steel teeth of the trap dug into her flesh. Licking the blood, it started to throb and hurt even more.

She whined and yelped and paced with worry.

Without her protection, her cubs would either starve or become prey to the many predators in the mountains.

Without her, her family would die.

Lying down, she felt the weight of the situation on her shoulders. She was trapped and would most certainly be killed by the humans. She had seen it before. Other wolves lying dead in the desert sand, their tongues hanging from their mouths—killed for their fur and left to die in the dust and sand to be eaten by the vultures.

She whimpered and cried in despair. All she wanted was to be free and to care for her cubs.

For hours she lay in the sand, gently licking her wound, trying to figure a way out.

There was none.

Her tongue became heavy with thirst and she panted vigorously.

In the distance, she thought she heard men's voices. Undoubtedly they were checking their traps and would soon find her.

Whimpering even more, Shiva bit at the trap to no avail.

She then smelled something. It was a human smell, but not as pungent as usual.

Looking up, she saw a small human—a cub. A boy.

Immediately, she growled, showing her teeth to let this human know she would not go down without a fight.

Yet the boy did nothing. He simply stared at her.

He was small by human standards, with brown hair that hung over his eyes and a soft look about his face.

She snapped her teeth more, yet the child did not move.

This confused her.

After a few moments, she stopped growling and lay in the sand, not understanding the intentions of this person.

With no other choice, she began whimpering and whining in an effort to show the boy that she was trapped and in pain. She licked her leg where the trap had set its teeth into her.

The boy edged a little closer, staring at the trap, and then at Shiva. Shiva could see the boy was scared of her, so she made every effort to let him know she would not bite or attack him.

Continuing to whimper and cry, she was hoping he would understand her.

The boy, still watching her, moved close enough so that she could attack him.

She did not.

She smiled to let him know it was safe.

With trembling fingers, the boy kept an eye on Shiva as he put his hands on the trap.

Shiva smiled even more. She gently licked the boy's hands to let him know he was safe. Finally feeling secure, the boy began to try to open the trap, but it was closed very tightly.

Shiva, seeing that he was trying to help her, tried her best to bite the trap and lick his hands, urging him on.

In the distance, the men's voices grew louder.

Shiva began to panic and whimper and whine.

The boy, using all his strength, gripped the trap on either side and managed to move the teeth apart.

Grimacing and struggling, his muscles fatigued, the boy edged open the trap until it was eventually wide enough for Shiva to pull her leg out.

She let out a little yelp and then ran off, trying to put as much distance as possible between her and the hunters. Her leg was injured, but it was not broken. Miraculously, the teeth had not shattered her bone or ripped any tendons. The muscle was torn but would heal quickly.

Running off, she forgot to thank the boy. All she could think of was her cubs and their safety. She purposely ran through a nearby river to throw off her scent and the blood trail. She doubled back several times until she was absolutely sure she had not been followed.

That night, she made it safely back to her cubs. They ran to her, licking her face and barking with delight. Seeing that their mother's leg was injured, the cubs licked her wound and slept safely next to her, grateful to have their mother safe in their den.

Shiva never forgot that boy. She never forgot that humans were not all killers.

Charles Owen lay in the filth and stench of the cage. He'd been shackled for almost a week with barely enough food and water to survive. Basil lay chained next to him and some other crewmembers sat across from them. They had been branded as pirates and sentenced to die without judge or jury. In the morning, they would be marched out in front of an immense crowd and hung for all to see. Charles had become despondent knowing that his life was about to end in this cage. He had tried to explain his circumstances to the French authorities, but they simply laughed at him. Nobody would believe he was a colonel in the British army.

"So, I guess this is it?" he said to Basil, who smiled.

"I suppose so, Charles. It's been a heck of a life. It has been a pleasure to fight beside you. Not many men would have sacrificed their career and their country for a cause they knew to be true and honest. I can never thank you enough," Basil replied, his voice filled with sadness and remorse.

Some of the men had written farewell notes in a faint hope that somebody might deliver them to their families. Charles knew that his death would be an anonymous one—his family left to wonder what had become of him. This gnawed at him more than anything else—that his family would never know the truth of his circumstances.

He would die a broken and dejected man.

Hanging his head, he wanted to cry, but thought better of it. He didn't want to show weakness in front of the other men.

Now, all he could do was count the hours until the sun rose and he was marched to the noose like a fat cow to the abattoir.

Staring at the cement floor, he thought of his beloved Louise and he longed to see her face one last time. Deep in a trance, he was startled by a voice coming from outside the cage.

It was a whisper, a faint whisper, but it was unmistakable.

"Father, pssst! Father, are you awake? I've come to rescue you."

Charles looked up as if being touched by an angel. Could this possibly be true? Could, against miracles of all miracles, this really be true?

The voice was that of his daughter.

———————— ✦ ————————

Tariq was going to attempt something very tricky.

He was going to try to fool the Caid's soldiers, who were frantically chasing him and Melbourne Jack.

Trapped on a cliff, with Jack unconscious next to him, and the rope of their hot air balloon about six feet away, Tariq knew if he could just reach the rope, he could probably float away to safety. However, that would mean leaving Melbourne Jack, and Tariq had no idea how to captain the balloon. Odds were that he might simply end up crashing to his death.

They found themselves in this predicament after Jack had rescued Tariq from the Caid's troops—only to crash into a mountainside when their hot air balloon couldn't climb fast enough.

It was dusk and the cliff they were stranded on was covered in shadows. He didn't know if the guards could see him or Jack. The guards were on horseback about two hundred feet below and some of them were riding around in a flank attempt. Still, he thought he and Melbourne Jack might be hidden from their sight.

He had an idea on how to distract the guards.

He took off Jack's jacket, pants and belt, and did his best job to make a lifelike dummy, which resembled a scarecrow. Then, staying in the shadows, he began to gingerly scale the face of the cliff. It was a straight drop down and he would surely die if he fell.

The dummy was tied to his waist like a kind of knapsack.

He wanted to be seen.

The face of the cliff provided some footholds to place his toes and there was enough grass to grab ahold of to hold his weight. He flattened his entire body next to the cliff, and he could feel his heartbeat pounding in his chest. He wasn't just scared—he was petrified! It was very precarious hanging from a cliff in the dark, and once he almost fell because he thought some grass would hold him, but it came loose and he was forced to scramble and find another hold.

"You see, they are trying to escape!" a guard yelled from below.

The other guards started yelling as well and pointing in the direction of Tariq and his dummy.

So far, his plan was working to perfection.

Reaching the hot air balloon rope, which was snagged on a branch, he carefully moved into a shadow and out of sight of the guards. With the darkness and distance, they wouldn't have a great view of him and would simply see some movements in the shadows.

Fastening the rope to the dummy, Tariq secured the rope as best he could and tried to make it as human-like as possible. Satisfied the dummy wouldn't come loose, he took his knife and sawed off the branch that held the balloon.

The branch snapped off and the balloon slowly sailed away with the dummy in tow.

That's when Tariq saw it, if only briefly, in the reflection of the moon.

An unmistakable handprint, painted in red, on the face of the cliff.

Quickly, Tariq stepped back into the shadows and out of eyesight, either from above or below.

"They are making their escape! The balloon is flying away!" he heard a guard yell.

There was much commotion and he heard the hooves of the guards' horses follow the balloon.

There was still the matter of the guards searching above him.

With the top of the cliff about twenty feet above Tariq's position, the guards wouldn't have a very good view downward, but he made sure he stayed in the shadows anyway.

After about five minutes, he heard voices above and footsteps going across the cliff. They were obviously looking for the two of them, but not finding anything.

He couldn't make out the guards' voices above the howling wind at the top of the cliff. Keeping hidden, he saw them light a torch as they searched down the cliff, but the torch wouldn't provide much light against the wind. They tried throwing a torch in the hope it would land on the ledge, but it fell harmlessly below, shining like a falling star until it hit the ground.

After a few more moments, the footsteps and voices above them had stopped.

The guards had given up and would probably join their comrades down below.

He and Melbourne Jack were safe.

For the moment.

It had been two years since Shiva the wolf had been saved by that boy. She never saw him again. Her cubs were now full-grown and together they ruled this area of the mountains.

Up early, she was hunting as usual and getting a quick start to the day. She decided to venture out into the desert to search for food. She enjoyed the open space of the desert in the early morning.

Walking slowly, she noticed the unmistakable smell of humans. The scent was far off, perhaps one hundred yards downwind. Normally, she would run in the opposite direction to avoid any direct contact with the humans.

This scent was different.

This scent was the smell of pure fear.

Curious, she crawled up to a ridge to peek into the beyond. A sixth sense told her to investigate this smell.

She saw the most peculiar sight.

There were humans, but only their heads!

How could this be?

Studying the scene for a few moments, she gingerly crawled to a patch of sagebrush about twenty feet in front of her. Camouflaged by the brush, she wanted to get a better view of these humans and ensure this wasn't a trap.

It was true! There were two humans, but only their heads were visible.

After twenty minutes, with no other humans in sight, she decided to investigate further.

Walking from behind the sagebrush, she allowed the two humans to see her for the first time.

Immediately, the two started to scream and yell at her and she retreated a bit. They continued to yell and shout at her, but the tone of their voices was different.

She could hear their fear.

"Go away wolf, go!" Malik yelled.

"HAAAAAA!" Sanaa screamed.

They had been buried for almost two hours and the sun had come up from behind the mountain range. In another ten minutes, the sun would be high enough to start burning their eyes—which had been brutally stitched open by the Black Mamba. Only an hour of direct sunlight could blind them forever.

Sanaa started to cry as she continued to yell at the wolf.

Malik screamed as loud and long as he could.

Yet the wolf would not go away. It stayed in front of them, pacing back and forth.

Sanaa studied the wolf. It didn't seem to want to attack them.

It simply seemed intrigued by their situation.

Continuing to cry, Sanaa felt all the emotion inside of her that had been walled away for years and years. She had proclaimed her love for

Malik, and he had proclaimed his love for her. After all this wasted time over a silly competition did they finally trust one another. Finally, she could be with the man she loved, only to die and rot in the desert by his side.

She did not want to die.

Forcing herself to stop crying, she did something that even surprised Malik.

She begged the wolf.

"Please, please help us. I know you cannot understand us, but we need your help," Sanaa pleaded, her voice full of hurt.

All those years ago, Shiva had sounded the same as she begged that young boy for help.

This was a sound a mother could understand.

Perhaps this human had her own cubs to save?

Shiva remembered the boy and how he had risked himself to save her. How he had helped her, even though it meant he had come close enough to be attacked. She stared at these humans—they didn't seem to want to hurt her. They appeared to be trapped and very, very scared.

After a few moments, she decided to act.

Walking slowly forward, she went to Sanaa and did something that amazed both Sanaa and Malik.

She started to dig.

CHAPTER
— 2 —

SCATTERED

OUTSKIRTS OF THE RIF MOUNTAINS. MOROCCO. 1914

Zijuan was dressed completely in black. A large walking stick made of oak rested in her right hand. The stick was almost six and a half feet in length. To the outsider it looked like a walking stick, but to the more initiated, it was something far different.

It was a weapon.

For two days, she had walked along mountain roads at a brisk pace, barely stopping to eat or sleep or drink water. She'd received word on the whereabouts of a certain gypsy witch who was somehow involved with Tariq and the clan. She understood the gypsies were forever on the move and might not be in any one place for long.

After walking over a hill and around a bend, Zijuan came upon the gypsy caravan of tents and wagons. The caravan was nestled around an oasis of trees and water, and the villagers performed their chores and played games in the safety of their clan.

When they saw Zijuan walking towards them, the women screamed and dragged their children into the confines of their tents. A posse of men came out to meet Zijuan. Some held knives, and all were wary of the outsider.

The leader, a large man with a bushy beard and a red silk shirt unbuttoned to his mid-section, spoke to her.

"What brings you to our camp?" he asked.

"I seek the witch," she answered, lowering her veil to reveal her face.

The men looked at one another, as they had not prepared themselves for a woman.

"I am her son—you can talk to me," the large man replied.

"I seek an audience with your mother, not you. Now take me to her!" Zijuan said in a stern voice.

"Woman, you do not give me orders," the man replied, in an effort to save face to his comrades.

"You will take me to her now, or you will regret your decision," Zijuan hissed.

The man lunged at her with his right fist, but Zijuan easily swung her walking stick sharply at the man, breaking his nose and sending him to the ground in pain. Another man lunged at her. Moving backwards slightly, Zijuan brought her foot up to meet his jaw, knocking him to the ground and knocking out two of his teeth.

The other men were paralyzed by this sudden turn of events.

Zijuan was about to attack another villager when a voice came from behind the group.

"You seek my counsel, Zijuan?" the voice asked.

The men parted to reveal a tiny and elderly woman, who walked in front of them to stand facing Zijuan.

"I do."

"I have been expecting you. Come, let's get you some dinner and tea and I will do my best to answer your questions."

The gypsy witch took Zijuan by the elbow and guided her back through the group of men and into the village. The men, suddenly deferential, sheepishly walked behind the two women.

Zijuan followed the witch into her tent and soon a complete meal of lamb, vegetables, and couscous was presented to them. Warm mint tea was provided in a large silver pitcher. Zijuan welcomed the nourishment and the sweetness of the tea after such a long, fast-paced hike.

"You are here because of the Black Mamba?" the witch asked.

"Yes, and because of my friends."

The witch studied Zijuan. She liked her immediately and could feel the power of Zijuan's presence.

"I placed a dark curse on your friends," the witch said.

Zijuan nodded slowly and kept looking at the ground.

"I suspected as much."

"The Mamba gave me no choice. He demanded I curse them, or he would slaughter my people. I am sorry."

Zijuan did not reply and took a few moments to take in this information.

"And where is the Mamba now?"

"I do not know exactly. The curse is powerful, Zijuan. The Mamba has captured some of your people, but not all of them. As I speak, they are in much agony. I do not know if they will survive."

"And you can see this?" Zijuan asked, lifting her head and making eye contact with the witch.

"I see much. I see the present, the past, and sometimes even the future."

"And what else do you see?"

The witch drank her tea and cleared her throat. Taking a stick, she dragged it along the carpet in a circle.

"There is much confusion and chaos in the future. It could be extremely evil and dark. Or, it could be full of light. It is constantly in motion."

"So how do I lift this curse?"

The witch continued to allow her stick to play along the carpet.

"You must kill the Mamba. That is the only way to lift the curse."

Zijuan nodded her head in understanding.

"One more question. I have a boy, a boy who is very special to me. His name is Tariq; do you know where he is?"

The witch nodded her head.

"He is being protected; that's all I can see."

"Protected?"

"From the curse and from evil."

"How?" Zijuan asked.

"I do not know."

Zijuan finished her meal and emptied her cup.

"I wish you well with your journey, Zijuan. Do not take the Mamba lightly—he is very, very powerful."

Zijuan smiled a bit and looked back at the witch.

"That's what I'm counting on."

"One more thing. I have something for you."

The witch went to the back of her tent and returned with an object in her hand, which she gave to Zijuan. Upon seeing this object, Zijuan's expectant expression changed to one of concern.

"Tariq's pendant…" she whispered.

In her hand Zijuan held the pendant of the panther that the witch had received from Jawad and used to place a curse on Tariq and the tribe. It had been Tariq's most prized possession and had belonged to his best friend, Aji, before he died in the streets.

"Return it to Tariq when you see him again," said the witch.

Caid Ali Tamzali sat across from the Black Mamba.

"You have done your job well, my old friend. The tribes have been eliminated and soon the French will invade Morocco. The countryside will then be ours to rule," the Caid said, sitting back in his massive chair, his fat belly rubbing against the wood table.

The Mamba sat erect and stoic, not showing any emotion one way or another. He simply bowed his head in acknowledgement.

The Caid continued, "I have word that French forces will invade in a week's time. I have already guaranteed them that we will protect their forces from attacks by the tribes. I want you to take control of security and see that every town, every trail, every road is patrolled by our troops. Any kind of insolence or rebellion must be dealt with swiftly and unmercifully. Do you understand?"

"Yes, my lord," the Black Mamba replied.

"Good. I will continue to work with the French. They have sent us a fresh supply of mercenaries and rifles. The mercenaries of the French Foreign Legion are yours to command. Ensure our troops have adequate rifles and ammunition."

"We will rule the countryside with an iron fist."

"Excellent, excellent. What of the boy Jawad? Has he met your satisfaction?"

The Mamba thought for a second before answering.

"He is an able apprentice and we may want to give him some more important duties."

"Good, have him continue to work closely with you. I see the same traits in him that I saw in you so long ago."

The Mamba bowed his head again.

Thoroughly satisfied with the crushing of the rebellion and the impending invasion by the French, the Caid reclined in his chair. If all went as planned, the French would dispose of the current Sultan and replace him with the Caid as the ruler of Morocco.

The country would be his to command.

───────────── ✦ ─────────────

Fez and Aseem wandered among the mountains looking for their tribe, but were unable to locate them. They had been wandering for seven days, and it was starting to grow colder. Their bodies suffered terribly in the cold during the night. What could possibly have happened to their people since they left on their excursion to Chaouen? It was as if the entire tribe had been wiped off the earth.

Saddened, they continued to patrol the trails, searching familiar locations. When they had almost given up hope, a familiar voice greeted them from behind a group of oak trees.

"Fez? Aseem?"

The boys saw movement from where they had heard the voice. Suddenly, a figure came from behind the tree and ran out to greet them.

It was Khafid, a scout and a member of their tribe.

"Khafid!" the boys yelled and ran to embrace him.

"We thought you had both been captured," Khafid exclaimed, delighted to see the two boys.

"Khafid, where is everyone? We've been searching for a week!" Fez asked.

Khafid released from the embrace and he grew solemn.

"The tribe is hiding. The Caid's troops are hunting us, and we had to move to higher ground. I am sorry we did not leave word, but we left in such a hurry."

"Have you seen Tariq? We were separated from him in Chaouen," Aseem asked.

"No, Tariq has not returned, I am sorry to say," Khafid explained, and he saw the blood drain from the boys' faces. Tariq not returning could only mean that he was dead, or had been captured by the Caid's troops.

"There is more bad news," Khafid said, as the boys' mouths opened wide.

"The Black Mamba ambushed one of our details. Most of our best warriors were killed and…" Khafid stopped midsentence, and emotion choked his voice.

"What happened?" Fez asked.

"He killed Malik and Sanaa," he said and with this news both the boys' eyes filled with tears.

Fez fell to the ground as if all this news was simply too much for him to bear. The life seemed to drain out of his body.

"I am sorry, boys," Khafid said and tried to console them, but both boys appeared to be entering a state of shock.

"I do not believe it. I do not believe that anyone could kill Sanaa or Malik. How do you know this is true?" Aseem asked.

"They never returned from their patrol and we found dead bodies at the ambush site."

"You found their bodies? Where are they buried?"

"We found everyone's bodies but Sanaa and Malik's. Everyone else we gave a proper burial."

"So there is hope they are alive?" Aseem asked.

Khafid tried to understand, but he was still going through the acceptance and grieving process.

"No, most likely the Black Mamba tortured them before killing them. He does not take prisoners," Khafid explained softly.

Aseem said nothing. The thought of Malik and Sanaa being tortured made him sick.

"Come, boys. Let's return to camp and get you warm and fed."

The three walked for almost five hours up into higher country. As they climbed higher, the air turned even colder and the landscape became more and more desolate. There were not as many places to hide up high in the mountains, but the Caid's troops would have a difficult time in the terrain. A sneak attack would be practically impossible to execute.

The climb was steep, and a couple of times they had to scale a rock cliff with a rope ladder that had been carefully hidden by Khafid.

Finally, they made their way to the camp, but as they approached, the boys were stunned to see that it wasn't the camp the boys had left behind. This looked more like a refugee camp.

The tents were thrown together and unorganized. People walked around with blankets thrown over their bodies and dire looks on their faces. Normally, the camp would be alive with singing and fires and bustling activity. Now, everyone moved as if they were mice being hunted by a hawk. There were no fires, as the tribe didn't want to attract attention. What was really strange was the apparent absence of men in the camp, which was now occupied mostly by women, the elderly, and children.

Seeing Aseem and Fez, everyone stopped what they were doing and ran to the two boys.

"We are so happy you are safe! We all thought you had been captured!" one of the women yelled.

Soon, Fez and Aseem settled into a tent with some cold, dried fish and rice. Understandably, they were despondent and saddened by the state of affairs. Neither could believe that Tariq, Sanaa, and Malik were all gone from their lives.

Fez was reminded of the plight of his people—they were little more than refugees when they were hunted and killed by the Caid's troops. Being in the camp now, around these people who had been through so much, brought it all back—the worst time of his life. In Chaouen, he had so much energy and felt he was a part of an important movement. In this village, there was so much remorse, he felt only sadness.

His father had a saying, "movement in life," which meant that to stay in one place would bring certain death. One always had to keep moving and adjusting. Just as his tribe followed the seasons and the migration of the animals, Fez knew must also keep moving.

And, because he possessed a keen intellect, Fez understood that to defeat the Caid the work must be done in the cities. After exchanging a knowing glance with Aseem, Fez finally spoke up.

"Khafid…Aseem and I are going to return to Chaouen."

Khafid, eating silently next to them all this time, barely lifted his eyes from his food.

"Why?" was all he asked.

"We have met with some boys who were slaves with us in the Caid's palace. They are as against the Caid as we are and also want to defeat him. We have already begun organizing an underground army to fight him."

Khafid laughed at this news.

"But you are just boys, and the Caid has grown so powerful."

Fez and Aseem both looked at one another. They were just boys, but what choice did they have?

"I know, Khafid, but this is our only hope. We cannot sit in these mountains and wait to die. Soon it will be winter, and then how will we survive?" Fez said.

Khafid spat on the ground.

"I do not know how we will survive the winter. Most of our hunters have been killed and we have scarcely enough food to survive another month. Go to Chaouen and perhaps a miracle will happen. I will stay in the camp to look after our people the best that I can."

Fez and Aseem stayed the night and then set off for the city of Chaouen in the early morning. They really didn't feel like being in the village, as there was hardly anything to do but to try to keep warm. The walk back to Chaouen was solemn, as both boys sensed that their lives were changing dramatically. Without Malik and Sanaa to lead them, how could the tribe possibly survive? For all they knew, they might be joining the street orphans as beggars if they no longer had a home with the tribe.

Margaret, Sophie, Inez, Alice, and Etienne lay hidden behind a five-story brick building on the corner of an alley and a main thoroughfare. The French sky was now very dark and the moon was hiding behind many gray clouds. Margaret and Alice had their horses with them, and had tied a chain to each saddle. The plan was a simple one—when they thought the time was right, they would attach the chains to the cage doors and break them open using the weight and strength of the horses.

Well, it seemed like a simple plan.

Except the girls weren't sure if the chains would hold. They also had no idea if the doors would actually come off, or if the strength of the horses would be enough.

Then there was the little problem of the guards who were standing around smoking about three hundred feet from the cage. Their plan was for three of the girls to distract the guards while Alice and Margaret pulled off the doors and made their escape.

The girls nervously looked at one another.

"It will work, I promise it will work. I have to try! He is my father," Margaret pleaded, her eyes welling with tears.

"Do not worry, Margaret. We know it will work. You are our friend and we will help you," Inez explained.

In truth, the girls were very nervous about everything. They were nervous about getting caught and being expelled. Or even worse, being thrown in jail as pirate conspirators. They were nervous the plan wouldn't work at all and they would end up being chased by the police.

But Margaret was their friend, and the look in her eyes erased their fears.

"Okay, Sophie, Inez, and Etienne, as we discussed, you distract the guards, and Alice and I will break off the doors. We'll rendezvous at the road leading back to the school, just on the outskirts of town. If you're caught, do not mention the school or any of us," Margaret explained, and all the girls nodded in agreement.

"Ah, this will be an adventure for all time. I am sure it will be a success and then we will get to be with actual pirates!" Inez exclaimed and all the girls smiled. Margaret was glad she had broken the ice a bit, which allowed the girls to relax.

"Okay then, let's get going," Margaret whispered, and the girls began to come out from behind the building and out into the street.

That's when they heard it. A voice, a man's voice, came from behind them.

"And where do you girls think you're going?"

The girls froze in fear.

They had been discovered.

Melbourne Jack sat on the edge of the cliff rubbing his head and feeling every bit of a nasty headache. He'd been knocked unconscious for over twenty minutes and had only just come to. It took him a few moments even to remember where he was and why he was lying on a steep ledge more than a hundred feet off the ground.

Tariq had to do some explaining to make Jack understand why his pants were missing.

"Nice work distracting the guards, Tariq. Now let's get the heck out of here," Jack said as he stood up. He quickly sat back down.

Tariq stared at him with a pensive look on his face.

"Whoa, my head is a mess like someone used it for a punching bag. Give me a few seconds," Jack said.

Tariq smiled as he watched Jack try to stand up. At one point Tariq thought that he might be dead because he had been unconscious for what felt like a long time. Tariq was grateful and relieved that his friend was alive.

Jack took a few more moments and then made his plan.

"Okay then, we're going to need to scale this cliff. It looks like there are enough holds to make it to the top and the moonlight should guide us on our way. I'll go ahead and go first and you follow. Don't worry, we'll be fine," he said, hoping to make Tariq feel comfortable.

The truth was, he was the one who felt nervous about the climb. Not because it was especially difficult, but because his head was in such bad shape he might lose his equilibrium.

Still, they had to make their escape, in case the guards figured out they had been tricked and circled back around.

Slowly, Jack grasped a groove in the cliff and hoisted himself up. Placing his right toe on a rock, he began to scale the wall and move up with ease. He was surprised at how easy it was. Within ten minutes he was safely at the top.

"Okay, Tariq, now it's your turn!" he yelled down, happy that he had scaled the cliff and tested its safety for Tariq.

Tariq followed his exact path and soon was standing next to Jack on top of the cliff.

They had made it!

"Okay mate, let's get a move on," Jack said and both of them smiled.

The two began their walk and made quick time to distance themselves from the cliff. In the darkness it would be very difficult to track them. However, in daylight, it would be relatively easy, so they had to find some kind of protection before the sun rose in eight hours' time.

Tariq and Jack practically ran for an hour, keeping up a brutal pace. Tariq was already thirsty, but there was no water to speak of. Before he allowed the balloon to float away, he hadn't thought to cut loose a canteen. His legs were heavy with fatigue and his throat was parched.

Still, he was in very good spirits.

Finally, they slowed to a brisk walk.

"Jack, can you tell me about that diary?" Tariq asked.

"What do you want to know?"

"Why is it so important? It took you years to find it, so now what are you going to do with it?"

Jack felt the diary of Alexander the Great in his pocket, for about the tenth time since he'd woken up, to ensure it was safe.

"I'm going to give it to Foster Crowe. He'll know what to do with it."

"Who is Foster Crowe?"

"He's the man who rescued me and the proprietor of the circus where I was raised. He's a very wise and good man. The only thing I really know about the diary is that it holds very important secrets in a battle against evil."

"And this circus, it's in Australia?"

"Not really sure where it is now. It moves around a bit. Last I heard it was in India or Ceylon."

"India or Ceylon?"

"You've never heard of India or Ceylon?" Jack asked.

"No, where are they?"

"The subcontinent. India is a huge country, and Ceylon is an island off India's southern coast. The last I heard, word was that was the circus's next destination, just not sure where exactly they are. Still, shouldn't be too hard to find them."

"Why?"

"That's just the way it works. See, everything is connected, Tariq—in this world and the next. There are no accidents."

"There aren't?"

"No, everything has a reason, and the world is exactly as it is supposed to be. The world, the universe, the afterlife, they are all like a living breathing thing and everything is connected. There is a natural law of behavior."

"What is it?"

"It's the idea that if you do something good, or bad, to someone or something, that it will come back to you."

"So, if I steal something, something will be stolen from me?"

"Yes, that's it exactly. Only it's much deeper than that. It extends into the afterlife. If you were evil and wicked in this life, then you'll be tortured in the afterlife and in your next life. All things are interconnected—even thoughts and feelings! Have you ever just had a feeling that someone you loved was in trouble and it turned out to be true?"

Tariq thought about this for a moment.

"Yes, once my friend Aji was being chased by a gang of street thugs and I felt something in my stomach. I knew exactly where to find him."

"That's exactly it. Most people are too busy to pay attention to their feelings or their surroundings. There's a saying I've learned, "all know the path, but few take it." Everyone knows the difference between right and wrong or good and evil, but in reality, temptation and laziness prevent people from following the right path."

Tariq listened intently, as this was one of many of the same lessons that Zijuan was trying to teach him. For most of his life, he'd been a survivor, giving little thought to what was right or wrong in life. When he realized there was a difference between right and wrong, his life changed for the better.

Tariq enjoyed talking with Jack and felt safe with him. Ever since Melbourne Jack had come into his life, Tariq had felt different, like he was on an important path. When he had been separated from Jack, he'd felt afraid and hopeless.

"Jack, it was kind of strange how we met," Tariq said.

"Yes, I was thinking about that too. How did you come to hide in my wagon?"

"I was running from the Caid's guards and was about to go down an alley when I heard a voice in my head. It was the voice of my friend Aji who died. Aji told me to go a different way, and then I saw these red handprints on a wall and I took off down that alley instead. I was just kind of guided to your wagon."

Jack stopped in the sand, staring at Tariq, an astonished look on his face.

"Did you say red handprints?"

"Yes, and when I was untying the balloon from the cliff, I saw another red handprint. What does it mean?"

As Jack took in this news a broad smile came across his face. "It means, little brother, that you are being watched. You have never heard the Legend of the Red Hand?"

"No, what is it?"

"Your friend, what was his name?"

"Aji."

"Your friend Aji is watching out for you, Tariq. There may be more to you than I had originally thought."

Tariq was riveted by the conversation.

"Jack, can you tell me about the Red Hand legend?"

Jack smiled even more and looked over at Tariq.

"Well, we've got a pretty long hike in front of us, so why not?"

CHAPTER
— *3* —

THE LEGEND OF THE RED HAND

AS TOLD TO TARIQ BY MELBOURNE JACK

Many, many centuries ago in Kerala, India, a girl awakened with a start, feeling raindrops on her face as she let out a huge yawn. Pulling a blanket over her shoulders, she stepped outside her family's hut into the early morning. Dew covered the many plants and trees and the jungle was alive with sound. Monkeys screeched in the distance and the nearby sound of crickets and frogs was deafening. It was not yet light, and the sun wouldn't rise for another half an hour.

Her name was Lakshi.

She headed over to her fire pit, where she prepared the kindling and then chipped two rocks together until a spark was produced. Soon she had a small fire started. Gently, she placed larger and larger sticks on the fire until it was of suitable strength.

Kneeling next to the fire, she rubbed her hands together to keep warm and watched the flames intently, placing wood in strategic locations to keep the fire strong.

Lakshi was the only one in her village who was awake at this hour. She rose early every day because she preferred the quiet. Although she was only twelve, she was wise, and mature beyond her years.

As she sat staring at the fire, she felt as if she were being watched.

Looking over her shoulder, she could see nothing but the jungle darkness and the faint outlines of the trees against the sky.

A chill came over her.

Continuing to stare into the early morning mists of the Indian jungle, she could barely make out a pair of eyes reflected by the fire.

The eyes were green and they blinked twice.

Lakshi saw the unmistakable outline of a cat—a very large cat— whose green eyes were staring right at her.

She felt her heart race in her chest and her breaths shorten. The cat moved closer to her.

It was a tiger.

An enormous tiger.

It moved towards her in small steps until she saw its full body and color. Only ten feet away, it could easily pounce and kill her in a matter of seconds.

Yet, it didn't move. It stared at her and then, to her surprise, it retreated to the jungle. The tiger's expression wasn't one of fierceness, but one of compassion. Suddenly, Lakshi was no longer afraid. In fact, she felt herself walking towards the cat, intrigued by its sudden retreat.

As the tiger moved back into the jungle, she felt herself being called towards it. The tiger vanished into the jungle mist, and Lakshi ran after it, completely overwhelmed by this calling from deep inside of her.

She scarcely felt the mud beneath her feet or the branches that scraped her skin. She was now sprinting at full speed to find the tiger.

The mist was thick, and before long she had to stop, her lungs heaving. As she caught her breath, Lakshi realized she was lost.

That's when she saw her.

Her mother.

Her dead mother.

It had been six months since her mother died giving birth to Lakshi's younger brother. Lakshi had not been the same since her mother's death. She had shut herself off from her remaining family and her tribe.

Her mother's image was surrounded by a white glow, and her mother looked younger than Lakshi remembered. Gesturing with her right index finger, Lakshi's mother urged her daughter to come closer. Slowly, Lakshi approached the vision and saw the smile on her mother's face. Instantly the girl burst into tears. Her mother, seeing her daughter's grief, looked at her with nothing but compassion in her eyes. All Lakshi wanted to do was melt into the arms of her deceased mother—to feel that safety and comfort once again.

Her mother, seeing her desperation, put a finger to her lips as if to say, "You must be quiet," and pointed to the base of an elm tree. Lakshi, confused by this, looked over at her mother for guidance, who continued to point to the tree.

Walking closer, Lakshi noticed something at the base of the tree. It looked like an old, wooden, rectangular box. Picking up the box, Lakshi could feel that it wasn't very heavy, but it was awkward to hold. She had to hold it upside down to open it, and as she did, a scroll fell out. It looked to be very old, yet it was in pristine condition. Lakshi looked inside the box and realized there were others still rolled up inside. She left them alone and set the box down. The loose scroll was long, and Lakshi unrolled it very carefully. She scanned over it quickly, and saw that it contained many symbols and scientific diagrams, and many, many sentences. Only a portion of it did she understand. However, at the end of the scroll, as if to replace a signature, was a red handprint.

Looking back at her mother for guidance, she noticed that her mother was fading away into thin air as she slowly waved to Lakshi.

She was saying goodbye.

In an instant, Lakshi cried out for her mother, forgetting about the scroll entirely. Within seconds, her mother's image had completely disappeared from sight. Lakshi shrieked with despair. Sobbing, she placed the scroll back in its container with the others. Staring at the spot where her mother had been standing, she waited for several minutes in the hopes her mother would return.

She did not.

Lakshi was confused by these events, and wasn't even sure she had actually seen her mother. Except that she had this wooden box as evidence. Then, something strange started to happen. She began to feel a sense of calm inside of her. A feeling as if everything would be fine. All the anxiety and worry she had felt so acutely in the past six months seemed to melt away.

She felt at peace.

The mist lifted and she easily found her way home, now encouraged by the sighting of her mother. She was sure the whole experience was a sign of some kind.

While walking back to her hut, she saw that her father was busy preparing the morning's breakfast. He was a slight man, balding, and always moved deliberately and slowly. He was considered the wisest man in the village. In fact, he was considered the wisest man in the entire region.

He scolded Lakshi for allowing the fire to go out and asked her what she was holding, intrigued by the box.

Lakshi tried to explain how her mother had given it to her, or rather, had pointed to where it could be found.

Lakshi's father stopped piling on wood, turned and stared at his daughter. He then asked her to repeat what she had just said.

Lakshi told her father exactly what had happened to her, starting with the tiger and ending with finding the scrolls. He questioned her completely and exhaustively for almost ten minutes. The fact that a tiger hadn't attacked her and the fact that she seemed to see her dead mother didn't surprise him. He didn't laugh at her story or question it. In fact, the more she spoke, the more he tended to believe her.

After asking about every detail, her father took the box from Lakshi and together they went to their hut, where he unfurled the scrolls on a table and began reading them one at a time. The scrolls appeared to be a series, with each scroll focusing on a different area of expertise. Some went on about chemistry or biology, while another discussed theology, and others detailed mathematics, physics, and astronomy. There were countless subjects.

It was the most marvelous thing he had ever read.

A man of logic and science, he was constantly examining the physical world and performing experiments of all kinds. Although never formally educated, he possessed a rare and refined intellect.

As he read, Lakshi's father laughed out loud and began talking to himself. Taking out a tablet and pencil, he began scribbling down equations, scratching his head, laughing some more, and continuing to jot down more equations and notes.

Lakshi asked her father what the scrolls contained, and he replied that she had discovered something that even he could not fathom.

Lakshi pressed further for an explanation of their meaning, but he could only describe the scrolls as the *answer to everything*. He then warmly hugged and kissed his daughter, and went back to examining the scrolls.

Lakshi left the hut, poured herself some tea, and was even more confused than she had been earlier in the morning. Back in the hut, her baby brother cried, so she hurried in, wrapped him in a warmer blanket, brought him outside and gave him his breakfast. She sang him a lullaby, just as her mother had always sung to her, and soon he was asleep.

All day and night her father wrote furiously and didn't once leave the hut. Over the next month, he would busy himself with all manner of experiments and soon became the talk of the village. The curiosity of the tribe was palpable—what could he possibly be working on that consumed so much of his time?

Emerging from his hut, Lakshi's father produced a series of charts that mapped not only the earth's solar system, but also three adjacent solar systems. He then went on to explain a chart that would predict the exact weather patterns for the next hundred years.

For his next trick, he produced an invention that nobody in his village had ever seen. He uncovered a square box approximately twelve inches by twelve inches. The box had numbers on it, placed in a circular fashion, with two sticks pointing in opposite directions.

It was a clock.

He then explained to the villagers how the clock could keep track of time. The clock even had a counter in the lower left corner that tracked both the sunrise and sundown for that particular day with tiny brass numbers that were barely visible, unless the person was less than a foot away.

Over the next several days, he showed the tribe how the clock worked and they all began to understand the concept of time as it related to their daily lives. Before, they simply tracked time by how high the sun or moon was in the sky. It was a crude method, and it had worked for generations, but this was more definitive.

He explained how time was invaluable to human beings as it allowed two people in completely different locations to make plans to meet at a certain place at a certain time.

In another week's time, he had developed a calendar of days, months, and years.

He began to conduct experiments with plants and devised a number of medicines to cure infection, viruses, and colds. He explained the importance of boiling water to kill pollutants and bacteria.

Gradually, his theories and inventions made their way to neighboring villages. People would travel for miles and miles to hear him teach about medicine, architecture, science, geology, astronomy, philosophy, and many other subjects.

He explained their world to them in a way that was both captivating and exciting.

All the villages improved with his teachings. He taught mothers how to deliver their babies safely. He built a blueprint for indoor plumbing and sanitation. In the fields, he showed farmers how to plant and grow more abundant crops. Their region thrived.

Soon, the king heard of his exploits and invited him to his palace. The man, who refused to give his name, stunned the royal subjects with his many theories and inventions. The king's scholars were baffled and astounded. Soon, these scholars became his pupils, and he instructed them in each of the complex disciplines.

Not once did he ever mention the scrolls—to anyone—and he made Lakshi swear an oath that she would never mention them either. The man intrinsically understood that the scrolls could be used for evil as well as for good. He kept them a secret, only read them on special occasions, and made sure they were very well hidden. Portions of the scrolls were used in his teachings, depending upon the scholar's particular field of expertise.

The king was most interested in the subject of warfare. He knew the man could provide him with inventions that would allow him to crush his enemies. This was true; the scrolls did contain sections on warfare that would propel the king to new heights if implemented correctly in battle.

But the man refused to divulge them. He did not want this wondrous source of knowledge being used to massacre and butcher other men.

The king grew frustrated, and one day had his troops throw Lakshi's father into a prison where he remained locked up for almost three years, never talking to anyone, until one day he simply vanished. No one knew exactly how he escaped, as there was no trace of his exit.

Lakshi and her father made their departure in the dark of night shortly after the prison break. They stowed away on a fishing boat and made their way down to Ceylon, an island just south of India. Soon they set up a school just outside of the capital. Lakshi's father identified top scholars from around the country to study under him. Still, he never made mention of the scrolls and only taught a portion of the knowledge contained within them.

It was around this time he decided that the scrolls must be protected forever. He trained a select few to both teach and preserve the secrets of the scrolls. This exclusive group consisted of his most trusted pupils—those who were not just smart, but also ethical and honorable. He made it clear to each of his pupils that any knowledge learned from him must not be used for the destruction of mankind. For he knew, the wisdom of the scrolls must be used solely for the betterment of the world.

From that point on, preserving the revelations contained in the scrolls became his life's work. With Lakshi and his son by his side, the man set out on a pilgrimage around the world, setting up very small schools and teaching only the very best and most honorable students. Soon, his top students—each sworn to an oath of secrecy—were allowed to establish their own schools.

After the man's death, much care was taken to protect his identity and the scrolls themselves. They were moved to one secret location after another, and only a handful of people were ever allowed to look at them. The man had even planned to destroy the scrolls before his death by setting a match to them, but he simply could not bring himself to destroy such knowledge. In the end, he put his faith in mankind to protect and honor the wisdom in their pages.

The scrolls seemed to have a life of their own. Their formulas, diagrams, calculations and verbiage managed to bend and twist, depending upon who was reading them. In one sentence, the scrolls could explain a subject that would take an expert an entire book to cover.

Over the centuries, the mark of the Red Hand Scrolls would make their presence known.

All over the globe, new inventions and philosophies emerged, each contributing to a drastic improvement in the world.

The Renaissance in Italy.

The establishment of the university system around Europe.

The creation of the first globe.

The discovery of electricity and the subsequent invention of the light bulb, battery, and refrigeration.

The development of the metric system in France.

The invention of the microscope, which facilitated major advances in medical science around the world.

The wisdom contained in the scrolls caused the world to become not just a more positive place, but a fascinating place filled with artistic wonder and beauty.

After centuries of darkness, mankind began to flourish and move forward. Not just from these inventions, but from a moral and practical standpoint.

It was rumored that most great thinkers throughout history had unique knowledge related to teachings of the Red Hand Scrolls. Scholars and artists such as Galileo, da Vinci, Mozart, Michelangelo, Shakespeare, Isaac Newton, Benjamin Franklin, and others seemed to possess a divinely-inspired brilliance that many attributed to the scrolls.

But there was also a darkness—an evil force—that acted against the positive teachings of the Red Hand Scrolls. Some argued that another set of scrolls existed that was being used for power and the forces of darkness.

Around the world, evidence proving the existence of a systematic evil force began to emerge.

The Spanish Inquisition.

The massacre and enslavement of indigenous people in Australia, Africa, South America, Asia, and North America.

The invention of instruments of war—far more devastating than anything seen in history—such as the revolver, the Gatling gun, the tank, and the submarine.

Others surmised that the teachings of the scrolls were being manipulated by unscrupulous people.

Yet throughout history, the secret of the scrolls remained, as did generations of people sworn to protect them.

The Red Hand Scrolls slowly became more myth than reality, which is what the society protecting them had intended all along. Soon, the scrolls represented little more than a fairy tale for children.

But they were real.

The most powerful evidence of their existence was the occasional sighting of a red handprint, believed to be left by those living in the afterlife. The red handprint represented a method of communication between the living and the dead. Many times, people who swore they had communicated with long-departed loved ones mentioned seeing a red handprint, or prints, at the scene of their vision.

Red Hand scholars determined that Lakshi's vision of the tiger was a sign that cats were a natural medium between the living and dead. The scholars used cats to better their understanding of the scrolls, to ward off evil spirits, and to communicate with the afterworld.

The prevailing thought among the Red Hand scholars was that our ancestors were trying to show mankind the right path. To do this, departed souls left a red handprint to mark the way. Sometimes, this was done simply to show that there was, indeed, life after death and that life had a purpose.

The Red Hand was meant to be seen as a symbol of hope in times of great danger or despair.

CHAPTER
— 4 —

STRANGERS IN A STRANGE LAND

Margaret, Alice, Inez, Etienne, and Sophie turned around expecting to find the Marseilles police. Instead, they looked straight into the face of Henri—the French anarchist from Ile d'Yeu.

"Who are you?" Henri asked the girls in a hurried tone.

"My name is Margaret Owen. Charles Owen is my father and we're here to rescue him."

Henri stared at the girls with a dumbfounded look on his face. They were still dressed in their school uniforms and each looked completely out-of-place. They were obviously terrified in his presence, and a couple of the girls looked ready to burst into tears. Henri was joined by three of his compatriots, and all were dressed the part of a rogue.

"Your father is Charles?" he asked.

"Yes."

Henri took a few moments to take in this information, assess the situation, and devise a plan of action.

"Okay. My name is Henri and these are my men. We are also here to free your father. What kind of plan do you girls have?"

Margaret looked at the other girls and then explained her plan to Henri. Listening intently, he nodded, rubbed his chin, and turned to discuss it with his men.

"It's not a bad plan. However, I think we can improve it a little bit and together we can free your father. What do you say we work together?'

Margaret assembled the other girls for a quick discussion, and provided an answer to Henri.

"Okay, what do you have in mind?"

Shiva the Wolf furiously dug in the sand to the appreciation and urging of Malik and Sanaa. The sun had now come up over the mountains and was shining directly in both their faces. Shiva, sensing their urgency to be freed, whimpered as she dug. She was almost a third of the way to digging out Sanaa.

Malik felt the heat on his eyes and tears began to drip down his face and sting his cheeks. He desperately wanted to close his eyes, but the stitches holding his eyes wide open made it impossible. The heat was becoming more and more unbearable with each passing moment and he felt his breathing become increasingly labored. His body was in shock, and he had begun to hyperventilate. Malik could feel panic setting in, as it was apparent that within a few more minutes he would be rendered permanently blind.

Shiva dug and dug until Sanaa was finally able to free her hands, which had been bound behind her. Pushing from behind, she used her leverage to bring up her knees and free her legs. It was excruciatingly hard and took over ten attempts before she was finally able to wiggle her legs free, slowly bringing them up and out of the sand. The entire time, the sun was searing her eyes, and she wondered if she would go blind at any moment. Malik had begun to scream and cry for her help. After fifteen minutes of struggling, she was finally free. Tears had run down her face, but her eyesight appeared to be intact.

Pulling herself up out of the sand, she shielded Malik's eyes from the sun by placing a piece of her shirt over his face and began to help Shiva dig. Sanaa heard his muffled cries beneath the cloth. Together, she and the wolf dug him out in ten minutes. Finally free, the two hugged one another, and Sanaa removed the cloth from his eyes to kiss his mouth and face.

They were free!

Shiva paced beside them for a minute and then went on her way— just as the boy had done so long ago.

Sanaa continued to hug Malik, holding him close, when he uttered the words she would never forget.

"Sanaa, it is too late—I am blind!"

The girls huddled together on an apartment roof overlooking the town square below. At the center of the square was a cage that held Charles Owen, Captain Basil, and a number of other crewmembers. Directly below the girls, two French soldiers paced and shared a cigarette, stomping their feet to warm themselves in the cold night. It didn't make sense that there would only be two guards. Someone in the French police had made a mistake, one that Henri planned to take full advantage of.

At their feet, the girls had buckets full of fruits and vegetables. After making eye contact with each of the girls, Etienne grinned slyly and shouted, "Go!"

The girls began throwing with all their might at the guards below while shouting obscenities and abusive language. Rotten cabbage, carrots, tomatoes, potatoes, squash, and pumpkins were hurled at the two guards, hitting them square several times. The startled guards scrambled to see what the commotion was and why they were being bombarded with rotten food.

"Free Morocco!" Etienne screamed.

"Imperialist swine!" Margaret yelled and giggled as she launched a potato that hit one of the guards right in the face.

"Nice one, Margaret!" Sophie congratulated her.

"Thanks!"

Alice threw a series of tomatoes that left red stains all over one of the guards' uniforms.

Furious, the guards decided to end this commotion and charged into the apartment building—exactly what the girls were hoping would happen. Wasting no time, the girls walked across a strategically-placed wooden plank that led to an adjacent apartment building. When they had all safely reached the building next door, Alice and Etienne shoved the plank over the edge and watched it drop to the ground below.

There would be no way for the guards to follow them.

As the girls made their way down the stairs, they hoped by the time they reached street level, the guards would just be reaching the top of the other building, enabling them to make an easy getaway.

Meanwhile, Henri and his men, with their horses, snuck over to the cage when the vegetable-covered guards abandoned their posts. Henri had decided to follow the girls' plan to use horses to knock the door off its hinges. The horses would also allow for a quick escape; however, they had no idea how long it might take to open the cage. Once the guards realized what had happened, they would come out firing. Not that Henri and his men couldn't handle two guards, but there was a police garrison only two blocks away, and if they heard the commotion in the square, dozens of police would rain down on them.

Henri quickly wrapped a chain around the cage door and locked it. He wrapped another one around the cage's upper hinge and around the two weakest points in the door.

"Who is there?" It was Charles's voice.

"Charles, it is Henri—prepare your men for escape."

"Are you with Margaret?"

"Yes, she is safe. Come, we must hurry!"

Two of the horses, each with a chain attached to its saddle, were urged to run. The pressure on the chains kept them running in place—at a standstill. Their first effort shook the door, but it did not come off its hinges. The second produced a tiny squeak from the door. They tried again and again, and their third and fourth efforts moved the entire cage, but still did not remove the door.

"C'mon on lads, push against the door, we just need a little more force," Charles said, and from inside the cage, Basil and the crew threw all their weight against the door and pushed as hard as their bodies would allow.

Henri slapped a mare on the hindquarters. The horse bolted forward but was stopped again by force of the chain. Soon, the French soldiers on the apartment roof began shouting, and shots rang out around the group.

They had been spotted!

"We've only got seconds before that police garrison is notified—we must go now!" one of Henri's colleagues yelled.

Henri, undeterred, set up the horses again while Charles and the crew desperately put all their weight against the door.

"Okay my friend, this one is for France," Henri whispered in the horse's ear. The horse shook his head as if to understand. Then, with a launch that would have done Pegasus proud, tore the door clean off its hinges.

Charles and the crew tumbled to the ground and quickly jumped to their feet.

Everyone jumped on the horses and made their hasty exit out of the square. Bullets continued to buzz by their ears, but they passed another building, finally out of range of the soldiers' gunfire.

Riding through the streets of Marseilles, the horses continued at a full gallop until they were out of the city and onto a country road. Shortly thereafter they came to rest at a group of trees and hunched down in hiding.

"This is where we are to rendezvous with Margaret," Henri explained to Charles.

"What took you so long?" the voice came from behind them.

Margaret and the rest of the girls all giggled as they emerged from behind some trees. Somehow, they had managed to get to the rendezvous point before the group.

Charles ran to Margaret and hugged her tightly, swinging her so her feet left the ground.

"I thought I'd never see you again," he said, tears rolling down his cheeks.

"I know," she said, beaming at her father through tears of joy and relief.

"You're not going to believe what's happened to me," Charles exclaimed, still in disbelief that he was in the presence of his daughter.

"Oh, I've got some stories of my own," Margaret replied as they embraced long and hard and Margaret melted in the chest of her father.

His embrace brought her more comfort and security than anything else in the world.

——————— ⚜ ———————

Sanaa walked with Malik through the desert. She'd fastened a bandage around his eyes in the hope that the condition would be temporary. After a day of travel, Malik still had not regained any of his eyesight. The two of them were hot, hungry, and very thirsty. Trudging through the desert, Sanaa knew they had to find water—and find it fast—or they wouldn't last another day.

That night, they huddled together behind a sand dune to keep one another warm. Thankfully, the weather was cooperative; the night wasn't too cold and there wasn't a cloud in the sky. A sandstorm surely would have done them in, but the sky was clear and full of stars.

Malik placed his head on Sanaa's shoulders and they held one another.

"You're not saying anything," Sanaa commented.

"I'm afraid, Sanaa. I'm afraid of going blind," he answered with obvious worry in his voice.

She held him tighter and kissed his head.

"Even if you are blind—and I believe you will regain your eyesight—it does not change my feelings for you. I will never leave your side, Malik," she promised with determination in her voice to show him she was serious.

"But I'll be blind and crippled."

"Malik, you will never be a cripple. You are fierce and a leader. You will always be those things…"

"Even without my eyesight?" he interrupted.

"Especially without your eyesight. Sometimes, our eyes deceive us and you will not have that disadvantage. You will learn to use your other senses and be that much more able."

Malik nodded his head—that was his Sanaa. She never felt an ounce of self-pity for herself or anyone else. It was the quality he most admired in her. She would never, ever play the victim and would not allow him to feel sorry for himself—not for a second! There they were, stranded in the desert with no food or water. He was blind, yet Sanaa simply focused on the positive and absolutely refused to dwell on the negative parts of their situation.

He took a few breaths, gathered himself, and then changed the subject completely.

"I imagine our tribe is scattered like the wind. No doubt the Mamba is hunting them. We must find them and get them organized, and then we must unite the other tribes. Divided, we will never defeat the Caid and the French. United, however, we can."

This is the voice that Sanaa respected, from the man she fell in love with. She would follow him anywhere on earth.

"Listen, someone is with us," Malik whispered.

Malik could hear the clear sound of footsteps in the sand. His hearing had already improved as the result of his lost eyesight. It sounded to him like more than one person was behind them, although he couldn't be sure how many.

Just then, they both heard some scurrying from behind them.

"The Mamba must have somehow followed us," Sanaa whispered.

Malik's heart sank, as she was probably right. The Mamba must have doubled back to check on them, found their trail, and followed them.

It was clear they needed to prepare themselves for an attack.

Sanaa started to stand up.

"No Sanaa, you cannot defeat them," Malik whispered to her.

"Then I will die trying. We surrendered once before, and I will not make that mistake again."

Standing up, Sanaa tried to find the source of the footsteps and readied herself for a fight.

She would not go down without a battle.

As she took her position in front of Malik, she was willing to fight the Mamba to the death.

Instead, someone very different from the Mamba appeared over the dune. A man wearing a blue robe, with his face covered by a blue veil and turban, came right up to Sanaa. Removing his veil, Sanaa could see that his face was very black, with a long goatee that hung from his chin. His bloodshot eyes seemed to look straight through her. He showed no fear towards Sanaa, and his entire expression was one of fierceness.

After staring at her awhile, the man's expression changed—from one of suspicion to one of empathy. Bringing his hand up slowly to Sanaa's face, he gently rubbed his thumb over the spot where Sanaa had pulled out the stitches from her eyelids. Blood had dried on her face. He glanced over at Malik sitting in the sand with his face bandaged, and understood that Sanaa and Malik were in a good deal of distress.

"Who is there?" Malik asked.

A sly smile came over Sanaa's face before she replied.

"Tuareg," she answered.

The man in the blue veil standing in front of her smiled as well.

Fez and Aseem returned to Chaouen and were soon in the company of their friend Timin. He had set up an underground headquarters in the alley behind a café. It wasn't really a headquarters at all, just some crates stacked together for them to sit on.

On the other hand, what Timin was planning while sitting on those crates was indeed masterful.

Over the past two months since meeting Tariq, Timin had organized almost every orphan and beggar in Chaouen to join the resistance as spies. He developed a series of secret codes and hand signals they used to communicate. He divided the city into various sectors and designated certain orphans to patrol each sector and report back on the happenings in their area. They monitored the police, the government, shopkeepers, and the military.

He even set up a school to explain how to spy, what to report, and how to identify what kind of intelligence was valuable.

Remembering how his family had been torn from him by the evil Zahir, and how he'd been thrown in prison for a crime he did not commit,

Timin devoted each and every waking moment to thinking of ways to defeat the Caid. Once a broken man, he was now a man with a mission.

He set up the foundation for his network of spies, and then he expanded.

Timin had twelve of his most intelligent and trusted spies move to Tangier to begin monitoring that city in the same way they were monitoring Chaouen. Each week, an intelligence report was delivered to him via a messenger wagon.

His spies moved in and out of society without so much as a look from the police or the military. They were the unwanted and the poorest of the poor. No one ever noticed them. More accurately, nobody wanted to notice them.

After a while, Timin had amassed an excellent collection of intelligence on the movements of the police and the strength of the military. He knew which shopkeepers were informers. He tracked delivery times and schedules for the businesses in town, and even managed to document the home addresses of most police and military officers.

He set up his network in such a way that even if a spy were to be captured, he wouldn't be able to give up much information.

He named his group 'the forgotten resistance' and saw it flourish before his eyes. Orphans and street urchins, who just weeks before had no reason or purpose in life, suddenly felt important because of their new roles. They felt empowered and needed.

"How was your visit?" Timin asked.

Fez and Aseem looked solemnly at the ground.

"Not good," Fez answered.

"What happened?"

"The Mamba has killed Sanaa and Malik and our tribe is scattered. They are barely surviving in the mountains. Things are very desperate."

Timin looked at the boys and their expressions showed their frustration and their sadness. They seemed completely defeated, and a far cry from the determined boys who had left just weeks earlier.

"Fez and Aseem, I know what it is to lose your family, and my heart is with you both. Please, do not give in to despair. Rather, take your anger and energy and put it into defeating the Caid."

Aseem and Fez both stared blankly ahead, nodding slightly but barely acknowledging Timin. The fact was, neither of them had much enthusiasm for anything. First Margaret, then Tariq, and now Sanaa and Malik—their entire family was disappearing before their eyes and both boys felt the weight of such terrible losses.

"I'll get you a nice hot meal, and then we'll go over the most recent developments. There is much to discuss and plan," Timin said, putting his arms around both boys and then departing to prepare some food.

Fez in particular was despondent. Losing his family and living through this latest catastrophe was proving too much for him. Aseem was very concerned about him and made a point to stick close to him and to make as many positive comments as possible.

"I'm sure Tariq is fine. You know him; he can get out of any trap. I'm sure he'll come smiling down the road any day now as if nothing has happened," he told Fez.

Fez merely stared at the ground.

"What about Sanaa and Malik?" he whispered.

Aseem didn't exactly know what to say to this.

"We don't know what happened to them, right? Sanaa is the greatest warrior I have ever seen, and Malik is almost her match. They could be in hiding and just waiting for the right moment to pounce!"

Fez stood up a little straighter.

"Do you really think so?"

"I only know that they are both very smart. Do not give up hope, Fez. Things are bad now, but they can get much better."

Fez actually smiled and his spirits appeared to pick up. Secretly, Aseem did not even know if he believed what he was saying, but he needed to give his little friend some hope.

"Come, let's get a meal and then start planning with Timin. You're the smartest one around here, and he will definitely need your help," Aseem explained. This made Fez perk up even more.

Soon, the boys were munching on lunch and going over plans with Timin, with both their spirits raised a bit.

———————— ❦ ————————

Louise Owen and Matthew Hatrider sat across from one another in the London Library, poring over documents and books, completely absorbed in their work. Despite doing research for months, they had yet to piece together this increasingly difficult puzzle.

Their goal was to clear the name and reputation of Louise's husband Charles Owen. Charles had been labeled a traitor by the British government and a reward had been offered for his capture. It was pure luck that the French authorities had no idea that Charles was wanted by the British—the French had actually captured Charles and labeled him a pirate.

There was much more to the story.

Louise had received word from Charles that off the coast of Africa, a British naval officer named Lieutenant Dreyfuss was marauding villages and sinking fishing boats. Dreyfuss was acting like a pirate, and all the while blaming it on actual pirates.

Louise and Matthew were trying to figure out why Dreyfuss was doing this. He couldn't possibly be acting alone. Someone high up in the British navy, or the British government, must be giving him orders to attack innocent merchant ships and fishing villages.

Their job was to find out who might be giving those orders.

Suddenly, Louise looked up and exclaimed, "Wait just one moment!"

"What is it?" Matthew asked.

Louise was reading a newspaper clipping from the *London Times*, dating back to July, 1910. She had been reading every newspaper and every article, going back the past three years, in an effort to find a clue.

"It's a clipping from the social page of the July 21, 1910 *Times*. The Far Indian Trading Company was hosting a party for government and military dignitaries. It says that 'Alexander Dreyfuss, a lieutenant in the

British Royal Navy, and Admiral Roy Ferguson, are the esteemed guests of Lionel Hedgecock—president of the Far Indian Trading Company.'"

She handed the paper to Matthew, who read it carefully three times over.

"It might be nothing. However, generally lowly lieutenants aren't invited to such high-powered social functions. This might mean something."

"Do you think we should look into it further?" Louise asked.

"Absolutely. What's interesting is that Dreyfuss isn't even under the command of Admiral Ferguson. It could be a coincidence, or it could be something more sinister. I'd like to have a closer look at this Ferguson, and Hedgecock as well."

Louise sat back, rather pleased with her detective work. Her research provided a much-needed relief from her daily life and took her mind off of her so-called fall from grace within London society. She found that most of her old friends had completely shunned her and as a result, she was alone a good deal of the time. Their situation was also proving very difficult for her son, David, as he had been ostracized at school. His friends barely spoke to him. Still, he was a very durable boy and simply went about reading more books and occupying his time with other activities. The one thing he had going for him was that he was far and away the best football player in his school. Because of this, the other boys didn't exclude him completely.

"How are you going to go about looking into it?" Louise asked.

"Very carefully. We'll need some kind of proof that orders signed by someone in the British navy had been given to Dreyfuss, instructing him to attack these villages and ships. What's more, given this news, no doubt the navy will try to hush it up as much as possible. So we'll need to be very considerate of whom we present any evidence to. We'll need to make completely sure they can be trusted."

Louise nodded along. She was so grateful for Matthew's help. Like a chess master, he always thought four moves ahead of everyone else. She was sure that if anyone could, he could get to the bottom of this mystery.

"You haven't heard from Charles, have you?" he asked in a whispered tone.

"No, not since that telegram."

He nodded and his face showed no expression.

"Well, I'm sure we would have heard something if he had been captured. We'll just keep digging, and hopefully we'll eventually find something."

Louise appreciated Matthew's confidence and his calm demeanor. She agreed—if Charles had been captured, it would have made all the London papers. She only hoped he was safe.

Inez stared at Captain Basil and inspected him closely. He had almost ten days of growth on his chin, his clothes were dirty and tattered, and he smelled of body odor and mold.

She wrinkled her nose at him.

"Are you sure you're a pirate? You look more like a bum to me," she told him.

Basil smirked at her comment.

"I assure you that I am a pirate, young lady. In fact, I'm the most wanted pirate in all the Mediterranean."

She continued to study him up and down. Inez was still dressed in her prim and proper school uniform, with her red hair brushed down to her shoulders and her black shoes still shiny and new.

"You don't have an eye patch, or a parrot, or even a sword. You're not what I was expecting to see in a pirate," she told him, most unimpressed with his appearance.

"Yes, well, my parrot is still with my ship and the French military took my sword. I can't do anything about the eye patch," he tried to convince her.

"Do you have any buried treasure?" she asked.

"Oh, yes, tons of it, buried all over the sands of Africa."

"Really?" she exclaimed, more excited by the conversation.

"Gold medallions, Spanish pieces of eight, diamonds and rubies by the fistful," he told her, obviously having some fun at her expense.

"Diamonds and rubies! I've never seen a diamond. Where is this treasure exactly?" she asked, almost jumping up and down.

"Well, I don't specifically remember—I need to see my map," he sheepishly answered.

"Where's your map?"

"Well, I can't remember where I left that either. I was trying to be so secretive that I've forgotten where I've hidden it."

Her expression turned to pure disdain.

"You mean you've got all this treasure and you can't remember where the map is? What kind of stupid pirate are you anyhow?"

"Inez, enough!" Sophie scolded her. Inez turned and walked away, still glaring at Basil, who was smiling at the conversation.

Charles walked up holding his wrists; he'd spent the last thirty minutes pounding his chains off with a hammer they'd "borrowed" from a nearby farm. His wrists were sore and red from where the shackles had dug into his skin.

The group had ridden for hours in a zigzagging fashion to throw off their trail. They'd stuck to country roads and done everything they could to avoid any kind of civilization. Now, they had a camp all set up in a cluster of trees, safely tucked away from any roads.

"The police and military will be hunting us," he said to Basil.

"I know. They'll undoubtedly go house to house asking about us, and we're not exactly the easiest group to hide."

Charles paced nervously and tried to think. Somehow, they were going to have to hide so nobody would suspect their true identities. What their next move was, he still wasn't sure. He only knew that he wouldn't leave Margaret again.

"Our biggest concern is not just getting captured. We've also got to conceal our identities so we do not arouse suspicion."

Cortez kept quiet throughout the entire affair. Even during the jailbreak, he scarcely said a word, yet stayed close to Basil or Charles at all times. He took care not to draw attention to himself, to the point that he seemed almost invisible at times. He played the part of the poor fisherman to perfection. He never fussed, did as he was told, and was loyal as a Labrador puppy to its master. Hardly ever looking anyone in the eye, Cortez always kept his focus on the ground, and took on a completely submissive presence.

Margaret, who had been listening attentively to the conversation, came up to her father and Basil.

"You could hide at our school," she answered.

Charles shook his head at the idea.

"Margaret, I appreciate the gesture, but it would just put you in more danger. Besides, I doubt your schoolmistress would approve of having wanted fugitives around her school girls."

"You might be surprised. Saint Catherine's is a very progressive school," Sophie interjected.

Charles, who had only just been introduced to Sophie, appreciated the gesture.

"I am thankful for your thoughts, Sophie, but it just isn't possible."

"It's the perfect disguise! Who would suspect a bunch of wanted pirates at a French girl's school? You could be hired hands and we could say you are the groundskeepers. It is perfect!" Inez said, excited about the idea of having pirates at her school.

"I don't know…" Charles was beginning to feel as if he had been ambushed.

"It's not a bad idea, Charles," Basil interjected. "Besides, it would allow us to rest awhile and have the time to form a plan for our next moves. Being at the school would also allow you to watch over Margaret."

Charles knew when he was outgunned. Rubbing his whiskers, he thought dutifully for a full twenty seconds before replying.

"Well, I could use a good bath," he commented and the girls all jumped with joy.

"Yes, you could!" Margaret squealed and hugged her father. More than anything, she just wanted to be with him. She never wanted to leave his side again.

"Okay then, we'll need a backup plan for a hasty retreat in the event your schoolmistress isn't for the idea—which is highly probable," he continued.

"Don't worry, we'll convince her," Inez said with a devilish grin.

The group made the decision to leave straightaway for Saint Catherine's in the morning. The girls would already be in hot water with Sister Anne, considering they'd already been reported as missing. Lost in the conversation was Cortez, who sat in a corner away from the group, staring at the ground and listening. He wasn't interested in any family reunions. He was a bounty hunter only interested in one thing—the reward on the heads of Charles and Basil put there by the British Empire. Somehow, he needed to get word to Dreyfuss that he was in the company of both Basil and Charles. How could he do that? He had no idea.

Regardless, he would surely find a way to turn them in at the first opportunity.

CHAPTER
— 5 —

E PLURIBUS UNUM

Caid Ali Tamzali sat triumphantly on his horse. In front of him were rows and rows of soldiers, both on foot and on horseback. Many of them were his own troops, and many more were part of the French Foreign Legion, or Legionnaires as they were called, dispatched by the French government. They numbered in the thousands, and each soldier had been outfitted with a new uniform and guns—all courtesy of the French.

The Caid had received word that the French would be launching an attack on Morocco in two days' time. Their navies and armies planned to attack Tangier before moving through the country to attack Marrakesh. The Caid expected they would run through the Moroccan troops like a finger through water.

At the same time, the Caid would increase his hold on tribal villages and continue his personal reign of terror through the Moroccan countryside. He would continue to squash any kind of resistance.

"Already we control the countryside and every village within two hundred miles of this kasbah. The French will invade Morocco tomorrow and will we assist them in any manner possible. You all have your assignments—do not disappoint me or there will be consequences," he ordered, surveying his assembled troops.

The Caid's army, while looking impressive, was made up mostly of boys and men he had kidnapped and forced into battle. The soldiers sent by the French were not actually soldiers, but mostly criminals and vagrants who joined the French Foreign Legion as a way to escape the gallows or extreme poverty.

The French Foreign Legion, for the uninitiated, is a mercenary army controlled by the French government. It is made up almost entirely of immigrants and, generally, attracts the lowest of the low of society. The

French Foreign Legion was a haven for criminals, paupers, and anyone else looking to escape from their normal life. One benefit of joining "The Legion" was that once a soldier had fulfilled his time and duty, he was offered an entirely new identity and full French citizenship.

As a result of having mostly malcontents amongst its membership, The Legion was renowned for its brutal and harsh training methods. The men were tortured and hardened to the point where they felt no compassion for anyone. These were some of the most vicious soldiers on the planet.

Fighting alongside the French troops was a large group of young boys, forcibly recruited by the Caid to join his army. Many of these boys were no older than sixteen and some even as young as twelve. At first, a number of them deserted and returned to their villages. After that, the Caid instituted a policy stating that he would kill three boys for every boy who escaped. It was a harsh and vicious policy, but it was effective, as desertions almost completely stopped. Yes, they looked fine and had the latest weapons—but that was all for show. Beneath the surface lurked a serious morale problem.

The Black Mamba rode next to the Caid, and behind him Jawad sat proudly on a new horse equipped with the latest Italian leather riding saddle. He looked coolly at the troops and appeared to enjoy his newly-appointed power.

The Mamba got off of his horse and Jawad followed his lead. In his right hand, the Mamba held a hard stick made of bamboo, which had been sanded down to remove any splinters and painted with a brown varnish. He walked among the rows of troops, inspecting them, and quickly bringing the stick down on anyone who failed to meet his stringent requirements. Sometimes, the stick was brought down on the calves of the recruit, bringing him to his knees wincing in pain. Or the stick was aimed at the elbow or wrist of the man with such force that it even broke bones.

The Mamba had a stick made for Jawad fashioned after his own. Once in a while, he would simply nod at a recruit and allow Jawad to hit the man, doing the Mamba's dirty deed for him. He was training Jawad to be completely merciless.

The men grew to fear Jawad almost as much as they feared the Caid and the Mamba.

———————— ❧✦❧ ————————

The Tuareg people were a band of nomads migrating across the Sahara desert. Their caravans typically resembled a traveling clan of gypsies. The men wore a headdress called an *alasho*—a combination of a veil and a turban. Its most distinctive feature was its beautiful indigo blue color, which the Tuareg believed would ward off evil spirits. In fact, their entire robe was colored in indigo blue. They called themselves *imohag*—which means "free men."

The women typically wore very colorful clothing and adorned themselves with large gold earrings and henna tattoos on their faces. Many wore multiple rings and bracelets, and were usually chanting and singing. Some of their songs were prayers, but others were sung simply as a way to pass the day.

The Tuareg frequented all of Africa and rode from country to country in camel caravans. They felt as comfortable in the hot desert as a duck in a cool lake. The Tuareg were renowned traders and bought and sold goods from one country to the next.

Talented celestial navigators, while traveling the Tuareg kept track of distance by measuring the night sky and the stars.

Well-known for their generosity, they were perhaps some of the happiest people on earth and it was difficult to find a Tuareg without a smile on his or her face. Generous to a fault, the Tuareg spoiled their guests with all manner of gifts and feasts. To the Tuareg, physical things meant very little and a man's wealth was often measured in how much he could give away in his lifetime.

On the flip side of the coin, the Tuareg were fierce warriors and their bravery was unmatched in the Arab kingdom. Like most clans, they fought together—an insult to one Tuareg was an insult to them all.

Sanaa and Malik sat around a campfire, drinking gunpowder tea—a tea poured three times out of the pot and served with honey and sugar—and eating some delicious *taguella*, a millet flatbread served with goat milk and dipped in spicy pomegranate gravy. Surrounding them were approximately fifty people from this particular Tuareg caravan. The group included men, women, children, and the elderly, and all were fascinated by Sanaa and Malik.

The tribe had immediately taken pity on Malik and had done everything they could do to mend his eyes. The village chieftain placed a combination of herbs in small cotton sack and insisted that Malik hold it on his eyes for the better part of an hour. Although it did help the pain considerably, it did nothing for his eyesight—he was still blind.

Sanaa also used the herbs on her eyes to keep down the swelling and hopefully preventing any scars from developing where the Mamba had carelessly stitched her eyelids open. Thankfully, he had used a small thread and needle and the chances of a full recovery were very good.

Next to them sat a man by the name of Moussa Ag Arshaman. He was in his late thirties, his skin had a light, creamy color, and he said little. He wasn't fat, but he wasn't thin either. The sides of his face had a little bit of drooping skin, and he too was dressed in an *alasho*.

This man was a legend in the Sahara.

He was also a fierce enemy of the French.

In 1900, his tribe was defeated by the French and forced to surrender in Mali. His broadswords were no match for the artillery and rifles of the French army. In disgrace, Arshaman was forced to surrender his people to the French generals, while they mocked his veil and robes.

In torment, he watched as his people were rounded up, imprisoned in a labor camp, and forced to work grueling jobs as slaves and servants. After a year in the camp, he escaped with some of his people and fled to the Ahaggar Mountains, his tribe's natural habitat. The French had slaughtered thousands of his people and it had taken the Tuareg a decade to finally rebuild their tribe.

"Caid Ali Tamzali is aligning himself with the French. Soon, they will invade Morocco—if they haven't already—and seize the countryside.

No doubt they will come for you and your people," Malik explained, as Arshaman listened intently. Puffing on a water pipe, Arshaman took in all the information and allowed Malik to complete his explanation.

Afterwards, he stared into the desert for two minutes, collecting his thoughts and calculating his strategy.

When he finally spoke, his voice was deep and raspy and flowed like molasses. His words carried weight and could easily force the listener into mesmerized obedience.

"We were defeated by the French because of their rifles and their machines. I would not take one hundred French soldiers for just one of my own. But against their machinery, we will be no match for their army," he said and Malik nodded in agreement. Although he couldn't see him, Malik knew of his reputation and the tenor of his voice was that of a man not to be trifled with.

"In the open desert, as we Tuareg fight, it will be too easy for the French to cut us down. But, if we fight in the mountains and the cities, then our chances and our opportunities for success will increase," he said before concluding.

"There is one other thing we must do..." Sanaa began.

"What is that?"

"We must kill the Caid and the Mamba. Cut off the head of the snake and the body will die along with it."

Arshaman smiled at this and blew apricot-flavored smoke into the night air.

"You would make an excellent war chieftain, Sanaa."

Malik smiled at this remark.

"Many men have underestimated Sanaa because of her beauty. She is the best fighter in our clan, even better than I, and her strategic skills rival that of any French general," Malik said.

Arshaman slapped Sanaa on the back and she choked on some of her food.

"That is what I like to hear. So how are we going to defeat the French and this Caid?" he asked, getting more and more animated as the conversation went along.

"You will join us?" Sanaa asked as she recovered from her slap on the back.

"My dear Sanaa, I have waited twelve years for an opportunity to fight the French, and I finally have my chance. When we fought the French all those years ago, we were alone. Now, as we are aligned with you, we can and will defeat them."

The Tuareg people behind them started to become more and more excited as the talk of fighting the French continued. Many of them had lost loved ones in the last war and some of the older ones had been forced to work in the labor camps. For years they had been a defeated people; those who escaped with Arshaman were continually hunted by the Caid's troops along their trade routes.

Some of the men began to holler and whistle and the women made a kind of high-pitched scream that resembled a hyena's laugh. Soon, drums were produced and the tribe gathered around Sanaa and Malik and insisted they dance with them. In anticipation of sharing the battle-field, the tribespeople taught them a traditional Tuareg war chant.

Even Sanaa, who was accustomed to being emotionless and stoic, smiled at their generosity and at the sight of so much excitement. Just hours ago she thought that she and Malik would surely die and now they were dancing with a nomadic people who had just agreed to go to war with them.

"Tomorrow we will escort you back to your tribe, and when we arrive we shall discuss how we will go to war together," Arshaman told them.

"There is something we must do first," Sanaa told him.

"What is that?"

"You must marry Malik and me."

At this, all the dancing and drumming came to a stop and everyone looked at Malik and Sanaa.

"Sanaa, are you sure? I will probably be blind for the rest of my life. You do not want a cripple for a husband," Malik responded, sheepish in his answer.

Sanaa took his face in her hands.

"Malik, you are the only man I will ever love, and I don't want to go one more day without you for my husband. Blind or not, you will never be a cripple in my eyes."

Malik was more humbled by these words than by any others he'd heard in his lifetime. He was trying to be strong and brave, but secretly he was still in shock that he might be permanently blind. In spite of his shock, hearing that Sanaa wanted to be his wife filled his heart with warmth and kindness.

"Of course I will marry you, Sanaa," he said and kissed her in full view of the tribe.

This made the tribe cheer with appreciation and holler with excitement.

"Okay then, we will marry you right now and then depart for your tribe's camp at first sunlight. I'm sure your people are missing you," said Arshaman.

That night, under the moon and stars, Malik and Sanaa became husband and wife under the guidance of Arshaman. Sanaa had never been happier in her life. She felt as if, for the first time in years, she could finally breathe without worry.

Zijuan traveled at night, avoiding well-traveled roads. She stuck to back-country trails and often camped by a stream or under a cluster of trees. Her thoughts drifted to Tariq, Malik, and Sanaa, and she felt worried about what the future might hold for them. In fact, she had no idea if they were alive or dead. Lately, her dreams had been dark and foreboding and oftentimes she woke in a cold sweat in the dark of night, her heart beating fast and her breathing labored.

Between trying to run her orphanage and trying to find Tariq and avoiding the Caid and his troops, Zijuan often felt like a hunted animal—panicked and wary of everything around her. Every time she traveled, she was constantly on guard for any sound or movement—anything that seemed out of the ordinary.

She had no doubt the Caid would be hunting her.

Her objective was simple: make it back to the tribe. She had not received word from Sanaa or Malik in weeks, and that could only mean they were in some kind of trouble. There were rumors that the Black Mamba had massacred the entire tribe, but those were only rumors… she hoped.

Finally reaching the base of the Rif Mountains, Zijuan began the long and arduous climb up the steep mountain trails. She was careful to switch back often and to hide her footprints by walking on rock and through water. It had been some time since she had been to the encampment, but she could always find her way back.

But after two days of searching, she wasn't so sure.

The tribe had six general camp locations and all were empty. Not just empty—it looked as if they had been abandoned for some time. She could tell that one of them had been left in haste, as there were still tracks and cold ashes from a fire. Still, it looked as if it hadn't been used in weeks.

There was one more place she thought to look.

In the case of an extreme emergency, the tribe had identified a spot on the adjoining mountainside to use as a retreat from danger. It was situated in a desolate spot at the top of many very steep trails. It was, in fact, a very poor place for a camp, but it was extremely safe because it provided a vantage point in all directions. The conditions made it practically impossible for a large army to follow.

If the tribe had gone there, it could only mean they were very desperate.

Zijuan decided to follow her hunch. She would set off the following morning. It was a three-day hike and she would need an early start.

She only hoped she could find the tribe and finally get some answers.

Tariq and Melbourne Jack stood on the outskirts of a town called Tetouan, located about forty miles south of Tangier and, along with Tangier, was one of two major ports on the Mediterranean Sea. Known for its white buildings and apartments, the city's appearance reflected the influence of the Spanish, who had successfully captured Tetouan in the nineteenth century. Many of the city's inhabitants spoke Spanish as their native tongue.

Jack had decided that it would be best to disappear into a big city. He hoped to arrange for some kind of transport and then rendezvous with Tariq and his tribe back in the Rif Mountains. He had managed to find some pants when they passed a house on the outskirts of town. Seeing him without any pants, the owner took pity on him and gave him a pair, along with a blessing for safe travels.

Tariq was exhausted from the long hike. They had been walking for almost a week, and his shoes were worn to little more than threads on his feet. In many places, they had worn completely through to the point that his feet were directly exposed to the sand. On the bottom of both heels, his skin had been rubbed raw, and blood had started to ooze more with each step. For the last half mile, he had been in considerable pain and needed to stop every hundred feet or so to rest. Nonetheless, he didn't complain—not even once—and rejected Jack's offer to carry him on his shoulders. He was determined to make the journey under his own power.

"We've got to get some shoes for you and get those feet taken care of," Jack told him with concern in his voice. Tariq nodded in agreement. They had finally arrived in Tetouan and it was clear Tariq needed to rest. In fact, he could no longer walk and as he sat at the side of a town fountain, he gingerly took off his shoes and placed his feet in the cool water. The relief was instant.

"Okay, mate. I'll tell you what, you wait here and I'm going to go rustle you up a pair of shoes and some food."

Tariq smiled and allowed the water to cool his feet while he took in the sights of the city.

It was beautiful.

All around him, merchants buzzed with their latest wares. To his right, a group gathered around a fish merchant who was hawking a freshly caught mackerel to the highest bidder. The men yelled and raised their fingers to bid until finally a winner was declared, to the discouragement of the other men. Tariq could smell some freshly baked pita bread at another stall and his stomach whined with emptiness.

Nobody paid him any attention as he soaked his feet and relaxed. He had an immensely satisfied look on his face. Already his feet were starting to feel better, and he felt ever so grateful to have them plunged in a cool pool of water. He remained seated on the bank of the pool, allowing the cold water to heal his feet, and practically fell asleep when…

"Is your name Tariq?" a voice whispered in his ear.

"Wha—?" he said with a start, instantly awake.

"Do not make any noise. I was instructed to look out for a boy that looked like you."

Tariq turned around and saw a boy standing there. The boy was a bit older than he was, about seventeen, but dressed in rags like a street urchin.

"Why would anyone tell you to look for me?"

The boy sat next to Tariq and, continuing to whisper, he pretended to look busy.

"It is not safe for you here—you must return to Chaouen at once."

"Chaouen? But why?"

"I do not know. I was only instructed that if I were to see you, I was to urge you to go directly to Chaouen."

Tariq was completely puzzled by the conversation.

"Trust me," the boy said and looked directly in his eyes. Tariq could see the sincerity in his face.

"This is not a trap?" Tariq asked.

The boy smiled.

"No, if I wanted to capture you then I would have simply alerted the soldiers to your presence. Go to Chaouen, Tariq—please!" the boy asked and then, without warning, left as quickly as he had appeared.

Melbourne Jack returned to the fountain and looked at Tariq, who still had a puzzled look on his face.

"What happened, Tariq? You look like you just saw Julius Caesar," he said before sitting down and placing down a balm of some sort and some food and shoes.

"A boy just sat down and whispered to me that we must leave at once and return to Chaouen," Tariq said, scarcely believing it himself.

Jack did a double take before replying.

"What are you talking about, mate? What boy?" he asked, looking around but seeing nothing but the blur of activity from the many denizens of the marketplace.

"I didn't know him, but he was on the lookout for me. Jack, I feel he was being honest—we need to return to Chaouen."

"Tariq, I thought we were returning to your tribe. They will be worried about you. Besides, it will be dangerous for you in Chaouen. The Caid's troops will be on the lookout for you."

"Yes, I know, but clearly there's something happening, and it probably has to do with Fez and Aseem. I don't know if they're in trouble or need my help or what."

Jack listened to Tariq's barrage of arguments, but he still felt it was too dangerous to return to Chaouen. He understood Tariq's reasoning, but he felt the safer road would be going to find the tribe.

"Tariq, I want you to think this through. The Caid's troops are hunting you. It is much safer to remain with your tribe in the mountains than to be seen in the city streets," he tried to explain.

"*That's* why we have to return to Fez and Aseem. If they are discovered as spies, they will need my help more than ever. I am not worried about any danger to myself—I am only concerned with helping my friends!" Tariq tried to explain, and Jack, for the first time, understood the depth of loyalty felt by this young man.

Jack sighed heavily before answering.

"Okay, then. I'll escort you back to Chaouen, but then I must return to my people. Let's leave first thing in the morning."

"No, we should leave now. This town is too dangerous for us, anyway."

"But Tariq, your feet are bloody and torn—there's no way we can walk to Chaouen. You wouldn't make it one mile, even with these shoes."

"Then we must make other arrangements," Tariq answered and smiled.

That night they set out for Chaouen. Jack chose a route that circumvented the route they had taken on their way into Tetouan. He hoped they could avoid running into many of the Caid's troops. It was slow going, as Jack was on foot. As they left town, Jack had managed to haggle a good price for a small donkey, which now carried Tariq on its back, along with some supplies and food so their walk would go that much faster.

Tariq was secretly relieved that Jack had decided to continue with the journey. He had been afraid that, since recovering the diary of Alexander the Great, Jack might decide to leave him and return to Australia. Jack wasn't just a close friend, he was a kind of protector and Tariq felt terribly safe in his presence.

Jack and Tariq traveled through the night and rested only a little. This was Tariq's favorite part of the day. He loved to hear the desert animals come alive during the night and to watch the stars fade into the distance overhead. The next morning, they set out before sunrise to take advantage of the coolness in the air. It was cold, but he enjoyed the chill on his cheeks and fingers and toes. He felt alive. He noticed a bat to his left flying in an erratic fashion as it ate bugs and flies. It amazed him that the bat didn't make a sound. Tariq watched the bat for some time and was thankful for its company. As the sun rose once again against the Rif Mountains, Tariq felt as if he were in God's presence. Some people went to a mosque or a church to find God, but Tariq felt as if he found God in nature; all he had to do was be quiet and listen.

He no longer felt alone.

"Tariq, have you heard of Latin?" Jack asked him, awakening Tariq from his daydreaming.

"I think so."

"It's a very old language. So old, in fact, that Latin is the basis for many modern languages such as French, Spanish, and Italian. These are called Romance languages," Jack explained. Tariq was always riveted when Jack talked about anything. Jack had a way of making the world such an interesting place.

"Anyway, there's a phrase that I want you to learn. Are you ready?" Tariq nodded.

"*E pluribus unum*," Jack said.

"*E pluribus enum?*" Tariq repeated.

"No, *e pluribus unum.*"

Tariq repeated the phrase four times.

"What does it mean?" Tariq asked.

"It means 'Out of many, one.'"

"Out of many, one," Tariq repeated.

He thought about it for a minute.

"It means we are all connected, right?" Tariq asked.

Jack smiled with appreciation. He was continually astounded at how Tariq picked up ideas.

"That's exactly what it means," Jack answered.

"It means that out of many people, we are all one," Tariq continued, now totally transfixed with the idea.

"Not just people—everything! Everything is connected—all of our actions, our dreams, and even our afterlife. Look around this desert and listen—see how it seems as if there is a rhythm to the sounds? If you just close your eyes, it's almost as if you can feel everything, and everything is exactly as it should be. Every flutter of a dragonfly's wings, every falling star, and every breath of wind is in perfect harmony."

Tariq closed his eyes and it was true—he could feel everything happening around him.

"Listen to your own heart. It has a beat and a rhythm. That beat and rhythm is in everything, you just need to listen for it."

Jack was silent once again. Many lessons went this way. Jack would say something, repeat it a few times, and then let Tariq think about it. He didn't pound Tariq with information; he gave him tiny nuggets and allowed him to thoroughly understand each piece before continuing with anything new. Most important, he wanted Tariq to form his own opinions on matters rather than simply repeating what he was taught.

Jack noticed if he forced his teachings on Tariq, then Tariq was much less interested—probably due to his naturally rebellious and independent nature. But if Jack merely mentioned something in passing, and allowed Tariq to come to it on his own, he found Tariq to be willing and intelligent student.

All the talk about the Legend of the Red Hand had piqued Tariq's interest in Jack's world and the secrets that lay across the ocean. He felt as if Jack had given him just a small crumb of knowledge and he was hungry for the entire piece of bread.

Being with Jack had started Tariq thinking about his own life. He considered the decisions he'd made so far, and wondered if he would consider himself a good person. He'd been an orphan his entire life and had thought about nothing but survival. If he had to steal or beat up another boy to protect himself, he never gave it a second thought. Everything he did revolved around just trying to get through each day.

He thought about being a protector of the Red Hand Scrolls and about having the opportunity to learn their secrets. The more he thought about it, the more the idea appealed to him. There was an entire world out there and he had experienced so little of it.

For the first time, Tariq realized that life wasn't just about day-to-day survival. There was something much, much bigger than himself out there. He suddenly felt his life wasn't just a series of meaningless decisions, but that he was part of something—and whatever that something was, it had rules and paths that led to good or evil.

It was all terribly exciting and thought-provoking.

————————— ⁂ —————————

Charles and Basil stood on a ledge overlooking Saint Catherine's, the private boarding school attended by Margaret, Sophie, Etienne, Inez, and Alice. It hadn't taken them long to travel to the school and they now stood looking down on it. It was absolutely beautiful, nestled in a French valley surrounded by long and narrow rows of sycamore trees, with a light fog rolling in off the valley's edge. The buildings were very old, built in the traditional French brick style. Charles thought to himself that Claude Monet would very much have liked to paint the scene in front of him.

Moments later, they stood facing Sister Anne in her pristine office.

"Absolutely not!" Sister Anne roared when confronted with the motley crew in front of her.

Charles, Henri, and Basil looked sheepishly at the ground. They had wanted to wait before explaining their predicament to Sister Anne, but the girls insisted they do it at that instant.

"Sister, do you remember the story of the Louise-Renée Leduc? She was a simple woman who led the March on Versailles, was eventually imprisoned, and made a heroine of the Revolution?" Inez asked loudly and urgently.

"Yes, Inez, of course I remember—" Sister Anne tried to answer.

"We are taught that the truth is not always clear and that there are many sides to justice. This is our chance to prove ourselves worthy as students of Saint Catherine and her legacy. If we do not stand up to this injustice, then how can any of us honestly take anything that you teach us seriously?"

Sister Anne stood staring at Inez with her mouth open, as did everyone else.

Then Sophie stepped forward.

"I stand with my friend Inez. Just because the French authorities want Colonel Owen and Captain Basil does not mean that they are guilty. In fact, I am convinced they are innocent and being framed by a sinister conspiracy. It is our responsibility to help them, regardless of the risks. Justice must be served!"

Sister Anne felt ambushed as the other girls joined their hands and stood in front of her, defiant in their position. Looking at the girls, and then at the raggedy group of men behind them, Sister Anne felt she was at an impasse.

"Harboring pirates and fugitives is hardly what I had imagined I'd be doing during my tenure at Saint Catherine's. And you, Monsieur Henri—you're practically an enemy to France," she said, trying to convince herself of her reasoning.

She tapped her finger on her desk before continuing.

"However, you make an interesting argument. After talking with you, Colonel Owen, I have no doubt you have been improperly charged by the British Crown. Still, there are the other girls to consider. And how will you conceal yourselves?"

She did a quick glance at Cortez, who hadn't said a word the entire time.

"We've figured that out, Sister. They could hide in the far barn away from the school. If anyone asks, they are our new farm hands and groundskeepers," Margaret interrupted.

"If the French authorities catch them, they will shut down this school," she said with desperation in her voice.

Charles stepped forward and tried to make his point in passable French.

"Sister Anne, I cannot thank you enough for taking the time to meet with us. We are tired and hungry and, up until yesterday, I thought my time on this earth was finished. We don't mean for any harm to come to you and your school. In fact, that's the last thing I would ever allow to happen. Therefore, I cannot allow you to take on such a risk, even at the insistence of these brave girls. If you could allow us a bath and a meal, we'll be on our way. But I must insist that Margaret come with me. I will not leave her side after such a long time away."

The girls gasped and started crying and Margaret ran to her father and hugged him tightly. She was so sorry to leave her friends, but she wasn't about to leave her father's side.

Charles, Basil, and Henri bowed deeply to Sister Anne and were about to leave her office when she spoke up.

"Oh, very well! You may take up your quarters in the barn furthest away from the school and we'll masquerade that you are our new help. Do not reveal your real names to the other girls, and Colonel, you must keep the fact that you are Margaret's father a secret. I'll see to it that you two get to spend plenty of time together," Sister Anne said as the girls shrieked again and ran to each other, joining arms and hugging in a tight circle. Basil and Charles winked at one another.

"Merci, Sister Anne. We'll do our best to stay completely invisible," Basil said in excellent French. Sister Anne beamed with appreciation.

"Okay then, let's get you some breakfast. But first, you must take a bath, as even the cows are complaining of your smell," Sister Anne said, giggling as she made her way past them.

The girls returned to their quarters, quickly changed into clean uniforms, and made their way to breakfast. The men were shown to a barn on the outskirts of the school and a proper bed was made for them (if a proper bed means sheets stuffed with straw and a blanket to keep warm). Still, it was a sight better than a prison cell and the hangman's noose. They were provided clean clothes, and after they had a bath, they were served a generous breakfast of ham and cheese omelets, some nice warm bread, coffee, and a side of strawberry preserves. The men devoured their food so fast it barely touched their lips. Cortez sat quietly in a corner, eating his food, his head buried over his plate.

"I forgot what bloody good cooks the French are. This is amazing," Charles said between bites. Basil nodded along with him.

Once dressed and fed, the men took to surveying the land. Soon, Sister Anne had them working a till and preparing the school garden for the spring planting. It was hard work, and their muscles ached, but it was the best Charles had felt in some time. To simply be alive and working and with his daughter was a dream come true.

At a distance, Sister Anne studied the men. She had liked Charles and Basil immediately, and even the scoundrel Henri. But there was something about that man Cortez that she didn't trust. He wouldn't meet her eyes, and he was always a distance away from the group.

She decided that she would need to keep an eye on him.

Back in the courtyard, Henri prepared his men for the journey home.

"Charles, my goal was to see you safely here, and it's obvious you're in good hands. Take care, my friend. It was a pleasure to meet you," Henri said and the two men embraced. They had already agreed that once Charles and Basil were safe at Saint Catherine's, Henri would return to his island and his people.

"Henri, you're as brave a man as I've ever known. I can't thank you enough for seeing after my daughter and me. I am forever in your debt," Charles replied.

Basil then stepped up with his own crew.

"I've instructed my men to venture back with Henri, and I'll meet up with them outside of Marseilles. It is safer for them this way," Basil explained.

Charles remained eminently impressed with Henri and his crew. It was a rare man who would risk his life to help a man he barely knew—all to return a favor. Charles took his time thanking each man, as did Basil, and soon the group of French anarchists disappeared down the road and out of sight.

All except for the man named Cortez, who insisted on staying with Charles and Basil.

Back in England, in a four-story brick house on one of the nicest streets in London, two men were enjoying a glass of fine cognac and smoking huge cigars. Each sat in an oversized leather chair and allowed his lungs to take in the heavy cigar smoke and his lips to savor the complex burn of the cognac.

One man was about sixty and very heavyset. Despite his age, his hair was not yet gray—it was still a fiery red. A walrus moustache covered his upper lip and a nose that looked to have been broken about a dozen times sat crooked on his face. His eyes were narrow, and he had dark, blue circles under them. Rolls of fat drooped down his neck and over his collar. His suit was custom-made by the finest tailor in all of England. His shoes were custom as well, and he had six pair at home identical to the ones he now wore.

His companion was also about sixty. He was tall—almost six-foot-three—and going increasingly bald. He attempted to hide this fact of nature by habitually combing what little hair remained in such a way that it attempted to cover up his bald spot, but he never accomplished his mission. The effect was quite the opposite—it looked like someone had speedily glued patches of hair across his head, and it now resembled some kind of jigsaw puzzle.

The second man's skin was pasty white from the long English winter. The first man's skin was a bit tanner, as he had just returned from holiday in Italy.

The first man—the large man—was Lionel Hedgecock, president of the Far Indian Trading Company, and the second man was Admiral Roy Ferguson of the British Royal Navy.

The two sat drinking and smoking and seemed altogether pleased with themselves. Mr. Hedgecock produced some papers and shared a few of them with Admiral Ferguson. As they looked over the papers, they both chuckled and smiled.

"Are these figures really correct?" Ferguson asked.

"Yes, Roy, we are making more money right now than at any time in our history! It's all thanks to Lieutenant Dreyfuss. He has done a masterful job patrolling the Mediterranean and blowing our competitor's ships out of the water. Our fishing revenue has gone through the roof, as has our spice trade. Our plan has been simply masterful," Hedgecock said excitedly.

"Yes, well, if all it takes is sinking some Spanish trading boats and attacking some peasant fishing villages, maybe we should have thought of this long ago," he answered and the two men toasted one another.

Hedgecock continued to chew on his cigar, and a couple drops of drool fell from his fat lip onto his suit jacket. He ignored the drool from the cigar and continued to feverishly scan the paper in front of him.

Greed was in his eyes.

"I'll have the funds transferred to your account in the usual manner. I imagine it will be over one hundred thousand this month. Have you heard from Dreyfuss?" Hedgecock asked, as a sinister grin crossed Ferguson's face.

"The usual stuff. He sank two Belgian trading boats last week and sacked an Algerian fishing port," Ferguson answered in the drollest of voices.

"What about Owen?"

"No word yet on that bit of unpleasantness. Still, the damage is already done, with all the stories in the press. Right now, Charles is the most hated man in all of England," Ferguson answered matter-of-factly.

Hedgecock snorted his approval before putting down the papers. He had dreamed up this scheme three years ago, and now they were reaping the profits at last. Dreyfuss was their "strong man" in the Mediterranean and literally blew any kind of competition out of the water. Ferguson was his man in the British navy, who saw to it that nobody snooped around Dreyfuss or asked any unsavory questions. In return, Hedgecock had made Ferguson a very rich man.

The unpleasant part of this operation was that Lieutenant Dreyfuss was also killing innocent African fishermen to ensure that the Far Indian fishing fleets caught all the fish. They were sinking trading boats right and left in order to drive up the price of spices and other goods, all of which were willingly supplied by the Far Indian Trading Company to the hungry English public.

Charles Owen was another matter. Since they couldn't kill him, they had destroyed his reputation through the English papers instead. Even if he were to appear and implicate Dreyfuss, hardly anyone would take his word that the lieutenant was engaged in any kind of criminal activity.

The two men sat and laughed, plotting and scheming about how they could become wealthier—and more and more powerful.

Zijuan crossed the mountain pass with nary a spot of trouble. Yes, it was cold, but the spring weather meant the midday was warm. Even flowers were beginning to show themselves through the morning frost. Ordinarily, she would enjoy the pleasant surroundings and take time to appreciate their beauty. However, today she walked with urgency, feeling a bit frantic but completely focused on finding the tribe.

She kept up a brisk pace, aided by her walking stick, until she finally reached the ridge; she desperately hoped she would find the tribe once she made it to the other side. The climb had been very steep and treacherous. She could see why a large army would have so much difficulty finding the camp. There were places on the trail where it seemed impossible for any livestock to pass through, and many areas where it was only possible to proceed in single file. It made sense that the tribe would retreat to this ridge, as there were so many opportune places to stage an ambush.

In spite of its strategic effectiveness, Zijuan noticed that the farther she climbed, the more desolate the landscape became. Trees and plants became more and more scarce, and with the increase in altitude, her breathing began to feel labored.

It would be a very tough place for the camp.

As she crested the ridge, Zijuan was unprepared for the sight in front of her. Yes, she had found the camp, but it was not the camp she was expecting. Even from a distance, it looked defeated. There were no roaring fires or laughing children. In fact, no one was outside—the tribespeople were most likely huddled in their tents to protect themselves from the howling and biting wind. It concerned her that she hadn't even seen any scouts, which should have been the norm.

Zijuan walked directly over to the first tent and announced herself without entering. She could hear rustling from inside, but it took a few moments for the inhabitant to emerge.

It was Nawwaf, a younger man. His wife and his two children followed him outside, and all four hugged and greeted Zijuan with tears in their eyes.

"Zijuan, please come inside and let me tell you what has happened," Nawwaf suggested.

Soon Zijuan was seated inside with a wool blanket wrapped around her. It was warmer inside, but it wasn't comforting. Usually, a fire would be going, along with a teakettle and perhaps a pot of stew. However, the tribe had forbidden people from making fires, as the smoke might signal their location to outsiders. Because of this, everyone in the village had been reduced to keeping warm by wrapping themselves in blankets and furs. Most days they didn't venture outside at all and simply huddled together in their respective tents. Food was being rationed; there was hardly ever enough for more than one meal a day, which usually consisted of cold lentils and perhaps a little dried fish.

Nawwaf looked as if he had aged ten years since Zijuan had last seen him. He looked tired and hungry and altogether miserable. His children, usually gregarious and happy, simply stared at the ground without saying a word.

"Many of our most able warriors are dead—ambushed and killed by the Black Mamba. We have heard he tortured and slaughtered Malik and Sanaa. We moved to this location because the Black Mamba continues to hunt us, and it was the only way we could keep safe. However, we cannot hunt, and it's so windy outside that we almost never leave our tents. Zijuan, I fear our time is coming to an end. If the Mamba finds us, he will cut us down for sure," Nawwaf explained, and Zijuan could hear the despair in his voice.

Things were much worse than she had anticipated.

"I will stay with the tribe until such time as you are safe and can begin to rebuild. We must move from this site as soon as possible, as it's not feasible to stay here for the long term. I will begin scouting the countryside for a suitable replacement. In the meantime, we must have scouts set up on the perimeter. It is too risky to leave the camp exposed like this," she said, and Nawwaf nodded his head in agreement.

The next morning Zijuan met with each and every camp inhabitant and heard the same story. They were hungry and tired and depressed. Nary a person smiled, but Zijuan's presence did slightly improve the tribe's morale. She established sentries at various points on the trails to ensure any visitors, wanted or not, would alert the camp.

The morning after, she set out by herself to find a new camp. It was a slow and arduous trek through the mountains and valleys. Each time she thought she had discovered a proper spot, she found some problem with it. She had to find a location that would not only be very difficult to attack, but also suitable for shelter, with an appropriate level of shade. It needed to be near a water source, and the tribe needed to be able to hunt and gather food.

After four days of searching, she finally found a clearing she felt was acceptable. The area was just large enough to hold the entire tribe, and a stream was only a short five-minute walk. It was only approachable from two directions and, in both cases, access was by a trail that crisscrossed through a series of valleys. Walking was treacherous. It would be difficult to launch a surprise attack on this location, and it offered an emergency escape exit in the event of a hasty retreat. More than enough oak trees added protection and shelter.

That night, Zijuan set up a small camp and slept in the clearing to ensure the wind didn't cut too much into the shelter. In the morning, she continued to measure the vantage points they might use to launch an ambush. She found that the creek was just big enough to catch a few fish, but too small to supply fish for the entire tribe. She saw evidence of animals on several trails, which confirmed her hunch that the hunting would be excellent.

Settling under her blanket, Zijuan was just drifting into sleep when she heard the distant sound of voices. In the background she could hear the trampling of horse hooves on the hard ground.

Someone had been following her, and they were closing in on her location. Nobody would find this spot by accident—they were clearly traveling there for a purpose. And the only person who might have cause to follow her was the Black Mamba. Had he discovered the tribe's camp, massacred the people, and followed her tracks up to the ridge? Her mind raced with possibilities.

Drawing her dagger, she knew one thing for sure: she would not go down without a fight.

Crouching beneath a cliff and hiding in the shadows, she waited for her pursuers and promised to give them a surprise they would never forget. If it was her time to die, she was going to take more than a few of them with her!

CHAPTER
— *6* —

INVASION

Wave after wave of French military boats crossed the Mediterranean Sea. There were cruisers and ironclad battleships, as well as the new dreadnoughts—a faster and sleeker class of battleship. In addition, the French had various troop transport ships and support ships to provide reinforcements to the larger war ships. French officers stood on each ship's deck smoking cigarettes, the collars of their black pea coats pulled up high around their faces. They watched the horizon with the intensity of an osprey hunting for a tasty bit of mackerel.

All night the ships thundered across the water, looking like a fat flock of metal geese as far as the eye could see. Smoke billowed from their stacks and French flags proudly flew in the wind.

By daybreak, the majority of one group of ships had reached Tangier and began bombarding the city. Shells fell on buildings and soon massive fires broke out across the entire city.

Shortly afterward, the troop transport ships arrived, and French marines attacked the city, battling street by street. The Sultan's troops met them with resistance, but they were no match for the superior French army. The battle soon raged through city squares and business districts. Urban guerrilla fighting broke out, with the Moroccan troops firing from the shadows of apartment building windows. All around Tangier, chaos developed as the city's inhabitants ran to put out flames that threatened to engulf their city, all the while dodging bombs and bullets from the French.

Within the day, the French had taken Tangier, with the exception of the Sultan's palace.

The second fleet landed at Casablanca the following day, and it took just four hours to capture that coastal city.

The French generals had their orders. Some of the troops from Tangier would march down and capture Marrakesh, since Casablanca was already secure.

Soon, the French would capture all of Morocco's major cities.

Caid Ali Tamzali monitored these developments with great glee and anticipation. He knew the French had plans to attack this week, and the resistance had turned out to be even less than they had anticipated. His troops had already secured the surrounding areas of his kasbah and had subdued the nearby tribes.

There would be no further resistance from any of the tribes.

All the Caid had to do now was to wait for the French to capture the Sultan. Then he would be named the new Sultan of Morocco and allowed to rule with an iron fist.

Tariq and Melbourne Jack stood on the outskirts of Chaouen. The journey had been relatively easy and the donkey had proven to be an excellent purchase. Tariq's feet were nearly healed, and his new shoes fit wonderfully over his bandaged skin.

Jack was nervous.

They had so far managed to avoid bandits; now they were returning to a city where the Caid's troops would be hunting for Tariq. It would be very dangerous, and Jack wasn't sure exactly how Tariq might make it through town unnoticed. This problem had been bothering him since the previous day, when he had suddenly come up with this plan.

"Tariq, I've got an idea about how we can hide you from the troops, but you've got to trust me, okay?"

Tariq nodded, as this issue had been bothering him as well.

They walked the final mile or so to the edge of the city. Before they entered, Jack stopped and told Tariq to hide out with the donkey until his return.

It was half an hour before Jack returned with something in his hand.

"What's that?" Tariq asked.

"It's a burqa," he announced before unveiling a large black robe with a matching headdress and veil.

"A burqa! But that's for girls!" Tariq protested.

"It doesn't matter who it's for—it will keep you protected from view and your identity secret."

Tariq took a look at the burqa. It was so long that it would cover every inch of skin on his body. The veil completely covered his head and face. Trying it on, he realized it was way too long. Cloth hung from his arms and dragged on the ground.

"Are you kidding me, Jack? I can't wear this thing," he continued to protest.

Jack began making some adjustments at Tariq's feet and, producing a needle and thread, he quickly stitched up the fabric so it wouldn't drag on the ground so much. Satisfied, he pulled up the veil to see Tariq's face and proceeded to put black kohl around his eyes.

"Jack! Are you serious?" Tariq whined.

"If anyone takes a close look, we've got to have you looking like a girl. Nobody will be so bold as to pull up your veil, but they might take a closer look through it."

Tariq sat in his burqa, completely covered from head to toe and feeling very silly.

"Tariq, if it makes you feel any better, I've got to wear one as well," Jack told him.

"What?"

"It wouldn't look proper to have a western man walking around with a Moroccan girl dressed in a burqa, now would it? We'll pretend we're mother and daughter out strolling through the city."

Tariq started laughing at the thought of Jack wearing a burqa.

"I thought you might like that," Jack answered and began putting on his own robe.

"The donkey and our provisions should be safe. It's my hope that we can find your friends in short order. If anyone suspects us and calls the guards, we've got to be ready to make a quick exit and get out of town—understood?" Jack said in a stern voice.

"Yes," Tariq answered, suddenly remembering they were in a great deal of danger.

"Okay then—let's go find your friends."

Jack and Tariq walked the city streets of Chaouen completely shrouded by their burqas. They tried their best to walk in a feminine manner, which was made easier by the fact the burqas didn't allow for much room to walk. Tariq's head was hot, and it was very itchy. He had no idea how girls did this every single day of their lives! It would be completely miserable to have to walk in public all the time completely covered. Only a small number of Moroccan women wore burqas, but he still felt empathy for the women who did. Although the fabric was lightweight, it was still a burden to grab or hold anything. He felt his own breath against the veil and decided he really, really needed to brush his teeth. His breath smelled awful, which only made the experience that much more miserable. Attempting to see was also a difficult challenge. He felt as if he lived permanently behind a window drawn with cotton shades. He could only see that which was right in front of him; things at a distance were almost impossible to make out.

For two hours they walked the city streets, and nobody paid them any amount of attention. They hadn't found any sign of Fez or Aseem, and both of them were now sweating profusely through their burqas. A couple of times, they had to stop in an alley and ensure nobody was watching before they took off their veils just to cool down their heads. Jack was even sweatier than Tariq, and his face had flushed a deep red.

They were stopped at a village market to get a better vantage point of the square. Tariq's feet were still bothering him a bit so Jack decided to allow him to rest at the market while he scouted around by himself. Tariq, trying to be inconspicuous, stood just outside the market next to a brick wall.

Suddenly, a feminine voice spoke to Tariq as he was looking around the square. It was a soft voice, melodic, and very sweet.

"You're not a girl, are you?" she asked.

Tariq didn't know what to say. If he answered in his normal voice, undoubtedly she would know he was pretending. If he tried to imitate a girl, it's possible he would come off as a complete idiot.

So he just stood there ignoring her.

"It's okay, I promise I won't tell on you. It's just that your feet are those of a boy."

Tariq looked down and it was true—his shoes were poking out from under the burqa and they were undoubtedly boy's shoes as they were leather and dirty. There hadn't been time to find him proper shoes for a girl—besides, how many people actually look at a girl's feet?

Tariq squinted through his burqa to catch a glimpse of the face of his new coconspirator, and he was shocked by what he saw.

The girl was also dressed in a black burqa from head to toe. Only her eyes peeked out from a cutout in her veil. They were the most beautiful eyes he had ever seen in his life: green and mesmerizing and completely exotic. Black kohl outlined her eyes, which made them look even more intoxicating.

"Thank you," was all he managed to say, and the girl giggled with delight.

"You're the first boy I've talked with in over two years who wasn't my uncle. I used to have loads of friends who were boys. But since I've reached marrying age, I'm not allowed to talk to any of them."

Tariq didn't know what to say to this. This girl had absolutely no idea what he looked like or who he was, and now she was spilling all her secrets to him.

"I'm on a secret mission," he replied, trying to sound important.

"A secret mission?" she repeated, her tone rising with excitement.

"Umm…yes."

"What kind of secret mission?" she asked.

"Well, if I told you, it wouldn't be a secret mission, would it?"

She punched Tariq in the arm after that reply, and he yelped in surprise. A couple of people in the market looked at the two of them but then went about their business.

"Tell me about your mission or I'm going to start yelling and you'll be exposed for sure," she scolded.

"I can't."

"Okay, I'm going to count to three. If you don't tell me, then I'm going to start yelling."

Tariq couldn't believe what was happening. Who was this girl and why was she talking to him?

"One."

He couldn't think of anything to say that might appease her.

"Two."

She was about to count three when he finally gave in.

"Okay, okay—but we've got to go somewhere more secluded before I can tell you."

"Why not here?" she asked.

"Because I'm terribly hot, and I'm about to suffocate in this thing. I don't know how you girls can wear this thing all day."

"You get used to it. Okay, follow me—but you better tell me about your secret mission!"

"I will, I will," Tariq promised.

Tariq followed the girl down a small alley. Once they were safe from being spied on by others, he lifted up his veil and let out a deep breath. His face was so hot, and it was a relief to feel the cool air against his skin. Tariq paused after taking a couple of breaths, expecting this new girl to lift her veil as well. She simply stood there staring at him.

"Aren't you going to take off your veil?"

"No," she answered tersely with a puzzled look, as if she were trying to place him from somewhere.

"I know you," she told him.

"No you don't, I'm not from Chaouen," he answered.

"I don't know you, but I know of you. You're the boy who is wanted by the Caid, aren't you?" she asked him.

Tariq almost fainted. He knew he was wanted in Chaouen, but he had no idea just how aggressively the Caid was hunting him. He suddenly felt sick—as if he might vomit and pass out all at the same moment.

"Don't worry," she said, trying to reassure him, "your identity is safe with me."

"How did you know?" he asked, not even wanting to go through the effort of protesting.

"Wanted posters are up everywhere with pictures of you and your friends. Also, my uncle is in the police force. A reward has been offered to anyone who captures you."

Tariq was sure he was going to pass out upon hearing this news.

Just then there was a moment of silence. The girl paused, wondering if she should tell Tariq something.

"I hate my uncle. He is brutal and a very corrupt policeman. My father and mother were killed in a fire and I was forced to live with him. My father was a very kind man, but his brother is evil. He is already trying to find the highest price for my hand so he can marry me off."

Tariq could hear the hurt and sorrow in her voice. He suddenly felt such empathy for this girl.

"Is this really why you were forced to wear a burqa? It wasn't that you reached marrying age, it was that your father died and your uncle made you wear one."

Tariq could see the sadness in her eyes as she nodded that this was the truth.

"If you help me, then perhaps I can help you," he said, without even thinking of why he was saying it. In fact, the entire conversation had left him dizzy. He felt a kind of magnetic pull to this girl, as if she could get him to say and do anything she wanted.

"How could you help me?"

"I'm not sure, but I know I can."

"How can I help you?" the girl asked.

"I'm looking for two friends of mine, and it's very important that I find them. One is as tall as me—with dark skin and short hair. The other is short with round glasses. They would probably be together."

The girl nodded her head.

"If it's the boys on the poster, I know where they are," she answered.

"What? How?" Tariq answered, exhilarated by her answer.

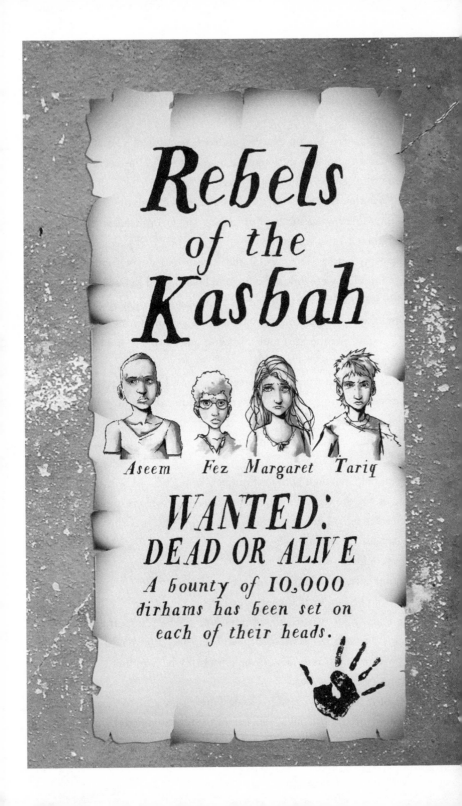

Just then, they both heard a woman's voice call out.

"Azmiya? Azmiya?"

She quickly turned, obviously worried that someone would find her talking with a strange girl. It was uncommon that she ever had a moment of privacy when she was outside her uncle's home. Most times, the head servant wouldn't let her get away from her side. However, today she had been haggling with a garment merchant, which allowed Azmiya time to step away.

"Azmiya? That is your name?' Tariq asked.

"Yes! Go to the blue fountain with koi and you will find your friends," she answered before hurrying away.

"How will I find you?" he asked, but she was already running down the alley.

Just like that, she was gone. Tariq just stood there with a stupid look on his face, a bit stunned by what had just happened. Putting his veil back on, he went to the market to look for Melbourne Jack. He suddenly realized he had a predicament on his hands. How could he possibly find Jack when many women were wearing burqas? They all looked alike to him. He couldn't just walk up to some woman and call out Jack's name. He'd be found out for sure.

For fifteen minutes he stood by himself and he began feel very nervous. It wasn't normal for a Moroccan girl to be by herself for such a long time, and people were starting to stare at him. But something else also held his attention. He couldn't stop thinking of Azmiya. They'd only talked for a minute or two, but still he found himself going over every moment of their conversation.

A shopkeeper kept eyeing him suspiciously. After a few more moments, he came directly up to Tariq and began to pester him.

"Are you lost? Where is your mother?" he asked, to no response from Tariq.

"It's not proper for a girl to be standing by herself. You will come and wait with my wife until we can find out what to do with you," the man said. Still Tariq said nothing.

That's when the man looked down and saw Tariq's shoes peeking out from under the burqa. Tariq tried to shuffle them back under the robe, but the damage was already done.

The man reached up and snatched the veil off of Tariq's head, completely exposing his face.

"What in the name of—" the man stammered when, inexplicably, a fist came out of nowhere and punched the man square in the face. The man went flying across a table, his legs tumbling over his torso as he landed with a somersault.

"Come on!" Jack yelled, grabbing Tariq by the hand and pulling him along.

"Wait!" Tariq said, yanking his veil from the man's fist before running after Jack. He put the veil on as best he could while running at a full sprint.

"Wait, stop them!" He heard a woman's voice call out from behind them and soon everyone in the square stopped to watch as the two robed figures broke through the crowd like Moses parting the Red Sea.

"This way!" Jack yelled, and they turned right and ran out of the square at a full sprint. Tariq looked behind him, and to his surprise, saw there were two guards chasing after them.

"We're being followed!" Tariq yelled. Jack turned around and shook his head. Although they had both hiked their robes up to their thighs so they could run at all, they were no match for the two guards running at them at full speed. He knew they would be caught in moments.

Without warning, Jack stopped, whirled around Tariq, and in one motion, his robe exploded in a cloud of fabric, twisting around him like a cyclone devouring a tree. Out of this whirlwind, two wooden boomerangs flew out at full speed, crisscrossed in midair, and struck the guards directly in their heads. Both were knocked backwards with such force that their legs lifted completely off the ground and their bodies landed in the dirt with a loud thump. Jack ran to them, made sure they were unconscious, and gathered his boomerangs.

"Let's go! They'll have friends!" Jack yelled and they walked briskly away, their disguises back intact, trying to put as much distance between themselves and the unconscious guards as possible.

"We have to find the blue pool with koi," Tariq told him.

"What?" Jack asked.

"A girl told me."

Jack stopped in mid stride. Although he couldn't see Tariq through his veil, he tried to picture his face.

"What girl? What are you talking about?"

"A girl told me that's where we could find Fez and Aseem. That's all I know."

"I leave you alone for two minutes, and you talk to some girl and find out where your friends are?" Jack said and then laughed with appreciation. Life was never boring with Tariq around.

"Okay then, let's find this blue pool after we secure the donkey," he said and the two of them walked off in search of the mystical pond with the Japanese fish.

The Black Mamba stood staring over the marsh as fog rolled in and enveloped the tall grass a gray mist. The ground was soft and muddy and his boots were sucked in with each step. The marsh stunk of the entrails of many animals that had met their death in the mud.

Across the marsh, the Mamba could see numerous campfires flickering in the night. He could hear the voices of men and the occasional beating of drums. Flanking him on each side were two lines of fifty fighters each, all of whom he knew to be capable in battle. Directly to his left stood Jawad, dressed in black with his sword in his hand. Behind him were five more rows of soldiers and the French Legionnaires.

Silently the group made their way across the marsh, crouching low in the night, each man trying not to make a sound.

The closer they crept in the darkness, the campfires grew bigger and bigger and the men's voices grew louder. The Mamba's eyes narrowed and he looked every bit the predator poised to pounce on its unsuspecting prey.

Two days ago, the Mamba received word from one of his spies that a small resistance force was gathering to fight the French. Mostly, these were farmers and peasants who were ill-prepared to fight an organized army. They were a motley crew from many small villages that dotted the countryside. The Caid was had been taxing them to starvation and as a result, most simply felt they had nothing to lose and chose to fight. Despite these weaknesses, they still remained a threat and needed to be dealt with swiftly and unmercifully.

The Mamba welcomed this fight; it had been too long since he had tasted the sweetness of battle.

The soldiers drew near, until finally they were within fifty feet of the group. There were maybe two hundred of them—a ragtag bunch, by the looks of them—and they hadn't had the good sense to post a sentry as a lookout. Undoubtedly, they were scared and unorganized, more accustomed to feeding goats than waging war.

Reaching down, he grabbed a fistful of mud and rubbed it between his hands. He took one final breath, allowing the foul stench to fill his nostrils, then bellowed to his troops in his most threatening voice.

"Attack!" he screamed.

He and his men fell into a full sprint as the group of rebels stared wide-eyed at the marsh, suddenly spotting hundreds of soldiers charging on them, ready to attack. Most of the rebels scattered. Some fell down, clawing for a weapon, and a few tried to fight, but most simply began running as fast they could in the opposite direction.

The ones who stayed to fight were cut down within seconds. Others, who were asleep, jumped up from their blankets only to be trampled and slashed to their deaths with sharp and swift blades.

The Mamba and his soldiers followed the others into the night, killing anyone they found. Only a few slipped from their fingers into the safety of the adjoining hills.

Surveying the remains of the camp, the Mamba stepped over any corpses in his path. Wiping blood from his sword, he picked up a piece of rabbit still roasting on a stick and took a bite of the juicy meat. It was a little overdone, but delicious—not too gamey. The juices dribbled down his chin as he continued to take one huge bite after another.

Battle always made him hungry.

Jawad walked up next to him. Blood was splattered on his shirt, and his pants and boots were muddy and filthy from the bog.

The Mamba smiled at him.

"I see you managed to get one," he said, thoroughly happy with his apprentice.

"Three," Jawad said proudly.

"Excellent! Well, they weren't much competition, but they do make a tasty rabbit," he mentioned and allowed Jawad to tear off a hunk of meat from the stick.

"What should we do with the bodies?" Jawad asked.

The Mamba eyed the corpses and continued to eat.

"The buzzards must eat, as must the hyenas," he said with a shrug before continuing to eat his rabbit.

Jawad took a bite of the rabbit, and it was very hot to his tongue. He didn't want to appear weak to the Mamba, so he carefully chewed the flesh and tried to blow on it without making it obvious.

"I have word of your friend Tariq," the Mamba said.

Jawad was astonished at this news.

"Where?"

"In Chaouen. Apparently a boy who matched his description broke into the local garrison and caused a commotion. Some guards captured him in the mountains, but he managed to escape," the Mamba explained, his expression so intense that he seemed to be in a trance.

Jawad was excited by this news. He understood that to kill Tariq would put him on a pedestal with his master.

"We will leave for Chaouen tomorrow. Perhaps we can learn some news that will lead us to him."

Jawad was even more excited about this bit of information.

"I cannot wait to find him," he said.

The Mamba stared at him and a smile formed on his face.

"Good! We must track down any rebel filth that dares to defy the Caid. Tariq is gaining quite a reputation and killing him would be a powerful and symbolic blow to any who oppose us."

The Mamba and his soldiers slept on the battleground that night. By morning, buzzards had begun devouring the many carcasses left behind to rot. The giant birds hovered over the bodies—sometimes fifteen at a time—and picked apart the fleshy parts. The bodies had already started to decompose, and the smell was nauseating.

Jawad was glad when they were finally back on the road, away from the carnage of battle.

Zijuan was crouched in the darkness, waiting for her pursuers, when she saw the first few come up over the ridge. Even in the moonlight, she could see they were dressed completely in blue—the Tuareg! But what were they doing in the mountains? Relieved, she watched as they walked along the trail.

That's when she saw them—Malik and Sanaa!

"Sanaa!" she shouted, jumping out from the shadows and completely frightening everyone in the group.

"Zijuan?" Sanaa replied and ran to her mentor. Both women hugged one another tightly.

"I thought you were dead," Zijuan whispered in her ear.

"I thought I was as well."

"The Mamba?" Zijuan asked.

"Yes," Sanaa answered in a weak voice.

Zijuan released her grip and saw that Sanaa was crying. Zijuan could not remember a time in her life that she had ever seen Sanaa cry. Perhaps when Sanaa had been a young child, but certainly not in many years.

Whatever happened on the trail put a look of fear in Sanaa's eyes that Zijuan had never seen before.

Zijuan finally looked at Malik, noticing the bandages around his eyes and the walking stick he held in his right hand.

"Malik," she said and went to him.

Malik smiled and held out his arms to embrace Zijuan.

"What happened?" she whispered.

"The Mamba blinded me," he answered, in a voice so sad that it nearly made Zijuan weep on the spot.

"What?"

"He stitched our eyes open so the sun would blind us. Sanaa was lucky, but I was the unfortunate one."

Zijuan looked at Sanaa and saw the stitch marks in her eyes. They were mostly healed, but were still visible if one looked closely.

"There is one more thing to tell you," he added.

"What is that?"

"Sanaa and I are married," he explained and a wide smile broke out on his face.

"It's about time," Zijuan answered and hugged him again.

"What are you doing on this trail?" Sanaa asked.

"Looking for a new place for the tribe. I found a place just around the bend."

Malik smiled at this.

"Great minds think alike. I know the exact spot you are referring to, and that is where I was headed with the Tuareg. No doubt the tribe is scattered and hiding in desolation," Malik replied.

"Yes, they are in bad sorts," she agreed.

"And what about Tariq, how is he?" Malik asked.

Zijuan lowered her head and did not answer.

"What is wrong, Zijuan?"

"I did not find Tariq. His friends returned to the camp for a short while before returning to Chaouen," she replied solemnly.

"He wasn't with them?" he asked.

"No, they came alone."

Malik allowed himself to ponder the consequences of this news.

"That can only mean he is dead or has been captured," he said, his voice falling to a whisper, as if this news knocked the wind from him.

Zijuan placed her hand on his shoulder for reassurance. She understood the news about Tariq would hit him almost as hard as it had her.

"Come, let us set up camp and you can introduce me to your new friends," Zijuan said, turning to meet some of the Tuareg who had gathered close. Their indigo veils and robes were majestic, as were their friendly smiles and mesmerizing dark eyes. Zijuan had only met the Tuareg once—a long, long time ago—and came away impressed by their fighting spirit and their generosity.

"I am Moussa Ag Arshaman," a fair-skinned man said, as he approached and bowed to Zijuan.

She returned his bow and continued to study him. Moussa Ag Arshaman was renowned throughout Africa as a genius on the battlefield and as a fearless warrior.

"I have heard of you," Zijuan said with a measure of respect.

"And I have heard of you, Zijuan," he said with conviction, as if to show he respected her all the more because she was a woman, not in spite of it.

"Let's set up camp; we have much to discuss," Sanaa said, and soon the clearing was alive with activity as the Tuareg soldiers established a makeshift camp and began preparing the night's dinner.

Marrakesh fell soon after Tangier and Casablanca. The French quickly seized control of most of the major cities in Morocco. French troops marched from street to street rounding up any suspected resistance soldiers and placing them in makeshift concentration camps.

Only one stronghold was left.

Moroccan troops had garrisoned in the Sultan's palace as a last resort. They stood twenty or thirty deep in areas—ready to fight to the death for their leader.

The French, now fully organized, realized they had to capture the Sultan's palace to truly cripple the Moroccan forces.

The battalions gathered just outside the Tangier city limits as generals organized their troops and companies. Soldiers were each given a fresh supply of bullets and ordered to sharpen their bayonet blades until they were sharp enough to easily cut through a tough piece of meat. The men were replenished and now stood ready for a fight.

The French set up their artillery positions to shell the Sultan's palace at daybreak, just before twenty thousand French troops arrived to attack in a coordinated strike of biblical proportions. Attacking in waves, the French planned to engage the Moroccan troops in fierce hand-to-hand combat until the Sultan's palace had been overtaken and the French flag—the *drapeau tricolore*—flew overhead.

The Sultan, a young man of twenty, paced in his chambers and frantically tried to think of an escape. He, by birthright, had inherited the position of Sultan, the supreme ruler of Morocco. This title had been handed down for generations, going back hundreds and hundreds of years.

He had been given the title of Sultan when he was just sixteen.

Of course, he was completely ill-prepared for such a responsibility and mostly allowed his many advisors to run the country. He was, for all intents and purposes, little more than a figurehead. Still, to the Moroccan people, he was a historical symbol of their strength and courage. If he died, many Moroccans would see it as the symbolic death of their country.

Dressed in the finest silk, with an ivory bracelet on both wrists and eight heavy gold chains hanging from his neck, the Sultan considered his options over and over in his head.

He didn't have any.

The French had no intention of cutting a deal with him. They wanted to install their own ruler. It would be, to them, a moral victory to take out the Sultan.

In truth, he wasn't a very good leader; he was more interested in the many spoils and luxuries his position afforded him. He squandered millions on fine clothes and jewelry and the latest western fashions. While his country starved, the Sultan engaged in four-month-long tours of Europe and entertained anyone with a royal title.

He wasn't a tyrant, that much was true, and he didn't rob the treasury as completely as many of his ancestors had done. Yet, he didn't make any improvements either. He was as plain-vanilla a ruler as anyone could be. He simply wanted to be left alone with his toys.

All that was about to change. He had been given word that French forces were organizing outside the city gates and would attack his position at dawn.

Images of Marie Antoinette flowed through his head. Would they behead him as well, and parade his severed head around town in a kind of sick ritual?

At that moment, he wanted to be anyone other than the Sultan of Morocco.

CHAPTER
— 7 —

THE BUDDHA'S TOOTH

Foster Crowe set up his circus on the outskirts of the city of Kandy in the country of Ceylon. Ceylon was a tiny island country just off the southern coast of India. The island was mostly dense jungle and mountains, save for a handful of cities. The indigenous people were poor and had never seen a circus in their lives. But once they learned the show had free admission, they flocked from miles and miles to take in the magnificent sights and the displays of magic that stupefied their imaginations.

Crowe had more important matters at hand and a very real purpose for making the long and arduous trek to Ceylon.

Amanda Seigfried was the one who, so long ago, had befriended Melbourne Jack when he was sold to the circus by the British army. She was an animal whisperer who could not only talk with animals, but could also get them to follow her commands and instructions. Like most animal whisperers, she was astute and terribly sensitive to her surroundings and had an intuitive sense of the "feeling" of a place or person.

Amanda had felt something six months ago that forced the circus to pack up and head for Ceylon. She was extremely sensitive to good and evil, both in the world and in people. When she was first taken by this feeling, she doubled over in stomach pain and remained curled up in a ball for the better part of three hours. For the next week, she lay in bed, too sad to leave her tent and barely able to drink the cups of miso soup and ginger tea brought to her by Foster himself.

Everyone in the circus was terribly worried about Amanda.

Amanda was the one who announced that they needed to move the circus to Kandy. Her "spells," as she called them, grew stronger and longer as they approached the shores of Ceylon. Resting in the stalls of an old Hong Kong livestock ship, she could scarcely make it up to the deck to take in the sight of the majestic Indian Ocean. As they ventured to

Kandy, their wagons pulled by mules and dozens of Ceylonese workers, Amanda broke out in a fever and fell into a kind of trance.

Foster had wanted to turn back, but she insisted they stay the course.

He had heard that there was an unspeakable evil in the darkness of the Ceylonese jungles just outside of Kandy. Rumors of villagers being strangled in the night and talk of human sacrifice had made the rounds in the many villages. People started to completely avoid that part of the dense jungle. The snake hunters ceased to look for their cobras and pythons in the many trees and anthills that populated that part of the jungle. Even the wild elephants began to detour around that section of jungle. Wild monkeys fled from the trees.

Whatever person, or force, that was in that jungle emanated pure and concentrated evil. A force more powerful than anything Amanda had ever felt in her life.

But they also had designs on something else: the tooth of the Buddha, reported to be housed at the Sri Dalada Maligawa temple.

The Buddha's tooth was considered the most sacred and holy artifact in all of Asia. It remains the only surviving relic of the Buddha and has been passed down for thousands of centuries. This tooth was considered so sacred that an entire fortress was built around it to protect it from bandits and marauders. The Buddhist monks who guarded it were some of the most lethal martial artists in the world—each hand-picked for special training at the age of seven. These chosen ones practiced martial arts in every form for six hours a day until their twenty-first birthdays. Only then were they allowed to guard the Buddha's tooth.

The tooth itself was locked away in a room and guarded twenty-four hours a day. The only entrance into the chamber was through a steel door guarded by senior monks. Four of the Buddhist elders were allowed to actually view the tooth, once a year, and on this date each year, the monks held a sacred festival. The whole country celebrated, while the Buddhist masters spent an entire day praying as they gazed upon the tooth.

A moat—filled with crocodiles—was built around the fortress housing the tooth. Criminals were thrown into the moat as punishment, and those prehistoric animals learned to love the taste of human flesh.

It was said the Buddha's tooth held unimaginable power and kept harmony in the world. It was believed that if the tooth were to fall into evil hands, there would be no limit to the amount of devastation it might cause. Other legends told of a scroll written by the Buddha himself that always accompanied the tooth. No one could confirm or deny the existence of the scroll—it was rumored that only a handful of Buddhist masters had ever laid eyes on it. The Buddha's tooth and the mysterious scroll were more myth than reality.

Fortunately, Foster Crowe believed in myths almost more than he believed in reality.

He strongly believed they had traveled to Kandy to confirm that the tooth was safe in its resting place, as well to as attempt, if he could, to actually see the mythical scroll of the Buddha.

The only problem was the matter of breaking into the Sri Dalada Maligawa. As far as fortresses went, it was the most well-guarded building in all of Asia. In fact, it offered more protection than the Taj Mahal.

If the tooth was missing, as was his suspicion, then he must find out who had stolen it, and why. His greatest fear was that someone had discovered the secrets of the Red Hand and was using them for evil.

One night, after the circus had closed, he carefully watched the temple and the two sentries who stood watch over the only bridge leading in or out. At one precise moment, he walked over the bridge in full view of them, yet they didn't see a thing. Even from a distance away, he was able to momentarily hypnotize them—making them believe they wouldn't *want* to see him.

Once past the guards, he opened the door to the temple and silently made his way inside. Moving from shadow to shadow, he entered the main building, moved around some hallways, and finally found the room that housed the tooth.

Two monks guarded it, and they were both undoubtedly trained to kill.

He attempted to hypnotize them as well, but they were too strong-minded. He'd have to fight them instead.

As Foster emerged from the shadows, the guards instantly spotted him and came to attention. Each had a longbow staff, approximately seven feet in length. They quickly surrounded him. Bowing his head, Foster didn't make a sound, but simply waited for the monks to attack him.

After several moments, and after yelling at him in Singhalese—a language he didn't understand—the monk behind him stabbed at his lower back in a series of rapid thrusts. The attack was so fast and brutal it would have instantly crippled most men. Foster, however, simply parried the blows, grabbed the stick with his left hand, and broke it with his right elbow. Then, with two quick steps, he hit the monk with a series of pressure point blows and the monk crumpled to the ground in a heap.

The other monk, shocked at such a display, kept his distance and didn't attack.

Foster moved to the door of the room and produced a skeleton key from his pocket, which he immediately inserted into the lock.

The monk, seeing that Foster was trying to enter the room that held the Buddha's tooth, attacked with a vengeance.

Sticks and deadly kicks and elbow thrusts flew at Foster with hummingbird-like speed and accuracy. These monks were some of the best martial artists in the world. Just one of them had the strength and power of a dozen normal men.

Yet, in a manner of seconds, Foster had disarmed and disabled the second monk as well. He didn't kill either of them, or really even hurt them—he simply hit pressure points on their necks that would put them in a deep sleep for a couple of hours.

Turning back to the door, he jiggled and adjusted the skeleton key until he heard a click as the lock released. Quietly, he entered the room.

It was completely dark and a musty smell entered his nostrils. Lighting a match, he could see that the room was empty, except for a cement stand directly in the middle of the room. The stand had a curved base, and stood about three and a half feet off the ground, with a glass container on top, covering a purple pillow. In the center of the pillow sat a tooth.

Foster gently removed the glass top and examined the tooth. To the naked eye, it certainly looked like a human tooth. However, upon closer inspection, it was not a tooth at all.

It was a plaster fabrication made to look like an ancient tooth.

Foster carefully lifted the pillow. Underneath, he saw a clear outline—the perfect shape and size of a page. Something that had been hidden under the pillow was now missing.

It was true—the tooth had been stolen and a scroll did exist!

Whoever had stolen it hadn't been too concerned about alerting the monks to its absence. The replacement tooth was a poor replica and, if there had been a scroll, they hadn't even bothered to replace it.

After putting everything back in place, Foster quickly vacated the room, locked it up, and removed a small bottle from his pocket. The bottle was almost filled to the brim with an odorless liquid. Opening the bottle, Foster produced a handkerchief, dropped some of the liquid on the fabric, and rubbed it just beneath each guard's nostrils. It was an amnesia potion designed to fog their short-term memory.

The guards would wake up with no recollection of Foster Crowe or of having been defeated. They would simply be in a confused daze as to why they had been unconscious.

Foster left the temple as quietly as he had entered it.

Back at the circus, he sat quietly in his tent and tried to think of a possible explanation for what he had discovered.

There was only one.

His worst fears were being realized.

Someone else knew of the Red Hand Scrolls.

Someone who was very, very evil.

Foster sat in his tent and made the decision to call in Raja the Seer.

Raja was a gypsy from Bombay. Foster had found him in an Indian slum and convinced him to join the circus.

Raja was a fortune teller—a man with an incredible ability to see into the future. Although Foster also had considerable powers, lately his psychic powers had deserted him. He tried meditating and relaxing, but the images just didn't come to him.

"Raja, I need your powers. I feel there is so much disruption in the world and the circus is in much danger."

Raja bowed, exited the tent, and returned with an object hidden under a green velvet cloth. He removed the cloth to reveal a glass ball on an ancient mahogany stand, which he placed on the table in front of Foster.

Raja closed his eyes, placed both of his palms around the glass ball, and quietly focused for three solid minutes. Removing his palms, he stared into the ball.

To Foster, the glass still looked empty, but to Raja, something entirely different was happening.

"I see three warriors in the sand. One is blind. They are fighting a great battle, but the outcome is unclear. Jack is with them."

"Jack!" Foster exclaimed. "He is protecting someone or something."

Raja leaned back and breathed deeply.

"That is all I can see, my friend."

Foster furrowed his eyebrows.

"Nothing of the circus? Nothing of this new evil?"

"I'm sorry, Foster, but no. I do not control what I see, and today this is all the ball had to show me."

Foster nodded his head.

"Thank you, my old friend."

Raja bowed and left the tent.

Foster sat back and tried to digest the information he had been given. A great battle in the sand? Three warriors? And what did Jack have to do with it?

None of it made any sense.

He would need to seek out the darkness in the jungle.

CHAPTER
— *8* —

NOT INVISIBLE

Tariq and Jack soon found their way to the blue pool with the Japanese koi fish. It sat underneath a grouping of weeping willows. As they approached, a light breeze brushed the branches of the trees. The fountain was in a secluded part of town, away from the hustle and bustle of the main area, and surrounded by a group of blue apartments. The pool itself was only about three feet deep and constructed from tiny tiles in different shades of blue. Scattered across the bottom were numerous coins—it was obviously also used as a wishing well. The large koi swam effortlessly in the clear water, occasionally eating a bit of food, perfectly content in their world.

For two hours they stood near the fountain, trying to look as inconspicuous as possible. The last thing they needed was to attract any attention. They had ditched their burqas and hoped they wouldn't run into any guards in this section of town.

It was obvious why Fez and Aseem would want to stay around here. The area was peaceful and there wasn't a great deal of security. Mostly, they saw the occasional mosque and families keeping to themselves.

At last, Tariq saw them. The boys were with an older man and another street urchin. All four walked close together at a brisk pace. Not wanting to shout, he and Jack took off after them.

They walked through a series of alleyways and finally stopped behind a building. Tariq ran to them and tapped Fez on the shoulder.

"Fez!" he exclaimed with a smile.

Fez looked around, saw it was Tariq, and immediately hugged him tight. In fact, Fez was crying, he was so happy to see his friend.

Aseem had to do a double take to convince himself that Tariq was really alive and standing next to him. His eyes opened widely and a huge smile broke across his face.

"I cannot believe you are alive!" Fez said and shook his head in disbelief.

"What happened to you?" Aseem asked.

"It is a very long story. This is my friend Melbourne Jack. We were in Tetouan and a boy said we needed to return here. It was all very mysterious. We were on our way back to join the tribe, but decided it was more important to check on you," Tariq explained.

Fez and Aseem looked at one another.

"Yes, we put out word to the various street boys to be on the lookout for you. You are wanted by the Caid and his police—it's incredibly fortunate you haven't been captured," Fez explained. Tariq understood this and nodded in agreement.

"There's something else," Fez continued.

"What is it?"

"The tribe has been scattered. The Black Mamba attacked them and slaughtered most of our best fighters. And there is something else..." he tried to explain, but had to stop.

Tariq was speechless. The tribe had been attacked?

Fez couldn't continue. Tariq saw the despair in his friend's eyes.

"What is it?" Tariq whispered, with concern in his voice.

"Malik and Sanaa are dead, Tariq," Aseem finished.

Tariq almost fainted. Jack grabbed him and helped him to a step where he could sit down.

"What? Are you sure?" Tariq asked, tears forming in his eyes.

"The Mamba killed them. That's all we know."

Tariq began to cry, burying his face in his hands. Malik was like a father to him, and Sanaa was the one who had rescued him from the Caid. He considered both of them to be completely fearless and totally incapable of being killed. How could this have happened?

Fez was the one who sat next to Tariq and put his arm around him.

"We feel the same way. We couldn't stay with the tribe. We are determined to avenge Malik and Sanaa's deaths, and that is why we are in Chaouen. This is our friend Timin. And you remember Jamal from the kasbah. We are establishing a spy network and we *will* kill the Caid and his men."

"A spy network?" Jack asked and stepped forward.

Timin glanced at Jack and was suddenly suspicious.

"Fez, perhaps this isn't the best venue to explain—" he started.

"Tariq is our friend. If he says that Jack can be trusted, then he can be trusted," Fez replied, eyeing Timin with a seriousness that made the old man take a step backward.

Jack, assessing the situation, attempted to calm Timin's fears.

"Do not worry. I am an enemy of the Caid as well," he explained.

Timin nodded in understanding and allowed Fez to continue.

"We have put together a spy network using beggars and street boys. Timin is the one who has organized it all. We are establishing a set of codes and maps to track everything the Caid does. We're already set up in most of the major cities in the north, including Tangier."

Jack thought about it for a second.

"It's ingenious! The homeless and the street urchins are almost invisible in society, so they will make the perfect spies."

Timin was becoming less skeptical of Jack. He decided to provide a bit more detail.

"We've set up a number of countermeasures to prevent any double agents. We've also designed the system so that no one person really knows very much about the network. In the event a spy is captured, there's really not much information he could give the Caid. Only the four of us really know how it all works."

Tariq wiped his tears and listened intently to Timin's explanation.

"I heard the French attacked Tangier?" he asked.

"Yes, as well as Marrakesh and Casablanca. They expect the Sultan's palace to fall any day now," Timin replied.

"The French have an agreement with the Caid and are now his allies," Tariq explained.

Timin looked astonished.

"How do you know this?"

"Because I overheard a French general talking with the Caid's advisors."

Timin paced back and forth before replying.

"This is worse than I thought."

"Which means your spy network will become more important than ever," Jack interrupted.

Timin nodded in agreement.

"What are your current plans for the spy network?" Jack asked.

"To gather as much information as possible and then begin a series of strategic attacks against the Caid—and now the French."

Tariq stood up, and with anger on his face, dried his tears.

"I want to defeat the Caid and to kill this Black Mamba. We will avenge Sanaa and Malik. We will become not just a thorn in the Caid's side, but a knife in his ribs. We will cripple him."

Aseem and Fez exchanged glances. They had seen Tariq like this before, and it frightened them. When Tariq got very angry, it was as if a demon had entered his body. The other boys knew never to mess with Tariq when he had this look on his face.

"We need a way to let the Caid know who we are. A symbol of some sort," Fez said.

"Yes, yes—we must put fear in the heart of his soldiers and hope in the hearts of the people," Jack answered.

Buckets of paint, in several different colors, sat next to a window sill on a nearby apartment building. The painters had broken for lunch and had left their supplies behind. Tariq went over to the work site, looked through all the paint, and plunged his hand inside one bucket. The paint was slippery on his hand and droplets of paint fell from his fingers to the ground.

Walking back to the group, he placed his hand on a nearby wall, leaving a perfect handprint in red paint on the blue stucco.

"That is our symbol," he said without emotion.

Everyone looked at the red handprint on the wall.

Jack laughed and nodded in agreement. The others looked at the print with puzzled looks—what did it mean?

"We'll explain the significance of the Red Hand. In the meantime, trust me; it is the perfect symbol of our resistance. Wherever we go, we will be sure to leave behind red handprints as reminders of our existence and as a warning to the Caid. The Red Hand will come to mean freedom and resistance to tyranny and oppression. It will become a symbol that will be feared by oppressors, but seen as a sign of strength to the many impoverished people of Morocco."

Everyone stared at the wall and a feeling came over the group—a kind of unity.

They had their symbol.

That night, Tariq sat alone on a rooftop overlooking the city of Chaouen. The sun was setting in the distance, creating a collage of red, orange, and yellow against the beautiful blue paint on the city's buildings. It was warm outside, and his entire body was flushed from the heat.

Jack came up from behind and sat next to Tariq.

Looking over, Jack could see little dried streaks on Tariq's cheeks, created by tears.

They sat together for five minutes without saying a word. Finally, Jack felt compelled to speak.

"I understand that Sanaa saved you from the Caid?" Jack asked.

Tariq nodded his head without saying anything.

"She sounds like an amazing person. And this Malik character sounds like a brave leader."

Once again, Tariq nodded his head without saying a word.

Jack could see how upset he was. He could see the sadness in his face and in his slumped shoulders.

"Tariq, I know you have experienced so much loss in your life, and I know it seems like everything is against you in times like these. But Sanaa and Malik were warriors who stood up against a vicious tyrant. Unfortunately, death is a very real possibility in this ugly business of ours. Try not to remember how they died, but how they lived—fighting for what is right and always being courageous."

Tariq swallowed hard.

Finally, after a few moments, he spoke up.

"I do not remember anything about my family. I do not remember my mother or father or even if I had any siblings. As far back as I can remember I have been an orphan. I keep trying to remember the face of my mother or father, but I cannot."

Jack put his hand on Tariq's shoulder for reassurance before speaking.

"I remember the day the Brits took me from my aboriginal family in Australia. Mostly, I remember my grandmother's face. But it's all blurry now, like a dream. I don't remember my father's face at all."

Tariq shifted in his seat.

"All I've ever wanted is a family. I look at other children and I see how they smile and play and I realize that will never be me. I am too young to be this hardened, Jack," Tariq sighed.

Jack exhaled deeply at that sentence he genuinely felt for Tariq. Tariq was right—he was too young. Jack himself had found a surrogate family in the circus and a surrogate mother in Amanda. That's what had saved him. But what did Tariq have? He had the tribe, but now they were scattered like the wind.

"I've been talking with your friends Aseem and Fez. They really love you, Tariq, and they have been terribly worried about you. All of you have been through a tremendous amount. *They* are your family, Tariq. Zijuan obviously cares for you deeply. And I know how tough it is to want to get close to anyone once you suffer a terrible loss like this, but you must live your life. You must not give in to doubt and anger."

Tariq continued to stare into the distance.

"There is a boy named Jawad who we met when we were slaves in the kasbah. Originally, I thought he was our friend, but he betrayed us. I understand he is now the apprentice of the Black Mamba," he explained. Turning to Jack, he continued.

"Is there good and evil in the world, Jack? Is there a path I should follow? Because I feel lost right now. Does it make a difference if we struggle and rebel, or should we just give up and join the Caid? He and his forces are gaining momentum—no matter what we do, they will always win."

Jack looked Tariq in the eyes and understood, for the first time, the completeness of the turmoil inside of his young friend. This wasn't just about losing Malik and Sanaa—this was about the path of his entire life.

He took his time before answering.

"Remember how we talked about the saying, 'We all know the path, but few of us follow it'? And how we are all born with an intrinsic understanding of the difference between good and evil? We all know the right decisions to make, but we are swayed by riches, or prestige, or even grief and hatred. Here, let me show you."

Jack began a simple drawing of a path and on either side of the path, he drew trees with words such as "wealth," "power," "grief," and "anger" written inside the trees. The path led to a drawing of a sun.

"Life is easy, Tariq," Jack began, "many people think it is complex or difficult, but it is actually easy. Look at the path. If you follow the path it will lead to lightness. It is that simple. If you give in to anger, or grief, or to the desire for power or wealth, then you will always be lost in the forest. It may take you years to find your way back onto the path, or you may never find your way. The longer you stay in the forest, the harder it is to return."

Tariq stared at the drawing—it seemed so simple.

"You have not had an easy life, Tariq. You are an orphan, you are poor, and you have had to deal with so much death at such an early age. But life is not fair, Tariq. Never expect it to be. As a result of your upbringing, you are tough and wise beyond your years. And you are an interesting person, Tariq. You are the stuff that life is made of. Other children may have easier lives, but you are actually living your life. You are making a difference."

Tariq looked at the diagram and suddenly felt so much better.

"Honor Malik and Sanaa by living your life completely and fully. Continue their legacy."

They both heard footsteps approaching from behind. Aseem and Fez joined them, sitting down the other side of Tariq. They had both been worried about him.

"Aseem and I were thinking that perhaps we could say a prayer and give an offering for Malik and Sanaa," Fez began. "Jack helped us make these special lanterns that rise up to the sky when they are lit. We could light two of them and then say our goodbyes to Malik and Sanaa."

Tariq smiled and nodded.

"I would like that very much."

All four of them stood up on the roof and Fez produced two white lanterns. They resembled very small hot air balloons with a small candle in the basket. It was almost dark now. Lighting each candle, Fez said a small prayer and then they released the lanterns into the sky. The four of them watched as the baskets rose over the city and up into the stars.

Tariq watched them disappear, then bowed his head and said a silent prayer. Aseem put his arms around Tariq's shoulder to let him know he was not alone in the world.

That was all Tariq needed.

Charles and Basil had been working as farm hands at Saint Catherine's for almost two weeks. Each day they performed a myriad of chores that included repairing buildings, planting crops, and digging new wells. The work was hard but they both enjoyed it. Charles especially appreciated having work to do, as Margaret had taken it upon herself to be his personal apprentice. They spent their days together laughing and working— simply being father and daughter. Basil was thoroughly pleased watching Charles relax and enjoy his time with Margaret.

One morning, before the school had awakened, the three of them set out to repair a fence. Basil and Charles enjoyed waking up early to watch the valley come to life before the school woke up. It had been the same when they were at sea. Basil and Charles would sit on the deck of the *Angelina Rouge* watching the sunrise on the horizon before the crew stirred. Usually they drank some warm tea and sat in silence enjoying the view. They almost never said a word.

Just then, Margaret said something that had also been bothering Charles.

"Father, we must get word to Mother that you are safe," she said.

"I know. I've been thinking the same thing. But telegraph offices are constantly watched by the police and we are fugitives. No doubt the British authorities will be watching them as well," he replied.

"I think we have to take that chance. What if you went in disguise and wrote something in code?" she asked.

Charles gave this some thought. He already knew the answer before the conversation had begun.

"Okay," he said and his daughter smiled with satisfaction.

"Can we go now? There's a telegraph office about ten miles from here. It will take the better part of the day to reach it and return. That will give us enough time to write the letter in code."

Basil shook his head and laughed along with Charles.

"What do you say, Captain Basil? Want to partake in a little excursion?" Charles asked.

"Why not? I could use a nice walk," Basil replied.

Margaret left a note for Sister Anne and all three headed out before the students awoke. It was a beautiful walk through the French countryside, and every mile or so there was a charming little farmhouse with crops of grapevines in neatly planted rectangles. The dirt road was soft and made for a very easy walk. Charles enjoyed the simplicity of such a walk—it allowed his mind to wander freely. For once, he felt completely unencumbered by his many challenges and responsibilities.

He also felt almost giddy that he was finally going to be able to get word to his wife that he was alive and well. He went over and over in his head thinking of what he could say to her in as few as words as possible.

They arrived at a tiny house made of stones on top of a hill. There were two sets of wires leading from the roof to a telegraph pole. The telegraph wires led to another pole and then another, until they stretched out for miles. Charles and Basil didn't have much of a disguise. They had pulled their hoods over their heads and hoped that a week's worth of growth on their face would be enough camouflage.

The door was open and the three travelers walked in. The little house was just one room containing a large wooden table, which faced them. A telegraph machine sat directly in the middle. Directly to the left of the machine was a blue book with a pencil on top of it. A man sat behind the table, carving something out of a small piece of wood with a pocket-knife and looking very bored. He was older, perhaps in his early sixties, with a gray handlebar moustache. Directly in front of the table were two wooden chairs.

"Come in, come in," he said and waved to them to sit down.

Margaret and Charles sat down, while Basil stood in back.

"I suppose you want to send a telegraph; it's been busy in here lately. Simply write down your message in that blue book, along with the correspondence number where you want it sent. The charge is ten francs for every fifty words," he explained, barely lifting his eyes from his woodworking.

Charles had already crafted the letter in his head and began writing the message neatly on the paper. It was written in code—to a layperson, it would appear to be gibberish. Margaret watched him appreciatively. She was so excited that her mother would finally know she was with her father.

Charles finished writing the note when he noticed something on the opposite page. The name 'Montaro' could be seen. He was familiar with the last name, as the British authorities had long sought a man named Sharif Al Montaro for murdering a British ambassador in Madrid.

Flipping the page over, Charles was shocked by what he read.

Dreyfuss—

Have located Owen and Basil at a French school called Saint Catherine's outside of Marseilles. Await your arrival.

Montaro

Charles reread the note three times and then looked for the date it had been sent—a week prior!

With that head start, Dreyfuss might have enough time to find the school, depending upon where he started his travels.

"Excuse me," Charles asked, "do you remember exactly who sent this prior message?"

The man looked up from his woodcutting.

"Yes, he was in here a week ago in a hurry. Skinny man, black goatee—sounded like he was from Algeria or someplace."

Charles nodded in understanding—it was Cortez! Cortez was really Sharif Al Montaro. Charles stood up to talk to Basil, and at the same time, Basil motioned for Charles to come stand next to him.

"We've got a real problem," Charles whispered.

"You're telling me," Basil replied and shifted his eyes for Charles to look at the wall.

There, recently posted, was a wanted poster with the faces of four men—and Charles and Basil were two of them! Cortez was another.

Charles studied the poster closely and then whispered in Basil's ear.

"Cortez is a bounty hunter, a man by the name of Sharif Al Montaro. Heard of him?"

"Everyone knows of Montaro," Basil replied, concern in his eyes.

"We've got to get out of here," Charles said and returned to the man behind the table.

The man had put down his knife and wood, suddenly taking a bit more of an interest in Charles and Basil.

"Where did you say you were from?" he asked with a bit of suspicion.

Margaret, sensing that something was wrong, decided to speak up.

"We're vacationing from Scotland, my father and uncle and me. We just love France—my father can't get enough of the brie and red wine. Unfortunately, my mother couldn't join us this trip—taking care of my little brother and all. She'll be so happy to hear from us—she is such a worrier. You know how mothers are. She's staying with her mother in London. It's so lonely where we live in the Highlands, and London is so busy and exciting this time of the year," she explained and the man stood, mouth open, at the amount of information.

This was clearly exasperating to the telegraph operator, but he began sending out the telegraph via Morse code anyway. Charles knew Morse code, as did every British officer, and easily followed along as the man tapped out the message. The man was transmitting it verbatim from Charles's note, so it seemed possible he didn't suspect a thing. He did, at one point, stop and reread the telegraph, briefly furrowing his brow.

"That will be twenty francs," he said when finished.

Margaret laid down the exact amount; they said their goodbyes and hurried out of the office.

"What is going on, Father?" Margaret asked, once they were a safe distance away.

"Cortez is an imposter. He's a bounty hunter who has turned Basil and me in to the British lieutenant, who's now hunting us," he explained, quickening his pace and clearly worried.

"What?" she exclaimed.

"There's something else. I saw a wanted poster on the wall back at that office. It had our pictures on it. No doubt the French authorities are scouring the countryside for Basil and me, and it's only a matter of time before they come upon Saint Catherine's."

Margaret began walking as fast as her father and she now clearly had worry in her eyes. Basil walked quietly behind them, watching the countryside, suddenly extremely wary of their situation.

It would take them three or four hours to return to the school.

Back at the telegraph office, the man with the handlebar moustache emerged from his desk and slowly walked across the wood floor to take a look at the wanted poster. The photographs of Basil and Charles stared back at him. They looked different in the poster—tired and downtrodden. The photo had been taken when they were in Marseilles and had already been prisoners for a week. In large block letters below the photographs, the poster advertised a giant reward of 1,000 francs for the return of the two men.

The telegraph operator licked his lips and studied the photographs. The poster had just been nailed up the previous day by a French policeman passing through town. He hadn't noticed it until now, but there was also a picture of Cortez was right below the one of Charles. It was the same man who had visited the telegraph office last week.

The man stroked the gray whiskers on his chin and rubbed his face as he thought about what to do.

He returned to his desk, picked up the logbook, and studied the two messages that had been sent. Then, he began to send a wire of his own.

To the Marseilles police headquarters.

CHAPTER
— 9 —

THE BEGINNING

The French soldiers stood waiting, anticipating the moment they would hear the whistle signaling it was time to storm the Sultan's kasbah. There were tens of thousands of them surrounding the kasbah, bayonets fixed at the ready, Chassepot rifles locked and loaded. The kasbah, called the Dar el Makhzen, stood high on a hill, overlooking the entire city of Tangier.

This would make for a very difficult assault, as the French troops would need to march uphill in order to take an elevated position.

All eyes were fixed on the prize in front of them: a kasbah of resplendent beauty with thirty-foot-high stone walls.

From their position, the French troops could see thousands of Moroccan troops standing between them and the kasbah and it was assumed that thousands more stood inside the kasbah's high walls.

The Moroccan troops had constructed barricades along the entire perimeter of the kasbah. They had strewn large stones and logs across every street, and had troops positioned on the other side. On the rooftops of nearby buildings, Moroccan snipers took strategic positions, ready to fire on command.

Just past dawn, whistles were blown, launching the French soldiers on a surge forward through the Tangier city blocks. Bayonets at their sides, the troops ran wildly and aggressively toward the Moroccans' positions. The Moroccan troops, expecting an attack, fired directly into the surging French troops.

Many French immediately went down, as bullets ripped through their uniforms. Others, frightened, turned and retreated. Most, however, continued to run straight at the Moroccan barricades with bullets ringing out all around them and smoke stinging their eyes.

The first set of troops was cut down, but the second wave managed to cross over most of the barricades and was now engaged in hand-to-hand fighting. Saif blades ripped through French flesh as the Moroccan troops stood their ground. Snipers hit their marks, and many of the French troops fell in a heap of blood and bullets.

All through the morning, wave after wave of French troops attacked the Moroccan positions. The fighting was fierce, and continued until the outside positions were exhausted—some of them were forced to cease fire because they literally ran out of bullets. Hand-to-hand combat continued across the perimeter of the kasbah. The French were exhausted from climbing and fighting uphill; the troops were drenched in dirt and sweat, and their muscles ached and whined, begging for mercy. The initial rush of adrenaline from the fight had worn off and they found themselves entrenched in a battle that most hadn't anticipated.

They had thought it was going to be easy.

But by early afternoon, the outer perimeter had been secured and the French now surrounded the kasbah. However, they had suffered far too many casualties, and many of their troops were tired, hungry, and emotionally spent. Fighting for six hours in constant threat of death will drain one's excitement.

Desertion was another problem, as many of the French troops simply turned tail and ran—they did not want to die in a foreign country for a cause they didn't understand.

The French generals paced up and down among the troops, screaming at them and hoping to raise their spirits higher as they braced for another attack.

The Moroccan troops positioned themselves high on the palace walls and began shooting at the French. First, they shot at anyone resembling an officer and managed to kill a general, a colonel, and three captains. The French hid behind barricades and their officers quickly ran to the rear, and from a safe distance, yelled instructions to the front line. The French also hid behind anything that might deflect a bullet. They brought cannons to the front and placed them directly in front of the kasbah door. Crowds of French soldiers stood around the five cannons—they would need to rush them to the door as Moroccan troops fired upon them.

Another whistle was blown and thousands of Moroccan troops ran across the empty courtyard and attacked from atop the kasbah walls and gate. Outside, dozens of French troops pulled and pushed the five cannons to within firing range of the kasbah door. Many were shot as they struggled to drag the heavy cannons across the battlefield. French snipers were in position and fired at the soldiers on the kasbah walls—managing to hit a few and to scare many others.

Smoke from rifle fire was so prevalent that a light haze had descended above the kasbah in a gray cloud, like an omnipresent vulture hovering over a carcass.

Once the first cannon was locked into position, a shell burst out of its turret and smashed into the kasbah gate, splintering the gate and leaving a massive hole behind. A second cannon was fired, hitting its mark about six feet to the right of the first blast. This shot caused much more damage than the first—the hole was now big enough for troops to run through.

The French began rushing through the hole they'd blasted in the kasbah door, only to be met by hundreds of Moroccan fighters waiting on the other side. More cannon shells were fired, some of them killing both French and Moroccan soldiers. The cannon blasts continued until the door and gates were left with several giant holes.

Once the fighting spilled into the kasbah, it became strictly hand-to-hand combat. The French fought with their sharpened bayonets and the Moroccans used their saifs. Rows and rows of soldiers fought so close together they could have smelled one another's breath. The French, already tired, began to lose the battle, until reinforcements arrived to strengthen their position and again they began pushing the Moroccans back. After twenty minutes, the French had pushed the Moroccans so far back that the battle reached the interior of the kasbah, spilling into its hallways and rooms.

By midafternoon it was over.

Bodies lay strewn all around the kasbah and its outside courtyard. The wounded were gathered and treated, and the ones who were so seriously injured that medical help couldn't save them were mercifully given a bayonet to the gut and died quickly.

The French troops garrisoned the kasbah and took the remaining Moroccan troops as prisoners. Once the kasbah was secure, the French command entered and ordered every room searched. Their only objective was to find their ultimate prize—the Sultan!

The problem was, the Sultan was nowhere to be found. Every room, every hallway, every cabinet and floorboard was checked and double-checked.

The Sultan had simply vanished.

All through that night and into the next day, the kasbah was searched and all the prisoners were interrogated. It was fruitless. The Sultan was gone.

The French leadership and its troops were dejected. They had lost twice as many men as they had expected, and the Sultan wasn't even in the kasbah. As long as the Sultan was alive, the Moroccan people would continue to see him as their true ruler.

Zijuan, Malik, Sanaa, and the Tuareg walked into the tribe's camp one warm morning, bringing with them cooked food and supplies. People came out of their tents and greeted Malik and Sanaa like prophets descending from heaven. Most cried and screamed when they saw them. They were alive! Many more fell to the ground and prayed in appreciation. A feast and party was thrown that night, and for the first time in a long time, the people forgot their troubles. Laughter and songs could be heard under the Moroccan sky.

The next morning, the tribe moved to its new site, which provided needed shelter, a plentiful amount of water, and opportunities for hunting. Tents were easily assembled and it wasn't long before the camp resembled its former self, as children played outside and there was a bustle within the community.

That night, the leaders held a meeting. Sanaa, Malik, Zijuan, and Arshaman sat around a campfire drinking tea and discussing the future.

"We must unify the many mountain and desert clans in order to be able to fight the Caid. He has taken advantage of the fact that we are unorganized and prefer to fight with one another," Arshaman began.

Everyone nodded in agreement.

"In an open battle, even united, we will be no match for the artillery and modern technology of the French," Malik replied, pausing before continuing. "If we are to fight them in a field, we must secure some weaponry. Otherwise, our only course of action will be to remain guerrilla fighters and attack in small numbers where they are most vulnerable."

"We must kill their leaders—starting with the Mamba and the Caid. Kill the head and the body will follow," Zijuan replied in a stoic voice.

Sanaa, as she had throughout most of the night, sat silent, smoking a water pipe and staring into the fire.

"Sanaa, what are your thoughts?" Zijuan asked.

"I promised myself that if Malik and I somehow lived, I would not stop until the Black Mamba lay dead by my sword. For too long, all of the tribes have lived in fear of the Mamba and the Caid. It is time for us to stop living in fear and it is time to start making them fear us."

This sent chills down Malik's spine. Most of the others were accustomed to Sanaa's strength and seriousness, but tonight her tone was different—it came from a place deep within her. A place reserved for pain and sorrow.

"The Caid has already taken many of the men and boys from most of the tribes. The tribes that reside deeper in the mountains have so far been unaffected, as have the ones in the desert," Zijuan explained.

"Then we must start with those tribes. We must find a way to be unified, and must convince them to fight with us under one flag," Malik answered.

Arshaman nodded in agreement.

"I can unify the desert tribes," he said. "We have good relations with many of them. And as to the ones that we don't, they hate the Caid more than the Tuareg, so I'm certain they will join us."

"Malik, you are the one with good relations with the mountain tribes. Are you in a strong enough condition to make the peace?" Zijuan asked.

"Zijuan, I have lost my eyesight but not my brain or my voice. I will depart first thing in the morning. I only require an escort."

"You know you have one," Sanaa replied and Malik smiled.

"We should meet at Raven's Valley in three weeks' time," Arshaman suggested.

Deep into the night they worked, finalizing their plans and analyzing which tribes would probably join them and how the leadership of the unified tribes would be organized. They discussed logistics and battle strategy until their heads were dizzy. In the morning, Arshaman and his Tuareg departed for the desert. Malik, Sanaa, and a small contingency of soldiers began their trek through the mountains to attempt to gather support from the various mountain tribes.

Before they departed, Zijuan gathered Sanaa for a brief conversation.

"I want you to continue your training and swordplay with Malik. Just because he is blind does not mean he is useless. His other senses will be enhanced by the loss of his sight, and he can still be an excellent scout and warrior."

Sanaa hugged her mentor and wished her farewell.

The next three weeks would be vitally important to the survival of the tribes.

Through the days to come, Malik and Sanaa visited with every mountain tribe within a hundred miles. All of these tribes already paid taxes to the Caid and had been victims of his treachery and deceit. They had all heard the stories of the Caid's atrocities and violence against the many tribes in the Rif and beyond.

One by one, they agreed to join the newly-formed alliance. Even the tribes that had been hostile toward Malik in the past joined them, as they realized the bigger threat they faced from the Caid and his armies.

Slowly, an army grew out of a group of ragtag and unorganized tribes.

Louise Owen needed proof.

Proof that the Far Indian Trading Company was working with the British navy to slaughter innocent villagers and hijack fishing boats. She needed evidence strong enough to tie everything together in such a concrete and unimpeachable way that the British authorities would be forced to listen to her.

For weeks, her work with Matthew had come to a standstill. At the moment, even after all their research, all they knew was that there might be a connection between the two, but they had no real way to actually prove any collaboration.

Then, to her surprise, an opportunity presented itself in the form of an invitation to yet another party (although she was receiving fewer and fewer of them of late).

The event was a cocktail party at the London Yachting Club. By itself, that didn't mean much. However, the yacht club was housed in the same building as the offices of the Far Indian Trading Company and their president—Lionel Hedgecock.

If she could find a way into his office, then she might be able to find some kind of proof connecting his company's activities to the British navy.

It was risky and dangerous. If she were to be caught, she would likely be tried as an accomplice to her husband and as a traitor to Britain.

With a cup of steaming-hot Earl Grey tea warming her hands, Louise peered out of her window, its glass dusted with frost, and thought of her husband. She remembered the life they'd had together and the family they had raised. She thought about how much she missed him, and about how their family was ever so slowly falling apart without him.

Taking a sip of the bitter tea, at that moment Louise decided that if there was proof of a conspiracy between the Far Indian Trading Company and the British navy to be found, she was going to be the one to find it.

She was going to clear her name. She was going to clear her husband's name.

She was going to get her life back.

_____ ❦ _____

For weeks the newly-formed resistance worked tirelessly in secrecy and in the shadows. Complex codes were created. Spy networks were established and organized. New recruits were thoroughly and exhaustively interviewed and interrogated to be sure they were not agents of the Caid.

In almost every major city in Morocco, a spy network had been set up, comprised solely of transients, beggars, outcasts, and orphans. They were the refuse of the world—the forgotten and unwanted castoffs from society. They were invisible, or at least most people wished they were.

Yet they heard and saw everything.

A vagrant begging for coins on a sidewalk in Marrakesh overheard a seemingly innocent conversation between two French officers concerning the impending arrival of more French marines.

The delivery schedule of supply trucks was closely scrutinized by a band of urchins in Casablanca.

The number of troops, and their details, were counted by a one-armed snake charmer in Tangier.

All messages were delivered in code by carrier pigeon, an old gambler's trick that Timin had used to deliver odds to his various betting stands.

Melbourne Jack and Tariq spent much of their day learning codes, working with Timin, and trying to remain incognito under the scrutiny of the Caid's troops. As long as they were still in Chaouen, they kept constantly on guard and often chose to remain inside during the day for fear of being recognized.

One day, while sitting around the fountain, Tariq looked up into a window across the courtyard. A girl with beautiful long hair who looked to be about his age stood in the window. She was staring at him! Once Tariq made eye contact with her, she raised her hand and waved.

Was this Azmiya? Tariq had been searching for her since their first encounter, but he had no idea what she looked like. She'd been wearing a burqa the whole time they spoke.

He waved back, and he saw her point downward towards the apartment door. Tariq walked over, but she disappeared back into her apartment. He was about to knock on the door when it opened just an inch.

"Go around back to the alley. I will meet you there," the girl whispered, and just like that, the door closed again.

Tariq ventured around to the alley, where he saw another door that led to the apartment—most likely this was the servant's door.

Sure enough, after a minute, the door opened and a girl slipped out. But now she was dressed in a burqa and her face was covered. Even in the secrecy of the alley, she didn't want to be seen in public without her veil.

"Azmiya?" Tariq asked.

"Yes," she replied.

Tariq felt his heart race and his breath shorten. Since their first encounter, he had been able to hear her voice in his head. Even though he didn't know what she looked like, he couldn't keep from thinking about her.

"This is where you live?" he asked.

"Yes!" she replied and looked around to be sure none of her neighbors could see them. It was obvious she was very nervous.

"So you've been watching us? How come it took you so long to wave?"

"I am almost never alone. My uncle or our servants are always watching me. This is the first time I have been alone since I last saw you, but it will only be for a few moments."

"I'm glad you waved to me. I've been thinking about you," Tariq blurted out, suddenly feeling stupid for being so honest.

"I've been thinking about you, too," Azmiya whispered, and Tariq could almost feel her blushing from beneath her burqa.

"Can I see your face?" Tariq asked.

"I do not think it is proper."

"I don't care."

Slowly, she took off her burqa and Tariq could see she was embarrassed. Not just because she was allowing him to see her face, but because she had a long scar that ran down the left side of her cheek, about five inches in length. Other than that, she was a lovely girl. Her face was narrow, with beautiful olive skin, and her eyes seemed to see right through him.

"Did your uncle do that to you?" Tariq asked.

Azmiya stared at the ground and nodded.

"Where is the head servant?"

"She is shopping. I told her I didn't feel well and wanted to stay at home."

Tariq didn't know what to say. He could tell she was embarrassed and ashamed of her scar.

"I've got scars, too. They're not as good as yours, but they're not bad," he said, as he lifted up his shirt and turned around to show her. On his back were long scars from the whip that Zahir had beaten him with when he had been imprisoned in the kasbah. He had six of them, all around his back. They were burgundy-colored now and mostly healed, but still protruded visibly from his flesh.

"What happened?" she asked, clearly impressed.

"The Caid and his men did this to me. I was a slave at the kasbah," he replied, lowering his shirt and turning back around to face her.

"Is that why you fight him?"

"Yes, and we're going to win!"

"I see you and the other street boys talking and meeting around the square. Nobody else notices, but I do. What you are doing?"

Tariq did not know what to say. Her uncle was a policeman. If he learned of their plans, it could ruin everything they had worked for. Still, he had a strong sense that he could trust Azmiya. He could see that she hated her uncle and her life at home.

"We're planning on defeating the Caid," he replied.

She shifted on her feet and waited a bit to reply.

"Can I help?" she asked.

"How can you help?"

"My uncle always has his police friends at our house. I'm not allowed to be in the same room with them, but I can hear their conversations through the walls. Usually they just get drunk and act stupid, but sometimes they talk of the French and what is happening within the police force. I would be happy to be a spy for you."

"Really?" Tariq answered excitedly.

"Sure. You see this space over here in the wall? I will put a note behind this brick whenever there is news. You can leave me notes here as well," she said, lifting up a small brick to reveal a tiny space behind it.

"Brilliant!" Tariq responded, overjoyed that he would have a way to communicate with her.

"Okay, then. I should return. The servants are due back soon, and I mustn't risk being caught," she said and turned to open the door.

"Azmiya, I have to leave for a while to return to my tribe in the Rif. I'll return as soon as possible. I hope to see you again soon," he said, thoroughly sad to watch her leave so soon.

"I hope to see you again as well, Tariq," she replied before shutting the door behind her.

Tariq left the alley, and as he looked back at her window, she was nowhere to be seen.

He walked across the square, down yet another alley, down a long stairway until he reached a wooden door. The door was locked, and Tariq had to use a secret knock to identify himself. Soon the door was opened by Melbourne Jack.

Tariq said "hello" to Jack and walked into an abandoned apartment. The apartment had been transformed into a makeshift command center, with an old apple crate serving as a conference table and a blank wall on which to write codes in chalk. Once they had been written on the wall, the codes were quickly committed to memory and immediately erased. Everything was memorized—even maps of the cities—and nothing was ever permanently recorded. Not only were codes used, but the network used code names as well. Nobody knew Tariq by name, only by his code name—Desert Fox.

Hardly anyone knew anyone's true identity or appearance. Only a few people knew of Timin—his identity was kept secret from everyone. All the codes were organized this way to protect one another. If captured, no one person had much specific information to provide to the police. Even the codes were designed to rely upon correlating pages in books and the books they referred to were changed every week or two. If the police somehow learned of the code, they would also have to figure out the titles of the changing books.

"Are you ready?" Jack asked.

"Yes," Tariq answered. He was still thinking of Azmiya, but he didn't want anyone to know. He was deliriously happy, but before he let himself truly feel these feelings, there was something else he must accomplish.

Tariq and Jack were joined by Timin, Fez, and Aseem, who had been out collecting some horses. Timin had wanted to dispatch a bigger group, but didn't want to jeopardize anyone's identity. For the mission at hand, it would just be the five of them.

"Okay then, we all know our roles," said Timin. "We ride in and then split up. I will return to Chaouen while Tariq and Jack return to the tribe. Aseem and Fez, you know what to do. We'll rendezvous back in Chaouen in two weeks' time. If one of us is captured, the rest of us will all meet on the outskirts of town and form a plan to free him. Whatever you do, do not give up any vital information. Provide the false information you were given."

Just before nightfall, they rode on their horses out of Chaouen until they reached a trail that led them into the small town of Bab Taza.

Bab Taza was a short distance from Chaouen and had a population of only about 5,000 people. Yet it was an important strategic waypoint for the Caid and his troops, who used it to store food before distributing it to various outposts in the Rif. Tariq and his spy network had obtained intelligence that a food delivery was overdue and would likely arrive sometime around midnight tonight.

A delivery they planned to intercept.

"Do you think the plan is a good one?" Fez asked.

"Yes," Aseem answered.

"As do I. Timin has proven to be very smart. I think this is going to be the first in a series of successful victories."

Tariq rode behind them. He was so happy to see his old friends, but being in Chaouen had proven to be very stressful. He felt so paranoid—always worrying that the police would learn of his true identity. It was even rumored that the Black Mamba was returning to Chaouen and would be looking specifically for him. It would be a relief to leave and return to the tribe—even if the tribe had been scattered.

They rode for another two hours, making excellent time, until they finally saw the lights of Bab Taza in the distance.

The group grew more excited. They all had their plans clearly set out in their minds. If all went well, they would be in and out very quickly.

Cutting across the desert, they found the dirt road the supply convoy would be traveling from Tangier into Bab Taza. There were two small hills on either side—perfect spots for an ambush.

"If anything goes wrong, hop on your horse and ride like the wind. Our intelligence says that only three guards are with the shipment, so, it should make easy pickings," Timin explained.

Tariq nodded in agreement. The fact was, he, Aseem, and Fez had been well-schooled in these kinds of maneuvers by Malik and had already participated in one ambush. This, however, felt different. Malik was so well-organized, but he hadn't even allowed them to do anything on the first ambush. They were merely witnesses, there to learn. This time, they were expected to actively engage the enemy and play a central role. While this excited them, it also scared them.

Were they ready? Did they have the nerve and conviction to actually face the Caid's soldiers? They were, after all, still boys. What if there were more troops than they had anticipated? What if there were a dozen guards? Would they then be defeated?

Despite all these questions, they knew they had to step up. They'd been planning for months, and now it was time for action.

Patiently they waited, with Jack and Tariq crouched on one side of the road and Timin, Fez, and Aseem on the other.

Just then, up ahead, they heard the snorting of a horse and the sound of men's voices. The group leaned against the hills, tense with anticipation. Jack produced two boomerangs and allowed his breathing to slow and his mind to focus on the moment.

Each of them had a burlap bag with holes punched out for their eyes and mouths—this would disguise them in case one of the guards happened to catch a glimpse of them up close.

The voices grew louder and louder until they were just feet away from them. Jack took a quick peek from behind the hill—it was nothing more than a wagon with two guards riding on top and another guard riding next to the wagon on horseback. They were traveling slowly and not paying attention to their surroundings.

A costly mistake.

In one quick and effortless movement, Jack appeared from behind the hill and launched a boomerang at each of the two guards in the wagon, striking them perfectly in the head, knocking both men to the ground. Before the guard on the horse could even react, Aseem jumped from a hill up above, traveled about ten feet in the air, and as he landed, smashed a stone on the guard's skull—knocking the man from his horse.

All three guards had been knocked unconscious in a matter of seconds.

Timin checked to ensure they were, indeed, knocked out and began tying up their hands and blindfolding their eyes. Jack collected his boomerangs while Tariq and Fez controlled the horses.

Jack opened the back of the wagon and sure enough, there was a nice shipment of food.

Aseem, dusting himself off, helped Timin with tying up the guards, then mounted his steed.

It was all completed in less than two minutes.

Timin quickly produced some red powder from his satchel and began brushing it on the hands of one of the guards.

Aseem and Fez smiled with delight as they sat on top of their horses.

"Nice job Aseem! That was a brilliantly-timed jump!" Tariq congratulated him and Aseem beamed with pride.

Jack procured some food from the wagon and attached it to the guard's horse before taking the reins.

Aseem, Fez, and Tariq stared at one another. They hated knowing they would need to leave one another yet again. But the boys all understood they were on a mission much bigger than themselves.

"See you soon, Tariq," Fez said with just a whisper of regret.

"Before you know it," Tariq replied and smiled at his friend.

Aseem didn't know what to say until he just blurted it out.

"Don't do anything stupid!"

Tariq laughed.

"Then it wouldn't be any fun, would it?"

Jack rode up to Tariq and saw that Timin was already on top of the wagon—he'd quickly hitched his horse up to add more speed.

"Okay, we know the plan, Godspeed to all of you," Jack said.

"See you soon, Jack. Thank you for joining us—we couldn't have done this without you," Timin said and gave him a quick nod of respect.

Tariq and Jack urged on their horses and were soon in a full gallop across the desert sands.

Timin, along with Aseem and Fez, rode directly to the town of Bab Taza. They weren't worried about the guards, as they were both blindfolded and their hands were tied. Besides, judging from the size of the bumps on their heads, they might still be unconscious.

Coming to a group of houses, Timin, Aseem and Fez hurried and offloaded some crates of food and placed them at the back of each house. Then they each dipped their hands in some of the red powder and placed handprints on the walls all around the houses. They made sure that they smudged each print a bit to make their hands appear to be bigger than they were—all in an effort to conceal their identities in case the police tried to match up the handprints with actual human hands.

Everyone would know that the Red Hand was responsible for leaving this food.

They continued in the same manner in different neighborhoods until all the food was gone. It only took about an hour, so the three of them were able to leave Bab Taza for Chaouen far before the sun came up.

Before leaving, all three vigorously washed the red powder from their hands until not a trace was left.

The next morning, some of the villagers awoke to their daily routine. Most were starving, as the Caid left them little food and taxed them so unmercifully many families had no money left. As they opened their doors, they were surprised and amazed to see the boxes of food that had been left for them, and quickly brought them inside. They opened the boxes to find dried fruits and meats and wonderful cheeses—these were all swiftly collected and hidden around their houses. Entire families ate well for the first time in months, and many of them cried at the sight of such a feast. Stepping out their front doors, they saw the red handprints left behind by Fez, Aseem, and Timin.

What did it all mean?

Gossip spread fast as to the mystery of the red handprints and the meaning of it all. Not that any of the villagers cared where the food had come from. They were so happy to have been fed and to get a bit of relief from their constant hunger. All this food could last most of them a few weeks, if not a month!

The red handprints were seen as a blessing.

Later that day, the guards stumbled back to their outpost in Bab Taza, each with a headache caused by the visible bumps on their heads. They had managed to get their hands untied and their blindfolds off by the time they walked into the outpost delirious with thirst and famished.

After eating some stale bread and grapes and chugging down a gallon of water, the guards explained the day's events to their sergeant. He listened to their story and noticed that one of the guard's hands was red.

"What is that?" he asked.

The guard stared at his hand and stammered for an answer.

"I do not know, sir. I just woke up and it was there," he answered.

"This morning there were red handprints all over the town. The rumor is that some of the villagers were given shipments of food—the Caid's food!" he screamed, pounding his fist on the table.

"Sir, I—" the guard blubbered without an answer.

"Arrest these three!" the sergeant ordered and all three soldiers were quickly arrested and placed in the small jail in the headquarters.

"But sir, we were knocked out and tied up—just look at our heads!" one of them pleaded.

"Ha! I see you have a simple plan to make yourselves look like you were ambushed. I do not believe you for one second. It is a criminal offense to steal food from the Caid—punishable by death!"

All three guards lay down in the dirty cell, their heads still throbbing and their bellies still empty.

What had happened to them?

Tariq and Jack made quick time to the Rif Mountains and were soon on the trail leading to the camp. They packed an ample amount of supplies, along with a dozen carrier pigeons, which they planned to use to communicate with Timin. With any luck, they would find the tribe on the following day. Tariq should have been happy, but he was not. He did not want to see the tribe without Malik and Sanaa there. Fez and Aseem had made it seem as if the entire tribe was desolate and depressed. Honestly, he would have preferred to stay in Chaouen with Fez and Aseem to help with the resistance. But in the end, he had to agree that it was too dangerous for him.

Still, he was always glad to spend time with Jack and so thankful that Jack had decided to stay a while before returning to Australia. He didn't want to lose another friend.

Back in Chaouen, Fez and Aseem woke early, ate some breakfast, and then walked solemnly to an army headquarters. They both were very thoughtful and quiet. Even though they had been planning this for some time, neither of them was excited about what they were about to do. In fact, they were both sick with worry.

An army captain stood outside the headquarters, drinking some tea and swatting at flies. He looked middle-aged, maybe forty, and had a small potbelly and a tiny black moustache.

Aseem and Fez walked up to him, but he tried to ignore them.

"We want to join the army," Aseem said.

The captain stopped swatting flies and stared at them.

"We have no need for little street urchins," he replied and resumed swatting.

"But we have information on these rebels. We can help you," Fez answered.

The captain again stopped swatting flies and stared at them.

"What do you mean, you have information?" he asked.

"Last night there was an attack in Bab Taza. We know who did it, and we can help you find them," Aseem replied.

Fez stared at the ground, apparently too frightened, or ashamed, of what they were doing.

"You know of this attack?" the captain replied.

"Yes. We just want to join the army and fight for the Caid. It would be a great honor for us. We are tired of living on the streets and we will fight very hard for you. We have no home and no family," Fez said.

"Hold on just one moment," the captain answered and disappeared behind a wall. Soon, he was joined by two other officers.

One, a burly man with a bushy beard, stared at them and whispered some questions to the captain.

"What's this about you two knowing something about the attack in Bab Taza?" he asked.

"We can tell you everything. We just want to join the army and fight," Aseem replied.

Fez shifted in his feet before adding, "We also know of this boy Tariq who is wanted, and we know where he is hiding."

The man stared at them; the boys had no doubt he was a high-ranking officer. He rubbed his chin and continued to stare.

"Okay, you can join us. We'll get you both a hot bath, and then you can join my regiment. First, I want you to tell me everything about this attack."

Fez and Aseem looked at one another before answering.

"Okay," Fez replied.

Both boys disappeared into the building, as the door shut behind them.

CHAPTER
— *10* —

FOUND!

Charles, Basil, and Margaret walked as fast as possible back to Saint Catherine's. By midafternoon they were back overlooking the valley and the school. Hiding behind brush and trees, they surveyed the area to ensure that Dreyfuss had not already found their position. For fifteen minutes they stared at the school, but nothing seemed out of the ordinary.

They decided to split up. Margaret would go down first, and then Basil and Charles would flank her position and sneak around the back. Margaret was to give a hand signal if anything went wrong.

Margaret walked down with more than a little worry. She was afraid of leaving her father, and even more afraid of what she might find in the school. She walked directly to her room, where Inez was casually reading a book on the bed.

"Where have you been?" she asked.

"Um, nowhere, have you seen Cortez?" Margaret asked.

"No, maybe—I don't know. He was at the barn the last I remember, but that was yesterday."

Margaret nervously looked out the window and paced around the room.

"What is wrong?" Inez asked suspiciously.

"Nothing," Margaret replied.

"I know when something is wrong. Where were you all day?" Inez said, getting up from the bed, her eyes narrowed, ready for the inquisition.

"It was just a walk, that's all and nothing more," Margaret replied. She wasn't much of a liar, and Inez was renowned for sniffing out a lie.

"Why do you want Cortez?"

Margaret, already exasperated, threw up her hands.

"Okay, fine, but you must agree to keep it a secret."

Inez moved in even closer, as she could smell there was trouble brewing about. If there was one thing Inez enjoyed more than anything else, it was trouble.

"What is it?" she asked.

"Cortez isn't Cortez at all. His real name is Sharif Al Montaro, and he's the most ruthless bounty hunter in all the Mediterranean. He's working for a man named Dreyfuss and has come here to set a trap for my father and Captain Basil. Dreyfuss is an English sea captain, or something, and he is hunting my father and wants to kill him. He should be here any day now, if he's not already here."

Inez stood silent for several moments and then shrieked with delight. In fact, she was so excited that she started jumping on the bed.

"I knew it! I *knew* you were hiding something. Oh, this is so wonderful—I can't believe it! A real live pirate-hunting bounty hunter—and he's been under our noses the entire time!"

Then, just as suddenly, Inez got very serious, hopped off the bed, and looked at Margaret with her big brown eyes. Her face was a mess of freckles, and as she looked at Margaret, she pursed her lips with the most critical of intent.

"We must set a trap for this Dreyfuss and also capture Cortez."

Margaret was taken aback by the strength and determination in her friend's voice.

"Yes, I know. I have been watching to see if Dreyfuss has already found us, but so far I haven't seen any sign of him."

"Any sign of who?" Alice asked, walking into the room with Sophie and Etienne.

"Whom," Sophie corrected her.

"Oh my goodness," Inez began, "you won't believe what has happened! Cortez is not Cortez at all, but a vicious bounty hunter who is setting a trap for Colonel Owen and Captain Basil. A ruthless English sea captain named Dreyfuss is coming for them—but we're going to set a trap!" Inez screamed and jumped up and down all around the other girls, whose mouths now hung open in disbelief.

"So much for keeping a secret," Margaret said sarcastically.

"Is this true?" Sophie asked with concern as she went to Margaret.

"Yes, I'm afraid it is."

Alice walked over to them.

"How did you find out?" she asked.

"The telegraph office. We figured out that Cortez sent a message about his whereabouts to Dreyfuss about a week ago.

Inez was still running back and forth.

"Ha! We will set a trap for Cortez, and then we'll wait for this Dreyfuss. They won't know what hit them. I'll bet there's a bounty for Cortez. We'll all be filthy stinking rich!" Inez exclaimed.

The other girls watched Inez as she resumed shrieking and bouncing up and down on her bed.

"How are we going to set a trap for him? He's one of the most wanted men in Europe, and we're just some schoolgirls," Etienne questioned, not at all convinced by Inez's enthusiasm.

Inez continued jumping and shrieking.

"Don't worry, I have it all figured out," she answered. At once, she stopped jumping around and gathered all the girls around her. They giggled with delight as she described how they were going to trap the intrepid Sharif Al Montaro.

Five minutes later, the five girls walked out to the barn where Cortez was tossing some hay. He didn't look to be working too hard and seemed to resent their presence.

Inez grabbed a rope, managed to tie a loop, and began throwing it rather awkwardly at Alice. She threw it five times, each time missing on purpose. Exasperated, she gave up and allowed Etienne to try to lasso Alice. Again, she missed every time on purpose and walked away in a huff.

"What are you doing?" Cortez asked finally, intrigued by the girls' rope throwing.

"Well, we have a competition coming up, and one of the skills is to rope a baby calf. But, none of us is very good at it," Sophie explained.

Cortez stopped shoveling and watched as Margaret managed to get herself tangled in the rope on her first try.

"No, no," Cortez said, his competitive nature getting the best of him. Grabbing the rope, he made a proper knot and wound it tightly.

"You see, if you tie the knot this way, it tightens quickly. Throw the rope over your head three times, letting out a little line each time, and then let it go as you release your hand," he explained, while winding up the rope again and tossing it perfectly around Alice. It landed right around her arms and then he tightened it—completely trapping her.

"Oh, I think I see, let me try that," Inez said, grabbing the rope. She walked with her back towards Cortez and focused intently on twirling the rope over her head before turning around to face Cortez. He stood there impatiently, waiting for her to throw it, when he saw something in her eyes. It was a different look than before, it was—

Before he could finish his thought, Inez had thrown the rope perfectly, encircling his arms. She tightened it immediately and effortlessly.

"What is happen—" he asked, now tied up and thoroughly confused.

"Ha! We have you, Sharif Al Montaro!" Inez screamed with glee.

The look on Cortez's face went from disbelief to surprise to fear. If these girls knew who he was, then so did Owen and Basil.

He had been trapped.

Just as he was about to say something, the entire world went black and he crumpled to the ground.

Margaret stood over him with a shovel in her hands. She had snuck behind him, hit him as hard as she could, and knocked him unconscious.

The girls wasted no time tying his wrists and feet, then tied another rope around his waist, blindfolded him, and stuck a rag in his mouth. Then, all five lifted him into a wheelbarrow. They pushed him up through the school roads, down a dirt path, and then up a hill past some trees.

"Sophie and Alice, you go up the road and keep a lookout for any British soldiers. I'll meet with my father and we'll come up with a plan," Margaret directed.

"That sounds perfect! Let's go, Alice!" Sophie replied, and soon the two girls were running down the dirt road outside the school.

"Ugghh, he's awfully heavy," Inez complained as the three remaining girls pushed him up a slight hill.

"He smells of fish and tobacco!" Etienne said disgustedly.

They made their way up the hill with some difficulty and finally came to rest at the spot where Margaret was to rendezvous with the men.

Basil and Charles came from behind some trees to greet the girls, who were drenched with sweat and breathing very hard from the work.

"Who is this?" Basil asked.

"Sharif Al Montaro, who do you think?" Inez answered.

Charles and Basil looked at one another and then at the unconscious and gagged Sharif Al Montaro.

Both burst into laughter.

"Margaret, I just wanted you to tell me the coast was clear. You didn't need to knock him out," he joked, hugging her tightly, obviously very proud of his daughter.

"It was all Inez's idea. She tricked him into thinking she couldn't throw a rope. It was brilliant!"

Inez's cheeks turned even redder from the attention.

"Well, it did seem like a good plan," she answered sheepishly.

"Look at this! The most wanted man in the Mediterranean subdued by schoolgirls. I never would have believed it," Basil continued to laugh and stare at Montaro, who was still unconscious.

"Yes, and we will even share in the reward with you!" Inez said proudly.

"Reward?" Basil asked.

"Of course, a tyrant like this must have a huge reward on his head—even bigger than the reward on yours, Captain Basil," Inez explained and all the girls looked at him with a look of expectation.

"I hadn't thought of a reward. You're right, there must be a huge reward for him," he answered, still amazed by the gumption and intellect of the girls.

"It's settled, then. We'll keep this Montaro as our prisoner and then turn him in for a fat reward. Then we'll lay a trap for Dreyfuss," Inez continued, who now seemed to be running the show and delighted in making even more plans.

"You told them about Dreyfuss?" Charles asked Margaret.

"Well, it kind of slipped out," Margaret answered with a bit of embarrassment.

Montaro lay unconscious in the wheelbarrow until he was rolled down to an empty barn. Basil threw a huge bucket of water on him and he slowly regained consciousness. As he gathered his senses, his vision was still blurry, but he could see the faces of Basil, Charles, Etienne, Margaret, and Inez staring back at him.

"Mmmmpphh," he mumbled from beneath the rag in his mouth.

Charles went to Montaro and pulled the rag out, allowing him to talk freely.

"I won't waste your time trying to argue my innocence," Montaro remarked, with a hint of arrogance.

"Good, because that will save us all a lot of time," Charles replied.

"What do you want?" Montaro asked.

"I don't need anything from you. In fact, you've already let me know that Dreyfuss will be on us in short order. You've given us far more information than I could hope to get from you."

Montaro stared at him, seething with hatred.

Basil stepped forward and patted Montaro on the thigh.

"Didn't you kill a prince in Barcelona? Well, I have to imagine there's a handsome reward for you in that part of the world. The kind of reward that would make a man—or girl—very, very rich," he said and winked at Inez, who was busy trying to look fierce, with her arms folded and a scowl on her face.

Montaro said nothing.

"Unless you have something to share with us, there's no further use for this conversation," Charles explained and shoved the rag back in Montaro's mouth. Montaro continued to glare at Charles with nothing but hatred in his eyes.

"Let's saddle up and leave for Spain first thing in the morning. It's too dangerous for us here, and Dreyfuss will soon be on our tail."

Margaret ran to her father and hugged him.

"I'm coming with you. I won't leave you again."

Charles hugged her back, enjoying the warmth of her embrace and being with his daughter again. He had thoroughly enjoyed every minute with her.

"Margaret, it's going to be very dangerous, and I can't risk losing you to a man like Dreyfuss—there's no telling what he's capable of. You'll be much safer in the school with your teachers and your friends. I'll return for you once I've settled things in England," he explained softly, smoothing her hair and hugging her tightly.

"You're going back to England?" she asked.

"I must return and attempt to clear my name. I can't continue to run like a scared deer."

They heard footsteps from outside the barn, and Alice ran in, breathing heavily and wide-eyed with panic.

"We've spotted them about half a mile away. There are at least twenty of them, maybe more," she said between breaths.

"British soldiers?" Charles asked.

"Yes," Alice replied, and then bent over with exhaustion.

Basil and Charles looked at one another and then looked at Montaro.

"We can make it if we run, Charles," Basil said, obviously concerned.

Charles looked again at Montaro and then at Margaret.

He had perhaps a thirty-minute head start if he wanted to run. He could also stay and try to hide, but Dreyfuss would probably tear the place to shreds looking for him. And then there was the issue of Montaro and what to do with him.

Charles had a decision to make, and he had to make it fast.

He immediately decided the best thing to do was to make a run for it. He and Basil quickly saddled three horses, threw Montaro on one, and led the other two out of the barn. Margaret assisted in finding a couple of sleeping sacks for them to take on the journey. She didn't say much during her preparations, and was solemn as she fully realized her father was leaving was once again. He wouldn't tell Margaret—or anyone else, for that matter—exactly where he was going. It was safer for both of them that way.

He was about to jump on his horse when he heard a most familiar voice coming from behind him.

"Going somewhere, Charles?"

It was Dreyfuss!

To make matters worse, twenty British soldiers had surrounded them. One of them had grabbed Sophie, who was now gagged. The soldier let her go, and she threw down the rag and ran to Margaret.

"I'm sorry, they snuck up on me," she explained, with so much regret that Margaret thought she was going to cry.

"It's okay," Margaret whispered back to her.

Charles and Basil put their hands on their heads and dropped to their knees. They knew that fighting was fruitless. Besides, they wouldn't dare endanger this school or its students.

"This is between you and me, Dreyfuss. Leave the others alone," Charles warned.

"You're not exactly in a position to negotiate, are you Charles?" Dreyfuss said as he walked up to him. Charles could see the intensity in his eyes and the conviction in his walk.

"I've followed you around the Mediterranean for months now. You have eluded me at every stop and now, after all this time, I finally have you," Dreyfuss hissed, as he walked up to Charles. Then, without warning, he reared back his hand and struck Charles as hard as he could in the face. The blow took Charles by surprise, sending him down face first into the dirt.

"No!" Margaret yelled, trying to run to her father as Inez and Alice held her back.

Blood dripped from Charles's lip as he stood back up. His jaw was throbbing and he felt a tooth loosened in his mouth. He tried to weigh his options, but he had none—Dreyfuss had captured him! The only thing he could do now was to attempt to negotiate the release of the school.

He was about to speak when Sister Anne came dashing down the road, flanked by dozens of students. There had been quite a stir in the school, and the girls and teachers were all very frightened.

"What is the meaning of this?" she demanded of Dreyfuss.

"These are wanted pirates and fugitives, and you have been harboring them at this school," Dreyfuss scolded her. Sister Anne, not accustomed to being spoken to in such a tone, stopped just short of him.

"Leave my school at once. Take these prisoners, but leave these grounds and never return. This is a place of refuge and learning," she barked at Dreyfuss.

Dreyfuss paced in the dirt, thoroughly enjoying the little exchange.

"My dear, I have no intention of leaving with the prisoners. I have every intention of hanging them. As for this school, you made your decision when you decided to harbor these insolent renegades. We will burn this school to the ground until not a stick is standing," he growled.

Sister Anne could feel the conviction—in his eyes and in his voice.

Composing herself, she stood right up to Dreyfuss.

"Charles Owen was right about you. You are nothing but a common criminal and a murderer. I was right to harbor these brave and innocent men," she practically yelled at him.

Staring at her, Dreyfuss smiled a bit and then yelled to one of his men.

"Smythe, prepare two nooses and throw them over that tree. Wesley, prepare a number of torches and prepare to burn every building on the school grounds," he ordered and walked straight to Sister Anne.

"You should think about your students, my dear. I wouldn't want anything unfortunate to happen to them," he whispered in her ear, and Sister Anne shuddered with fear.

Holding her tongue, Sister Anne stepped back and held a few of the girls, most of who had gone pale with fear and were now crying.

Dreyfuss sneered at Sister Anne. He turned to his men and nodded, instructing them to get Basil and Charles mounted on their horses and to bind their hands behind their backs. Basil and Charles were then marched over to a large tree, where two nooses had been strung up from a high and sturdy branch.

Margaret screamed in terror as she watched this happening. Her father tried to be stoic and strong for her and never showed an ounce of fear towards Dreyfuss.

Basil stared at the ground and prepared for the inevitable.

He and Charles would hang as pirates after all.

CHAPTER
— *II* —

A NEW IDEA

Louise Owen arrived late for the party at the London Yacht Club. She was dressed to the nines in a burgundy raw silk evening dress complete with a matching hat adorned with a feather on one side.

The party was like every other party in the British upper class. Every patron knew —or knew of—one another by first and last name. Everyone was dressed in their finest evening wear. Champagne and the most elegant of hors d'oeuvres were served. Tonight, it was fresh crab on buttermilk crackers and a roasted sea bass.

More than a few eyes did a double take when they saw Louise enter by herself. Whispers were pointed her way like daggers being thrown at her chest.

Trying not to attract any more attention, Louise grabbed a glass of champagne and headed to the northeast corner of the room. Usually, she would have made the rounds and chatted with dozens of her acquaintances. At this time, she simply wanted to be as anonymous as possible and to blend into the background.

She wasn't there on a social call—she had an agenda!

Louise planned to break into the office of Lionel Hedgecock to see if she could find any evidence she could use to incriminate Dreyfuss. She knew it was a desperate plan, but what other choice did she have? The Far Indian Trading Company and the British navy would certainly never come forward and admit to any kind of conspiracy. She had to have hard proof, even if it meant breaking the law to obtain it.

Standing with her back to the wall, she was suddenly confronted with Mildred Dansbury—Hillie Dansbury's mother.

The Dansburys had essentially declared war on Louise Owen and her family after it became common knowledge that Margaret and her friend Alice had spiked the tea at Hillie's birthday party with an especially strong laxative. The toilets at the Dansbury resident were backed up for a week and a pungent smell still permeated throughout the house. Mrs. Dansbury had done everything in her power to diffuse the smell, to no avail. No amount of detergents or perfume—or even huge bouquets of flowers—seemed to lessen the awful stench. It had gotten to the point where they no longer even invited houseguests, to avoid any further embarrassment.

Mildred Dansbury glared at Louise.

"I'm surprised to find your sort here. I'm sure the invitation found you by mistake," she hissed sarcastically.

Louise stared back at her. She was in no mood for Mildred or her dramatics. It was so odd to Louise that they had been friends for almost twenty years, but were now reduced to bitter enemies. She didn't want to cause an unnecessary scene.

"Hello Mildred, you look lovely this evening," she replied in her most pleasant voice.

Mildred continued to glare at her.

"So, I hear Margaret and that Irish girl have been shipped off to France. Well, that's probably a proper place for them."

"Yes, they are both very happy, and thank you for asking."

"And what of your husband being a traitor to the crown? No doubt he'll be hanging from the gates of Buckingham Palace any day now."

"Do they hang people from the gates of Buckingham Palace? I shouldn't imagine the King would be keen on that. As for Charles, it's all just a simple misunderstanding. It will all be cleared up shortly."

Mildred, knowing she wasn't going to get a rise from Louise, simply turned around and walked away, losing herself among the many partygoers.

Louise continued to stand in the corner until the whispers turned to silence and people simply bored of gossiping about her. She waited another five minutes and was about to go upstairs when she heard someone behind her.

"What are you up to, Louise? You can't be here by accident."

It was Matthew Hatrider! Louise hadn't mentioned to him that she would be here, and she didn't want to involve him, in case she was apprehended.

"Oh nothing—just taking in a little social gathering," she replied as casually as possible.

"I don't believe that for a second. You just happen to be at a party at the same headquarters as the Far Indian Trading Company after you haven't attended any social functions in months? This can't be a coincidence."

His voice was firm and demanding, and Louise stared demurely at him. If she was one thing, it was a very bad liar.

"Very well, Matthew. Yes, it's true that I am here because the offices of the Far Indian Trading Company are in this building. I'm desperate, Matthew. I just don't know how else to get proof of their involvement."

He nodded his head in agreement.

"In about five minutes, one of the admirals is going to make a toast. When he does, you're going to need to act fast. Lionel Hedgecock's office is on the fourth floor. Take a right when you reach the top of the staircase and it will be the last office on the left. The door will obviously be locked—do you know how to pick a lock?"

She shook her head and he sighed heavily.

"Okay, then I'm going to need to help you. We'll need to be quick about it. I can probably get you into the office, but you'll have to hurry. If you're caught, they'll likely throw you in prison as a traitor."

Matthew said the last word with a steely seriousness, to be sure Louise fully understood the real danger she was putting herself into.

"I know, Matthew," she whispered.

"Is it worth it, Louise? If you're caught, what will happen to your son and your daughter? I won't be able to protect you. Given Charles's dubious reputation, it's likely they'll conclude you were a coconspirator the entire time."

"Matthew, my family is slowly disintegrating before my eyes. Margaret is away in France and David has been ostracized by his schoolmates. I'm a pariah in our circle of friends—not that I have any friends left. I have to do something drastic. I know it's dangerous, but it's the only hope I've got."

He heard the defeat in her voice and he knew she was probably right. Without some kind of hard proof, there's no way that Charles Owen could ever clear his name.

"All right then, when the Admiral starts his toast, we'll hurry upstairs. But Louise, after the door is open, I can't help you anymore. I have my own family to think about. I do hope you understand."

"Of course, Matthew. You've already done far more than I could ever have imagined. I'll be grateful to you forever."

They continued to make small talk until a tiny bell was rung and one of the many British admirals began to make a long-winded speech. Matthew and Louise took their cue and hurried up the back stairs, which were made of solid marble and were slippery to the touch. Louise could almost feel her heart leap from her chest as she made her way to the fourth floor. Matthew lit a tiny lantern, and they carefully headed down the hallway to a door with a glass plate. "L. Hedgecock, President" was stenciled on the glass in black letters.

Matthew produced a tiny paper clip and began jiggling it in the lock. Around the office he'd become a jack-of-all-trades and was frequently called on to pick locks when some officer had misplaced his keys. The locks really weren't that complicated and could usually be picked open in a matter of minutes.

Luckily, this one was no different.

After two minutes, they heard a click. Matthew turned the doorknob, and the door opened right up.

"Okay, Louise, you're on your own now. Please do be careful and you'll need to be quick. I wouldn't want anything to happen to you," he said, handing her the lantern.

Taking the lantern, she squeezed his hand and closed the door behind her. Matthew made his way quickly down the hall and rejoined the party. As if nothing had happened, he began mingling with guests—all the while wondering how Louise was faring.

The office was massive! Three mahogany file cabinets were on her right. In the center of the office sat an oak desk with two chairs directly in front of it for visitors. A tall and comfortable leather chair was behind the desk. On the walls were various maps and accolades from papers, as well as some awards from the British ministry.

Louise placed the lantern on top of the first file cabinet and tried to open the drawer—but it was locked!

Quickly, she went to the desk and opened the drawers. In the middle drawer, she found a key ring with three tiny keys hanging from it. Returning to the cabinet, she tried the first two keys without success. The third, however, unlocked the cabinet easily.

"Not much of a security system," she thought to herself.

Without delay, Louise began rifling through the hundreds of folders. Most were labeled with customers' accounts or names of ships. Satisfied, she closed and locked the drawer and proceeded to the next filing cabinet to repeat the process.

Nothing.

She opened the third and final cabinet and was about to lose hope of finding anything at all when a folder caught her eye. It was jammed in the back and had the word "Dreyfuss" on the tab. She pulled out the folder and looked inside. It contained a small black notebook and many newspaper clippings. The clippings included stories of hijackings and pirating around the Mediterranean Sea.

She took the folder and the lantern over to the table. When she opened the notebook, she could see it was a ledger of some sort. It listed ships' names, along with specific dates and descriptions such as "2 tons tuna" or "500 pounds of salt."

This was it! This was the evidence she needed. It was a gold mine. Just as she was getting excited about her discovery, she heard voices outside the office. One of them was unmistakably Mildred Dansbury's! Immediately, she blew out the lantern. Closing and locking the last cabinet, Louise returned the keys to the drawer and looked around the office. There was absolutely no hiding place. The only way she could escape was through a huge glass window. Tucking the folder safely in her dress, she unlocked the window and stepped outside onto a ledge. She closed the window behind her but couldn't lock it.

Moving to one side, she realized she didn't have anywhere to go. She was four stories up and the ledge ended with the sculpture of a huge eagle—she wouldn't have the space to cross it! With her back pressed against the cement wall, Louise could hear voices and could see light emanating from inside the office.

Louise stared ahead into the darkness. She had no escape—all it would take is one look outside the office window, and she would be caught.

Inside the office, Mildred Dansbury was searching for Louise, along with Lionel Hedgecock and his assistant. Mildred had seen Louise and Matthew disappear up the stairway. When Matthew returned without Louise, Mildred became suspicious. It had taken her the better part of ten minutes to locate Lionel Hedgecock, as he was outside smoking a cigar with some school chums. Once she explained what she had witnessed, he quickly gathered his assistant and together they raced up the stairs. After opening his office, Hedgecock searched through his desk, but everything seemed to be in order. Taking his keys from the desk drawer, he found the cabinets locked, just as they should have been.

Nothing was out of order.

"Well, everything looks to be in place. There's only one way out and we would have seen her."

"What about the window?" Mildred practically screamed.

Lionel looked at the window—it was odd that it was unlocked. He slowly walked towards it, curious. Why it would be unlatched?

From outside, Louise could see that Hedgecock was about to open the window. She was frozen with fear. The wind was biting into her and she knew she was trapped.

She only had one choice.

Louise stepped off the ledge into the darkness. She allowed her body to float through space towards the earth. The feeling of falling through the air and gaining momentum was frightening. The fear of dropping, of falling, of losing control, had always been terrifying for Louise. The idea of leaping off a ledge and leaving everything to chance went against her every instinct.

Faster and farther she fell until she hit the surface.

Only she didn't hit the ground.

She plummeted into the frigid water of the River Thames.

Her body plunged below the surface and instantly she felt as if she were going into shock, the water was so cold. She swam as long as she could beneath the surface and then abruptly came up for a gulp of air before retreating again below the surface. Everything was dark. The current was very strong and she could feel herself being pulled under. She tried desperately to swim against the current, but she felt helpless. The pull was just too strong.

Louise was terrified. Given the temperature of the water, she knew she would only survive for about twenty minutes before her body would retreat into hypothermia and she would certainly drown.

Up above, Hedgecock opened the window and glanced to either side. He scanned outside and then looked both above and below him. He could hear the river beneath him, but as he looked down, all he could see was darkness.

Shutting and bolting the window, he took one last glance around the office, looked at Mildred and shook his head.

They were alone in the office.

Tariq and Melbourne Jack made their way through the Rif Mountains to the area where the tribe should have been—but the site was completely empty! They searched the area for over two hours but there was no sign of the tribe or their trail. They were about to give up hope when a voice called out from a distant tree.

"Tariq?"

Tariq and Jack both stood up and looked into the direction of the tree. A man came from behind it and approached them both.

It was Himli, one of the tribe's scouts!

Tariq ran to him and they hugged each other in a welcome embrace.

"Himli, where is everyone? Where have they gone?"

Himli motioned into the distance. "Over beyond that point. And who is this?" Himli asked, eyeing Jack suspiciously.

"Ah, this is Melbourne Jack. He is a sworn enemy of the Caid and a good friend of mine. Do not worry, he is on our side," Tariq said with a smile.

"Good to meet you, mate," Jack said and extended his arm.

Himli nodded and shook Jack's hand. This man was definitely not from Morocco—and he looked different from anyone Himli had ever met. As Jack was an Aborigine from Australia, his darker skin, curly hair, and moustache were definitely alien to most Moroccans.

"Come, gather your things. We can make camp before nightfall," Himli ordered and soon all three of them were walking down a valley trail. Himli made an effort to cover their tracks and they proceeded, taking a series of alternate trails and routes to throw off any followers.

"Himli, I am so sorry to hear of Malik and Sanaa. My heart is still hurting from the news," Tariq explained in a very sad voice.

"Tariq, have you not heard?"

"Heard what?"

"Malik and Sanaa are alive! They have returned to the camp with Zijuan. Oh, I can see there is much to tell you."

Tariq stopped in his tracks and stared at Himli.

"Are you joking with me, Himli?"

"No, they have been asking for you. They will be overjoyed to see you!"

Tariq suddenly screamed with delight, raised his hands, and started jumping up and down. He hugged Himli tightly and then hugged Melbourne Jack. He didn't stop yelling and hollering for thirty seconds.

Himli and Jack simply stood and smiled at Tariq's joy.

"This is the best news I could ever receive! I am so happy, Himli! All of my prayers have been answered."

"But Tariq, there is one other thing I must tell you. Malik is blind," Himli explained as his voice retreated to a whisper.

Tariq stopped jumping around.

"Blind? What are you saying?"

"The Black Mamba captured Malik and Sanaa. He tied them up and buried them up to their heads in sand. He then stitched their eyes wide open so the sun would blind them. Sanaa managed to escape blindness, but Malik was not so fortunate."

Tariq stared at Himli with a quizzical look on his face.

"When did all this happen, Himli?"

"Come, I'll tell you on the way. We must hurry to make camp by nightfall."

The three continued to walk at a brisk pace while Himli recounted all the new happenings within the camp and the tribe.

By sunset, they made their way past a bend to the edge of the camp. Only, it was nothing like Tariq had ever seen before. The size of the camp was ten times the size it had been when he left. Tents covered almost every inch of the area, and people who looked very different from those in his tribe stopped to smile at Tariq.

"Who are these people, Himli?" Tariq asked.

"This, my friend, is an army preparing to fight the Caid."

The tents came in all sizes and shapes, and bonfires burned, many of them with roasted rabbit twirling on a spit. Smells of goat stew spiced with turmeric and pomegranate also filled Tariq's nostrils.

Children darted around, playing among the tents. It was nothing like Fez and Aseem had described to him.

The three walked through the camp, to the far end, where Tariq saw a figure sitting on a stool, calmly stitching a shirt.

"Zijuan!" Tariq yelled and sprinted to her.

Zijuan, seeing Tariq, covered her mouth and her eyes instantly welled with tears. In a moment she was off the stool with outstretched arms. Soon, Tariq was in her embrace and hugging her warmly. She held him close to her for a long time, holding his hair between her fingers, allowing herself to cry.

"I thought you were dead!" she said, releasing him just long enough to look at his face, before hugging him once again.

"I never thought I would see you again," he whispered.

Finally letting go of him, she continued to smile and size him up.

"Look at how you have grown since the last time I saw you!" she laughed and Tariq blushed.

"Zijuan, this is my friend Melbourne Jack—he saved my life!" Tariq excitedly introduced them.

"I've heard a lot about you, Zijuan. If half of what Tariq says about you is true, I'm more than impressed," Jack said and extended his hand.

"Well, Tariq never ceases to amaze me. It is nice to meet you, Melbourne Jack."

Just then, two figures emerged from a nearby tent. They were more than familiar to Tariq—it was Sanaa and Malik.

"Sanaa!" Tariq yelled and ran to her, embracing her tightly and then, without thinking, also embraced Malik, who was carrying a cane.

Sanaa, stoic as ever, hugged Tariq but did not show as much emotion as Zijuan had. Still, it was obvious she was very happy to see him.

Malik, however, hugged Tariq warmly and tightly and brought his cheek to Tariq's. He kept his cheek pressed to Tariq's for about ten seconds, allowing the warmth of Tariq's face to warm his own.

"How I have worried about you, Tariq," Malik whispered to him and then kissed him on both cheeks.

"I heard what the Mamba did to you. I will not rest until he is dead," Tariq replied and Malik smiled.

"Your safety is all that matters to me. Come, let's eat together. I can't wait to hear all about your adventures."

The five of them sat down to a gorgeous meal of roast partridge and pomegranate soup. Mint tea, as usual, was served along with some warm Moroccan bread called *khobz*. Tariq was famished and hungrily shoveled the food into his mouth. In between bites, he told of his exploits in Chaouen, how he met Melbourne Jack, and how they escaped the Caid's troops. When he began telling the story of Timin, Zijuan, Malik, and Sanaa became very interested and listened intently.

"Tell me again—who is this Timin?" Malik asked.

"The police falsely imprisoned him for running a betting parlor, but it was Zahir, the Caid's henchman, who turned him in. Timin is organizing an underground spy network of street kids and vagrants. He's really amazing—he has spies in almost every major city, and word is spreading fast. In fact, just four nights ago we were successful in our first raid on supplies being delivered to the Caid's outpost in Bab Taza. *And,* we left a symbol of our success," he said proudly.

"A symbol?" Sanaa asked.

"Red handprints—that is our symbol. Jack can tell you all about the Red Hand."

Zijuan smiled and nodded her head.

"Oh, I know all about the Legend of the Red Hand," she said softly and smiled.

Jack looked surprised.

"You do? Most do not, or they dismiss it as some kind of fairy tale."

"Oh, the Red Hand is very real. As for you Melbourne Jack, I would imagine you are not in Morocco by accident, but on some quest. Is that not correct?"

Jack, doubly impressed with Zijuan, nodded in agreement.

"Just as I am also sure it was no accident you happened to meet Tariq. I met a gypsy witch who told me Tariq was being protected by powerful forces—I suppose that would mean you."

"A gypsy witch?" Jack asked.

"Yes. She placed a curse on our tribe, which we believe to be the root of all our troubles. It is good you are here, Jack. Your presence will help protect us from dark forces."

Just then Aji the cat came from behind a tent and ran straight to Tariq. Aji purred and licked Tariq's face as he settled right into his lap.

"Hey, Aji, I have missed you," Tariq said as he played with him.

Zijuan watched the scene with interest.

"Tariq, when did you find that cat?" she asked.

"Well, it was more like he found me. One day, he just showed up at my tent and never left my side."

"Hmmm," Zijuan said, studying Tariq and Aji.

"Do you have other cats in the tribe?" Jack asked.

"No, just the one," Malik replied.

"Are you thinking what I'm thinking, Zijuan?" Jack asked and Zijuan smiled.

"I think Aji was placed here by someone in the afterlife, someone who is looking out for Tariq. Cats are natural protectors against evil spirits and this cat seems to have a special amount of strength."

"Who in the afterlife?" Tariq asked, suddenly intrigued.

"I do not know, but someone who cares about you a great deal," Zijuan explained.

"In our circus, we have dozens of cats for just that reason. The big cats—the lions and tigers—are our greatest protectors against evil," Jack said.

"Where is your circus now?" Zijuan asked Jack.

"Somewhere in Ceylon or India. I haven't heard from them in a few months, but I'm due to return soon. It's because of Tariq that I am still in Morocco," Jack told them and everyone smiled.

"So, your quest is complete?" Zijuan asked.

With that, Jack went silent, as did Tariq. Tariq had sworn never to say a word to anyone, even Zijuan, about Jack's quest or the diary of Alexander the Great.

"You could say that," Jack finally answered.

Zijuan was especially interested in Jack and studied him intently. She now understood why Tariq had been kept from harm. She also felt that somehow Jack was going to be involved in Tariq's future and in the future of this tribe. After weeks of worry and fear, she now sensed an inner calm and a feeling of relaxation, as if some nagging questions were finally being answered.

"I want to hear more of this underground resistance," Sanaa said, changing the subject.

Jack grinned and began explaining.

"It's ingenious. The codes are dependent upon information from a different book each week. It is organized this way so that if an operative is captured, it won't do the Caid much good. All communications and correspondence are in code. Every spy network is self-contained, meaning they don't know who the other spies are, or even where they are posted. You could be sitting down in a café talking to someone, and you would never know if he or she was part of the resistance. The spies all operate independently and have their own sectors of a city. Messages are communicated via carrier pigeon, and not even the spies know exactly where the pigeons go. Training is done one-on-one and usually takes a couple of weeks. It's all very anonymous."

As Malik, Sanaa, and Zijuan listened to Jack, it felt as if all of them were thinking the exact same thing.

"We may have finally found the solution we've been looking for," Zijuan finally said.

"I was thinking the exact same thing," Malik agreed.

"What are you talking about?" Tariq asked.

"Tariq, we can fight the French and the Caid in the mountains, but they'll slaughter us in the open desert. We have resources in the cities, but not nearly as substantial as this resistance you've been talking about. If we can work together with Timin, we will be able to begin concurrent attacks on the French and the Caid," Malik explained.

Sanaa stood up excitedly and exclaimed, "We can win this war. Don't you see? If we are able to obtain intelligence from the French about their plans—and the Caid's—we can begin attacking them where they are most vulnerable. It is masterful to have the spies be street boys and vagrants, as they are invisible to society."

Tariq suddenly understood. Everything around them, all these people, they were all gathered together for one purpose—to defeat the Caid!

"How many soldiers do you have?" Jack asked.

"Here, a little over two thousand. However, we expect our numbers to grow to four or five thousand in a few short weeks as we recruit more tribes to join us," Malik answered.

"The main issue will be arming and organizing them. These people are all from different tribes, and many even speak a different language. Without some organization, they will be little more than lambs for slaughter at an Easter feast," Jack reckoned, putting his hand to his chin as he pondered the consequences.

Zijuan looked at Jack and asked him a question.

"Jack, do you think, with your intelligence, that you could receive word of any arms shipments? If we knew when and where a shipment was due to arrive, then we might be able to hijack it and even the odds somewhat."

"Hmmm, I was thinking the same thing. We'll need modern rifles and time enough to teach the tribesmen how to shoot. I'll bet some of them have never even seen a rifle," Jack replied.

Malik continued to consider all possible consequences. Although his sight was gone, his mind was functioning as it always had, if not better. He could use his knowledge and imagination to visualize everything as he spoke.

"We will need to go beyond arms and men. We must have a location that works to our advantage. We will have morale on our side, as these people are fighting for their families and their lives, while the Caid's soldiers are little more than mercenaries and young boys who have been kidnapped and forced to fight. Most of these people have already felt the wrath of the Caid—they've watched loved ones butchered or forced to join the Caid's army against their will. It will be no trouble getting them to fight."

"Jack, can you send a message to the resistance and ask them if they've received any information on an arms shipment? Unfortunately it will only be a one-way message, as none of these pigeons have been trained to return to this spot. Would it be possible to train some of them to use this as their home base?" Zijuan asked.

"Sure, I can get a message to them. As for training pigeons, that's not my field of expertise."

"But it is mine," Malik interrupted.

Everyone looked at Malik.

"I've trained falcons since I was eight years old. Pigeons will be much, much easier to train. It should only take me about two or three weeks. I suggest we set up an expedition force to visit Chaouen to begin looking at arms to steal. In the meantime, we will have ample time to train this army."

Everyone nodded in agreement. Zijuan spoke first.

"Sanaa, you are the perfect person for such a mission. Could you escort Jack and Tariq back to Chaouen in three weeks' time? Meanwhile, I will remain with Malik and the other tribe leaders to begin the training. Malik, in order to keep the peace, we'll want to give every tribe leader an officer position within the army and run it as a democracy. We'll need to quickly develop a training program and begin training maneuvers as soon as possible. I think we'll need, at a minimum, six weeks before they'll be battle-ready."

Jack looked at the ground apprehensively and deep in thought.

"Jack, are you conflicted about returning to your people?" Zijuan asked.

"I want to help, I really do, but I need to think about this tonight," Jack replied. It was easy to see that the decision was weighing heavily on him. If the artifact were to fall into the wrong hands, it could be devastating.

"We understand, Jack. You've already helped so much, and it would be selfish to ask you to stay. Whether you decide to stay or leave, you are still my friend for life," Tariq explained, giving Jack a pat on the shoulder for reassurance.

Later that night, Zijuan came to Tariq and placed his pendant around his neck.

"Zijuan, I can't believe you have this—it is the only thing I have to remember Aji. I thought it was lost forever," he said as he rubbed the pendant between his fingers.

Zijuan hugged him again and brushed his hair with her hands.

"How did you find it?" he asked.

"I have my ways," she said and they both smiled.

The following morning, the camp woke early and was soon buzzing with excitement and anticipation. Fires were built and pots were put on to boil water for tea. Jack emerged from his tent, stretched his back, and went straight over to Tariq, who was sharpening a knife. Aji purred, asleep at his feet.

"Well mate, I guess you haven't gotten rid of me yet. I was up all night thinking it over, and I've decided I'll help your tribe defeat the Caid as best I can," he said.

Tariq jumped up and hugged him tightly—this was the best news he could have received. Tariq had been afraid that Jack might return to the circus. Soon, news spread to the other leaders that Jack was staying. Everyone congratulated and thanked him. He was especially struck by the Tuareg leader, Moussa Ag Arshaman, who was obviously a fierce warrior and a very intelligent fellow. He asked Jack about the hot air balloons and the Red Hand and his circus. He demanded a demonstration of Jack's boomerang-throwing prowess and was awed by his ability after Jack simultaneously threw four boomerangs—each finding its mark and returning effortlessly to his hands. Arshaman himself tried to throw the boomerang several times, and each time it failed to return, which made him even more impressed with Jack's ability.

That morning, a pigeon was released to Chaouen with a message written in code asking Timin to have his spies look for a large shipment of arms.

The movement to defeat the Caid was starting to grow—would it succeed like a small spark that ignites a roaring fire, or would it dwindle to ash like dying embers?

CHAPTER
— *12* —

IS THIS THE END?

Charles and Basil were led on horseback with hands tied behind their backs, to a tall oak tree, where two nooses had been thrown over one of its strong branches. The nooses lay in waiting for their victims. Margaret wailed and cried and many of the other girls were also crying—even Sister Anne shed a tear or two. Most of these girls had lived very sheltered lives and had never witnessed this form of cruelty.

Charles, his head hung low, glanced at Margaret through the corner of his eye and tried to raise a smile. He never, ever wanted this for his daughter and, as his horse stopped at the foot of the tree, he yelled.

"Margaret, I can't have you witness this. Please, cover your eyes and leave," he pleaded with her as she cried ever more forcefully. Nodding her head, she covered her eyes and allowed herself to be led up the hill by Sophie, Alice, Inez, and Etienne.

None of them wanted to witness this barbaric act.

Dreyfuss, from atop his horse, continued to smirk, enjoying the power he now held over Charles, Basil, and these schoolgirls. There was nothing, absolutely nothing he enjoyed more than wielding his power.

"Terry, prepare these prisoners for the noose," Dreyfuss ordered.

Young Steven Terry rode up on his horse and pretended to tighten the knot behind Charles's wrists. However, he had a small knife hidden in his palm and, without detection, quickly cut the rope.

"On my mark, Colonel, fall to the ground and take action," Terry whispered to Charles.

Charles, immensely surprised, showed no outward emotion.

Young Terry did the exact same thing to Captain Basil, who also showed no emotion.

Next, Terry positioned the horses directly beneath the nooses and was about to throw them around the necks of Charles and Basil when he suddenly shouted.

"Now!"

Charles and Basil flung themselves off their horses, while Terry produced a Colt revolver and pointed it straight at Lieutenant Dreyfuss's head.

The expression of Dreyfuss's face was one of complete shock and outrage.

"Terry, what are you doing?" he demanded.

"I've had enough of your killing and marauding. I should have set the colonel free back in that village. I promised myself that if I ever had the chance again, I would free him. I didn't join His Majesty's navy to be little more than a pirate and murderer. I don't care if I hang for this, but I'm not taking orders from you any longer."

Seeing a rifle on the back of Terry's horse, Charles quickly grabbed it and pointed it at another British soldier.

Suddenly, Charles remembered young Terry from his first encounter with Dreyfuss. He was the seaman who had hesitated when Dreyfuss ordered him to kill Charles.

The rest of the soldiers looked at one another with panic on their faces. Most drew their weapons and began shouting at Seaman Terry.

"Terry, have you lost your mind? What are you doing?" they screamed.

"This here is Charles Owen and he's a colonel in the British army. He outranks Lieutenant Dreyfuss over there. If you draw a weapon on him, you're committing treason," Terry barked back at them.

"That's right, ain't it, Colonel?" Terry whispered to him.

"Quite right," Charles whispered back.

Then, one of the other young soldiers broke rank.

"I'm with Terry. I've had enough of this marauding and killing. If this 'ere is a colonel, then I'm with him," the young lad said and pointed his gun directly at Dreyfuss.

This began a surge of panic with the other soldiers. Who was with Dreyfuss, and who was with Charles?

It became apparent soon enough.

Half the soldiers either rode or stood next to Charles while the other half remained next to Dreyfuss.

It was a classic standoff, with each group pointing guns or swords at the other with only about thirty feet separating them.

The soldiers were stunned and in utter disbelief. Many of them were friends and had trained and served together. But now, they were suddenly faced with killing one another.

They were about to slaughter one another when Charles spoke up.

"Lads, I don't want to see you butcher each other. I know most of you are confused and scared and just trying to do your duty. This is between Lieutenant Dreyfuss and me. Rather than a bloodbath, I suggest he and I settle it the old-fashioned way."

"Which way is that?" one of the soldiers with Dreyfuss asked.

"With swords," Charles replied.

The soldiers looked around and murmured to one another.

"Sounds right and fair to me," the same soldier replied.

Dreyfuss looked at his group and shouted at them.

"You are committing insubordination. By the British Crown you are to follow my orders or risk being court-martialed and sentenced to death for treason. This isn't some pub fight or backyard pugilistic endeavor," he began.

"I've got to agree with the Colonel here, if he is a colonel. Whoever is still standing at the end of the duel is the man we'll follow. Agreed, boys?"

The other soldiers discussed it quickly.

"Fair enough," young Terry said, and soon all the soldiers had dismounted. Two swords were produced, of the 1908 Pattern Cavalry Trooper variety. This sword was not standard issue for the British navy, but it was considered the finest cavalry sword ever made. A few of the lads had traded for them back in training and offered them for the duel. Dreyfuss and the other officers looked them over.

163

Margaret and the other girls had overheard the yelling match between the men and ran back down the hill to join the scene. All the soldiers, teachers, and schoolgirls backed away from the two swordsmen, forming a wide circle around them. Charles and Dreyfuss were each given a sword. Both men rolled up their sleeves and practiced a few swipes in the air.

"Very well then—to the death!" Dreyfuss screamed and charged at Charles with his sword held high and a murderous look in his eyes.

Charles moved away from the charging Dreyfuss in the nick of time and parried the blow. He used angles to keep him at bay and played a defensive position, quickly discovering that Dreyfuss was skilled with the sword and fought extremely aggressively.

Parrying five quick blows, Charles mounted a counterattack of his own, driving Dreyfuss back to the edge of the circle. He distantly heard Margaret urging him on, along with the screams of the other girls. Some of the soldiers were rooting on Dreyfuss and others were cheering for Charles.

Lunging at Dreyfuss, Charles instantly knew he'd made a mistake by getting off balance and reaching too far with his outstretched arm. Dreyfuss, seeing the mistake, moved to one side and sliced the side of Charles's left shoulder with his blade, creating a gash about four inches long. Right away, blood started to drip from the wound, turning his white shirt red.

He heard Margaret scream.

Luckily, it was his left shoulder and not his right—that would have been catastrophic!

Dreyfuss continued in a frenzied attack and launched nine straight blows at Charles, driving him backwards. Charles was forced to simultaneously deflect the attacks with his sword and move his body at different angles to avoid the blows.

The two continued to move backward and forward, and to thrust and hack at one another. Charles then realized that while Dreyfuss was very aggressive, he was also very angry, and Charles decided to use that against him.

Allowing Dreyfuss to get closer and closer, he drew him in and then, suddenly, launched a straight left punch right into Dreyfuss's nose. It was a direct hit! Charles had caught Dreyfuss completely by surprise, leaving the lieutenant totally exposed.

His nose was broken!

Dreyfuss's eyes swelled up and blood gushed from his nostrils and down his chin.

Taking five steps backwards, Dreyfuss tried to gather his wits, but Charles was on him once more with thrust after thrust and attack after attack. Dreyfuss, unaccustomed to playing defense, and beginning to feel the throbbing sensation in his nose, began to panic.

Dreyfuss moved forward in a blind rage, waving his sword in wide sweeping motions in an attempt to decapitate Charles, but these blows were easily deflected and Charles could see that Dreyfuss had become unhinged.

He waited for the opportune moment, and when Dreyfuss brought his sword high above his head, leaving his torso completely exposed, that's when Charles struck. He simply leaned forward, extended his sword, and plunged it straight through Dreyfuss's left kidney. Quickly pulling out the blade, Charles knew it was over.

Dreyfuss's face went ghostly white and blood dribbled from his lips. He took three steps forward, fell to his knees, and made one last gurgling sound as he collapsed onto the dirt, landing on his face.

Dreyfuss was dead.

Charles continued to circle him, not yet believing he had won. After months of being hunted, he had finally killed his pursuer. Immediately, he felt an enormous sense of relief. Dropping his sword to the ground, Charles brought both hands to his knees and said a quick prayer.

Margaret ran to him and hugged him tightly.

"Ow, that wound is deep," he complained and she released her embrace a bit.

The British soldiers surrounded Dreyfuss's body, completely flabbergasted by the events that had unfolded in front of their eyes.

To many of the soldiers, Dreyfuss had been a bully. He had been invincible to them—watching him get beaten and killed was quite sobering.

Steven Terry walked up to Charles and saluted him.

"Sir! We are now under your command. What are the orders, sir?"

"You have a ship?" Charles asked.

"Yes, sir!"

"Then we depart for Liverpool at dawn," he replied and Terry smiled.

"It's back home we go, lads—we leave for Liverpool at first light!" Charles called out.

The crew smiled and threw their hats in the air and let out a cry of "hip hip hooray" for Charles. They had been away from home for almost two years and most were very homesick.

The ones who had originally been against Charles quickly changed positions. Each and every soldier came to salute him and to swear their allegiance.

"I guess you now have a ship and a crew, Charles," Basil said, and came up and shook Charles's good hand.

"You're coming with us, Basil."

"I can't, Charles. I am a wanted man and would not want to see my head on the inside of a British guillotine."

"Well, I don't think we use guillotines anymore. You've been unfairly hunted and branded a pirate, and the British public needs to know the truth. I'll back you up one hundred percent, and with the testimony of the crew, I think we both have an excellent chance of being pardoned."

"An excellent chance?" Basil asked suspiciously.

"Well, Dreyfuss has powerful friends who will want to protect themselves."

Basil thought about it for a moment and then replied to Charles.

"Charles, I am a wanted pirate. The British have been hunting me for years. I cannot chance spending my life in prison, or being put to death. You are my friend for life, but I must find a ship and make my way back to be with my family."

Charles heaved a sigh and nodded. He now understood that Basil couldn't make the trip back with him to England.

"You're the bravest man I've ever fought with, Basil. I will miss your camaraderie more than you know, and I do hope we will meet one another again."

The two men hugged and shook hands.

"I will see Montaro to a garrison in Spain and return the reward to the school," Basil said.

"No, no, you've earned that reward—" Charles tried to interrupt him.

"Ha! What do I need with money when I have friendship, the wind in my face, and a ship under my feet? Besides, God smiles on those who give, not those who take," he replied and Charles had to laugh at his wisdom.

"Okay, my friend. Have a safe journey. I will leave you a way to reach me in England, and should you ever need any assistance, I will always be there to help you."

"I will do that Charles," Basil replied, as a feeling of melancholy came over him. He realized just how close he and Charles had become and how much he was going to miss him.

"What are you going to do now?" Charles asked.

"After I return Montaro, I'll try to meet up with Henri. He has family in Avignon, and he mentioned he was going to take a sojourn there for a couple of months to tend to his family's vineyard. Perhaps he can help me find a ship."

"A fine plan. Godspeed, Basil."

"Godspeed, Charles."

Louise Owen continued to fight against the river current that threatened to drown her. She tried to keep swimming, but she was extremely fatigued. In fact, all she could do now was dog paddle, in the hope of simply keeping her head above the frigid surface. Darkness was everywhere, and she could scarcely see five feet in front of her face. As the current continued to pull her, she felt her hand hit something solid. Swimming madly, she reached the area where her hand had hit and, indeed, there was something there—a buoy! Louise threw both hands around the floating orb and clung to it for dear life. Now, at least, she could rest, but if she didn't find a way to shore, it would only be a matter of minutes before she'd develop hypothermia and begin freezing to death.

For another five minutes, she hung onto the buoy. She felt her fingers begin to tingle, and her toes were now completely numb. Her breathing was starting to slow, and with every passing minute she felt herself lose strength. The sound of her chattering teeth was all she could hear.

Louise realized that she was going to die. It had never occurred to her when she jumped out the window that she would be unable to swim to shore. What a stupid and idiotic thing she had done! She thought of poor David and Margaret and what their lives would be like—first without their father and now without their mother.

They wouldn't stand a chance in life!

The more she thought of them, living alone in the world with nobody to guide and watch over them, the more determined she became.

Louise spotted a group of rocks about fifty yards away. She might be able to reach them.

Those rocks were her only hope.

She knew this was her one chance for survival. If she swam and missed the rocks, she would be dead within the hour. Taking five very deep breaths, she cleared her mind and thought of nothing except reaching the rocks. It was very difficult to force herself to let go of the buoy. It was her only lifeline, but she had to take the risk of letting go.

Releasing the buoy, she put her head down and swam as she had never swum in her life. With each stroke, she pulled harder with a sole purpose. Her fingers suddenly had feeling again. Rather than fighting the current, she allowed it to carry her and when it released its grip on her, she swam vigorously toward the rocks. All the time she thought of young David, and her beloved daughter, and how she had to survive to be there for them. Without her, they would drift aimlessly through life like a boat without a rudder.

Louise swam like this for several minutes until she raised her head from the water and could see that the rocks were only fifteen yards away.

The current was still strong, but she fought and resisted it, lunging toward the rocks with her arms.

Her efforts brought her closer to the rocks, only to have the outgoing current pull her back again. It was exhausting—two strokes forward and one stroke back. She propelled herself with sheer will, knowing this was her only chance. Any hesitation and the current would pull her down for sure.

Kicking hard and stretching her arms forward, she felt it—was it rock? Yes!

Both hands on the rock, she held on with her fingertips and pulled her body close to the rock, using all of her strength. Feeling the hard surface against her chest, she pulled herself up just high enough that her head was out of the water and she could finally relax.

She had made it!

For a few seconds she allowed herself a bit of elation and then, knowing she couldn't stay in the water much longer, she pulled herself up, cajoling her exhausted body out of the water onto the huge, black rocks that formed the river's edge.

Her body shivered and her teeth continued to chatter uncontrollably. On her hands and knees, she climbed over the rocks. She slipped more than once, scraping her elbows and smashing her knee into a rock. It took her almost twenty minutes to crawl her way up the embankment to street level. Both elbows dripped with blood and she had large welts all over her forearms. Her left knee throbbed with pain, with a huge gash just below her kneecap.

Hailing a cab, Louise made her way home. The cabby was shocked to see a well-dressed woman soaking wet and bloodied standing barefoot at the side of the road. He gave her a blanket to cover herself and insisted that the fare was free. She thanked him profusely when they stopped in front of her house—grateful for the small humanity bestowed upon her after such a harrowing ordeal.

Still soaked and trembling, she walked in the front door. Her nanny, a young girl by the name of Sara, was completely startled by the sight of Louise in such a condition. She immediately drew Louise a warm bath and fetched a spot of rum for her.

Before she could take a tub, however, Louise ran up to David's room. She gave him a kiss on the cheek and simply stared at him sleeping in his bed. He looked so innocent and peaceful, and she felt so lucky to have such a wonderful son.

After leaving David's room, Louise sat in the bath for over an hour, allowing her body to warm itself as she cleaned the grimy mud off her body. The notebook and papers had been lost, unfortunately, but at the moment, she just didn't care.

Sitting in the tub, she didn't cry. In fact, she did the opposite—she smiled with elation and relief.

What an adventure it had been.

Aseem and Fez were placed into basic training with the Caid's other recruits and began exercises and maneuvers at five o'clock each morning. Their sergeant was a Moroccan man with bushy eyebrows and a huge jaw that sported five days' worth of growth. He screamed at them in French, which they didn't understand, and generally ran around hitting things with a club or stabbing a bayonet into a dummy made of straw. They were given uniforms and two meals a day—mostly soup, rice, and bread. The other recruits were almost as young as they were, and some had been forced to join against their wishes.

One night, Fez and Aseem woke and crept out of their tent. There were sentries posted everywhere, so they tiptoed through the shadows to ensure they weren't caught. Making their way over a fence, they walked briskly for three blocks until they came to an old church with a graveyard in the middle. They found a grave with the name "Collins," and looked for a large rock which was supposed to be placed to the right of the gravestone. Picking up the rock, Aseem found a piece of paper that had been folded into squares and quickly opened it.

"Let me read it," Fez whispered.

Aseem gave the paper to Fez, who read it thoroughly.

"It's in code," Fez whispered.

"Of course it's in code. What does it say?"

Fez began deciphering the code in his head. Unlike most people, he didn't need a pencil and paper to easily assign letters to a corresponding line and place in the poem they used to crack the code.

After just a minute, he had it figured out.

"It's from Timin. Tariq is safe and Malik and Sanaa are alive! They need for us to find a large shipment of arms to steal and they need it fast. We're to report back in a week's time about the exact place of the shipment," Fez whispered.

Aseem thought about this for a moment.

"We don't need a week. I know exactly where they are."

"Where?" Fez asked.

"A ship is due in eight days' time. I was washing the floors in the officers' area when I overheard them talking."

"You don't speak French!" Fez questioned.

"No, not the French, the Caid's troops who are working with the French. They were saying how the new recruits weren't ready for guns and we should continue to train with sticks, and they also talked about a shipment coming in."

"How big is the shipment?"

"I don't know."

"Well, where is it going to dock? And when?" Fez asked.

"I don't know that either."

"What's the name of the ship?"

"How should I know?" Aseem responded, clearly frustrated.

Fez furrowed his eyebrows and gave Aseem the stink eye.

"Well, I guess it's better than nothing. I'll leave them a note to begin looking for a ship that's due in about eight days' time. Maybe they have spies on the docks who can help them find out more," Fez answered, obviously agitated, and began writing a reply to the note.

He moved the rock to the other side of the gravestone, as instructed, and left his note underneath the rock. Quickly, the two boys made their way through the shadows and back to their barracks without detection. They were soon nestled safely in their beds.

CHAPTER
— *13* —

OLD SHATAM TEACHES A LESSON

The Black Mamba sat in his tent, sharpening a dagger and seething with anger in his thoughts.

It was rumored that the tribes had been gathering together to defy both he and the Caid. Even worse, it was also rumored that Malik and Sanaa were leading them.

He was being made to look the fool.

It was his responsibility to control the countryside, and if the tribes were organizing and banding together, his job would be that much more difficult.

And to top it off, the Caid was growing impatient, as he had not yet been named the absolute ruler of Morocco. The fighting between the French and the Sultan's troops had been much, much more difficult than they had originally anticipated. To everyone's surprise, the French still had not captured the Sultan, who had disappeared into hiding—this fact infuriated the Caid more than anything else.

With the Sultan still alive, the Moroccan people would still have a leader and would never recognize the French, or the Caid, as their rightful leader.

All of this made the Mamba very testy.

Jawad came into the tent unannounced.

"Sire, did you hear of the raid in Bab Taza?" Jawad asked.

"What raid?"

"Apparently some of our own soldiers planned a raid on a supply wagon. It seems they call themselves the "Red Hand," and they left red handprints everywhere. The townspeople are very excited."

The Mamba stared at Jawad and then, without warning, rose to his feet and smacked Jawad hard across the face, sending him to the ground.

Jawad stared up at him—terrified!

"What did you hear of the Red Hand?" he spat.

"I'm sorry my lord, I was just—" Jawad stammered.

"Well, what do you know?" he screamed, about to hit Jawad again.

"I know nothing of the Red Hand, my lord. I am simply reporting what I was told."

"And that is all?"

"Yes, my lord, I swear."

The Mamba stared at him and then turned his back on Jawad.

"Get out," he hissed.

Jawad quickly scampered to his feet and ran out of the tent. Lately, his master had been so angry with him, scolding him at every opportunity. The more Jawad tried to impress him, the more the Mamba seemed disappointed in him.

Jawad walked alone to the other end of camp, sat on a tree stump, and started to cry. He was a tough and seasoned slave and had endured numerous beatings and hardships, yet all he lived for now was the appreciation and acceptance of the Mamba.

When the Mamba rejected him, it tore at his heart.

"Power isn't what you had hoped for, is it, young Jawad?" a voice spoke from behind.

Quickly wiping his tears, Jawad turned to face the person who had interrupted his silence.

It was an old man he vaguely recognized. The man was stooped over, with sad eyes and wrinkles so deep that his face resembled a dried-up prune.

"You dare speak to me, old man?" Jawad yelled at him and raised his fist to him.

Yet the old man simply stared at him and didn't cower for an instant.

"You don't remember me? Surprising, since we spent years together at the kasbah."

Jawad studied his face. He did know him; he just couldn't manage to put his face with a name.

"Old Shatam?" he blurted out, finally remembering him.

"Very good," Old Shatam said, coming up next to Jawad.

Old Shatam had been a slave at the kasbah and had performed the lowliest of duties. He had been a slave for far longer than anyone cared to remember, and for the most part, he was all but invisible to everyone. He came and went like the wind.

"As I said, power isn't what you thought it might be, is it?"

Jawad didn't know what to say to this question. What was he talking about?

"How do you mean?"

"Oh, I watch you mimic your master. I see you beat people and treat them brutally as he does, but you are not he. He has an evil heart, while deep down, I think you are a good person," Old Shatam told him and looked him straight in the eyes.

Jawad was completely speechless at this line of reasoning.

"What do you know of me? You're a silly and stupid slave," he told him and turned his back.

"You know who the worst slave masters are, Jawad? Former slaves. One would think they would have an understanding of what it is like being a slave, and the hardships, and would want to treat everyone with decency and kindness as a result. Yet former slaves are always the most brutal and vicious to those beneath them. I do not understand why this is. Once a former slave gets a little power, it always goes straight to his head."

Jawad said nothing to this, as Old Shatam's voice did not show an ounce of fear.

"I think these former slaves have so much anger in them, that looking at slaves reminds them of who they once were, and the horrible experiences they endured, so they can't help but beat and brutalize those lower than them. Or, it could simply be they are very insecure with themselves and must beat others to feel powerful."

Jawad continued to listen to the old man, although his back was still turned to him.

"Why do you hate these villagers, Jawad? They are the ones who always showed you kindness. It is the Caid, and the Mamba, and the Caid's soldiers who used to beat and humiliate you, yet all you show them is affection and obedience. Why?"

Again, Jawad said nothing and continued to stare into the distance.

"I have watched you for a long time, Jawad. You were the best camel jockey I have ever seen and a natural leader. I saw how the other boys would follow you, and how you always helped the new boys learn to ride and looked after them. But, it seems you have decided on a path of wickedness and brutality. Why? I do not know. So, I ask you again: is power all that you had hoped it would be?"

Shifting on his toes, Jawad felt himself wanting to talk to Old Shatam. It had been so long since he talked with anyone about anything other than dominance and slaughter.

"At first it *was* all I'd hoped for. I loved the power and the wealth," he replied softly.

"And now?"

"It is like a new pair of shoes. At first, you admire them and take special care of them and they feel so good on your feet. After a while, they just become your everyday shoes and there is no longer anything special about them."

"That is a very good answer, Jawad. I hope you learn from it," Old Shatam said, and walked away.

Back in the tent, the Mamba paced apprehensively. Perhaps it had all been an honest mistake, and they chose the symbol of the Red Hand out of folly? Still, it was a strange coincidence and one he could not ignore. He had been taught of the Red Hand by a priest who had long since died. Mostly, it was thought to be superstition and folklore. Still, even the possibility that it could be real was frightening, as the Red Hand would be more powerful than he could imagine.

The Black Mamba, being very superstitious, felt a sense of dread.

CHAPTER
— *14* —

DARING

Foster Crowe stepped across a small brook and his boots sunk into some slimy mud. Lifting them up and out, he carefully walked across a bog. With every step, his feet sank into the mud, and he trudged along until he safely made it out onto more stable ground. It began to rain and, within minutes, he was drenched. He made his way over to a large mango tree—if he stood underneath, it allowed a little cover. The rain was so thick it came down in sheets, and he could scarcely see five feet in front of him. Soon, the ground was covered with blankets of water and his socks were completely soaked.

After fifteen minutes, the rain stopped altogether, and the sun began to shine through the branches and leaves of the dense jungle.

Looking down, he saw blood showing through his pants down by his shin. Quickly, he pulled up his pant leg and was shocked to see both of his legs completely covered in blood.

Leeches!

There were a dozen of them, sucking on his flesh, fat with his blood. He'd wiped his entire body with a fresh bar of soap, which usually worked as a deterrent and kept leeches off of him. He was, however, deep into a jungle in Ceylon, and these leeches were double the size of their ordinary brethren.

Retrieving a small canister from his pocket, Foster poured salt on each of the leeches, causing them to drop from his skin onto the jungle floor. He then stomped on them, causing their bodies to explode. Blood splattered all over the ground.

Checking his legs and thighs thoroughly to ensure he'd ridden himself of all the little vampires, he took off his boots and socks, only to discover two more nestled between his toes. After pouring salt on the last two leeches, he wrung out his socks. What seemed like a quart of water poured out from each one.

As he put his socks and boots back on his feet, Foster smelled the jungle air and listened to its sounds. The air was pure and fresh, as it should be after a good downpour. Yet he could smell just a hint of sulfur. Listening to the jungle, he thought it quieter than usual. The birds had fallen silent, and not even the monkeys were doing their usual squabbling and screeching.

Foster knew he was close to something.

He'd been traveling for three days in the muck and heat of the dense forest. He'd endured a blanket of mosquitoes, each as big as his thumb. He'd almost stepped on a cobra that was feasting on a nest of termites. Lucky for him, cobras were actually tranquil and calm and wouldn't usually attack unless severely provoked. The pit vipers, however, were a different story entirely. These extremely aggressive snakes were more poisonous than a cobra. It was no accident that more people died of snake bites in Ceylon than anywhere else in the world. Vipers, cobras, and kraits all slithered throughout the entirety of the Ceylonese countryside, and they were especially abundant in the heart of the jungle, away from civilization.

But he couldn't think about any of that.

Foster's sixth sense told him he was approaching something—or someone—very dangerous.

Crouching between the leaves and taking one careful step at a time, he didn't make a sound as he crept forward in the dense brush.

That's when he saw it.

Up ahead, perhaps a hundred yards away—the faintest outline of a roof.

Lying on his belly, he took out a monocular from his knapsack and brought the distant shape into focus.

It was an old temple. A very, very old temple that had been almost completely overrun by jungle foliage and creeping vines.

Whatever it was he was feeling was coming from that place.

As he inched towards it, he felt the dark presence from inside permeate through his heart and his skin. His breathing became labored and his pulse quickened. Foster had felt evil in his life, but nothing had ever compared to this.

He took a moment to breathe and collect his thoughts.

For years he had been tracking this source of evil. He had followed it through India, New Zealand, then to Australia, and finally here, to Ceylon. This force was mysterious and transparent and almost impossible to locate. It seemed to be everywhere at once. Foster believed there was a natural order to the universe wherein good and evil flowed freely, and generally, there was a balance between the two. But this thing—whatever it was—completely disrupted the harmony between good and evil. It created imbalance, which, in turn, transformed the world into a much more evil and darker place.

He understood that whatever he was about to confront was extremely powerful and very dangerous. He detected something foul in the air, yet he couldn't pinpoint what it was.

Completely camouflaged and just thirty feet from the entrance to the temple, Foster scanned for an alternate entrance. He decided it would be better to enter from a back door than to go in from the front—for both stealth and surprise.

He saw a slight hill to his left and decided on that route. Continuing to crawl on his belly, his movements were so slow and calculated that not a leaf or twig was disturbed. A guard could have been right on top of him and still not known that Foster was beneath him.

He continued on his belly for twenty minutes and made his way over the hill, when he came upon a most tragic and fearful scene.

There were dead bodies everywhere.

At least ten of them—and the odor they produced was nauseating. This was the foul smell he had detected earlier.

He could see the bodies just down the embankment to his left. They had been thrown there like trash in the rubbish bin. Most likely they were poor travelers or snake hunters who accidentally came upon the temple and were instantly massacred.

Some of the bodies were nothing but bones, while others had just started decomposing and were filled with maggots and flies. One of them still had flesh attached to its face and a massive knife wound ran from the upper left forehead down to the jaw. The cut was so deep it exposed bone! Foster tried not to look at the bodies and kept moving forward through the brush, around to the rear of the temple.

He immediately spied a wooden door in the rear and decided to enter through it.

Moving down the hillside, he was more cautious than ever and moved even slower than before. Seeing those dead bodies had unnerved him. His hands became clammy, and sweat began to drip from his forehead, stinging his eyes. He tried to control his breathing, but it was impossible—his breathing sped up until he was practically hyperventilating.

After taking a deep breath to calm his nerves, Foster reached up and grabbed the doorknob, but it was locked. Standing up, he produced a ring of skeleton keys, tried three that he thought might work, and on his second try, the door opened. He had a ring of twenty keys that could open almost any lock in existence—he had developed these skeleton keys with the help of a metalsmith in Kathmandu. He stayed alert and constantly looked around to be sure no one was approaching. He heard and saw nothing, just the normal sounds of the jungle and the distant singing of a parrot.

Moving inside, he closed the door behind him. The hallway was pitch-black. Rather than lighting a lantern or match, he waited a minute to allow his eyes to adjust to the darkness and then began to gingerly move ahead.

He produced a dagger from a sheath on his belt, and held it in his right hand. His back pressed firmly against the stone wall, Foster shuffled down the hallway until he came to an intersection. To his left, it was complete darkness, but to his right, he could see a tiny light flickering, just past a bend in the hallway. Deciding to follow the light, he pressed up against the wall and made his way down the hallway. Passing around the bend, he saw a solitary doorway from which the flickering light emanated.

Whatever being he sought was most likely inside that room.

Holding the knife even tighter, he moved slowly along the hallway until he came to the doorway. Steeling himself, he quickly peeked inside and hoped he wouldn't be seen.

What he saw surprised him.

Behind that door was a very big room. There was a solitary candle on a desk in the corner that provided enough light to illuminate the entire room. Along each wall sat a long wooden table and each table contained test tubes filled with unimaginable potions and concoctions. Shelves had been hung above the tables, and on those shelves sat collections of jars, beakers, and glass canisters.

Yet the room was uninhabited.

Before stepping inside, he took one last look around the hallway to ensure he wasn't being followed.

The room was indeed empty. It was made completely from stone and had no windows. The floor was also stone with some small puddles of water in places from leaky spots in the ceiling.

Whoever was working in this room was an apothecary—a medical professional who specialized in potions and remedies of various sorts.

On the wall, dozens of formulas had been written in chalk, and hundreds of books had been stacked in every corner.

Someone was definitely performing dozens of experiments in this makeshift laboratory.

On each table, there were also dissected rats, insects, frogs, and fish; dozens of snakes were stored in jars of formaldehyde. The instruments to perform the dissections were also on the table, along with a dirty towel that must have been used to wipe off the knives. The countertops were splattered with blood, guts, and entrails from the many experiments, along with hundreds of leaves from various plants and flowers. The beakers and test tubes were filled with every color of liquid—from brown to blue to red to green. On one table, Foster could see rows of small glass jars stacked high—each filled with a different powder.

The person responsible for this mess obviously wasn't concerned with cleanliness or order. Moreover, the condition of this room suggested the existence of a twisted and deformed mind. Scribbled notes in Latin and Hebrew were written on the walls in white chalk. Various charms and symbols littered the walls as well—as if a possessed witch doctor had scribbled barely legible notes in a frenzy of rapturous enlightenment.

Foster continued to worry about being caught. He didn't know what he was looking for, but he knew he had to be quick about it.

In the corner on the far right, there were several pieces of papers strewn about, along with a couple of drawing books and what looked like an old journal.

He picked up the journal, and its pages were yellowed with age. On several pages, there were splashes of black ink, which might suggest the writer was someone who was in a hurry, or perhaps someone so exhilarated he could hardly contain himself.

And, he noticed that the handwriting was different on different pages, and that some of the writings seemed to be quite old while others looked very recent.

But it was the content of the pages that caused his skin to crawl and his blood to run cold.

The book depicted a variety of potions and inventions—each of them more and more sinister.

Some of the writing was in Latin, and some was in French or German.

At the top of one page—a very old page—was a phrase in French that Foster roughly translated to mean "plague," along with a series of formulas and a drawing of a rat and some fleas. The page was dated 1344!

Could this be the formula for the bubonic plague that swept over Europe and killed twenty-five million people?

Continuing to flip through the pages, Foster came across a page for the formula to improve gunpowder, followed by four pages of illustrations for the Gatling gun—a machine gun so horrible it changed the face of warfare forever. The drawings went on and on. Crude torture devices used in the Spanish Inquisition were illustrated. And towards the back of the book, Foster read formulas for something called "sulfur mustard gas," and other types of gases he didn't recognize.

There were illustrations of armored vehicles with huge guns on the front and even a crude sketch of a submarine.

Foster quickly recognized the journal for what it was—a historical journal of inventions designed for torture, death, and destruction.

The illustrations and dates meant that, indeed, someone had found the Red Hand Scrolls and were using them for evil.

His worst fears had come to light in that room.

Still staring at the journal in disbelief, Foster startled as he heard something from the front of the temple—footsteps!

He had to escape immediately. He couldn't very well kill the man without some kind of proof. He had to gather enough evidence to justify an execution. Placing the journal in his pocket, he retreated to the back door, closing it quietly behind him, and disappeared into the jungle. Once he was clear of the temple, he ran in a full-on sprint to get as far away from the temple as possible.

Back in the room at the temple, a man entered, placed his jacket on a stool, and wearily looked at one of his experiments—one he had been working on for many months but still hadn't found success. He began assembling some tubes and methodically went about pouring the contents of several beakers into a glass canister. For an hour he worked, until, forgetting an ingredient, he went to find his journal to check the formula.

It wasn't on its desk.

Scanning the floor and everywhere else in the room, he realized it was nowhere to be found.

He searched everywhere in the temple, but the journal was definitely missing. Going outside, he searched all around the grounds to no avail. But that's when he saw them.

Footprints.

Someone had found him out. Someone knew what they were looking for and had stolen his journal.

He stood at the jungle entrance, and as he stared into its dense foliage and mists, he churned with anger.

He would find this thief and punish him. So much was riding on the contents of that journal. Whoever had it would now understand everything they were trying to accomplish.

Whoever had stolen it would wish they had never been born.

CHAPTER
— 15 —

SWEET AS HONEY

Margaret sat in her room, crying, and being comforted by Sophie, Inez, Etienne, and Alice. It had been two days since her father left.

"I should have gone with him," she mumbled softly between sobs.

"It is best that you stay with us, Margaret. Your father is going to be very busy; besides, it is going to be so dangerous. You must continue your studies," Sophie replied and stroked Margaret's hair.

"But I only just got him back and now he's off again!" she wailed and buried her face in her hands.

Inez sat on the bed and put her arm around her. Inez was, undoubtedly, the toughest one of the group, but she could be extremely caring and compassionate.

"We should get some fresh air," she told Margaret.

"No, I just want to be alone," Margaret, whispered back.

"Nonsense! You should be happy! Your father is now safe and he has the word of all those British soldiers to back up his story. It is a good day, Margaret," Sophie stated with confidence, and that caused Margaret to look up from her hands.

"I suppose that's one way of looking at it," she hesitantly agreed.

"Of course! Did you see your father? How he killed that Dreyfuss in a duel to the death! I'll bet not another schoolgirl in all of France has seen her father kill a scoundrel in a sword fight," Inez shrieked and started bouncing up and down on the bed.

Margaret forced a smile, as she was almost driven off the bed by the bouncing Inez.

"She's right, Margaret. Your father really was brave. It's not a day for sadness," Alice agreed.

"Okay then, now that we have that all settled, I have another adventure for us that will cheer Margaret up," Inez yelled and continued to jump on the bed.

"Oh no," Sophie moaned.

Inez continued to laugh and giggle, her red hair flopping about in the air as she continued to jump higher and higher on the bed.

"Oh yes, today we are going to get honey!" she yelled.

"Honey? That's not an adventure," Sophie answered.

"It is the way we're going to do it. We're going to get it straight from the beehive!" Inez laughed.

"Oh no, Alice and I have had enough of bees after what we did to Miss Cromwell at our old school," Margaret responded sternly.

"We're not going to release the bees into Sister Anne's office, silly. We're going to take the honey and honeycomb straight from the hive! Imagine how good it will taste dripping from our fingers and as we chew on the scrumptious honeycomb," Inez gleefully yelled. She finally stopped jumping on the bed, hopped down to Margaret, and began mimicking licking gobs of honey off her fingers.

"I don't want anything to do with stealing honey from a bee's nest. Are you mad?" Sophie scolded.

"Oh, don't worry, pretty Sophie, the bee stings won't ruin your beautiful looks," Inez replied and started rubbing Sophie's face and hair to the laughter of the other girls.

"I'm not vain, Inez," Sophie answered with disdain.

"Ha!" Inez yelled, and Sophie knew she was beaten. Trying to beat Inez in an argument was like trying to break a stone with a noodle—utterly hopeless.

"I will get the beekeeper's gear. I know where a fat and juicy hive with gobs and gobs of luscious honey is just waiting for us," Inez said, bounding out the door and down the hill to the maintenance shack, where she quickly gathered up the beekeeper's gear and two large mason jars. Running back up the hill, she looked like an overloaded truck chugging up the road.

"Okay, it's about two miles away along the lake," she said, throwing the gear into a waiting burlap bag, which she slung over her shoulder. She handed Alice and Etienne a mason jar each.

Soon, the five girls were headed off school grounds, walking through the dense forest and foliage and along a beautiful mountain lake. Margaret, more than the others, felt a weight lifted off of her shoulders. She had been feeling melancholy all morning, and her friends had certainly lifted her spirits. Walking along the dirt path, she noticed two butterflies playing among the cattails and water lilies. The sun bounced off the lake water, and she inhaled a deep breath of lilac and pine and relaxed in the safe confines of nature. Her thoughts drifted to a holiday in Switzerland three years ago, when she and her father had gone hiking in the Swiss Alps. For the first time in a long time, she felt completely at peace. She remembered how wonderful the holiday had been, recalling the smile on her mother's face and the joy in her father's eyes. This trail reminded her of that vacation—on that trip, her family had scarcely seen another person for two weeks, as they had stayed in a remote cabin. She hadn't minded one bit, as she and her brother had easily entertained themselves, hiking freely among the beautiful Alps and swimming in the many rivers and lakes. Her father had taught them so much, such as how to tie a bowline knot, and how to catch a fish with nothing but a safety pin and a bit of twine.

She was grateful for her life. She was thankful her parents were anything but ordinary. She was amazed by her friends and their loyalty. She was happy.

"Okay, the hive is just up there. I will put on the gear and gather the honey. All of you stay back so you're not stung. If they come after you, then you must jump in the lake," Inez said with immense seriousness.

"Jump in the lake?" Etienne protested.

"Better to get a little wet than stung by a bunch of bees," Sophie replied and Etienne nodded in agreement.

Inez dressed herself in the beekeeper's suit. It was completely white and covered her body from head to toe. The only problem was, it was about five sizes too big for her. The sleeves flapped over her hands and she had to bunch them up. Even the gloves were twice as big as her hands. The pant legs were scrunched up in rolls and the stockings were almost three times the size of of her feet. Sophie placed the helmet on her head and it almost rolled off, there was so much space. Quickly tightening the chinstrap, it barely stayed on her head.

"How do I look?" she mumbled from beneath the black mesh mask.

"Um," Sophie answered, not knowing how to respond.

"Just don't fall or let the helmet drop off your head," Alice said and Inez looked down at her feet mournfully.

"Here, you'll need the jars—can you even hold them?" Sophie asked and handed her the two mason jars.

"I think so," Inez answered and was barely able to hold onto the large jars with her two oversized gloves. In fact, she had to brace the jars against her body so they wouldn't fall to the ground.

"Be careful with those, if they break, the entire trip will be for nothing," Etienne reminded her and Inez shook her head in understanding.

She turned around and waddled towards the beehive, looking like a baby polar bear that had gone on a diet and was now much, much too skinny for its skin.

"Do you think she'll be okay?" Alice asked.

"I have no idea," Sophie replied and watched as Inez disappeared into a grouping of trees.

Inez walked fitfully into the forest, her hot breath bouncing off the mesh face mask directly back into her face. It was hot in the helmet and she started to sweat. Her eyesight was compromised as she tried to see through the tiny black wires. Up ahead was the beehive. It was nestled in a stump out in the open. A few bees hovered around the outside of it.

Walking towards it, she suddenly felt nervous. What if the suit didn't work? What if the helmet fell off and the bees swarmed her head? Steadying herself, she shook off her fears and continued to walk straight to the hive.

CHAPTER
— 16 —

A BRILLIANT PLAN

Sanaa led an expedition to Tangier that included Tariq, Melbourne Jack, and six other tribe members. Zijuan and Malik stayed back to help train the gathering army and to recruit new tribes to join the resistance.

The group avoided major towns by taking the back roads and by traveling mostly at night. They didn't know if Timin had identified a suitable arms shipment for hijacking, as the carrier pigeons hadn't yet been trained. However, they did know that in Tangier, Jack and Tariq had identified a holding place for any secret codes; Timin had been instructed to send any details to that spot.

Once they arrived in Tangier, they stayed in Zijuan's orphanage, which was being managed by an assistant named Baboo, and all slept soundly in the various vacant rooms. Tariq enjoyed seeing some of the children he had grown to know in the orphanage. He had become a sort of cult hero to them and they peppered him with many questions about his adventures. Being in the orphanage brought back many memories— both good and bad—from his time staying there as a young boy. Mostly, he thought back to when Zijuan had rescued him after Aji's death and gave him a safe place to call home. He remembered their many lessons together and how many times out of fear he had defied her or rebelled against her, and how each time, she patiently worked with him until he trusted her completely.

In the morning, Tariq and Jack ventured to the secure spot where they hoped a message might be waiting. The designated spot was a mosque, just four blocks from the orphanage, with a brick wall around the entire perimeter. One of the bricks was loose on the south end of the building, and any correspondence was to be placed behind that brick.

Walking around the mosque, Tariq and Jack surveyed the surrounding area to ensure the spot had not been compromised. Jack walked to the loose brick, knelt down as if to tie his shoe, and felt underneath for a note.

He found one!

Quickly putting the note in his pocket, he continued to walk alone for three blocks to make absolutely sure he wasn't being followed. He and Tariq met in an alley and read the note together.

It was in code, as expected, and took Tariq and Jack the better part of twenty minutes to decipher it.

"March 12th. Pier 38. Tangier Harbor."

"That's it?" Tariq asked.

"That's enough," Jack replied and immediately burned the note.

"That gives us five days to spend in Tangier. What should we do?" Tariq asked.

"Keep our heads down and stay out of sight. I'd like to take a look at the harbor tonight and begin planning our raid," Jack replied as they made their way back to the orphanage.

That night, Sanaa, Jack, and Tariq made their way to the Tangier harbor and staked out pier 38. There was nothing special about it—it looked like any other pier in the port.

"I would imagine they're going to have sentries posted in front of the pier. I doubt we'll be able to go in that way. Our best approach would be a seaside assault on either side of the pier," Jack surmised.

"We'll never be able to unload the shipment here, as there will likely be too much security. If we try to hijack the ship, the French navy will surely intercept us," she answered.

Tariq stood by silently and enjoyed listening to their strategizing.

"An amphibious assault might work, assuming we can silence the crew and offload the shipment to another boat before we rendezvous on land," Jack replied and Sanaa nodded in agreement.

"We can only guess how many guards they will have on the boat. I would imagine it will be heavily guarded if the shipment is a big one—I'd expect perhaps a dozen or more guards," she continued.

"Will that be a problem?" he asked.

"Not for me it won't," she answered matter-of-factly, bringing a smile to Jack's face.

"We'll need a transfer boat big enough to hold a large shipment of arms," she continued and all three of them looked around the harbor.

"What about that tug boat? We could even have a coal trolley on the back," Tariq suddenly said and pointed to a tugboat sitting innocently two piers away.

Tied to the rear of the tugboat was an empty coal trolley used to transport coal up and down the coast. It was very long, almost thirty yards, and almost twenty yards wide. It wasn't very deep, only five feet, and its surface was only four feet out of the water. Essentially, the trolley was a long barge that could be pulled or pushed by the tugboat.

"That would be perfect! Transporting arms to a coal trolley and covering them with a tarp—it will be the perfect cover. Also, I would imagine a tug boat can outmaneuver some of the larger cruisers," Jack said and patted Tariq on the head.

Tariq smiled broadly with pride.

"Okay, we have our plan. Let's work out the logistics over the next few nights and continue to analyze the harbor," Sanaa said and all three of them began walking back to the orphanage.

Jack was lost in thought when he suddenly realized he was standing next to a sail manufacturer's factory. It was a large brick building with a locked gate. Peering inside the gate, he could see huge rolls of fabric used to make sails.

"What are you looking at?" Tariq asked.

"Just wondering about something. You two go on ahead to the orphanage. I'm going to check something out," he replied.

Sanaa and Tariq continued to the orphanage, while Jack, after ensuring the coast was clear, scaled the metal fence. Soon he was inside the sail factory where rolls and rolls of sails were everywhere on the floor. Some of them were made from thick, sturdy canvas-like fabric, while others were thinner. An adjacent room housed a large number of long metal poles that were used to make masts for testing the sails. In still another room, he found sewing machines and materials used to make sails.

"This might just work," Jack thought to himself, before retreating over the fence and making his way back to the orphanage.

In five nights' time, Sanaa, Tariq, and Jack lay hidden in the shadows of a building just opposite pier 40. They watched as a large cargo ship slowly approached and tied up at pier 38. Six French navy crewmembers walked off the ship and set up a sentry at the entrance. After a few more minutes, several crewmembers made their way up the pier and into the city of Tangier, singing and laughing, no doubt enjoying their furlough.

Sanaa made a series of hand signals and the three slid into the water and began swimming underneath the pier. They were all dressed completely in black with black grease covering their faces—they were virtually invisible in the darkness and blue waves.

Swimming to the tugboat, Tariq hoisted himself onto the ramp, quietly untied the tug, and made his way to the wheelhouse. For three days, he had trained on how to operate the tugboat and hoped he was up to the task. They simply didn't have the number of men to spare and, besides, Sanaa wanted small numbers to avoid detection.

The coal trolley was already in place with lines attached to the tug, so all Tariq had to do was turn on the ignition and steer the tugboat about fifty yards. He'd never driven a boat before, but he had faith in himself that he could get the job done. Sanaa was hesitant to entrust such an important job to him, but Jack reminded her that Tariq thrived in dangerous situations. Finally, she relented and worked tirelessly with Tariq until she was confident he understood how to control the boat—at least until she and Jack could come aboard and take over.

Sanaa and Jack quickly swam under the cover of the piers and made their way to the port side of the French ship. Surveying the number of guards, they decided that Jack would make his way to the starboard side for a multi-directional assault. The assault was synchronized by each person counting to twenty and then both throwing up a rope with a grappling hook that attached to the railings on either side of the boat. The hook was covered in cloth to muffle any sound from the hook banging against the steel railing. Pulling themselves up, in a matter of seconds both were on board and safely hidden—Jack behind some cargo netting and Sanaa behind a rowboat.

Two guards paced back and forth at mid-ship, each enjoying a cigarette and talking endlessly about the best way to cook an omelet.

Sanaa, who had been patiently waiting in the shadows for the right moment to strike, crept up behind the guards and brought out a hard wooden stick, about eighteen inches long. Before either of the guards could make a sound, she had knocked them both unconscious. In one swift motion, she grabbed four ropes and bound their hands and feet. Once she had them immobilized, she gagged them, stuffing rags in their mouths.

Jack was most impressed.

They opened the companionway door and headed down a stairway. A voice came directly from her right side; without a second thought, Sanaa proceeded to knock out another unsuspecting crewman.

She left this one for Jack to bind.

Continuing through the boat, she found three more of the crew playing cards and within a moment had knocked them all out. She and Jack bound and gagged all the crew and threw them into crew's quarters— even the guards from the deck—and locked the door. The last thing they needed was one of them alerting the guards at the end of the pier. Clearing the floor, and now confident that there wasn't anyone else on board, they worked quickly and made their way to the cargo hold to find the arms shipment.

What they uncovered was much more than they had expected to find.

Wooden crates were stacked three high. Jack opened a crate and several rifles of the Berthier carbine variety fell to the floor.

"Jackpot!" he whispered.

A rope hung nearby that opened the cargo doors to the deck. Sanaa pulled on the rope and, within seconds, the cargo doors opened.

There was just one problem.

Getting the crates up onto the ship's deck would require the strength of four men, or the hoist on the pier, but they now realized that would draw too much attention.

"Oops," Sanaa apologized.

They had tried to think of every contingency, yet this was the one thing they hadn't considered.

Just then, they heard the sound of the tugboat outside.

What was Tariq doing? They hadn't given him the signal to start the engine.

Sanaa hoisted herself up to the deck with a rope and instantly saw why Tariq was heading their way.

A French destroyer was closing in on them from outside the marina. Several soldiers were on its deck and a spotlight flooded their position.

"Jack, we've got company!" Sanaa yelled.

Jack made his way up to the deck just as machine gun fire erupted from the destroyer. Bullets ripped all around Sanaa and Jack as they leapt to cover.

"Get us untied! I'll start her up!" Jack yelled.

Sanaa ran across the deck as bullets continued to bounce around her. She leapt to the pier and released the lines that tied the ship to the pier. Other guards were now running at her from the pier entrance, and one of them fired a pistol at her.

The ship drifted away from the pier, and Sanaa swung back aboard with one of the lines. Hoisting herself up, her arms and hands were covered with rope burns but she ignored the pain.

Jack was busy trying to start the engine. He wasn't much of a boater, and it took him a few moments to figure out the ignition. It was a motor ship and ran on petrol. Finally, the engine wheezed and sputtered and the boat roared to life.

The French destroyer, however, was getting closer and closer and continued to spray them with bullets—the ship would be on them in a matter of moments!

Tariq, seeing the danger, thrust the tugboat into full gear and headed past the cargo ship straight for the destroyer. Bullets ripped through the tug's wheelhouse glass as Tariq knelt below the steering column and prayed he was on a proper course.

A ramming course.

Jack, seeing what Tariq was doing, turned the wheel and chugged after him, but had difficulty maneuvering off the pier and sideswiped a ship that was docked on the next pier. The jolt threw Sanaa from her feet and she almost went overboard. Quickly correcting his position, Jack threw the throttle forward and the ship began to chase Tariq's tugboat.

The destroyer captain, seeing that Tariq was going to collide with them, ordered his machine gunner to take out the tugboat. The artilleryman squeezed the trigger hard and hot bullet shells littered the deck. The tugboat's wheelhouse exploded into shards of glass and steel.

Yet still, she kept coming forward.

"Captain, she's going to ram us!" a crewmember yelled as the French crew braced for impact.

"Yaaahhhhhh!" Tariq screamed.

The tugboat mowed forward and plowed into the destroyer at full throttle. Tariq was thrown from his position and hit the floor hard, smacking his head on the deck. Glass was everywhere and his hands and knees were cut up. A shard of glass found its way into his lip and he instantly tasted his own blood.

The impact was so severe that the destroyer was actually rocked back three feet. The tugboat, although much smaller, was designed to push ships of this size and much, much bigger. It continued to chug along like a duck pushing a log through the water. The destroyer was completely off course and at the mercy of the determined tugboat and her captain.

Dazed and dizzy, Tariq managed to rise to his feet, then ran to the back of the tugboat. He heard French voices screaming at him as bullets ricocheted off the steel railing to his right. Running as fast as he could, he jumped from the stern onto the coal trolley and ran to the back. He soon realized, however, this was a huge mistake.

Behind the tugboat, the trolley's momentum was causing it to swing into the path of the destroyer. Stopping at the trolley's edge, Tariq was about to jump in the ocean when he heard Sanaa call out.

"Tariq, catch this!"

Tariq looked up and saw the cargo ship barreling down on his position. From the deck above, Sanaa threw a rope directly at Tariq. The rope hit him in the face! Luckily he caught it and was able to get it tied around his waist while the cargo ship—captained by Jack, a complete novice—was coming much too close to the tugboat.

It rammed right into the side of the trolley, throwing Tariq off balance, and continued on her way to the open sea.

Tariq ran along the side and jumped into the ocean—hanging onto the rope, he was now being dragged alongside the cargo ship!

Bullets continued to ring past him, splashing all around him. Water pulverized his face and went up his nose. Grabbing the rope tightly, he worked his way up until his feet reached the side. Then, placing both feet on the side of the ship, he walked up the side to the safety of Sanaa's arms. She quickly pulled him over the side.

Dripping wet, cut up from glass, and dizzy, Tariq looked over at Sanaa, who burst out laughing.

"Now, tell me that wasn't fun!" she teased, and he began laughing along with her.

In the rear, the destroyer was still being pushed by the tugboat, well off course. Jack pushed the cargo ship engine to full throttle into the darkness of the night.

They had made their escape.

An hour later, they pulled up to an abandoned beach and gave a series of signals using a lantern. Jack allowed the cargo ship to drift in the waves until it finally beached itself on the sand. There, the alerted tribesmen emptied the crates onto six wagons that had been equipped with teams of donkeys. The work was quick, and in less than an hour, the entire contents of the cargo hold had been loaded onto the wagons and covered with tarps.

Tariq and Jack had one more thing to do—one final touch. Pulling out some red ink, they placed handprints all over the inside of the cargo ship.

"Well, I guess now they'll know who did this," Jack said and slapped Tariq on the back.

"What a thrilling escape Jack! One victory for the Red Hand!"

Sanaa noticed a seventh wagon covered with a white cloth.

"What is that?" she asked.

"You'll see," Jack replied, with a toothy grin.

The group headed out, on an old dirt road that led into the mouth of the Rif Mountains.

Their army now had their weaponry to compete with the Caid and the French.

CHAPTER
— *17* —

INCOGNITO

Inez continued to the beehive.

Standing over it and calming herself for a moment, she wasn't sure exactly what to do next. A few bees came up and buzzed around her, exploring her, but not yet aggravated by her presence. She stared at the hive. It looked like a gigantic brown Easter egg. A few more bees came out and buzzed around her helmet.

"Better now than never," she thought to herself and plunged her arm into the top of the beehive. She broke it wide open and allowed her hand to delve deep inside.

Instantly, hundreds of bees angrily swarmed around her. The buzzing was overwhelming and intense, and dozens of bees crowded around the outside of her mesh mask, trying to get inside. Hundreds more swarmed her body and harmlessly stung the beekeeper suit.

Inez didn't feel a thing.

For thirty seconds she reached her right hand deeper and deeper into the hive until at last she felt the liquid inside. Inez squeezed her right hand into a fist in the hive, and with her left she took a mason jar began scooping the golden liquid into the glass jar. Sinking her hand back into the hive, her fingers touched something brittle—she hoped it was the honeycomb! Digging her fingers in, she broke off a large piece and pulled it outside the hive to have a look at it.

Her fingers held a beautiful hunk of honeycomb with silky honey dripping from its hexagon-shaped slots.

Stuffing the honeycomb in the jar, she continued to scoop out more honey and comb until the jar was three-quarters full. She set the first jar on the ground carefully so it wouldn't spill, then took the other jar and filled it to the brim as well. Bees continued to swarm around her as she worked. She was now accustomed to their presence and buzzing and was no longer bothered by it.

When both jars were full, she held them carefully in her hands and pressed them tightly against her chest. As she walked back out of the forest, some of the bees continued to attack her, but most stayed at the hive, buzzing incessantly in anger that their home had been disrupted.

As she emerged from the forest, she could see the girls waiting for her next to the lake, about twenty yards away. The jars were slippery, so she clutched them to her body took her time with each step, careful not to slip on the baggy beekeeper suit.

By the time Inez reached the girls, only two or three bees were still flying around her. Honeybees are the only bees in existence that die after stinging, so most had died. Others had given up or had stayed to protect the hive.

Exhilarated by her adventure, Inez put the jars on the ground and proudly took off her mask, revealing a huge smile on her freckled face and her red hair cascading down her neck.

The girls stared at her, shocked she had actually pulled it off.

"Well, what are you waiting for?" Inez asked and giggled.

Alice was the first to come up. She dipped her index finger into the jar until it was covered with the yellow goodness. Stuffing her finger into her mouth, her face lit up at the sweet taste of the fresh honey.

"Mmmm, that's the best thing ever!" she yelled, and quickly plunged her hand back into the jar. She broke off a piece of honey comb dripping with liquid, and popped it into her mouth.

The other girls surrounded both jars and stuck their hands in, grabbing a taste of the honey and eagerly going back for more. Inez removed the beekeeper uniform, placed both gloves in the cold lake water to wash off the honey, and then excitedly joined her friends gorging on honey.

Margaret dipped her entire hand into one of the jars, laughed, and then happily lapped up the golden liquid, allowing some of it to drip down her chin.

"A most excellent idea, Inez. Let's get going, the other girls will love it!" Sophie exclaimed, and soon they were walking back to the school grounds, thoroughly satisfied with their afternoon adventure.

On their walk back, they passed over a hill to the small farmhouse where the school stored their horses. A gentle farmer by the name of Jacques lived in the farmhouse with his wife. He was a bit loopy and eccentric, but the girls enjoyed his company and he always gave them free cheese from one of his cows or goats. It was some of the best cheese in the valley and he created a series of delicious varieties such as Bleu d'Auvergne, Rocamadour, and even the occasional Gruyère (although it was, technically, a cheese from Switzerland and disdained by many of the French).

"I bet this honey would be divine with some of his Bleu d'Auvergne cheese. Do you think he would trade with us?" Sophie asked.

"Oh yes, and some fresh-made bread. That would be lovely," Etienne agreed, and soon the girls were heading up to the farmhouse.

The scene in front of them, however, wasn't what they expected.

Jacques had packed up a wagon; it was filled to the top with his belongings. A team of four horses led the front of the wagon and a cow was hitched to the back. Jacques was just closing up his barn door as the girls walked up.

"Hello, Monsieur Jacques. Are you going somewhere?" Inez asked.

"Oh yes, girls, Sister Anne will tell you everything. I'm off to the north to live near my relatives in Switzerland. Your school will be taking care of the farm animals and the house," he explained.

"But why are you going?" Margaret asked.

"The war, girls," he tersely answered.

"What war? There's no war around here," Sophie answered.

"Not now, but there will be. Just wait and see. The Germans are rattling their sabers and preparing for an onslaught," he calmly explained.

"The Germans?" Margaret asked.

"Oh, the Kaiser is spoiling for a good war. He's building up his armies and his navies and he means to attack France," he said while securing a knot on his load.

"You girls be careful now," his wife said as she came from inside the house and locked the door behind her.

"Are you sure?" Alice asked.

"One can never be sure, but there's hasn't been a good war in ages, since Napoleon really. Well, the Franco-Austrian war was a nice little tussle, but nothing world-changing," he said and came over to the girls.

"What's that you've got there?" he asked, looking over the two jars of honey.

"Fresh honey from a hive," Inez replied, no longer interested in the honey. She wanted to hear more about the Germans.

"Honey? Mind if I have a taste?" he asked, and before Inez could answer, he dipped his index finger into the jar and then right in his mouth.

"That is marvelous!" he exclaimed. "It would be perfect with some of our bleu cheese and a bit of bread," he thought aloud.

"Yes, that's what we thought as well," Etienne answered.

"Darling, get some of the bleu for the girls and a loaf of the bread," he yelled out. His wife went about rummaging through the front of the wagon, produced a huge hunk of bleu cheese wrapped in paper, and tore off a large piece of freshly-baked bread. It was so fresh that the girls could smell the delicious aroma, even from a good thirty feet away.

"Here you go darlings, this will be lovely with your honey," she said and gave the bread and cheese to Margaret, who nodded her head in thanks.

"Here, Monsieur Jacques, take this. We will miss you," Inez said, handing him a jar of the honey.

"No, no, that's too much," he protested but she wouldn't take back the jar.

"It will be a good snack for the road. You have been so kind to us," Sophie agreed and insisted they take the jar.

Jacques thanked them profusely and handed the jar to his wife, who stowed it in the wagon with the other food.

"Girls, please be careful and take care to look out for Germans. The winds of war are blowing across Europe. Please, please get out before they sweep across France. I would hate for anything to happen to any of you," he explained in dead seriousness. Then, in the French fashion, he kissed each of them on each cheek and bid them goodbye.

His wife did the same and added a bit of a hug.

Off they went in their wagon with their cow in tow. Disappearing over a hill, Jacques and his wagon faded out of sight.

The girls continued on their journey back to the school.

"Do you think it's true? Do you think the Germans will attack us?" Alice asked.

"I haven't heard anything of Germany attacking France, but then, I don't exactly read too many newspapers," Margaret replied.

"If the Germans do attack, then we must be prepared to leave at a moment's notice," Sophie said and the girls all agreed.

Inez made a little sandwich, wedging the bleu cheese between two pieces of fresh bread and then dipping it into the jar of honey. She popped the concoction in her mouth and her eyes went wide with excitement.

"You have to try this!" she squealed, but the other girls ignored her.

"Inez, this is no time to be eating. The Germans may attack us!" Sophie scolded her.

"I'm not afraid of any stinking Germans. If they try anything, our army will force them back to Berlin singing 'La Marseillaise' before their stupid Kaiser," she replied and the other girls laughed.

That night, the girls were back at school tucked safely in their beds, but Margaret couldn't sleep. Her thoughts drifted to her father and her mother and brother. She understood why her father felt she must stay at Saint Catherine's, but she already missed him terribly. The last couple of weeks had been wonderful; she had loved being in his presence again. Now, her father was gone and she worried about his fate. It would require more than luck to convince the British authorities of his innocence.

———————— ❦ ————————

Fez and Aseem went through their daily routine as soldiers in the Caid's army. Their biggest fear was someone recognizing them from their days as camel jockeys for the Caid. They were far enough from the kasbah that it wasn't very probable anyone would remember them. Besides, if someone did, they had an alibi—they had been asked to join the army and were released from slavery.

Each week, they left secret codes for Timin and placed them in the usual place. They tracked the army's movements and troop levels and its supply chains for arms and food. They were always listening for intelligence and, once, they even managed to copy a map of the exact locations of all the French troops in Morocco. This intelligence turned out to be a wealth of information for Timin and the resistance.

All along, Timin and his various groups continued to carry out raids, posing as the Red Hand and blaming the raids on the Caid's police force and soldiers.

Sergeant Abdul Maheida was a portly man with an enormous belly; in fact, it had taken him years to develop such girth. He had a sparse black beard around his full and chubby face. His eyes, ice blue, seemed to bore through a person when he spoke. He was, in all details, a very difficult man to get a handle on. He wasn't a disciplinarian, but he wasn't soft, either. He could be very flexible and even indifferent to rules, except when it came to certain things such as marching in a straight line. He enjoyed joking with the cadets, but he could issue a strong tongue-lashing when they did something wrong.

One night, after dinner, Fez and Aseem were polishing their boots in their barracks when the sergeant presented himself.

"Aseem and Fez, you're coming with me," he yelled and instantly the group of cadets stood at attention.

Fez and Aseem stared at each other—petrified.

"Sir?" Fez asked.

"You're coming with me," he said.

"With you, sir?" Aseem asked.

"Yes, yes, put on your boots and hurry."

Aseem and Fez quickly put on their boots and followed the sergeant out the door. The other boys watched them go but didn't think much of it. The Caid's soldiers were taught to act and not to think. If the sergeant wanted Fez and Aseem, he probably had a very good reason.

The boys followed the sergeant out of the barracks and along a city street. He was strolling purposefully, without much of a care, and almost seemed to forget the boys were following him.

"Sir, what is this regarding? Are we in trouble?" Fez asked.

"Shhhhh, young *loka*. All in good time," he replied and continued to stroll. He called all the boys *loka* as a term of affection, especially when he wanted them to do something as a favor. For instance, he might go to one of the younger recruits and say, "hey *loka*, fetch your *shiqa* a cup of tea," with *Shiqa* meaning "old man" in Arabic.

Suddenly Aseem stopped in his tracks.

"What is it?" Fez whispered, alarmed by his friend's appearance.

"What if we have been found out? He may be taking us to a secret place to torture us as spies," Aseem whispered and Fez turned just as pale.

"You might be right. They may have a secret location to keep us for days."

Both boys were deciding whether or not to run when Sergeant Abdul yelled at them.

"Hey you two, I'm not going to torture you. I need something to eat."

He then continued to walk down the road without a care in the world.

The boys cautiously followed him until he disappeared into a café. It was a nice little café, with white walls and a wooden door. The window-sills were painted blue, and even the windowpanes were a collage of blue and green colors.

Above the entrance to the café hung a sign painted with blue letters that read, "The Blue Cat," in Arabic.

Venturing inside, the boys adjusted their eyes, as the café was dark, illuminated only by the candlelight flickering on each table. As was the Moroccan custom, there were no chairs and everyone sat on the floor on kilim pillows. The café was packed with people, and smoke filtered to the top of the ceiling, creating a haze around the entire interior. In the corner, a musician played a *lotar*, a traditional Berber instrument similar to a lute. The song was a sad, slow ballad, drawn out from the instrument's strings in dramatic fashion. There were no women in the café, and most of the men ignored the boys, preferring to suck on their hookahs and eat plates of hot pita bread dipped in hummus. The hookah smoke was gentle to the eyes and tongue and had an exotic mix of apple, watermelon, apricot, and mint flavors.

Aseem spotted the sergeant getting seated at a far table and they both sat across from him.

A waiter placed down a jug of water and three glasses. Dusting off the table with his hand, he also set down a tray of food filled with slices of juicy watermelon, feta cheese, a variety of olives, sprigs of mint and basil, a huge dollop of baba ghanoush, and a generous helping of pita bread.

The sergeant motioned for the waiter to bend down. The sergeant whispered something in the waiter's ear, which caused him to look down at Fez and Aseem. At this, the sergeant gave the waiter a hand signal as if to say, "Forget about them."

With that, the waiter was off.

"Well, dig in, boys," the sergeant said and grabbed a nice slice of watermelon, popped it in his mouth, and then took another bite.

Aseem took a bit of cheese and nibbled on it while Fez ate a solitary olive.

"What? You boys aren't hungry? I've seen the slop they feed you. Go ahead. Eat! Eat!" the sergeant motioned.

Both boys were, in fact, famished and began devouring the food in front of them.

"That's more like it," the sergeant said, grinning with delight.

Soon, the waiter reappeared with a hookah pipe and placed it next to Sergeant Abdul's side. A large green bottle was delivered to the table, along with a small drinking glass. The sergeant filled the glass to the rim with some golden liquid from the bottle.

"Oh, this is for medicinal purposes," he told the boys and, in one gulp, emptied the glass and quickly refilled it.

"So," the sergeant began, sinking down as if to melt into his pillow, "you're my two little spies."

Fez and Aseem instantly stopped eating and stared at the sergeant.

"Do not worry, my little friends, I am not here to turn you in," he laughed and took another gulp from his glass, draining it again as he took another drag off of his hookah.

"Sir?" Aseem asked.

"Oh, I have been watching you. Your eyes give you away—they dart about as if taking notes. And, your little escapades outside the compound have not gone unnoticed," he told them. Fez thought he might pee in his pants right there at the table.

"Sir? We are not spies, we just like to explore the city," Aseem answered, trying to sound as innocent as possible.

The sergeant chuckled and drained another glass. The waiter brought a large plate of lamb to the table, along with roasted peppers and onions. More pita bread and a bowl of hummus were also delivered. The spices and smells from the lamb caused both boys' stomachs to gurgle with anticipation.

"Ah, look at this feast!" the sergeant exclaimed, his eyes sparkling with delight, as he dipped a particularly juicy piece of lamb into the bowl of hummus.

"Delicious," he exclaimed and licked the hummus from his fingers.

Both boys sat in silence.

He laughed again.

"Boys, if I were going to turn you in, I wouldn't have brought you to this café. Please, eat before this lovely lamb gets cold."

Fez gingerly reached out for a piece of the meat and popped it in his mouth. It might have been the most delicious thing he had ever tasted. The aromas of turmeric, basil, and garlic filled his nostrils.

Aseem followed, and after one bite of the lamb, the expression on his face matched his friend's.

The sergeant continued to drain glass after glass of the golden juice, and after the first bottle was empty, he ordered another. The boys continued to eat until their bellies were so full it seemed they might pop like an overinflated balloon.

The empty plates were taken away as glasses of lime juice and a bowl of sweet dates arrived for the boys.

"Ah, now we can get down to business," he laughed and took another drink.

"Sir?" Aseem asked.

"Business should only be discussed after a proper meal has been digested," he said.

Fez noticed his speech was beginning to slur.

"Yes, I know you are spies. No, I will not turn you in. The fact is, I have no love for the Caid and I detest the French. The Caid is turning this entire country into a civil war and it makes the feeling in my belly sour and sharp. I have no desire to slaughter my countrymen. Morocco is a corrupt country, but what country isn't? Sure, I may take a coin here and there, but that's nothing compared to the corruption of these Frenchmen. They would slaughter an entire people just for conversation at their dinner parties."

The boys stared at him, not exactly sure what he was talking about.

He stared at them with his steely blue eyes and suddenly became very serious.

"I'm going to help you boys."

Fez jerked backwards in surprise.

"Sir?" Aseem exclaimed.

"I don't know who you're working for, and I don't want to know. Whoever they are, they're very smart for having you join the Caid's army. What I *will* do is get you whatever information you need. For instance, I know that in three weeks' time, we are moving out to the desert and marching to Al Hoceima. I can give you our exact troop levels and any other information you need."

The boys just sat there, looking completely shocked. They didn't know what to say to this. This could be a trap—what if he was really just trying to get them to admit they were spies?

Again, he appeared to be reading their minds.

"Ah, but you think I am trying to trap you. No, boys, I am not that kind of man. I say it the way it is. I like both of you. You're tough and you're smart. Do not worry—this is not a trap. And if I ever think you're in danger, I will ensure your escape from the barracks. You don't even need to tell me for certain that you *are* spies, I'll simply give you information and you can do with it what you like," the sergeant said, now slurring his words a lot.

"Go ahead boys, eat your dates," he said, laughing and smoking and drinking more of the golden liquid.

In five minutes he had fallen asleep at the table and was snoring loudly.

"I think he's drunk," Fez whispered.

Aseem nodded in agreement. They both sat there for thirty seconds until the snoring grew so loud that patrons at other tables were starting to stare.

Fez reached across and poked him in the chest.

"Sir," he whispered to no response.

He poked him harder and tugged on his arm.

"Sir!" he said louder.

Still no response.

"Sir!" he practically yelled and poked him hard in the rib cage.

"Wha—? Oh, oh, boys. Sorry, I drifted off. Here, let me pay and let's be off. Remember what we talked about here," he slurred, and the boys had trouble understanding him.

Throwing down some coins, Sergeant Abdul rose to his feet and stumbled a bit before making his way to the door. Fez and Aseem joined him outside, only to find that the sergeant had fallen on the ground in the middle of the street. He was fast asleep and snoring.

"Sir, sir!" Aseem said, somehow managing to wake him and get him to his feet.

Sergeant Abdul was smiling and had his arms around Aseem and Fez, and all three were stumbling in the street—the boys could hardly hold him up! He was singing a song of some sort, but the lyrics were completely incomprehensible. He mumbled his words and put all his weight on the boys' shoulders. After only a block, their muscles ached and their legs were heavy from the weight.

Three times he fell to the street on the way home, and it was only four blocks to the barracks.

Stumbling into the compound, the boys took Sergeant Abdul to his bed, where he landed with a "thud" on the mattress. Before the boys left his room, the sergeant was fast asleep and his snoring had reached epic levels.

Their bellies stuffed and happy, Fez and Aseem settled themselves in their beds and drifted into a deep sleep.

CHAPTER
— *18* —

COMING IN FROM THE COLD

The next day at reveille, Sergeant Abdul showed up as if nothing had happened. Barking out orders at the cadets, he was as lucid as ever and had the energy of a sixteen-year-old. He put the new recruits through maneuvers and never so much as glanced at Fez and Aseem. For three days he trained with them as if nothing had happened. On the fourth day, he appeared at the barracks and asked for them. Again, they followed him to The Blue Cat. Once again, they found themselves sitting across from him as he ordered platters of food and more of the golden liquid. He was jovial in conversation and joked and laughed to his heart's content.

Midway through dinner, his words started to slur once again and his cheeks turned rosy. His eyes glazed over and he seemed to have a permanent grin on his face.

Then he got serious.

"You two must leave immediately," he told them before drinking more of the golden liquid, part of it sloshing down his chest and wetting his shirt.

"Excuse me, sir?" Fez asked.

"One of the officers thinks he has recognized you from the kasbah. He was asking about you today and mentioned something about camel races. Have either of you raced a camel?"

Aseem and Fez looked at each other; each had fear in their eyes.

"Yes, we were camel jockeys for the Caid," Aseem answered slowly.

Sergeant Abdul leaned back and drank more.

"That's it then—you must leave right now! Don't even go back to the barracks. There is a park up the block to the north with a solitary tree in the middle. I will leave any notes under that tree and beneath a rock. Every note will have the word "philistine" in it. If the note does not have that word, it means I have been discovered and you are to ignore any instructions in the note. Is that clear?"

Aseem and Fez nodded accordingly.

"Good, let me pay and you two can make your way out. Be careful you haven't been followed, and make sure you zigzag across many alleys. Get as far away from here as possible. Do you understand?"

"Yes, sir, but what will they say back at the barracks if they saw us leave with you? Won't they suspect you?" Fez asked.

Sergeant Abdul took another drink, this one a bit longer than the others, and wiped his lips with his sleeve.

"You let me worry about that, boys. Go now, leave and I'll pay up," he said and whisked them away with his hand.

Fez and Aseem left the café and turned right. They quickly walked down that street and then turned right again. They continued to zigzag across various alleys and to cross through courtyards. They even climbed up and over a couple of rooftops.

They were certain they had not been followed.

Without so much as stopping to gather food, the boys set off on foot for Chaouen that night, knowing they risked being caught by bandits.

"I'm glad we are going back to Chaouen," Fez said.

"I haven't slept a wink since we joined the Caid's troops. I thought for sure we would be pinched," Aseem agreed.

"It is a good thing we met Sergeant Abdul. He was a good friend," Fez said as they walked along the dirt road. The moon was almost full, and the distant howl of jackals startled them both. The boys each had knives and a bit of food wrapped up in a napkin from The Blue Cat café. They were not scared and did not feel tired.

"Do you think we can defeat the Caid?" Aseem asked.

Fez gave it some thought before answering.

"I think we can defeat the Caid, but I do not think we can defeat the French. They are too mighty, and their weapons are too superior to our own."

Aseem liked that answer and he continued to think as they walked.

"I would like to go to school one day. I remember when Margaret would teach us bits of English, and also math and history. I enjoy learning. It makes me feel…important somehow, not so useless," he said and his voice was full of sincerity.

Fez listened intently.

"I have never attended school, but my parents taught me about the ways of our village and the country. There is so much to learn in the world and it is always so interesting."

Aseem liked talking with Fez. He was, without a doubt, his best friend. Fez was much smarter than Aseem, but not arrogant at all.

"Do you think we are less than?" Aseem asked.

"Less than what?"

"I see the way that British people and French people look at us, like we are less than them."

Fez thought about this for a moment before answering.

"If they think they are better than us because of the color of their skin or the money in their pockets, then they deserve our pity. If they look down on those who perform hard work, then they have no understanding of life."

Aseem smiled broadly at the answer.

"Fez, you are an old man born into a boy's body. Only you could explain something so perfectly."

They continued to walk and enjoy the night air and the sounds of the desert.

"Are you afraid of dying?" Fez asked.

Aseem shook his head.

"No, I am afraid of being a coward."

"Why?"

"My father used to have a saying, 'A courageous man can live a fulfilling life in just one day, but a coward can live a lifetime and know only misery.'"

"Do you believe that?" Fez asked.

"Oh yes, I love the thrill of combat. I actually enjoyed the camel races—I just hated being a slave."

"Really? You enjoyed the camel races?" Fez asked, surprised.

"It was very fun to race, even though I was not very good. I did not enjoy being tied to the camels, but I greatly enjoyed the racing part. You were faster than both Tariq and me—and you didn't enjoy it?"

"No," Fez sheepishly answered.

"Why?"

"All I could think of was falling off and dying or hurting myself. Didn't you think about that?"

"No, not really. If I fall, then I fall. There is nothing to be done. I would rather go through life trying and falling than never doing anything."

As much as Aseem liked Fez for his intellect, Fez liked Aseem for his bravery.

"I very much like being a spy, and fighting the Caid, and being part of the Red Hand. It gives me a purpose. Yet something holds me back," Fez tried to explain.

"How do you mean?"

"I think too much. I always think about the outcome—what might happen," Fez explained with a bit of discouragement.

Aseem smiled at his friend's melancholy.

"Fez, you are a brave and courageous fellow. You avenged the death of your tribe and you were an excellent camel jockey. You may think a lot, but that is a blessing. It is a fool who rushes in. I think you will be a great leader one day," Aseem explained, and he meant every word. He did think that Fez would someday make a great leader because Fez was wise, but he was also compassionate.

"Sometimes I want an easier life, Aseem," he said and sighed as he said it.

"Do not wish for an easy life, Fez. Wish for a difficult life, and the strength to endure it," Aseem instructed him.

Fez repeated the phrase. "Do not wish for an easy life—wish for a difficult life and the strength to endure it," and smiled when he said it.

The next morning at the barracks, two officers came looking for Fez and Aseem. Walking straight to the boys' bunks and finding them empty, the officers began making inquiries as to their whereabouts. None of the other cadets had seen them since the previous night.

The officers walked to Sergeant Abdul's quarters and questioned him as he shaved with a straight razor over a metallic bowl filled with ice-cold water. He preferred a cold shave as it stiffened up his whiskers and made them easier to cut.

"Hmmm…no, I have not seen them. I took them out last night to discuss some disciplinary issues. The last I saw they were headed back to their barracks," he answered casually, as he scraped off a good bit of black whiskers and rinsed them off the razor.

"So you were the last one to see them?" one of the officers asked.

"Yes, I suppose so. It could be they got up early and are at the mess hall. Have you checked there?"

The officers shifted and whispered to one another.

"What's this all about, anyhow?" Sergeant Abdul asked.

"We think they may have escaped from the Caid's kasbah awhile back. One of the officers seemed to recognize them."

Sergeant Abdul shrugged his shoulders.

"So what if they escaped? They're still working for the Caid, so what's the difference?" he questioned in a stern and defiant tone. He didn't like officers and typically had no problem bullying them around. Today was no different.

"But why would they come back to join the Caid's army?" one of them asked, a small officer with skinny shoulders and a weak chin.

"Ah, they probably figured it was easier being in the army than living on the streets."

The two officers whispered to one another and then began to leave.

"You're right, sergeant. It's probably nothing," one of them said and they both turned and walked out of the sergeant's quarters.

Sergeant Abdul continued to shave while watching them from the corner of his eye. He didn't like that they were questioning him, and thankfully, Aseem and Fez had gotten out safely. Still, he knew he could now be under suspicion, and needed to watch his tracks. It had been a risk letting them go last night, as he was the last one to be seen with them. But it was a risk he had to take, and his intuition had proven correct.

He feared they had been discovered.

As he considered this recent turn of events, Sergeant Abdul continued to shave and suddenly pressed too hard on the razor's handle. The blade dug deeply into his skin, creating a gash about two inches in diameter. Blood streamed down his chin—a mistake caused by unsteady hands.

The game had just gotten much more dangerous.

CHAPTER
— 19 —

LOUISE'S NEW FRIENDS

Charles commanded *The Walcott* through the Mediterranean Sea, feeling the wind in his hair and the salt on his mouth. It had only taken a day to reach the boat, but he had been forced to launch it during the dead of night, as the French authorities still considered him a very wanted man. It felt good to be on a ship again and in the company of British soldiers. Once the crew learned of his experience during the Boer Wars and his exploits in India, they quickly warmed to him and accepted him as their commander.

Nevertheless, Charles was very apprehensive. He was still wanted in England as a traitor and a pirate. There was a good chance that he would be tried and hanged for offenses against the crown. All the running and hiding around the Mediterranean wasn't his style; he was an honorable man, and he simply wanted to return to his native land and take his chances in the courts.

Off the bow, a pod of bottlenose dolphins swam next to *The Walcott*, skimming over the surface of the water before diving under.

"They say dolphins are good luck," Seaman Terry said to Charles.

"Yes, I should say they are," Charles replied. He always enjoyed seeing dolphins; they always seemed to him like such happy and intelligent creatures.

Terry watched the horizon and stood next to Charles for a moment.

"Going through the Strait of Gibraltar in about an hour, and then it's off through the Channel. I reckon we'll make port in two or three days' time."

"It's a fine ship. I'm hoping the weather will cooperate," Charles replied.

"The entire crew knows how nervous you are, colonel. We'll all testify in your honor. Don't worry, sir. Once the courts see what really happened, you'll be given a full pardon," Terry said in his most understanding voice.

Charles nodded and smiled. He greatly liked Terry and all the boys on the crew. They were so eager and innocent and full of hope. Charles no longer shared their innocence. He understood that the world could be much more complex. There were powerful, wealthy men with vast resources within the British government, and once they were exposed, these men would fight for their lives.

———————— ❧❦❧ ————————

Louise Owen was led out of her house in handcuffs. She was flanked by two British policemen as a detective led her down the front steps of her house. Tears streaked down her face and her shoulders slumped in shame.

Behind her, a woman from Social Services was marching David out of the house.

Louise had pleaded and begged Social Services to allow David to go live with his grandparents in Newcastle, but the woman assigned to her case would have none of it. He'd be entered into their system.

In other words, David was going to be sent to an orphanage.

Louise had heard horror stories about the orphanages in Britain (sparked by the images in *Oliver Twist*) and she cried for her son rather than for herself.

Neighbors came out and watched the scene on their stoops as Louise was hustled into the back of a police carriage and taken away.

At police headquarters, Louise was made to wait for almost three hours before a detective came and escorted her to his desk. Her handcuffs were finally removed and she rubbed the red sores around her wrists where the steel had dug in.

"Where is my son?" she asked tersely.

"Social Services has him. I'm sure he's doing just fine," the detective answered, barely looking at her as he flipped through some papers.

The detective was a large man with a squalid face and he looked very English. He reeked of fish and chips and a little oil had dribbled and onto his white shirt leaving a greasy mark. His skin was pasty white and sweat dripped down from his lower lip.

Leaning forward, he lowered his voice when he spoke to Louise.

"You have something that doesn't belong to you, Mrs. Owen—a ledger I believe?" he asked, sounding rather serious.

Louise sat up in her chair, her back rigid, as she suddenly understood what was happening in this interview. This policeman worked for the Far Indian Trading Company. He had probably been bribed and instructed to bring her in.

"I don't know what you're talking about. What ledger?" she asked.

"C'mon now, Mrs. Owen. You've upset some very powerful people— you've taken something from them and they want it back. Give up the ledger and you can go right back to your life," he responded in a pleasing, soft voice.

Louise stared at him, not sure how to respond. There was no use lying, as the ledger was gone.

"I had the ledger, but now it's gone," she answered.

"What do you mean 'it's gone'? Where did it go?"

"I had to jump into the river and it was lost in the current," she explained.

The detective leaned back and took a sip of tea from a mug. He tapped a pen to his lips and stared at Louise.

"What do you mean when you say you 'jumped into the river'?"

"Exactly what I said. I jumped into the River Thames and the ledger was lost."

"Into the Thames? Are you mad? Do you know how cold that water is?" he asked.

"Yes, I know exactly how cold that water is. It took me soaking in a hot bath for two hours to warm myself back up to normal," she answered in a very condescending tone. She was not accustomed to being questioned in this manner.

The detective took another sip of tea and continued to stare at Louise. He wasn't expecting this answer from her. She had confessed to having the ledger, but this story about the sea was perplexing. He couldn't decide whether or not she was telling the truth.

"Okay, then. Let's put you in lockup for a day or two and see if you can't remember where that ledger is," he finally answered.

"I told you, it has been lost—it's probably at the bottom of the river."

"Yes, well, the problem is that I simply don't believe you Mrs. Owen—you being the wife of a traitor and all."

"My husband is not a traitor to his country. You, however, are a dishonest and corrupt officer of the law. I wish to speak to my barrister at once," Louise said sternly.

This time, it was the detective's turn to be surprised. He wasn't accustomed to being spoken to in such a manner, either.

"Take 'er away," he said, and soon Louise was taken by the wrists and led down a staircase, through a hallway, and into a room with two jail cells on either side. Both cells were filled with women, most of whom looked dirty and were dressed in rags caked with dirt and filth. The room smelled of foul breath, moldy cheese, vomit, and body odor.

Louise herself almost vomited when the toxic smells found her nostrils.

The guard opened up the cell on the right, the key scratching the edges of the lock as he clanked it around. Finally the door opened with a squeak and Louise was thrown inside.

Locking the door, the guard left without so much as a word and Louise was left alone in a room full of women. She was dressed very differently from her cellmates—her dress was freshly pressed, and she smelled of lavender oil. To them, she was obviously a "proper" woman of means. Standing in the cell, Louise felt the full weight of her circumstances. Her fall from grace was complete. She was alone in the world, and her husband was nowhere to be found. Her only son was being placed in an orphanage, and she was imprisoned in a rotten cell and surrounded by foul-smelling women of ill repute.

She didn't allow herself to cry. She just stood in the cell and stared at the ground.

"Oh, there's got to be a good story 'ere," one of the women from the back said, and all the women laughed.

"She looks like she just walked out of a Kay's catalogue and she smells like flowers," another said, to more laughter.

"Come now, luv, have a seat and unload your story on us," a woman said and gently took Louise by the shoulders and guided her to a bench. As Louise sat down, the other women—most with dirt on their faces and missing more than a few teeth—looked upon Louise with pity.

"You look like a proper sort, how'd you find yourself with our lot?" one of them asked.

Louise felt her body shaking and she wanted to cry, but she was determined not to allow herself to show weakness. She had heard stories of the nastiness of British prisons, even the ones with women, and she was deathly afraid these women might rip her to shreds.

"They took my son and placed him in an orphanage," she managed to say and then burst into tears.

"Oh, you poor, poor dear," one of them said and her voice was soft and understanding.

"That policeman is corrupt. The entire British government is corrupt," she managed to say between tears.

"You're telling us, love. Show me an honest copper and I'll show you a tour of the Vatican," one said and Louise managed to smile.

"Thank you," she answered and began to warm to the women around her.

"Would you like a spot of tea, m'dear?" another asked.

"Yes, that would be lovely," Louise answered.

"It's not very good and it's barely warm, but a little Earl Grey is just the thing in a time of crisis," one of them said. Soon Louise was given a cup of tea and a small biscuit and a hunk of cheddar cheese.

"Oh my, I wasn't expecting this," Louise said and was thoroughly surprised at the manners of these women. From their appearance, she had assumed them to be foul and vicious. In fact, they were surprisingly kind.

"Ah, just because we don't look the part doesn't mean we're not British," another mentioned and the girls laughed once again.

Louise brought the tea to her lips and it did taste delicious, although it was a bit cold. The biscuit was stale but she didn't mind. She was simply grateful to be the recipient of such civility and compassion.

Her entire life Louise had avoided "the poor" as they were called in British society. She looked down upon them and crossed the street when they walked towards her. She had purposely shielded her children from certain parts of town in order to protect them from seeing the underbelly of British society.

And now these people were consoling her.

"So, what are you doing here?" Louise asked one of them who was sitting right next to her. She had long, greasy hair and a mole on her chin. A thick, black hair grew out of the mole, and she was missing a front tooth. Her face told the story of a life that had been very hard. She smelled of rum.

"Oh, I pinched a couple loaves of bread and landed in 'ere. Not that it matters, the food in jail is better than what I usually eat."

"Do you have a family?" Louise asked.

"My husband was a fisherman lost at sea almost ten years ago. Sailed out of Liverpool, he did, and just didn't come back after one trip. My children were all taken from me and turned into servants," she answered.

This woman, although harsh looking, had more tenderness in her voice than Louise had experienced in some time. The look in her eyes was one of pure compassion.

"I'm so sorry," Louise replied and she genuinely was sorry.

"Ah, that's life though, isn't it? My children have a better life than I could have provided them. Been living on the streets for years now. How could I care for a family in my state?"

Louise suddenly felt stupid for breaking down and crying. In just a few moments Louise finally realized how charmed her life had been as compared to this woman's.

Yet, this lady wasn't jealous of her. She wasn't condemning Louise for having an easy life.

She was humane and caring, something that Louise couldn't say about her own class of people. In fact, her people, those of the upper class, were some of the most cold, manipulative, and conniving people she had met. Acceptance was based on status and connections, and people never thought twice about stabbing a friend in the back.

The most shocking part of her entire ordeal was that her friends had, for the most part, completely abandoned her just when she needed them the most. People she had known her entire life suddenly wouldn't return her letters or invitations to lunch.

It was such an awful and miserable feeling, being ostracized.

Laughed at.

Excluded.

At one time, she had treated Margaret so harshly, all because she wanted to keep up appearances to these people. How wrong she had been! She had scolded her daughter and taken sides against her. She felt ashamed and terribly sorry.

Sitting in the jail cell, having lost everything, she slowly realized that what was really important to her was not status, or possessions, or aristocracy.

It was choosing to do the right thing.

It was caring for her family.

She resolved, at that moment, to get out of this jail cell and right her family name, no matter the effort. She would not be made a victim and left to rot in a jail cell.

She would fight.

"Quite a sight, isn't it?" Jack said to Tariq as the two of them ate porridge and sipped hot lemon tea. The campground, which had once been so modest, was now full of a number of different tribes and people of almost every ethnicity and race. As far as the eye could see, tents and fire pits and tribespeople covered the landscape. One hundred men marched in groups of five down the valley to practice military maneuvers. Others were paired off in groups of two and sparred in hand-to-hand combat. A variety of smells could be detected throughout the camp—some delicious and others not so pleasing to the nose. The many tribes dressed very differently from one another. The Berbers from the mountains tended to dress in furs and brown leather in order to stay warm and blend in with the mountain scenery. The desert clans dressed in lightweight colorful cotton clothing, such as the Tuareg all in blue. Most spoke Arabic while others spoke a unique dialect.

At the center of it all was Malik.

Although he was blind, all recognized his military genius. Sanaa and Zijuan were almost constantly at his side discussing strategy with him.

They acted as his eyes.

A mammoth-sized map was laid before him and Malik used his hands to guide him along the length of the map. He placed tin figures at certain spots on the map, each representing the Caid's and the French troops, respectively. He calculated figures in his head and played out battle scenarios. In some ways, not having his eyesight was an advantage because it forced him to visualize everything in his head. He thought of many possible factors that escaped the other tribal leaders.

Eventually, all acknowledged Malik as their leader.

He diligently practiced martial arts with Sanaa each morning. Malik found that if he could touch someone, then the fighting was very easy, as it was all based on body movement. He had to listen to breathing and footsteps to gauge distance, and still had trouble with delivering punches with the fist, but he was getting better and was becoming more effective at making his opponents move and give away their positions.

His ground fighting was becoming more and more lethal.

Through it all, Sanaa would not allow him to feel sorry for himself. She never once allowed him to lament his situation or feel he was handicapped in any way. She gently but firmly made him adjust to his new life, until he had memorized every step and direction to the point where he could walk seamlessly through the entire camp without using his hands or a cane.

His hearing and sense of smell became more and more acute.

Malik formed a War Council with leaders of the other tribes so that all felt equally involved. They had almost eight thousand warriors at their disposal, and it took careful coordination for them to communicate and work with one another. Rather than intermingling the tribes, Malik decided that each tribe would establish its own hierarchy and coordinate its own movements in accordance with the unified army's plans.

"Tariq, can I see you and Jack in my tent?" Malik asked.

"Of course," Jack answered and the two followed Malik to his tent.

On the floor of the tent, the sizeable map had been laid out and the three sat down around it. Soon, Zijuan joined them and sat next to Tariq.

"We have intelligence that the Caid is going to move his troops and attack Marrakesh, which is the only major city in Morocco that the French and the Caid do not control. We even have reports that the Sultan is in hiding in Marrakesh and his troops are managing to hold the city. However, they won't be able to hold out for much longer," Malik showed them, pointing to the map as he spoke.

Tariq stared at the map, which showed various troops and columns spread out into position, and all were pointing toward Marrakesh.

"Do we have any idea how many troops to expect?" Jack asked.

"Preliminary reports are 15,000 to 20,000," Zijuan answered.

"So almost double our size?" Jack replied.

"Yes, and they have modern machine guns and perhaps even some airplanes," Malik answered.

Jack rubbed his chin and continued to stare at the map.

"Airplanes?" he asked.

"Yes, but only a couple. Airplanes might provide them with some advantage, but the real war will be fought on the ground. The French have a number of Gatling machine guns and their entire army is outfitted with rifles. The ammunition and weapons you stole will help us, but there are still many who will be fighting the old way—with swords and bows and arrows," Malik replied, his voice exuding authority.

"So what is your plan?" Jack asked.

"To engage in hand-to-hand combat as much as possible to negate the advantages of the French and their modern weapons. If we can get right on them, their soldiers will be no match for our tribes and their swordsmanship. We must get up close to win this battle."

Tariq stared at the map and was completely transfixed. How exciting it was to be discussing a battle with his trusted mentors. His mind buzzed with thoughts of warfare and sword fights and his dreams of becoming a hero.

"If we can win this battle, then we can defeat the Caid once and for all. If we lose, all of Morocco will be lost," Zijuan explained, and suddenly Tariq became fully aware of the consequences.

"Will we have the element of surprise?" Jack asked.

"Not with the size of our army. The time for guerrilla warfare and sneak attacks is over. This is going to be a battle of two armies looking one another in the eyes and seeing which one will fall," Malik said and asked Tariq to move all the pieces to face one another just outside of Marrakesh.

Jack quickly understood what was about to happen.

This was going to be a battle for the ages. A battle that would echo through eternity.

"When do we depart?" Jack asked.

"A week's time. I have already informed the other tribal leaders, and they are going to discuss the plan with their warriors today and prepare them for battle. You had mentioned a special project to me, and I think now is the time to pursue it. Take Tariq and ten warriors and make your way to Chaouen. We'll rendezvous as agreed upon," Malik said to Jack.

Jack smiled and nodded his head.

In Tangier, he'd had an idea that might be just the surprise element they needed to beat the Caid. He'd discussed the idea with Malik, who had readily agreed that they should put it into action.

There was no time to waste.

The Black Mamba sat with the Caid and the Caid's generals at his kasbah. The grounds were overflowing with soldiers.

"We have received intelligence that the Sultan is being held in Marrakesh. I have sent word to our leaders and all of our troops are meeting us at the kasbah. Then we will march together to capture Marrakesh. Once the city has fallen and the Sultan is dead, I will be named as the absolute ruler of Morocco!" the Caid explained, and his generals nodded their heads in agreement.

"What kind of forces will Marrakesh have to defend herself?" the Mamba asked.

"A few hundred of the Sultan's troops—at most. It should be an easy victory for us," the Caid answered.

The Mamba stared at the Caid and his generals. He didn't have much respect for any of them, as all were simple "yes men" to the Caid. In fact, there wasn't a military mind among them, and all were more concerned with the size of their harems and the fat of their lambs than they were with war.

"What of the Red Hand attacks?" the Mamba asked.

The Caid looked annoyed at this line of questioning.

"A series of attacks designed to annoy us and nothing more," he answered.

"Even the assault on the cache of weapons? They are better armed than you know. And I have heard a report that a resistance army grows in the Rif. If they are organized, they may be formidable."

The Caid stood up, clearly agitated with the Mamba.

"They are simple and stupid peasants and they will be slaughtered like pigs at a roast if they cross us. If Malik is still alive, and he is foolish enough to try to fight us, he will be cut down. Only then will our victory be complete."

The Mamba sat silently, as he knew the Caid did not want to hear any argument. Since the death of his son, the Caid had become singularly obsessed with ruling the land. So the Mamba simply nodded his head and said nothing more. Secretly, however, he was worried. How was it possible that Sanaa and Malik had lived? If there was an army forming in the Rif, how big was it, and how well organized? How motivated were they, and what weapons did they have?

He always made a point of knowing any opponent before the battle began, but he didn't understand this opponent well enough. He didn't have any advantage over them.

Worse, there was the issue of the Red Hand. Could this have been just a coincidence? Did it mean something else?

All of this worried him, and he was not a man accustomed to being worried.

Still, he had a duty to perform and he would prepare the troops to march into Marrakesh and sack it. With a victory in this battle, he and the Caid would rule all of Morocco.

Yet the Mamba's ambitions did not stop at Morocco.

He thought of conquering neighboring countries. Algeria, to the east, was ripe for the taking. Egypt could be next.

Morocco would be just the beginning.

He wanted all of Arabia under his thumb.

Timin received a message from Malik early one morning via carrier pigeon. He had to read it three times to be sure he deciphered the code correctly.

He called Fez and Aseem into a nearby alley.

"Your friends Tariq and Jack are returning to Chaouen. They have something very special to work on with the two of you," Timin told them.

"What is it?" Fez asked, obviously intrigued.

"They wouldn't say, only that they are going to meet with you, and some others, to begin a very important project."

Aseem and Fez looked at one another and smiled. It would be good to see Tariq, as always, and now he had them involved in some secret project!

228

"I need for you both to find a big warehouse of some kind where we can work on this project. It should be big enough to hold about thirty men or more, and it must have a very secret location. Can you do that?" Timin asked.

They both nodded in agreement.

"I have just the spot in mind. There's an abandoned rug warehouse on the outskirts of town. I don't think anyone is watching it," Aseem answered.

"Good. Go look at it today. They should be here in two days' time."

Fez and Aseem left in a hurry and Timin was left with his thoughts. What the note had said—that he hadn't shared with the boys—was that an army was coming, and that Timin was now responsible for carrying out a series of missions against the French and the Caid in various cities.

The note meant one thing and one thing only.

A war was coming that would determine the future of Morocco.

In two days' time, Tariq and Jack showed up in Chaouen with approximately ten other fighters. They appeared in the dead of night and were immediately shown the warehouse that Fez and Aseem had secured for them. They had a wagon full of supplies, as well as ten donkeys carrying large bags on their backs. The warehouse was huge, and it could fit more than three hundred men. Without a moment to waste, Jack lit torches and lanterns and immediately set everyone to work.

At dusk the next day, Aseem, Fez, and Tariq took a break and walked around Chaouen. They preferred to walk at night, as their faces were a little more concealed than when they walked during the day. Their muscles were tired and their fingers extremely sore. Adrenaline, however, surged through their veins and kept them going through hours and hours of laborious work. Walking through town, Tariq found himself staring up at Azmiya's apartment. It was no accident that this was where they found themselves, as he had quietly steered them in this direction.

He quickly went to the brick where Azmiya had agreed to leave him a note and lifted it up. Sure enough, there was a note folded up many times into a tiny square.

As Tariq read the note, the color drained from his face.

> T—
>
> I write this note wishing I could see your face. I am so lonely in this house and my uncle continues to terrorize me. I live in fear of him each and every day. I have no friends and I have no escape. I dearly wish I could leave with you, but I have not heard from you. I hope you find this note and I can see your face soon, as I am very sad.
>
> Yours, A

Fez and Aseem went to Tariq. He hadn't told them about Azmiya and they were curious about the note.

"What is it?" Fez asked.

Tariq sighed deeply and tore up the note.

"There's something I have to do, but it is really dangerous," he said.

"What is it?" Aseem asked excitedly.

"I have to rescue a girl," Tariq answered.

Fez and Aseem looked at one another and then turned back to question Tariq.

"What girl? What are you talking about?" Fez asked.

"Just a girl. Her uncle is a policeman and he is very cruel to her."

"A policeman? That is trouble for us, Tariq—we don't need the police snooping around us right now," Aseem replied.

"I know and I don't care," Tariq replied with conviction.

Whoever this girl was, she was obviously very important to Tariq.

"Well, if it's dangerous, count us in," Aseem said with a grin.

Tariq looked at them both. Somehow, he still felt responsible for them. Their lives were already in enough danger, and Tariq didn't make it any worse by getting them involved in this.

"I can't ask you to join me. If I am caught, you must continue to help Timin and Melbourne Jack."

Fez went to Tariq and put his arm around him.

"Tariq, if it is a dangerous mission, then Aseem and I insist on coming with you. Now, let's figure out a plan and rescue this princess of yours."

Tariq blushed with embarrassment.

"She's not a princess," he whispered and both Aseem and Fez laughed.

Up in her apartment, as she did every day, Azmiya sat alone in her room. Her uncle had forbidden her from going out in the city, so she was forced to stay in the apartment. It had become a prison cell to her. Her uncle berated and bullied her, calling her useless, stupid, and ungrateful. Unbeknownst to Azmiya, her uncle had once tried to marry her off, but the groom's parents cancelled at the last moment, insisting her dowry wasn't big enough. So her uncle was forced to continue to care for her—and caring for her meant money. To him, she was a drain on his finances and nothing more.

He began to despise her.

Azmiya tried her hardest to please him. She cleaned and cooked and ironed and helped to keep the house as tidy as possible. She never spoke or annoyed him in any manner, yet he still found fault with her at every turn. Once, she had mended a shirt for him and one of the threads had come undone. For that, he took off his belt and whipped her until she was huddled in a corner, sobbing and begging him to stop.

The food she prepared was always too hot, too cold, too spicy, or not spicy enough.

He found dirt no matter how hard she scrubbed and cleaned.

His clothes were never clean enough or sewn correctly. Sometimes, he would purposely rip a pair of trousers or shirt, just to blame it on her.

She felt so beat down and so useless that she was beginning to lose hope. Was this to be her life? Would she have nothing to look forward to?

The only thing that gave her hope was Tariq. In the weeks since she had last seen him, the abuse had gotten much worse. Every day she longed for just a glimpse of him, or a note, but day after day she found nothing. She thought of running away, but where would she go? How would she live? Her entire life depended upon her uncle and she knew it.

Lately, he had taken to drinking and one evening she heard him complaining about the "Red Hand" and how it was the cause of all his misery. His moods became more and more foul and dark with each passing day. She heard him cuss and scream and damn the infernal "Red Hand."

She didn't know what the "Red Hand" was, but she already liked it. Anything that caused her uncle embarrassment and annoyance was excellent in her mind. In fact, she would secretly eavesdrop on her uncle, and anytime he mentioned the words "Red Hand," a smile would come to her face. It was one of the few pleasures in her life.

One night, she had prepared a meal for her uncle consisting of roasted dove, couscous, and a bit of yoghurt. It was a simple meal, but delicious, as her cooking had improved greatly. The meal was prepared promptly at six o'clock, as her uncle had instructed.

Only this night he hadn't returned home until eight o'clock.

For two hours she fretted with each passing moment. The weight of the meal bore down on her shoulders, because she knew everything was getting cold and would not be to his satisfaction.

By seven o'clock, she sat in a corner, her knees hugging against her chest, knowing that the meal was ruined and she would be blamed.

Sure enough, when her uncle finally arrived, he sat down at the table, and she could hear him lifting dishes and slopping food onto his plate. After a moment, she heard him spit out the food and throw the plate against a wall.

"Azmiya!" he screamed and she slowly lifted herself from the floor and emerged from her room. Her shoulders slumped; she stared at the ground and tried not to cry.

"What is this filth you serve me?" he screamed, standing in front of her. She knew better than to argue or to try to provide an explanation, as that would simply make him angrier.

So she just stood there with her head down.

"Well?" he screamed at her.

"I am sorry. I will do better," she mumbled.

His eyes were bulging from their sockets and his breathing was hard and labored. The sight of her made him sick to his stomach. She was nothing but trouble to him, and he cursed the day his brother had died and he was forced to care for her. She was useless.

He picked up one of the doves and a handful of couscous, came up to Azmiya and rubbed the food in her face. She wanted so much to cry, but she knew it would only make things worse. So she stood there trembling with fear, with the evening's meal smeared all over her face, hoping he would not hit her.

"Now clean it up," he growled as he left her and returned to his study, where he would drink his whiskey and smoke his cigarettes.

She went about cleaning up the dishes and food and putting everything away in its proper place. Even the servants knew better than to help, or they might get the lash from her uncle.

It took Azmiya the better part of an hour before the kitchen was spotless and the food was put away. She returned to her room, and lay down and cried. She thought of her mother and father and how she missed them so. Her mother, beautiful and doting, putting freshly cut poppies on the kitchen counter and humming as she prepared dinner. And her father, always with a smile on his face, holding Azmiya on his knee and telling her a nursery rhyme, or teaching her a lyric to a song. She couldn't remember one instance when her father had yelled at her. He'd never done so, not even once. Her life had been full of joy and happiness and wonder. She went to school every day and never wore a veil.

She was free.

Now, however, she was a prisoner and she would remain one for the rest of her life. No doubt her uncle would sell her to the highest bidder for marriage, even if it was to a cruel and heartless man—and what other kind of man would her uncle know? All the policemen were just as cruel as he.

Falling asleep that night, she thought of her parents and her old house and it brought her a small bit of comfort.

At three o'clock in the morning she awoke with a start, her heart pounding.

Someone was in her room!

"Azmiya," came a faint whisper.

She froze, afraid to respond.

Who was it?

"Azmiya, it's me—Tariq!"

Sitting up, she allowed her eyes to adjust to the darkness until she saw a figure sitting next to her on the ground.

"Tariq?" she whispered.

"Yes, I've come to take you away," he whispered.

Without a second thought, she threw her arms around his shoulders and hugged him tightly. She didn't cry; she finally allowed herself to feel something other than misery.

Tariq, not prepared for such an embrace, had no idea what to do. He allowed her to hug him and after a few seconds, as she released him, he whispered,

"We have to go and go *now*. I don't know how long your uncle will remain asleep. What do you need?"

"I don't need anything. I just need to get away from this place."

"Okay, follow me."

They walked through the living room and were about to slip out an open window when Tariq stopped her.

"Oh, wait—just one more thing."

He produced a small cotton bag, plunged his right hand into it, and when he pulled it out, it was completely covered in red. He went to the closest wall and pressed down five perfect red handprints.

"Now we're ready," he whispered.

Azmiya stared at the red handprints and was instantly filled with joy. She smiled as she exited through the window. Fez was on the outside with a rope in his hands, waiting to help her down.

"Take this rope and hold on tightly—then push off. You'll swing over the courtyard to our friend on the other side," he whispered.

A sense of relief flooded over her. She forgot all about her uncle and her life in that apartment as she stood on its window ledge three floors above the ground. Grabbing the rope in her hands, she didn't just step off the ledge, she practically jumped off. She flew through the darkness; she wanted to scream with glee, but knew better.

She felt herself go down and lift up again, and in a few seconds, Aseem had grabbed her and led her onto another ledge on an adjacent building.

"Move over there and hold on tightly," he instructed her. She eagerly obeyed and walked about six feet down the ledge, where she held onto a pipe for safety.

Aseem swung the rope back across the dark abyss. He heard a bird whistle, which signaled that Tariq and Fez had the rope, and before long Fez came swinging across to Aseem. He grabbed Fez by the front of the trousers before he could slip backwards again. Aseem flung the rope back across to Tariq, and soon another whistle call could be heard. After a minute, Tariq flew through the darkness and landed on the ledge. Fez produced a knife and quickly cut the rope and tossed it away, in order to hide their escape route.

The four made their way to an open door and then down some stairs out of the building. After passing through some alleys, they disappeared in the darkness without a trace or a sound.

The next morning, Azmiya's uncle awoke with a headache and lazily dragged himself to his bathroom. Normally, Azmiya would have prepared him a cold basin to plunge his face into and a hot basin of water to shave.

But this morning, he saw neither.

"Azmiya!" he screamed.

No answer.

"Stupid girl," he thought to himself. After last night, she obviously hadn't learned a thing. He grabbed his brown leather belt—the one with a thick silver buckle—and was going to teach her a lesson she would not soon forget.

Entering the living room, he stopped in his tracks and dropped the belt.

Next to the open window were five red handprints on his white wall.

Going through the house, he called her name but heard no answer. He searched every room and closet.

Azmiya was gone.

Her uncle screamed her name and cursed the "Red Hand." In his fury, he went about destroying his living room. He smashed plates and vases and even managed to completely shatter his dining room table. When he finally stopped, his living room was nothing but a shambles of broken ceramic and splintered wood.

Only Azmiya wasn't there to clean it up.

CHAPTER
— *20* —

ON GROUND AND IN AIR

The Walcott lay docked in the port of Liverpool. It was early morning, and a fog had rolled in. Soon she was shrouded in mist. Liverpool was a military port and British naval vessels came and went in a steady stream. Because they possessed the world's greatest navy, the British prided themselves on both the quality and abundance of their warships. Liverpool was the city where the vast majority of their ships were built, and her inhabitants were some of the finest craftsmen in the world.

Charles Owen walked down a dock with three other sailors. He wore a black pea coat with the collar pulled up around his ears and a gray wool hat on his head. A tan scarf was wrapped around his neck and tucked inside his coat, so that only a small portion of his face was visible. Both hands were in his pockets and he kept his head down.

On their way down the dock, they passed two guards, who didn't even give them a cursory glance. Charles and the sailors continued down the dock and up into the Liverpool streets. The fog had rolled in and the city's brick buildings were mostly obscured by the thick mist. Puddles splashed under their shoes as they walked quickly away from the port and into the heart of the city.

After several blocks, they came to a small house built of red brick. It was a pleasant-looking house with a green door and white windowsills. A small apple tree grew just outside.

Just after young Seaman Terry knocked on the door, they heard footsteps approaching the door. They saw a woman of about fifty peer through lace curtains on a small window in the door. Her face was plump and her hair was starting to gray. The moment she saw Terry, she gasped and the door flew open. The woman threw her arms around Terry and hugged him tightly.

"Hello, Mum," he said with a smile. His mother grabbed her son's face, kissing both his cheeks. By this time, tears rolled down her face as she embraced him.

"Who is it, dear?" came from somewhere in the house.

"It's your son come back from the sea," she called out. Soon more footsteps could be heard, until a small and skinny man, with an almost bald head, came to the door. A huge smile appeared on his face at the sight of his son.

"Hello, Dad," Terry said. He embraced his father and then firmly shook his hand.

"Come in, come in," his mother urged and soon Charles and the rest of the soldiers were inside the house and sitting in the dining room.

"So you must introduce us to your friends," his mother asked, as she quickly prepared a pot of tea and began warming up fresh scones, sausages, beans, and hard-boiled eggs.

"This 'ere is Colonel Charles Owen. We've got to get him to London," Terry explained. At this, both his mother and his father stopped what they were doing and stared at Charles.

"*The* Charles Owen?" his father asked.

"Yes, sir," Charles answered and blushed a bit.

"Why, you're the most wanted man in Britain. Steven, what are you doing with this man? Do you know what he's done?" his father asked with more than a little bristle in his voice.

"It's all lies, Dad. Colonel Owen is innocent and was just doing his duty. Our commander, Dreyfuss, is the proper villain...that is, until the Colonel 'ere did him in with a sword."

"What do you mean he's innocent? What's this about 'doing in' Dreyfuss?" his father asked, still very defensive about having the notorious Charles Owen in his house.

"Dreyfuss was pillaging and murdering under orders. The Colonel just tried to stop him and was blamed for all the looting and pirating that's been happening. It's all lies. Me and the boys are going to testify in Colonel Owen's defense."

238

His father continued to look disdainfully at Charles as his son continued, "Dad, I'm ashamed of what I did, as are the other lads. Being out at sea, marauding with the Union Jack flying on our mast, it made me ashamed to be an Englishman. Colonel Owen is giving us our dignity back."

His father instantly understood that his son had been through some terrible experiences. His face softened, and looking at Charles, he gave him a small nod of his head. Without saying a word, he stepped over to Charles, patted him on the shoulder, and sat down. The gesture was understood by all—Charles was forgiven.

His mother sat down with the men at the dining room table.

"A conspiracy!" she whispered and her face seemed to light up.

"Oh no, dear—you with your conspiracy theories. Here we go again!" her husband stood up and took over making the tea.

"Innocent all along, you say?" she asked and looked at Charles.

"You should be very proud of your son, Mr. and Mrs. Terry. He showed a great amount of bravery, and in truth, he's the only reason I am alive," Charles explained and Mrs. Terry beamed as she looked at her son.

"Not soon enough," young Steven muttered under his breath.

"The world isn't as simple as you thought, eh?" his father said from the kitchen, where he had been preparing the portions of food he now brought to the table.

"Well, good. You should learn now rather than later. There's always a door behind the door; you know what I'm saying," Mr. Terry was now addressing Charles.

"Indeed, I do," he answered.

"Here, eat, eat! We have some lovely strawberry jam, and the sausages are fresh. You must all be starving," Mrs. Terry said and urged the men to eat.

"Indeed we are, thank you," Charles answered. Soon everyone was shoveling food in their mouths and going back for seconds.

After breakfast, the party retreated to the back garden and sat around a wooden table. It was still cold outside, but the fresh air felt good, and more tea was served.

"So what are your plans, Colonel Owen?" Mr. Terry asked.

"To make my way back to my family in London and try to clear my name. The testimony of your son and these fine cadets will certainly help my cause."

"It's not always easy to do the right thing, but we're proud of you, son," Mr. Terry said, causing young Terry to blush.

Just then, Mrs. Terry's face showed a look of complete shock and worry.

"I just thought of something," she said and hurried inside, returning with yesterday's paper. She unfolded a couple of pages and then showed it to Charles.

The headline read, "Louise Owen to be tried as traitor."

Charles quickly read the story. It was all about Louise and how she had broken into the Far Indian Trading Company offices. She was being tried as a coconspirator to her husband. If convicted, she would be given the death penalty.

Charles read the story twice more, and it was easy to see how upset it made him.

"She's to go to court tomorrow. They're trying for a quick trial," he mentioned as he continued to scan the article—as if he might possibly have missed something. His thoughts went to his poor wife and his son, David, who, the article said, was being held by Social Services.

Charles sat back in his chair. The color had drained from his face, and he looked as if he had aged ten years in the two minutes it took him to read that article.

"I've got to get to London," he said.

"Two steps ahead of you, colonel. I'll get the wagon hitched and we'll be there by morning," Mr. Terry said and stood up.

Charles looked at Terry and the other soldiers.

"Boys, I don't know how this is going to go. I can't ask you to do something that might jeopardize your futures. There are powerful forces lined up against me right now."

Terry and the other soldiers stood up.

"Sir, we've been doing some pretty awful things now under Lieutenant Dreyfuss. Things that make us feel horrible. Things that make us stay up at night. Clearing your name—it's the one right thing we have to do. The boys all agreed on that," Terry answered and the other soldiers agreed with him.

Charles put his hand on Terry's shoulder.

"You make the British navy proud," he said and shook the hands of the other boys.

"C'mon lads, London is calling!" Mr. Terry yelled, and soon the boys had boarded the wagon and were being led through the streets of Liverpool by the two horses in front. Charles kept his head down and his collar pulled up, and he crouched down low in the back to keep from being seen. Terry sat up front with his father, and the rest of the lads rode in the back of the wagon with Charles.

Back in her cell, Louise looked considerably worse for wear. It was very cold in the jail and she'd caught a bit of flu. Her clothes were tattered and dirty, and she had already lost five pounds from the pitiful portions of gruel and soup she was fed just once a day. Her cheeks were sunken and her hair was greasy from not having bathed in over a week.

She had met with both her barrister and Matthew Hatrider, but neither of them could provide much help. The charges against her were thin, at best. They didn't have any real proof that Louise had broken into the Far Indian offices, and they didn't have any proof at all that she was conspiring with Charles. It was obvious someone very powerful wanted to discredit Louise and to see her behind bars.

They needed to know if the judge would be corrupt or honest. If corrupt and pocketing bribes, then there was no hope for Louise. She would be tried as a traitor and hanged. If the judge was honest, then she might be set free, but her reputation would still be ruined. They just had to wait and see.

Louise had settled into jail life as best she could. She tried not to think of David and just hoped he was coping. She took to teaching some of the girls to read and write, and they played marathon games of cooncan—a card game that was currently all the rage. Mostly, she was just bored and passed the time staring at water dripping from the ceiling or observing the many rats and mice that frequented their cell.

Trying not to give up hope, she wondered if there was anything she could do to proclaim her innocence, but she could think of nothing.

Louise was trapped—and at the mercy of a corrupt justice system. Her court date the following day would determine her fate, and quite possibly, this ordeal would end with her hanging from a noose.

Lionel Hedgecock, president of the Far Indian Trading Company, sat across from Roy Ferguson, admiral in the British navy, and sipped on his glass of scotch. They were both seated in fat leather chairs and their bodies sunk into the down-filled cushions.

"So this Owen woman has been taken care of?" Ferguson asked.

"Yes, but she still maintains the ledger was lost in the Thames."

"That ledger could be the ruin of us. You're sure she doesn't have it?" the admiral asked.

"We've taken her family from her. Next is her house, and she's about to be tried as a traitor and hanged. It seems to me if she actually had the ledger, she would have handed it over by now."

Admiral Ferguson sipped on his glass of scotch, but he was still very concerned. He hadn't heard from Dreyfuss in over a month, and now there was this mess with Louise Owen. Some of the others in the navy were starting to inquire about Dreyfuss.

Lionel Hedgecock reached over and gave him a very full envelope. Ferguson opened it, and it was full of cash—the latest in a series of payments.

"Don't worry, Roy. This Owen woman doesn't have a case or any proof against us. It's her word against ours, and she is the wife of the most notorious criminal in England. Anything she says will be taken as a lie. We're making a handsome profit from our arrangement and we'll continue to profit handsomely. Wars have been started over money—the Boer War wasn't about anything other than diamonds being found in South Africa! What we're doing has been done since the dawn of time. So relax," Hedgecock told him. He could see that the admiral was nervous and worried.

Lionel Hedgecock wasn't nervous. He didn't get nervous. He had spent his entire life privileged and he had always gotten everything he had wanted. This Owen woman was a nuisance and nothing more.

He would squash her like he squashed everyone else who got in his way.

Caid Ali Tamzali led his army over the plains of Morocco. He rode in the rear on an enormous war camel, with the Black Mamba by his side on another. The Caid sat lazily to the side, with an umbrella hitched to the back of the camel that provided much-needed shade. A fine leather saddle was beneath him, and he sat on a thick cotton pillow to make his ride more comfortable. The camel was outfitted with actual leather armor that protected both its belly and front side. The saddle was adorned with a collage of colors in intricately sewed beads and glass buttons.

War camels were the largest and most aggressive of the pack and were bred to be especially brave in the face of battle. Each camel took years to train for battle, and today, as on all days in the battlefield, the Caid only rode the best of the best.

Just ahead of them, tens of thousands of soldiers marched in formation. Rows and rows of troops were dressed in fine military uniforms with modern rifles slung over their shoulders. A cavalry of almost one thousand rode camels, and other soldiers had mounted five Gatling machine guns on wagons that could be easily moved and positioned on the battlefield. Dozens of supply wagons picked up the rear.

The army marched over the dirt and clay, heading toward their destination—the city of Marrakesh. Once Marrakesh fell, and the Sultan had been killed, the Caid would rule Morocco. The Mamba was already preparing to march on Algeria and then on Egypt. Together, they could rule over Northern Africa, its people under their control.

Jawad rode a camel in front of them both. He had been given his own squadron of fifty riders to command, and he had done so with the brutality he learned at the hands of the Mamba. He watched them and berated them for even the smallest of mistakes. Jawad had driven fear into them so deeply, his troops feared him as much as they feared the Mamba.

The army marched over a hill until the soldiers in front suddenly stopped. The entire procession halted in back of them. A signal was given for the Caid to ride to the front.

"Follow me," he ordered the Mamba, and together they rode to the front of their giant army.

As they rode up a hill, they were unable to see what awaited them on the other side. It wasn't until they arrived at the front line that they could they see why the soldiers had stopped.

In front of them, spread out over the plains, was an army. Soldiers of every ethnicity stared back at them. Men, women, and even children stood ready to fight them.

Sanaa and Zijuan were on horses in the center, with their army surrounding them. They were joined by Moussa Ag Arshaman, the leader of the Tuareg people, and many leaders of other tribes. Malik was in the rear, and a soldier stood next to him whose job was to describe what was happening in the battle so Malik could help issue orders.

Although he was blind, Malik would not miss this battle for anything in the world.

Sanaa, dressed completely in black with her long hair blowing in the wind, held a rifle in her hand and a sword sheathed at her side. Zijuan was also dressed in black, except for a blue scarf that covered her neck. A saber was slung across her back, and she held a rifle in her right hand.

Around them, thousands of tribesmen and women stared at the Caid's army spread out before them, separated by only a quarter of mile of earth. Banners flew in the wind from the tribes—physical representations of their people and their culture that served as an affront to the Caid and his flag, whose colors represented the blanket of tyranny that reigned over them for an eternity. The faces on the tribespeople were cold and blank, as if every atrocity and tragedy they'd been subjected to over the decades had been etched and worn on their skin for all to witness. Their muscles flexed with anticipation, and their fists gripped their swords, rifles, and lances as though each weapon was an extension of themselves. They were beyond being afraid, or hesitant, or even logical about the battle in front of them. Everyone wanted to taste blood, and to release their angst and their misery and their oppression upon their enemies. The Caid's army was bigger, but it didn't matter an ounce. The tribes were desperate, and they knew they must defeat the Caid to win back their freedom and live out their lives in peace.

The Caid and the Mamba stared at the army in front of them. Yes, they had heard the rumors that an army was forming in the mountains, but they had never expected to meet them on this march. The truth was, they were unprepared for such a show of force. The sheer size of the army in front of them came as a shock.

"Prepare the cavalry," the Mamba ordered.

The Caid wisely allowed the Mamba to issue orders when it came to war. The Mamba's military expertise outweighed even his own.

Soon, the entire cavalry of camels and horses were in position at the front. The cavalry lined up across the plain for two hundred yards in columns ten thick. The camel riders rocked nervously in their saddles, with rifles in their hands, and sat staring at the army facing them.

Seeing this, Zijuan also ordered the cavalry to the front. Soon, a smaller contingent of horses and camels were positioned to face off against the Caid.

The Mamba could see the outline of Sanaa's body in the distance, and his anger only grew. It was true! She had lived and was now leading a force against his own army. He stared at the tribal army facing him and his muscles flexed with anticipation.

He would slaughter these people, and once and for all, completely squash these rebels and their filth.

Staring at Sanaa, he wanted one thing.

To see her dead.

The two armies stared at one another for a full minute. The Mamba waited for the Caid, who had drawn his own sword in preparation for battle.

"Attack!" the Caid yelled.

"Attack!" Zijuan yelled.

The two armies, each with their cavalry at the front, immediately charged towards one another. Instantly the ground was a sea of dust as the camel riders ran in full stride directly at the other.

Thousands upon thousands of soldiers charged at one another. First they rode on sweaty horses with drawn swords, screeching at the enemy, and then they continued on foot by the thousands, arms raised—every soldier ready to drive straight through their enemy's army. They charged like this for less than a minute, until at last they met face-to-face, colliding with one another like two bighorn sheep. Both armies were full of adrenaline and vigor and the battlefield soon became a canvas of dust, sweat, clanging steel, iron, and blood.

Melbourne Jack, Tariq, Aseem, Fez, and a host of other warriors had worked nonstop for a straight week, even through the nights, to complete the project at hand.

They needed an edge against the Caid, to turn the tide against their superior forces and weaponry—something he would never expect. Melbourne Jack had offered a suggestion weeks ago, and Malik had readily agreed to it, even though he thought it would be impossible to carry out.

Jack had built an air force—a fleet of hot air balloons.

Using material from the sailboat sails, spools of rope, planks of wood, and kerosene for fuel, he and the others had constructed exactly forty-four miniature hot air balloons. Most were only big enough to carry two soldiers: one to navigate and one to attack the Caid's army from the skies.

Using a mixture of water, sulfur, and limestone, they constructed rudimentary bombs to drop on the Caid's forces that would not only disrupt his army, but would also explode into a cloud of tear gas on impact. The group called them "blinders."

By calculating the wind speed and analyzing weather patterns, Jack had located the exact spot to launch the balloons that would place them directly over the Caid's army. Every detail of that day—Zijuan's position with the ground troops and exactly where they would meet the Caid's army—was planned down to the minute in order allow Jack to launch his aerial attack at just the right time from the ideal location.

All of Jack's balloon navigators were completely inexperienced, so it would be with a hope and a prayer that they would really be able to position themselves directly above the Caid's army. Jack had personally selected every one of the navigators and had spent hours and hours teaching them how to fly the balloons—but they still had little time actually flying them on their own. By attaching a one hundred-foot-long rope to one of the baskets and allowing the balloon to rise up in the air, Jack had been able to take his navigators up for small rides to give them an idea of what to expect. They couldn't risk having the balloons go up too high, as the Caid's scouts might spot them. Despite their inexperience, their basic training had really helped the soldiers understand how to maneuver a balloon, and each navigator felt fairly comfortable.

Jack had purposely made one of the balloons much larger than the rest—he would navigate that one.

The balloons stood at the ready as their navigators and bombardiers prepared all the materials and weaponry and began to inflate the balloons with hot air. Soon, the entire expedition was ready to launch. As the balloons slowly inflated, they were hitched to the ground with secure lines tied to stakes in the ground.

Jack found Tariq, Aseem, and Fez and told them it was time for the launch.

He had asked them to be his crew in his balloon. They worked well together and they were all small, so there would be much more room to move around inside the basket.

Azmiya stood next to some elders and children who would not be joining the battle. She had settled in nicely with the tribe and, as Tariq knew they would, the tribe had accepted her as one of their own. Malik and Sanaa had promised to look after her. Malik had even started teaching her the basics of combat and martial arts, and Azmiya greatly enjoyed his lessons. It was a welcome break for Malik, as he had been extremely busy organizing the army and strategizing for the battle.

Now, however, Azmiya's face was flush with worry watching Tariq prepare to fly off in that balloon to fight the Caid. To her, it all looked very dangerous. The balloons seemed like death traps as they launched into the air—they could plunge down to earth at any moment!

Tariq came up to her, but he didn't know what to say. He had spent time with her over the past week, but it hadn't been much time, as he had been busy preparing his balloon. Still, she was constantly on his mind and he often found himself glancing over his shoulder to make sure she was safe. Many times, their eyes met and they shared an awkward smile.

Azmiya, looking into Tariq's eyes, began to cry and rushed to hug him. Tariq, embarrassed, returned her embrace. Azmiya then felt herself kiss him on each cheek and then on the lips. It was a very small kiss, as their lips barely brushed, but Tariq felt electricity surge through his entire body. It was his first kiss, as it was hers. Azmiya quickly stepped back, a little embarrassed at such a display of affection.

Tariq walked away, but then gave one last glance to Azmiya, who was wiping away her tears.

Turning his back, he rushed to the basket with Jack, Fez, and Aseem, and soon they lifted off the ground. Tariq threw out some sandbags and the balloon slowly lifted higher into the sky. He waved goodbye to Azmiya, who waved back.

In the basket, Aseem and Fez were smiling at Tariq.

"Look who has a girlfriend, Fez. Our little lover boy over here," Aseem teased, which even made Jack grin a bit.

Tariq couldn't say anything in his own defense, so he just blushed and smiled awkwardly.

The balloon lifted higher off the ground and soon they were surrounded by dozens of other balloons. Jack led the charge and directed the other navigators to follow his lead to determine when to elevate and when to descend.

The balloons were colored every shade of red, blue, yellow, and orange. To many tribesmen, white meant the color of death or surrender, so they avoided it at all costs. The colors of their clan were sacred to each warrior, and flying their clan's colors in battle was considered an honor. As a result, the squadron of balloons resembled a splattering of paint drops across a light blue canvas. It was a beautiful sight to behold. On the ground below, many farmers and villagers rushed out, pointing at the balloons flying overhead. None of these people had ever seen a hot air balloon before, much less an entire squadron of them.

Over the horizon they drifted, with some of the navigators drifting below, and others flying higher, up into the white clouds. The wind was moderate and their speed was about twelve knots, which meant they would be directly above the Caid's army in only twenty minutes' time. Many of the bombardiers and navigators were smiling in amazement, as they had never been this high in the air. Others had terrified looks on their faces, as being this high up was a most new and discomforting experience.

Off they drifted into the rising red sun.

CHAPTER
— *21* —

VINDICATION

Louise Owen had been handcuffed and was now being led to a courtroom. Her clothes were dirty, and her hair was an oily and disheveled mess. In just a week's time, her appearance had transformed from a responsible English woman into a homeless street person. Dirt was caked on her face and her cheeks already looked gaunt from a lack of food. Dark bags had formed under her eyes.

Two guards led her up four flights of stairs into a stone hallway, where she was forced to wait for almost six hours with the other prisoners. Finally, a guard came, grabbed her by the elbow, and led her through a large oak door into a courtroom.

At first, she was startled by the amount of light and the number of people in the room.

She tried to hide her embarrassment, but she felt humiliated by her appearance. The audience sat hushed in their seats as they watched Louise being marched over to her barrister and given a seat next to him. Matthew Hatrider was in the audience, and he nodded and smiled at her. Unfortunately, he was her last friend in the world. She didn't have any extended family, and she hadn't heard from any of Charles's relatives.

Despite being mortified by her appearance, Louise's spirit was strong. There was nothing left for the government to take from her. She had begun to realize that all the things she thought were important—her house, possessions, and standing in society—didn't really mean that much to her anymore. Over the past few months, she had gained a belief in herself unlike anything she'd ever felt before. Charles used to tell her, "You have such strength, you just don't know it," but until now, she never knew what he was talking about. Yet now, in the face of such despair, she had finally managed to find her voice and her conviction.

Obviously she hoped she would be allowed bail and would be able to return home. Her barrister was already completely surprised that she had spent a week in jail without so much as a hearing beforehand.

Powerful forces were conspiring against her.

The judge wore the traditional gray wig and black robe and sat behind a massive wooden desk at the front of his courtroom. The faint smell of wood polish filled the room, along with a distinct odor of soap. The courtroom had recently been cleaned, and Louise hoped it wasn't on her account.

The judge looked very English. His chin was almost nonexistent and seemed to disappear into his neck. His face was skinny with an elongated nose, and his skin was pale and chalky from the long hours spent in court. The judge eyed Louise as she sat down. He was obviously familiar with her case, as well as with the notoriety it was receiving the local papers.

The judge tried his best to look unaffected by the attention and publicity surrounding the hearing.

Louise looked at the prosecution's table and saw there were four barristers present. All were very well-dressed and kept busy going through a myriad of books and papers. Normally the prosecution would bring one barrister, two at most, and they would appear to be bored.

Obviously, somebody was throwing a lot of money at the prosecution to ensure that Louise Owen would be convicted of a crime and put behind bars. Her heart sank as she realized just how far the Far Indian Trading Company and certain parties in the British government were willing to go to prosecute her.

The trial commenced with the judge banging his gavel. The courtroom went silent as he first read through a lengthy sermon on the rules of the court. Finally, he came to the heart of the matter.

"Louise Owen, you are being charged with two crimes: treason against the crown and His Majesty the King and conspiracy against the British government and the Far Indian Trading Company. How do you plead?"

Louise stood up and, in her strongest voice, answered the judge.

"Not guilty, Your Honour."

The courtroom became a murmur of discussion, as there was talk that Louise might have thrown herself at the mercy of the court by pleading guilty.

The judge banged his gavel for silence and then wrote some notes in his notebook.

"Very well. Considering the magnitude of the charges, and the notoriety of the case, I am withholding any offer of bail. You are sentenced to remain in the custody of the court until your hearing."

Louise stared at the ground and her hopes grew even dimmer. Without bail, she couldn't go home and she couldn't see David.

The judge was about to speak again when a door opened in the back and a group of men burst into the courtroom.

Louise turned her head and almost fainted.

"Oh my goodness!" she exclaimed.

Charles Owen walked through the center of the crowd, flanked by British soldiers, and practically ran to his wife's side. Before the bailiff or the guards could stop him, he hugged her tightly.

Soon, the crowd erupted into deafening noise—the entire courtroom was shouting.

No one could believe that Charles Owen—the most wanted man in England, a man branded as a traitor—had suddenly burst into their courtroom.

Two guards tried to grab him, but they were quickly subdued by the British soldiers.

Charles released Louise and strode to the center of the courtroom.

"Mr. Owen, I suppose you have an excellent reason for disrupting this proceeding?" the judge yelled at Charles while pounding his gavel.

Charles walked right up to the judge, grabbed the gavel, and threw it across the courtroom into the crowd. Suddenly, the judge fully understood the circumstances and sat back in his chair.

Charles Owen had seized control of the courtroom.

Leaping up onto the judge's desk, Charles now literally stood above the judge and everyone in the courtroom. The crowd continued to shout and talk. Many of the participants were journalists, and they were scribbling like mad in their notebooks.

Charles put up his hands to quiet the crowd, and soon the room grew silent.

"My name is Charles Owen. I am a colonel in the British army. It has been published in many of our papers that I am a traitor to my country and an outlaw and a pirate. I want to take this opportunity to tell you the truth. I'm here to throw myself on the mercy of this court, in the hope that the truth might be heard, and justice might find herself in the confines of this magnificent room."

The room was so silent that the beating of a moth's wings could have been heard. All eyes were fixed on Charles.

"Months ago, I was sailing off the coast of Morocco with my family. We were approached by pirates, and I sent my family overboard to swim to safety while I drew the pirates away. But shortly thereafter, I was captured and taken prisoner by a man by the name of Captain Basil. A week later, we were docked at a small village when the British navy, led by a Lieutenant Dreyfuss, ruthlessly attacked the village and began slaughtering its inhabitants. This was not an act of war—it was an act of an inhumane and vicious criminal."

The crowd began to whisper and murmur until Charles quieted them down so he could continue.

"I tried to reason with Lieutenant Dreyfuss, but he attempted to murder me in order to silence me forever. I had no choice but to remain in this group of pirates as they fled into the Mediterranean. For months, I witnessed the brutality and piracy performed by Lieutenant Dreyfuss against innocent villagers, merchants, and fishermen. He was acting on orders given to him by Admiral Roy Ferguson of the Royal Navy, in league with Lionel Hedgecock, president of the Far Indian Trading Company."

The courtroom burst into a sea of chatter and looks of disbelief. One of the prosecutors stood up to interrupt Charles, but he was quickly knocked down by one of the British soldiers.

"These men were on Lieutenant Dreyfuss's crew and were ordered by him to perform many of these acts of piracy. They are here to clear their consciences and to restore the good name of the British navy—the greatest navy the world has ever seen."

One of the prosecutors, a squat man, finally stood up and challenged Charles.

"This is atrocious. You are not on trial here, your wife is—" he said before the same soldier whacked him on the back of the head and he quickly sat down.

"These men will testify to the orders they were given by Lieutenant Dreyfuss. They also have ships' logs and manifests for every ship and village they pillaged, and even copies of wire communications between Dreyfuss and Admiral Ferguson. They will corroborate everything I am saying. These brave young men are risking their careers and their reputations by stepping forward to tell the truth and to testify on my behalf."

Charles then leapt off the desk and walked over to his wife.

"As for my wife, she is only on trial because she was trying to clear my name. She is only on trial because the Far Indian Trading Company wants her silenced and discredited."

The courtroom was again silent except for the many journalists excitedly scribbling in their notebooks.

Charles turned to face the judge, who had a shocked and surprised look on his face.

"Well, Your Honour?" Charles simply asked.

The judge sat up straight in his chair and tapped his finger on his desk for a full minute. He stared at Charles, and at Louise, and then at the prosecution. It was obvious he had taken in all the information he had just heard.

This judge had a secret that nobody in the courtroom could have guessed.

A veteran of the Boer Wars, he had witnessed, first hand, that the war was little more than a tool to secure diamonds for English merchants. He saw his friends and comrades struck down and killed in the name of commerce and profit. He was sickened by the corrupt nature of British politics and how the rich were continually favored over the poor. He was a man who believed in fairness, courage, honor, and justice. He entered the legal profession to try to combat some of this seemingly endless corruption.

He saw an opportunity to strike a blow at the diseased powers infecting his beloved England.

Taking a sip from a glass of water, he cleared his throat before addressing the court.

"This is, without a doubt, an unprecedented legal situation. Normally, there is a strict adherence to the letter of the law and a protocol for legal proceedings. However, given the magnitude of this trial, and the new evidence presented, I have no other choice but to enter charges against Admiral Roy Ferguson and Lionel Hedgecock and the Far Indian Trading Company for piracy, murder, treason, and corruption."

The crowd exploded into spontaneous chatter. The courtroom was so loud, it took the judge a full minute to finally quiet it to a point so he could be heard.

"Given this new information, I can't see it in my conscience to continue with the trial of Louise Owen, who, it seems, was put in an especially precarious situation. For too long, she has been unfairly ridiculed, publicly persecuted, and falsely imprisoned. She is now free of all charges."

There was a roar from the crowd and the courtroom reached a deafening volume. People stood up, journalists rushed out the door to meet deadlines, and grown men threw their hands behind their necks with open mouths, still unable to believe what had just transpired.

They were not all that shocked to discover that Charles Owen was an innocent man, or that Louise Owen had been unfairly imprisoned.

However, no one could believe that two of the most prestigious institutions in England—the British navy and the Far Indian Trading Company—were guilty of piracy, murder, thievery, and conspiracy.

Charles and his wife hugged and tears ran down Louise's face like droplets from a water lily after a long rain. Relief did not begin to describe their emotions.

Pure elation was perhaps a more honest description.

Charles seemed to grow younger before his wife's eyes, as the pressure of the last months started to recede from his shoulders. His eyes gained back their sparkle and his lips grew full with a grin. Louise continued to cry, as she realized she wouldn't be going to prison, that David would be returned to her, and she could go back to living a normal life. Holding Charles's face in her hands, she looked into his eyes and whispered.

"Somehow, I knew you would show up."

Charles kissed her and replied.

"You won't believe the stories I have to tell you."

The judge and the bailiff took down the names of the British soldiers who had been in the courtroom. They would be detained and questioned, and then their fates would rest with the British admiralty.

Journalists rushed up to Charles and Louise for a statement.

"Charles, how does it feel to go from being Britain's most wanted man to one of our greatest patriots?" one of them asked.

"Well, I don't know about all of that—" he answered before another one interrupted.

"Where is Lieutenant Dreyfuss currently?" another asked.

Charles took a moment before answering. It would come out soon enough, so he may as well come clean.

"He is dead," he answered.

"How did he die?"

"I killed him in a duel in France."

The journalists suddenly went quiet.

"A duel?" a younger one asked.

"Unfortunately, yes."

"Brilliant! Absolutely brilliant! You can't make this stuff up!" the journalist replied before rushing away to meet with his editor.

Charles and Louise continued to answer questions for another ten minutes. They both realized it was vital to get their stories in all the British papers in order to clear their names.

After they had finally finished answering questions, they headed out of the courtroom with their arms around one another. Matthew Hatrider stopped them in the hallway.

"Matthew!" Charles exclaimed, shaking Matthew's hand.

"Darling, Matthew has been in cahoots with me to clear your name. He's put himself in great danger—and he was the one who put together the connection between Hedgecock and Ferguson."

Charles stared at Matthew and a look of complete pride and gratitude came over him. Matthew Hatrider, who had been bullied all through cadet school. The boy who everyone picked on, it turned out, was more courageous than most of the men Charles fought with.

"Well, it was nothing, really," Matthew sheepishly answered.

Charles let go of his wife and, in a fit of emotion, hugged Matthew tightly to let him know just how much he appreciated his help.

"My friend, we're going to have you over for dinner as soon as this dust settles. I want to hear all about what you and Louise have been up to."

Matthew smiled and shifted in his shoes, feeling a bit of perspiration drip down his armpits from all the excitement.

"Well, that would be wonderful," he replied, and for once, he felt like a hero.

Louise and Charles collected David from Social Services first thing and returned to their home. The next day, the front pages of all the papers, their headlines glaring in black, declared Charles an innocent man and a hero to his country. A telegram was quickly sent to Margaret informing her of the good news.

The next week, the King and Queen of England invited Charles, Louise, and David over for high tea. Charles was now the biggest celebrity in England. They couldn't possibly attend all the dinner and party invitations that found their way to their mailbox.

They declined almost all of them.

The Black Mamba led the charge against the army of resistance. His war camel, whose body was protected by bamboo armor, charged ahead. The Mamba was steeled in his approach and had Sanaa clearly in his sights— she was on a camel of her own and charging just as hard directly at the Mamba. When they were perhaps fifty yards apart, with swords raised, the Mamba was about to bring his down when he was hit in the face by a projectile of some kind. Instantly blinded, he felt himself losing his balance, and in a fit of panic, brought the reins up over his head, jerking up the camel's head and causing it to stop in its tracks.

The Mamba was thrown ten feet in the air and landed on his back. He was completely blind and felt camels' hooves trampling all around him. The ground shook and he could smell the fear and labored breath of the horses and camels that ran around his body. A group of his soldiers, including Jawad, gathered around him to protect him from the onslaught of Sanaa and the cavalry. Sanaa, not expecting the Mamba to fall, had ridden right past him into the belly of the Caid's army.

Soon, both cavalries clashed, and the hundreds of horses and camels collided into a dust bowl of rage, sweat, screaming, and cold steel. Bullets whizzed through the air and smoke from the many pistols and rifles hovered in a cloud over the desert.

The Caid's army, however, was confused and shrouded in a strange haze of yellow dust. Projectiles rained down on them from the sky, blinding many of their soldiers and creating utter chaos on the battlefield.

The Mamba finally regained some of his eyesight and stood with his massive sword still in his hands.

"What happened?" he screamed.

"Look, Sire!" Jawad yelled and pointed upwards.

The Mamba looked to the sky to see it full of hot air balloons of every color dropping improvised smoke bombs and tear gas on his army.

Up above, Tariq, Fez, and Aseem were cheering like crazy. Fez had been the one to throw down the blinder that was a direct hit on the Mamba's head. All three boys cheered wildly and began throwing bombs right and left on the many soldiers on the ground below. The bombs exploded in a cloud of yellow smoke and soon the soldiers were coughing and covering their eyes, immobilized by the tear gas. Some stopped and shot their rifles at the balloons, but the balloons were too high and out of range of the useless bullets.

Soon, the battle below raged on the ground as every horseman dismounted to engage in hand-to-hand combat. Soldiers stood only inches from each other, swinging knives and daggers of every kind. Some grappled with one another, while the most skillful of them seemed to move through the battle with ease, cutting down the enemy in their path.

"Let's hear it for air superiority!" Fez yelled, as he threw another blinder. Tariq and Aseem shouted with him and continued to throw bombs overboard.

Jack was a master at understanding the wind, and he surfed little wind pockets that allowed him to keep his balloon positioned directly over the battle. He was completely focused on piloting the balloon when he heard something in the distance. While the boys continued to throw blinders he focused his eyes to the horizon, where the sound was coming from.

At once, he saw them.

A group of four French fighter airplanes flying in formation.

And they were headed right for them.

CHAPTER
— 22 —

A NEW ENEMY

Foster Crowe sat in his tent. He smoked a pipe made of birch wood, made strong with layers of lacquer, and allowed the tobacco to drift into the tent cloth over his head. He only smoked when he was worried—which was almost never—but lately he'd been smoking his pipe every night.

Sucking on the juicy tobacco, he sat and thought.

The man from whom he had stolen the journal was named Wu Chiang. As Foster studied the journal, that name appeared multiple times, and he deduced that Wu Chiang had been born in China, lived in Europe for decades, and only recently settled in Ceylon.

He'd been poring over many books and documents for an entire week in an attempt to decipher the journal, which contained a host of diagrams and formulas and many passages written in other languages—Latin, German, French, and even Chinese. The diagrams depicted detailed plans for devices and instruments designed for two things only—death or destruction.

The bubonic plague that stretched across Europe and killed over six million people in the fourteenth century.

The Gatling gun that was now dramatically changing how wars were fought.

Deadly gases that could kill with just one whiff.

Instruments of torture made popular during the Spanish Inquisition.

He read the names of people he assumed were agents intent on spreading this evil—these instruments, inventions, and philosophies. Some of the yellowed pages dated back nearly five hundred years, kept intact by the use of some kind of preservative. None of the names were familiar to him, so he assumed these agents worked in the background manipulating others.

Even the philosophies written down in the journal took on an incredibly evil tone. The general philosophy was that only a select few in the world were allowed to rule, and everyone else must be forced to bow down to them. The writings placed an emphasis on selfishness over thinking or caring for others.

The journal went on to state that the world was there for man to rule; man could choose to protect or to destroy the world. All animals and everything found in nature only existed to serve mankind, therefore the destruction of nature was deemed acceptable. These writings taught that man was inherently meant to be ruled, and to be ruled one way only—through ruthlessness and brutality. Especially repugnant was the view that all wild animals were vile and should be vanquished. That only mankind was civilized—anything else was considered to be uncivilized and unworthy of respect or sustainability.

Most disturbingly, the journal sketched out a kind of blueprint on how to create fear and insecurity in people. How to turn them against others, with the goal of having them become utterly obedient and subservient to one master. In chilling detail, the journal described exactly how to turn people into monsters who would kill and destroy without a second thought.

Foster wiped his eyes in disbelief at what he was reading. This was a master plan for self-destruction, either through war or through the decimation of the world and its natural surroundings.

The journal began to speak of modern times. He wrote down the names and dates of politicians and countries. Some of the sentences didn't made sense. Words like "civil unrest," "conspiracy," and "civilian manipulation."

When it suddenly all fit together.

This evil plan had been in formation for decades.

Foster could see it right in front of him.

Many countries were mentioned, but Germany above all others.

There was a map to create a world war unlike any the world had ever seen. It would make other wars look like mere skirmishes.

A war that could mean tens of millions of deaths.

Foster created a timeline and it all made sense.

It was ingenious.

After considering his options, he decided what must be done. He did not know when he might encounter Wu Chiang again, so he decided he must be killed as soon as possible. He sensed that Wu Chiang was as great a threat to the Red Hand as had ever walked the earth.

He had no choice but to go. He would leave by himself the following morning and return to the temple. He always hunted his foes by himself, as nobody else in camp was near his equal in martial arts, and he didn't want to be responsible for anyone else's death.

A voice came from outside asking to enter the tent. Foster put the journal in his top desk drawer and told the person to enter.

"A bit of tea, sir?"

It was Melgrave, a faithful servant to Foster. Melgrave was of Serbian descent—tall, old, and always wore a tuxedo. In fact, Foster could not recall one instance where Melgrave had not been dressed in a tuxedo.

"That would be perfect Melgrave, please set it down," Foster answered and motioned for Melgrave to put the tray on his desk. Melgrave obediently followed his instructions and placed the brown bamboo tray on the large desk. Adding a generous amount of black tea leaves to a small porcelain cup, Melgrave slowly drew a stream of water over the leaves, filling the cup to the brim, and allowing the tea leaves to begin soaking and releasing their flavor. Ceylon produced the best tea leaves in the world, and Foster had taken a liking to three or four cups of tea a day.

Just his one small cup instantly filled the tent with the pleasant aroma of freshly brewed tea and it brought a bit of relief to Foster.

"Hold on Melgrave, I'm going to fetch some biscuits from my other quarters," he said and stood up to leave the tent.

"Very well, sir," Melgrave replied while continuing to stir the tea.

Foster exited the tent into the Ceylon night and headed over to a small wagon where he kept many of his personal items and found a package of butter cookies that had arrived just that day from Australia. Foster dearly missed the comforts of home and it had taken this parcel almost two months to finally reach him. In it he found boxes and boxes of butter cookies, blackberry jam, toffee, and a host of other treats not available in Ceylon.

Grabbing the cookies, he suddenly felt a twinge in his neck. A sudden feeling of foreboding came over him. He tried to ignore it, but the feeling was so powerful, he had to sit down and take deep breaths for a few moments to regain his composure. Locking the door to the wagon behind him, he had a most awful feeling as he walked back to his tent.

Upon opening his tent flap, he suddenly understood the cause of his pain and the menacing feeling he'd had.

On the ground was Melgrave, spread out on his stomach, with a broken teacup at his lips.

"Melgrave!" he screamed and rushed to his side. Putting his right index finger to his neck, Foster felt no movement where Melgrave's pulse should have been. Turning him over, he straddled his body and began pumping up and down on his chest in an effort to revive him. He quickly began mouth-to-mouth resuscitation.

He continued for two full minutes, but it was useless.

Melgrave was dead.

Looking at the broken teacup, it was obvious what had killed him.

Someone had poisoned the tea and had intended it for Foster. Melgrave probably tasted it to ensure it had steeped properly, as he usually did for Foster.

That simple act of generosity had cost Melgrave his life.

The poison used must have been odorless and colorless and powerful enough to kill a grown man in a matter of seconds after just one sip. Only an advanced apothecary could have concocted such a poison.

Thoughts began rushing through Foster's head as he leapt to his desk and opened the top drawer.

The journal was gone!

Stolen!

Whoever had tried to poison him had stolen the journal and made off with it before finishing the job on Foster.

Wu Chiang was onto Foster and his circus.

They were no longer anonymous.

CHAPTER
— *23* —

SOMETHING ABOUT THE NEIGHBORS

Adeer bolted once it saw Margaret and Alice, jumping over a log and disappearing into the woods. They had been stalking it for half an hour.

"Darn!" Alice exclaimed and they both laughed.

They had decided to spend a Saturday finding animal tracks and attempting to find the responsible animal—a game taught to Margaret by her father to make their hikes more interesting.

By midday, they had walked over eight miles from Saint Catherine's, deep into their valley, when they found themselves overlooking a red farmhouse they hadn't seen previously. It was beautiful, with white trim, and a large stack of hay outside the northernmost wall. Smoke billowed from the chimney and it was obvious someone was home. A barn was next to the house.

"I've heard rumors there are strangers in that farmhouse. Nobody knows them. Even Sister Anne seemed concerned," Alice said.

"What kind of rumors?" Margaret asked.

"Just that nobody knows who has moved in…it's all very secretive."

"Hmmm…do you want to investigate? Perhaps introduce ourselves?"

"Of course! Life has been a bit boring around here since your father left."

They walked a quarter mile down a hill and, as they approached the house, Margaret thought she heard voices coming from the barn.

Walking closer, they both heard the same sound.

An unmistakably male voice.

An unmistakably German male voice.

Alice and Margaret both stopped and looked at one another. The Germans had been on everyone's mind, as the Kaiser was making threats of war against France and other European countries.

They carefully stepped into a shadow outside the barn and listened further.

It was most certainly German they heard. Margaret only understood a smattering of the language and she picked up words like "thank you," "please," and "Monday."

There were two distinct voices, both of them male. They continued to talk loudly and then exited the barn and disappeared into the farmhouse.

"Those are Germans! Are you game for seeing what's inside that barn?" Margaret asked, excited by the prospect of a challenge.

"Okay...but we have to be quick!" Alice replied, with more than a little nervousness. She wasn't as bold as Margaret or Inez, but she wasn't going to play chicken now.

Alice and Margaret slipped inside the barn. It was almost completely empty. There weren't any horses, or any sign that someone was living there. The only thing in the barn was a small table in the left corner with some plates of food and some papers on it.

It was a place setting for lunch.

Obviously the two men were planning to have lunch outside and had just slipped into the house for a moment to prepare their food.

The girls stole a look at the papers on the table. There were dozens of them, and all of them were in German. Acting quickly, Margaret grabbed what looked the most important document—a map with markings and some handwriting at the bottom. Stuffing it into her pocket, she heard the two men coming out of the farmhouse, laughing and making their way back to the barn.

They couldn't go out the way they came in or they would both be seen for sure!

They spotted a large barn door at the opposite end of the building and both girls sprinted for it.

It was locked, with a chain draped across the opening through the barn door handle.

However, there might be just enough space to squeeze through.

First Alice tried—she felt the door close in tightly on her stomach and had to hold her breath to fit through. She barely made it, and then

Margaret had to try to fit. She heard the men's voices grow louder and could tell they were only a few feet from the entrance. If they walked in now, they would see Margaret trying to squeeze through the door, and then they would both be caught.

Margaret was stuck! She couldn't fit through!

Margaret tried harder and harder to squeeze her body through, and was sure the men were going to see her, when inexplicably, they stopped. She heard one of them say something, and then the other man turned to go back to the house.

It gave her just a couple of seconds more.

With all of her strength, and with some help from Alice, she forced her body through the door and tumbled to the ground. Both she and Alice leaned up against the wall, out of breath and wide eyed with excitement.

"I guess I need to go on a diet," Margaret whispered and Alice almost giggled out loud.

As the two men sat down to lunch, Alice and Margaret carefully made their escape—away from the barn and into the neighboring trees. Circling around, they were careful not to be spotted.

They made their way back to the school before nightfall and up in their room, they gathered the other girls around Margaret's bed. Producing the piece of paper from her pocket, Margaret spread it out evenly on the bed and stared at it.

"We need someone who can speak German," Inez proclaimed and the other girls agreed.

"Where is Sophie? She can read it, I think," Etienne asked.

"She's helping with dinner," Margaret answered.

"Well, go get her!" Inez ordered with excitement.

Margaret disappeared to the kitchen and soon returned with an exasperated Sophie.

"Okay, what is this emergency? I'm going to get a scolding for sure," Sophie said, clearly annoyed at being pulled away.

"We need you to read something," Inez said and pulled Sophie to the bed.

"What does this map say?"

Sophie grew quiet as she picked up the document. She stayed quiet as she studied it. Her face contorted with worry as she read it three times over.

"Where did you get this?" she asked, clearly interested in the map.

"We stole it, now what does it say?" Alice replied, clearly excited as to the secrets behind the document.

"It's a map," Sophie answered and all the girls groaned.

"We know it's a map, but what does it say?" Inez pleaded.

"It's not clear exactly. The marking points are points of entry. It says something about ammunition storage and the dotted lines stand for trenches."

Sophie stopped to examine the document further.

"It says, 'The Kaiser is awaiting your report.'"

All the girls grew quiet.

"Do you know what this is?" Sophie asked.

Nobody answered.

"These are German plans to invade France. Where did you get this?" she asked and she grew very stern and serious.

"From a barn next to a farmhouse about seven or eight miles away," Margaret answered slowly.

"It's a spy document! So it's true, there *are* German spies in France," Inez exclamed, her eyes full of mischief.

"Inez, this is serious. We must alert Sister Anne. In the meantime, nobody goes near that farmhouse. Do you understand me?" Sophie ordered.

The girls all nodded their heads, except Inez, who didn't answer. She seemed lost in thought, almost distant and detached.

CHAPTER
— 24 —

THE SCENT GROWS COLD

Foster Crowe hiked back to the temple where he had first encountered Wu Chiang.

After watching the temple from hidden spots for the better part of an hour, he hadn't yet seen any movements. Foster had just decided to hike to the front of the temple when a sixth sense came over him.

Something, or someone, was warning him.

Stopping in his tracks, he looked around and then noticed something peculiar in the ground. The ground had a small indentation.

As if someone had planted something there.

Taking out his knife, he dug in a circle around the indentation, and in a few moments, his knife hit something hard and metallic.

Foster proceeded to carefully dig up this metallic object, reach underneath it, and then slowly pull it out and place it on the ground. It was only about a foot square, but it was heavy and relatively thick. On the top was a type of trigger.

Foster studied it. His familiarity with the Red Hand Scrolls had given him a keen understanding of mechanical objects. Whoever had designed this had the same understanding, as it was a modern device not usually seen by the civilized world.

Foster walked back about thirty feet, found a few small rocks, and proceeded to lob them at the device. The first two rocks missed their marks, but the third landed directly on top of the device.

Instantly, a loud explosion rocked the ground and threw Foster off his feet.

"Some kind of land bomb," he thought to himself.

Foster continued his walk to the front of the temple, his leather Clarks hiking boots making their way in the mud and grass as he scanned the ground for any more indentations.

He found six more on his journey to the front of the temple. Guessing that the front door might be booby-trapped as well, he made his way to the northernmost wall and scaled it, allowing his fingertips to easily grip the many brick edges, until he reached the roof. Once on the roof of the temple, he made his way on his belly to a hole in the center of the roof that went all the way to the floor. The hole was ten-foot by ten-foot square, and was used to collect rainwater and to allow sunlight into the temple.

Jumping down, Foster was now inside. As he stepped onto the floor, he noticed something flash before his eyes down low. Kneeling down, he saw it was a string stretched out across the room, about six inches above the ground—obviously another booby trap.

Carefully stepping over the string, Foster looked for others but saw none. Making his way down the hallway, he went to the room where he had stolen Wu Chiang's journal on his last visit to the temple.

It was completely empty!

Wu Chiang had obviously vacated the temple and attempted to kill Foster on his way out of town.

Where he was, and where he was going, was a complete mystery.

The trail had grown cold.

A shipping freighter was leaving Colombo harbor just before dawn one morning. The ship was long and wide, with her trim painted dark red. Smoke billowed from her two smokestacks as she edged away from the pier and headed out to sea.

A man sat below deck. His was in a small and cramped cabin. A bed, topped with a hard mattress with broken springs, sat in one corner. In another corner, there was a brown chest with a copper lock. The only light in the room came from a lantern on a small desk at the center wall.

A rat scurried across the room and a spider descended from a thread down to the floor. The smell of the sea came through a small porthole just above the desk.

The man sat at the desk writing in a notebook. He was a small but overweight man with round spectacles. His face was that of a boy, but on a man's body. Dipping his pen in black ink, he slowly wrote on the paper in long, flowing cursive letters. Periodically he would look at an open book in front of him, flip through some pages, and continue to write.

His skin was pasty and he sweat constantly. A bit of perspiration dripped from his large, full lower lip down to the roll of fat on his neck. Wiping his perspiration with an ever-present handkerchief, the man continued to write and flip through the pages.

This was the man named Wu Chiang.

The journal he was writing in was the same one that Foster Crowe had once possessed.

He spent almost the entire journey sequestered in his cabin writing, asking that his meals be left outside his door, rarely venturing to the deck of the ship during daylight hours.

The ship's destination was the seaport of Bremen.

In Germany.

Inez lay by herself watching the farmhouse below her.

Her red hair, brushed to one side, framed her many freckles. Although she was French, many mistook her for being Irish because of her red hair and fair complexion. Raised only by her mother and older brother, she learned from a young age to be tough and self-determined. She had always been the best athlete in her school and a constant troublemaker in the classroom.

Not a natural student, she barely managed to make the necessary grades to remain at Saint Catherine's. She saw school as an intrusion to the more important things in life such as playing football, fishing, skiing, and exploring the beautiful mountain regions around her. The other girls were exasperated with her natural athleticism and were envious that Inez could easily be the best at any sport without so much as practicing an hour.

It was also understood that Inez was the toughest one in the school, and that more than once she had knocked another girl down for what she perceived as injustices. For instance, if anyone made fun of her freckles or red hair, they could expect a good sock in the nose—as she was most sensitive about those two traits.

Today Inez was alone because she had decided that being stuck in a classroom on such a beautiful day was a waste; and besides, these Germans required watching at all times—in spite of the orders from Sophie.

So she had played hooky and ventured off alone with her "spying" supplies, as she called them: a black notebook and pencil, binoculars, and a lunch of apples and cheese.

For two hours she watched the farmhouse. Her notebook sat on the grass in front of her and she took fastidious notes.

10:00. No movement.

10:10. No movement.

10:20. No movement.

Normally, she couldn't sit still for two hours for anything. But, she loved spying and she pictured herself as a French resistance spy and imagined that the safety of her country depended on her learning the secrets of these Germans. More than anything else, she wanted to catch these Germans in the act of...something!

Finally, close to noon, two trucks rumbled down the dirt road and parked in front of the farmhouse. These were very large trucks with huge canopies on the back. Cloth was thrown over the canopy to prevent anyone from seeing the contents of the truck. Inez perked up with anticipation as two men emerged from the cab of each truck, opened up the back, and began unloading crates. Two other men came out of the farmhouse to help.

Inez used her binoculars to look at the crates. They were very big and made of wood. Most were closed, but a few were open and she could see what looked like cable spilling out. Another was marked "Transistor—Fragile" in huge black ink on the outside of the box. There were so many crates it took the better part of an hour to unload them all.

Inez wrote in her notebook:

Cables and transistor? Are Germans preparing a wire to communicate instructions to the Kaiser?

Watching the farmhouse, she thought she heard something from behind her. She shrugged it off—it was probably just a rabbit or a raccoon. She continued to stare at the farmhouse with her binoculars when suddenly, something blocked her view.

Lowering the binoculars, she raised her head up and a man's face stared right back at her. His face was square and three days' growth dotted his jaw.

His eyes were mean and fierce.

Before she could say anything, she felt something hit her head.

After that, she wouldn't remember anything.

For the next week, Foster scoured the docks and talked to every ship captain or dockworker he could find. He asked them all if they had seen an Asian man about a week ago. He didn't have a clear description of what Wu Chiang looked like—all he could say was that he was probably Asian and was likely traveling alone.

Finally, an old dockhand mentioned that he remembered seeing an Asian man about a week ago. He had been alone and carried a trunk. The dockhand described the man he saw on the docks as being slightly overweight, with thick glasses and a pudgy face, sweating profusely. Foster even sketched a face to the man's description in his notepad.

"Where did he go?" Foster asked.

"Let's see, that would have been pier 48. That ship would have gone to Bremen, Germany. I remember because the words all over the crates were in German."

"Is that all?" Foster asked.

The man thought hard.

"Well, just one more thing," he replied.

"What is it?"

"He was a peculiar fellow. I got a very bad feeling from him. He didn't say much of anything and seemed in a great hurry. I guess that's why I remember him. He gave orders not to be disturbed. The only Asian men I usually see are workers, so I thought it odd to see an Asian passenger."

"You got a bad feeling?"

"Yes, a real bad feeling. That, I definitely remember. Like I was sick in the stomach. I didn't like him, not one bit."

"Bremen, Germany you say?"

"Yes sir."

"Any idea when the next ship might be leaving for Germany?" Foster asked.

"Well, no other ships leave for Germany for another two weeks. But, a freighter leaves for Amsterdam in three days."

"Thank you," Foster said and quickly departed.

CHAPTER
— 25 —

A MOMENT IN ETERNITY

Caid Ali Tamzali was panicking. As he surveyed the battlefield, everywhere he looked was covered in the yellow gas. His troops were disorganized and spread out, no longer in formation of any kind. He yelled multiple directions that just confused his troops even more. Straight ahead, the fighting continued, and his army was holding its ground, but could they last? If they could not, he might be cut to shreds. From his position, he would wait and watch, and if the fighting came close to him, he would retreat with his royal guard.

He fired some shots at the hot air balloons above him, but they were out of range. Some of the tear gas hit his eyes and he screamed out in pain, dropped his rifle, and began rubbing his eyes in desperation. It stung like someone had poured chili peppers directly into the whites of his eyes. While focusing on rubbing his eyes, he lost his balance and slid off his camel. The camel, startled, bolted and ran in the opposite direction. The Caid dropped to his knees and continued to rub his eyes; one of his guards rushed to his side with a canteen of water and splashed some into his burning eyes. This helped some, and as the burning slowly subsided, the Caid regained full use of his eyesight.

Up ahead, perhaps sixty yards, the fighting was fierce, as both armies rushed at one another with full force and vigor. The Black Mamba had recovered from his fall and struck down his opponents with ease as he cut through the crowd. On the other side, Zijuan and Sanaa were crushing their foes at a similar rate, as none of the Caid's soldiers were a match for them. Backs to each other, they parried blows and thrust steel into unprotected bellies. All around them, swords flashed through the air and the smell of sweat, fear, adrenaline, and blood was everywhere. Bullets whizzed past them, but at this point in the battle, the majority of the fighting was hand-to-hand combat.

Melbourne Jack gave the other balloons the order to dive—they needed to descend before the airplanes could reach them. Each balloon had a rifle, and some of the soldiers prepared their rifle sights at the airplanes rather than continuing to rain down bombs on the battle below.

Jack, however, decided to power up his balloon in the hope of attracting some of the planes and diverting them from the other balloons.

"Tariq, I want you to navigate, take the rope!" he ordered, tossing the rope to Tariq.

As Tariq pulled down hard, the propane lit up and the balloon instantly started to rise towards the clouds. Melbourne Jack took one rifle for himself and handed another to Aseem.

"Wait until I tell you, then aim for the space in front of the plane. Don't shoot at where it is, shoot where it will be!" Jack ordered. His voice was loud and direct and the boys could hear how serious he was.

"Tariq, power up and see if we can reach that batch of clouds. We will make a much more difficult target in the clouds!"

Tariq continued to pull hard on the cord, and the balloon continued to rise, making its way towards some white and fluffy altocumulus clouds that were approximately a half-mile away.

Jack watched as the rest of the balloons descended towards the battle below. Muzzle fire could be seen coming from the basket of most of the balloons. One balloon lost control, went into a terrible spin, and crashed hard right into the middle of the battlefield. The others made a slower descent, attempting to stay above the battle to continue an air assault on the Caid.

Three of the planes followed the other balloons. One, however, decided to follow Jack into the clouds.

Jack watched as the plane came more clearly into view, close enough to see the leather helmet worn by the pilot and the plane's yellow finish. He was even able to recognize it as an early model Morane-Saulnier H, a very fast and agile single-seater. However, it was not especially outfitted for war. It lacked a mounted machine gun or even a crewman to fire.

The pilot, armed only with a revolver, fired at Jack and the boys, missing them on that attempt.

The plane continued to rise, and it was only fifty yards from the clouds when Jack and Tariq saw it come into sharper focus. The pilot maneuvered just above the balloon and then dove straight at them, turning away at the last possible second. The pilot came so close to the balloon basket that Tariq clearly saw that he had a brown moustache and was wearing black leather gloves.

The basket rocked back and forth as the plane passed by them. In fact, the rocking action saved them, as the pilot took dead aim at Jack's head and fired three rounds. Bouncing around in the basket, Jack was a moving target. The first bullet passed just under his chin and he ducked down into the basket before the other two passed harmlessly over him.

Standing up, he and Aseem quickly fired four rifle shots at the rear of the plane to no effect.

Drifting into the clouds, the balloon was now completely covered in white mist. They literally couldn't see three feet in front of them.

"Reload, Aseem! Tariq, see if you can stall us and keep us in these clouds for a bit. He'd be a fool to come after us in this soup!"

But a fool he was.

Soon, the boys heard the roar of the airplane in the clouds around them. The buzzing continued to get louder. Aseem and Jack were at the ready, positioned at either side of the basket, when out of nowhere, the white mist parted and suddenly the tips of the airplane's wings were only fifteen feet from the basket.

Firing wildly, Aseem managed to graze the paint, but that was all.

The French pilot, however, was much more accurate and managed to hit the fuel valve on the balloon.

Instantly, the propane tank shot up a huge, uncontrollable flame, and the balloon started to rise very high at an alarmingly fast rate.

"Tariq, slow us down! We want to stay in the clouds!" Jack ordered.

"I can't, it's broken!" Tariq replied.

Jack looked down and saw that the bullet had managed to completely rip off the top part of the propane release. It's a miracle, he thought, they hadn't burst into a giant ball of flames. If the bullet had hit three inches lower, it would have been curtains.

Jack tried to slow down the propane, but it was no use. There was absolutely no way to stop it from burning. The flame burned in full force, and they continued to rise at maximum rate. Soon, they were out of the clouds and headed up into the sky.

Looking below, Jack saw the plane emerge from the clouds, make a circle, and then begin climbing towards them.

The balloon was in a suicide climb, with no way to stop.

The French pilot would be on them any minute.

Sanaa continued to parry and fight, and her sword was crimson from her many victims.

"Sanaa, I'm going to move towards the Caid!" Zijuan yelled, and Sanaa nodded in agreement. Soon, Zijuan made her way through the crowds of soldiers, slicing her way through, until after a moment, Sanaa could no longer see her.

Shouting out orders, Sanaa was satisfied with their progress until suddenly, many of her soldiers fell back and some even retreated.

What was happening?

Why were they running?

Soon enough, Sanaa saw the answer.

The Black Mamba emerged from the crowd only twenty feet in front of her, and cut down two of her compatriots as he approached. The others backed away from him. Seeing Sanaa, he walked straight towards her, ignoring the other soldiers as he brought his sword in front of him, ready to fight.

His impressive body was covered in sweat and blood, and his eyes seemed to foam in anger. His extensive scars made him even more foreboding, and for a minute, even Sanaa thought of running away.

"I should have finished you when I left you to die in the desert," the Mamba screamed, walking to within six feet of her, putting his left foot forward, and raising his sword over his right shoulder like an axe.

"I should have fought you when I had the chance!" Sanaa screamed, and swung her sword with full force right at the Mamba's head. The Mamba, anticipating the blow, easily blocked it and countered with a swipe of his own, missing just two inches above Sanaa's head.

Like two full-grown lions, they pawed and sliced and swung at one another.

He is so strong! Sanaa thought, and decided she would need to use her agility to keep away from him. If she tried to fight him straight on, she didn't know if she would have the strength to deflect his blows. So she kept just out of range of his sword and counterattacked when she got an opening. The problem was, his long arms made it very difficult for Sanaa to land any attacking blows. He was also so fast that Sanaa barely had a chance to repel one strike before another was on her.

The fighting raged around them. With Sanaa now battling the Mamba, the resistance fighters found time to regroup and form a minor offensive. Around them, many hot air balloons crashed to the ground and bullets from the aircraft rained down. However, from their positions above the battle, the pilots weren't easily able to determine which soldiers fought for which side, so they shot just as many of the Caid's soldiers as resistance soldiers.

Sanaa and the Mamba fought on, with Sanaa playing more and more defense as his strength began to overwhelm her. He was so aggressive and filled with such anger that she had given up even trying to launch a counteroffensive. All she could do was to continue to ward off his many blows and play defense with dexterity.

As she retreated slightly, she felt herself starting to tire. Just then, without warning, her feet crumbled beneath her and she suddenly felt herself falling through the air and then landing on her feet on soft ground. The force of the fall was such that she had to bend her knees and roll to break her fall.

The Mamba had moved her so far backwards that they were now on the edge of the battlefield. Sanaa had fallen into a hole that she hadn't seen. The hole was surrounded by soft sand that was unable to hold her weight.

Gaining her composure, Sanaa stood up and saw the Mamba directly opposite her. They had both fallen into a cavern and were now about ten feet underground. It was a very small space, perhaps fifteen feet square, and Sanaa realized she would now have to fight in close quarters. There was no escape, as there were thick walls of stone going straight up on all sides of her.

She would have nowhere to run to be able to fight her kind of fight.

She would have to go straight at the Mamba, meeting his strength head on.

Covered with dirt and dust and sweat, she raised her sword just as the Mamba swung his sword at her head in a series of six blows. Somehow she managed to stay on her feet and move out of the way.

The Mamba was smiling at her.

"Nowhere to run now, Sanaa," he said, raising his sword to strike again.

Sanaa, now very tired, began to feel scared. She knew she was no match for the Mamba head on and his strength would eventually overwhelm her in such tight quarters.

She steeled herself and prepared for another onslaught.

Zijuan moved through the many soldiers like a leopard slicing through a thicket of long grass. Quick and deceptive, she easily deflected any attacks that came her way.

She had one objective and one objective only—to kill the Caid.

Kill the head and the body will fall.

She knew if she could kill the Caid, then his army might retreat once they realized he was dead. With their leadership gone, many of the soldiers could simply give up.

Crouching down, she clearly saw him up ahead. He had managed to get back on his camel and was directing the movements around him.

Zijuan drew her knife and launched it at the Caid's head. Her dagger was going straight for his nose when, at the last minute, he moved and it just missed him.

Turning his head, the Caid saw the unmistakable figure of Zijuan heading for him.

"Get her!" he ordered, and suddenly four soldiers surrounded Zijuan. They circled her the way a pack of wolves surrounds an innocent fawn.

One produced a revolver and took a shot at Zijuan. She ducked away from it, and in one swift movement, plunged her sword into the chest of her assailant, dropping him to the sand.

Moving in sweeping circles and motions, she was so fast and efficient that the Caid's soldiers barely had a chance to react.

In a matter of moments, she had taken them all down.

The Caid, visibly shaken, saw that Zijuan was better than his best and decided to do what all bullies do in a time of crisis.

He turned tail and ran.

Urging on his camel, he retreated from the battle and headed back to his kasbah at full speed.

Zijuan, seeing that the Caid was fleeing, ran to one of his soldiers on a camel, launched herself up and knocked the man down. Taking the reins, she turned the camel towards the Caid and urged it into a full gallop.

The two figures raced away from the battle and across the desert. The Caid had perhaps a minute's head start.

A fighter pilot, seeing what was happening from above, turned his plane and headed straight for Zijuan.

He would be on her in a matter of seconds. Aiming his revolver, he steadied his hand and focused his sight clearly on her head, which was bobbing up and down on the galloping camel.

The boys' balloon kept rising into the atmosphere with no way to stop. The plane was headed straight for them as Aseem and Jack fixed their rifles on the engine. They would have range and the possibility of getting off two shots each before the pilot reached them. Aseem squeezed off a shot that missed completely and then Jack pulled the trigger on his rifle. His bullet managed to hit a wing but did no real damage.

Aseem reloaded and brought the rifle to his shoulder. As he did so, he thought of his life, of being abandoned by his family, of being a slave in the kasbah, and of everything he had been through. He focused his rifle tightly on the small engine that powered the propeller. He did not want to die today. He wanted to live and go on to a better life.

Feeling his finger across the steel of the trigger, Aseem continued to focus on the plane, anticipating where it would be when he fired. The rifle butt dug sharply into his shoulder, but he relaxed, breathed, and squeezed the trigger.

The bullet sped out of the rifle's barrel and found its mark!

Instantly, black smoke poured out of the engine as it sputtered and whined and gargled.

Then it seized up and stopped completely.

The plane, with black smoke flowing out of the front, crossed right in front of them and began plummeting to earth.

"Nice shot, Aseem!" Jack said and slapped him on the shoulder.

The plane screamed towards the ground, picking up more and more speed as it fell. There was nothing to be done—it was in a straight nosedive. The French plane fell to the earth like a shooting star and crashed to the ground in a fireball of red and orange flames and black smoke.

That crisis averted, they still had a major problem. Their balloon continued to go straight up in the sky with absolutely no way to stop. Suddenly, they felt a huge jolt—the balloon was being tossed about and the basket began to violently swing back and forth.

"We're in a wind pocket. Hold on tightly, boys!" Jack instructed and all of them held onto the basket with both hands. The basket kicked and swung and the balloon continued to rise higher and higher into the atmosphere. Looking down, they could see the earth becoming smaller and smaller. Before too long, they couldn't even see the battle raging below them. Not only were they going up, they were drifting farther and farther away.

"What's going to happen?" Tariq asked Jack.

Jack was continuing to try to figure out some kind of clamp or seal to slow the flow of propane, but it was impossible.

"We're going to run out of fuel, and then we're going to start falling. There's no way I can stop it!" Jack replied and, instantly, all three boys felt a chill go up their spines. They understood what Jack was saying to them.

They were going to fall to their deaths from miles and miles above the earth.

Sanaa was backed into a corner. The Mamba continued to slash and hack and push her backwards. Bending her knees and using all of her weight, she deflected his blows as best she could. Moving rapidly, Sanaa kept trying to escape, but the Mamba was an excellent swordsman and cut off any escape route.

She was trapped.

How can I defeat someone who is so strong? I know I can beat him, but I cannot find his weakness!

As the Mamba stepped backwards, he seemed to be confused as to the best way to finish her. He still had to be mindful of her ability, as she was almost as good with a sword as he. One wrong move and he might pay with his life.

Suddenly, the Mamba sent an overhand thrust down towards Sanaa's head. She was forced to block it with one hand, and it took all of her strength just to stay on her feet. He continued this attack with four more swings at her head, and the last one finally forced her to her knees. Once down, she would be at a complete disadvantage.

After two more blows, she was completely backed into a corner with her back against the cavern wall. Her muscles were screaming with agony and sweat dripped down her face, stinging her eyes. Her lungs heaved, and her heart was beating relentlessly as her black hair fell down over her face.

The Mamba would not relent.

He grew frustrated with her resistance. Moving closer, he moved his legs a bit wider to gain leverage for a more powerful blow.

That's when she saw her opportunity.

As the Mamba brought his sword up, Sanaa pushed off the wall with her right leg and rolled in a somersault between the Mamba's legs. He was now behind her back, but they were almost touching. Quickly and blindly she thrust her sword between her torso and her armpit.

Directly into the small of the Mamba's back.

Sanaa had plunged her sword deeply and accurately to the spot just above the Mamba's tailbone where a bundle of nerve endings met in a tangled mass. She felt the sword go in deep, then removed it, and performed another somersault across the tiny room.

Spinning around, she saw the Mamba quickly fall to one knee, grunting with pain.

It had been a very deep cut.

As he stood, he screamed in blinding pain and anger and tried to charge at Sanaa, but the pain in his back was sharp and agonizing. He stumbled in his tracks, held his weight on his sword, and stared at her, seething.

The Mamba should have known right then that he had been beaten, but his ego and his pride prevailed. He refused to believe that he could ever be beaten by a man, much less a woman.

Trying to bring his left foot forward, he felt himself falling once again.

Sanaa circled him the way a cat circles an injured mouse, almost playing with him. Her expression was blank and hard as she watched her greatest adversary stumble to his knees. Her mind was blank. She did not think of Malik. She did not think of anything.

She simply watched him.

After three more tries he finally rose to his feet, clumsily raised his sword, and turned to meet her.

In one movement, her sword moved in for the kill and plunged into the Mamba's heart—a cut so hard and vicious and accurate that the blade emerged through the skin on his back.

Just as quickly, she removed the blade and circled out of harm's way.

The Mamba let out a gurgling sound, grabbed his heart, and stumbled forward on his stomach. His enormous body landed hard on the dirt, and his arms were spread out like a snow angel.

Sanaa stood over him, breathing heavily, her mouth open, staring in disbelief at what she was seeing. Her face was covered with dirt and sweat and her long, black hair stuck to her cheeks. Her heart pounded in her chest and her fingers trembled. She had overcome as tough an adversary as she could ever face—a man much stronger than she, with skills to match her own.

Yet she had beaten him.

She had beaten him through sheer will.

Watching the body for two full minutes, she finally composed herself enough to gingerly walk over and kick his leg, as if she didn't really believe he was dead.

But dead he was.

Turning him over, she took the Mamba's sword and secured it on her back, along with her own.

Then she began climbing up the wall and back into the battle.

Zijuan heard the plane and ducked low into her saddle. She felt a shot ring out over her head and another passed just in front of her. The plane screamed by overhead and in a few seconds, she distantly heard it begin its turn for another pass.

She would need to take the Caid—and take him soon.

Urging on her camel, she hoped since she was lighter than the Caid, this difference in weight would make up some time. Sure enough, she gradually edged closer to the Caid and was now only ten feet behind him. Hearing the airplane behind her, she could feel the pilot flying low to the ground off to her right. Pulling on her reins, she put herself directly between the plane and the Caid. She made herself very tall and listened for the crack of the gunshot.

Almost immediately she heard the gun blast and instantly ducked down low.

The bullet missed her by just inches, and up ahead, she saw the Caid suddenly arch his back, throw up his hands, and tumble off his camel.

As she had hoped, the bullet missed her and struck the Caid directly in the back.

The plane buzzed by her and Zijuan clearly saw the exasperated and surprised expression on the pilot's face.

He had killed the Caid!

The pilot no longer wanted anything to do with Zijuan—and certainly did not want to be found responsible for killing the Caid—so he turned the plane and flew off to rejoin the battle.

Zijuan stopped her camel well ahead of where the Caid had fallen, dismounted, and walked back where his body lay. Like Sanaa had been with the Mamba, Zijuan was in a state of disbelief that the Caid might be dying, or actually dead. He had been such a force for so long that he seemed immortal to her.

Walking slowly back to where the Caid had fallen, with her sword drawn, she came to find a dying man struggling to hold on to the last bit of his life.

He looked at her with one last dying gasp under the hot desert sun. As she stared at his face one last time, his black eyes seemed to lose all life. He was gone. Zijuan acted quickly. She took the crimson scarf from his neck, rolled it up, and placed it carefully in her right pocket. This was the Caid's scarf—having it in her possession would act as proof that he was dead. She then grabbed his sword and walked back to her camel, securing the sword safely behind her.

She mounted her camel and began riding hard, back to her fellow fighters. Up ahead, the battle raged in full glory as both armies continued to fight and claw at one another.

Riding to the outskirts of the battlefield, she stayed on her camel and in a quiet gesture of victory, raised the Caid's sword above her, holding it high above her head in her right hand. In her left hand, she raised his crimson scarf for all to see. Soon, some of the Caid's soldiers began to notice Zijuan with the Caid's sword and scarf, and suddenly stopped fighting.

This had a domino effect, as soldiers from both sides stopped fighting and turned to stare at Zijuan. Within moments, the entire battlefield was silent.

"Your Caid is dead!" she screamed.

One soldier screamed at her in defiance and charged at her camel. Anticipating such a reaction, with her left hand she reached down for her dagger and flung it right into the assailant's left leg—instantly disabling him.

"Many of you are fighting against your will. Many of you were kidnapped and forced to fight a war against your own people. You no longer have to be afraid. You can choose to throw down your weapons and return to your homes. Or, you may choose to fight alongside us— the true patriots of Morocco!" Zijuan screamed, still breathing deeply, adrenaline surging through her veins.

The Caid's soldiers looked stunned. Normally, the Black Mamba would be the first to scold them and whip them into shape. But he was nowhere to be found. Without the Mamba or the Caid, the army had no one to lead them.

"Where is the Mamba?" they whispered.

"He must be dead as well, or he would be among us," they surmised. Murmurs went through the crowd as soldiers figured out that both the Caid and Mamba were dead.

One by one, some of the soldiers dropped their weapons and walked off the battlefield. In moments, others joined them. Before too long, there were almost no soldiers left in the Caid's army. Without the

Mamba terrorizing them, many felt compelled to simply walk away. A few stayed and joined the resistance.

Watching this scene unfold, Jawad burst into tears. Everything he had wanted in life was now being taken from him. All the power he once held was now disappearing in front of his eyes.

And then he saw her.

Sanaa, standing with her back to Jawad, held the Mamba's sword triumphantly overhead.

His master really was dead.

Drawing a knife, Jawad ran at Sanaa from behind. Raising the dagger high, he was determined to avenge his master's death by killing the one who had killed him.

He was almost on her when she easily moved to one side, stuck out her foot, and tripped him to the ground.

"I remember you. You are the one who escaped our camp after we cared for you, and then you revealed our whereabouts to the Caid," she said to him coldly.

Jawad, lying on his belly, covered in dust, looked up at Sanaa with rage in his eyes.

"You are nothing but a peasant! I was destined for greatness and now I have nothing! Why don't you just kill me?"

Sanaa watched him and for a moment almost felt sorry for him. He was such a confused and pitiful boy.

"I don't kill children," she replied and simply walked away.

Jawad lay in the sand crying and feeling every bit the lost orphan. All his power and riches were being taken from him. His great plan—to gain power by joining the Caid—was now lost.

He was nobody once again.

Zijuan and Sanaa met in the middle of the battlefield. All around them lay bloody corpses of fallen soldiers. The healthy assisted the wounded. The dry sand was now a salvage yard of the dead and wounded—fallen weapons were everywhere and flags lay scattered on the ground. The two women were sweaty and dirty, and their wounds dripped blood and soaked their clothes. Without saying a word, they embraced and held one another tightly. Malik was brought up from the rear to join them, and he embraced Sanaa as if he would never let her go.

Too exhausted to celebrate, they didn't have to speak. Their eyes said it all.

They had done it.

They had defeated the mighty Caid and his army.

CHAPTER
— 26 —

CRASH

Foster Crowe packed his things and gave instructions for the circus to move to the Kerala province in India. Kerala was a sacred place and the circus would be protected by powerful forces. Amanda was already feeling much better since the departure of Wu Chiang. The color had returned to her cheeks and she was walking and smiling, jovial as ever.

However, upon hearing that Foster would be leaving them, Amanda's cheeks lost their color immediately.

"You're going after him, aren't you?" she asked.

"I have no choice. If I'm correct, he wants to plunge the world into a war that could cost tens of millions of innocent lives. I have to try to stop him," he explained, folding some clothes and remembering to pack his favorite hunting knife.

"That's all you're bringing? One little backpack?" she asked.

"I won't have time to check in and out of hotels. I'm hunting him, and I have to move faster than he does."

Amanda sat on the edge of his bed. The last few months had been so hard, but Foster's presence had kept up the morale of the circus. Now that he was leaving, what would happen to them?

"You can't bring anyone else?" she asked.

"No. The circus needs protecting right now and I don't want to spare anyone. Besides, a group is more conspicuous than just one man, and surprise will be a key advantage for me."

"Do you think you can kill him?" she asked.

Foster paused before answering.

"If I can find him, yes."

Amanda studied Foster and she could see the calmness in him, but she also sensed a bit of worry. She decided to change the subject.

"Why Kerala? Why not keep moving?"

"We need to be in a safe place and out of the spotlight. If I'm right, the world could quickly become a very dangerous place," he explained.

She nodded in agreement. She, more than anyone, understood that certain places in the world were safer than others. Kerala was, indeed, a place where the circus would be protected and would allow them time to reorganize and reenergize.

"Have you heard from Jack?" she asked.

"Not for months. Please leave him instructions in the usual manner regarding the circus's destination."

Amanda sighed and hung her head. Foster stopped what he was doing and put his hand on her shoulder.

"I know you miss Jack, and it's been years since you saw him. But I know he's alive. Just be patient," he explained, and then gently kissed her forehead.

Out of everyone in the circus, Amanda was the most sensitive and the most intuitive. She also knew that Jack was still alive; otherwise she would have felt his death. She understood that he had been diverted from his quest and was now on a different path. Where that path went, she did not know.

Two mornings later, Foster Crowe sat on the deck of *The Christina*—a cargo ship bound for Amsterdam, Holland. Resting his elbows on the steel railing, he watched as the city of Colombo faded in the distance and *The Christina* disappeared into the anonymity of the open ocean.

Foster knew Wu Chiang had something planned. Something very, very big, involving many different countries—some kind of world war. Millions of lives were at stake, and Foster was the only one capable of stopping him.

He knew he didn't have a lot of time.

He was alone now, hunting the most dangerous adversary he had ever encountered.

Inez woke up in the back of a moving truck. Her arms and ankles were bound behind her with a thick rope. A handkerchief had been tied around her mouth so she couldn't scream.

A throbbing pain pounded in her temples—she suddenly had an awful headache.

The truck rumbled beneath her, and its steel floor was cold and very uncomfortable. Her arms ached from being bound, and the ropes cut off her circulation.

At once, she felt very, very scared. Never in her life had she really been scared. She had always been the fearless one. Now, she found herself tied up and being transported to a completely unknown destination.

Nobody would know what happened to her. Nobody would know where to look for her.

She tried to scream, but the handkerchief made it impossible.

Inez was sure the man who had knocked her out had been a German. Was she being transported to Germany?

As the truck bounced along the rough road, Inez began to cry and miss her friends and her family.

She knew she was in serious danger. She knew the Germans thought her to be a spy and would probably throw her in prison. Or worse, she wondered, would they just kill her and leave her body on the side of the road or buried in a shallow grave in the forest?

Thinking of her mother, Inez missed her so painfully. She missed her school and even her brother. She thought of her mother's smile and the smell of lilac on her skin and even the scent of fresh flowers she placed in Inez's room each morning. Images flooded her mind of her friends at Saint Catherine's and the joy she had felt exploring the mountains and playing cricket or football with the other girls.

The truck continued down the road, rocks kicking out from under the tires. Inez listened to the engine hum and tried to picture her father's photograph in her head. She remembered how strong he had been. At that moment, she tried to imagine him beside her in that truck. Killed in an industrial accident when she was just ten years old, he had been the biggest influence on her life. He was the one who encouraged her to excel in sports when everyone else laughed at her because she was a girl. It was after her father died that she started getting into fights and rebelling against any kind of authority.

She hoped her father was looking down on her now, for she knew she was trapped and very alone—with men who wanted to kill her.

———————— ❧ ——————

The balloon edged higher and higher into the atmosphere until the land looked tiny and small beneath them. The ocean appeared omnipresent. Suddenly, everything below them was blue except for a few patches of white clouds.

Jack continued to check on the propane level. He feverishly calculated a strategy for what to do once the propane ran out. He figured their only hope was that the hot air in the balloon would last just long enough for them to descend to the ground. To slow down their descent, he would also need to try to glide on some wind pockets on the way down.

He had no idea if he could do it.

The boys had grown silent.

Everyone was scared.

There was nothing for them to do but to wait and see what happened. Going higher and higher into the sky was frightening, and eventually no one looked at the ground any longer. They sat in the basket, their backs against the side, paralyzed with fear.

Jack was their only hope.

Suddenly, the flame started to sputter and stall and eventually gave out altogether.

"This is it, boys! Stay down and hold on!" Jack yelled and all the boys held onto the basket with one hand and onto one another with the other. Everyone had a headache from the lack of oxygen and all were a bit sleepy. If the balloon had continued to rise, eventually they all would have passed out.

The balloon began to descend. Jack stood up and looked out, but there wasn't much for him to do. The balloon was completely unmanned.

It was very peaceful gliding through the air—the only sound was the wind against the sides of the balloon. Nobody spoke. They just listened and hoped and prayed.

Jack rocked the basket gently with his feet in an effort to guide the balloon in certain directions. It was a tumultuous task, as he didn't want to rock it too hard and lose control of it completely. He tried to spot pockets of air against clouds that might slow down their speed, as well as heat waves that signaled where the wind had completely stalled.

The balloon began to pick up speed and they all experienced the amazing sensation of falling. Tariq looked his two friends in the eyes and could see that they all were thinking the exact same thing.

We are going to die.

Tariq held Fez's hand and managed a small smile, but he couldn't bring himself to say any words. He had never been this scared in his life.

Not when he confronted Muhammad the street bully, who murdered his best friend, Aji.

Not when he was being beaten by Zahir.

Not when he had been tied to a camel and forced to race as his body screamed in agonizing pain.

The balloon continued to pick up speed and the basket continued to swing wildly back and forth. It passed through a thicket of clouds and seemed to pick up even more speed. Jack stood up, held on tightly, and stared at the horizon.

"Okay, boys, this is it. Hold on and brace yourselves!" he shouted, and the boys tried to hold on even tighter.

The balloon ripped through the air at a dizzying speed at a thirty-degree angle. It fell faster and faster until...

It hit hard, and everyone felt themselves being thrown from the basket. Suddenly, all four of them were underwater. White bubbles surrounded them all as they tossed under the surface. Tariq felt like he was a piece of wood being whipped through a raging river. He felt his head hit hard, and for the longest time he couldn't stop from going further underwater.

Finally, he stopped tossing, and from under the water, he looked to the sky. Tariq could see the faint outline of the balloon above. Streaks of sun edged through the sea and then eventually disappeared into darkness.

Frantically kicking his legs, Tariq swam as fast as he could up toward the surface, but began to feel a painful burning sensation in his lungs. He tried not to panic as his body cried out for a gulp of air.

Swimming upwards in huge strokes, he saw the surface slowly edge closer and closer and until, at last, he broke through, thrusting his mouth upwards and instantly taking in huge breaths of air and gasping. As his breathing slowed and he was able to gain his bearings, he saw that the basket was nearby, but turned on one side. The envelope of the balloon lay strewn across the sea.

He swam quickly to the basket, still stunned and disoriented by the crash.

Jack had grabbed the basket and was partly back on it, face down. Tariq could see blood coming from his side. As Tariq reached the basket Jack moaned. Tariq strained to roll Jack over, and as he lifted him, he saw that a huge piece of splintered wood had gone straight through Jack's rib cage.

"Jack, can you hear me?" Tariq screamed.

Jack seemed to wither before Tariq's eyes.

"Tariq, I fear this is the end," he muttered and Tariq stared at him with wanting, scared eyes.

"Don't say that, Jack. You'll be fine," he whispered.

"No, my artery has been severed. It's only a matter of time."

Tariq looked down and Jack's chest was a mess of blood.

"Tariq, there's something you must do," Jack told him.

"Anything, Jack."

"You must return Alexander the Great's diary to my circus. You must find Foster Crowe. I fear the world is coming into a very dark time. The diary has answers that may prevent millions of deaths."

Jack reached into his jacket and brought out the diary. It had been wrapped in both snake and crocodile skins to make it waterproof. He handed the diary to Tariq, who held it close to his body.

"Where do we find the circus?" Tariq asked.

"Go to Bangalore in India. Find an old mapmaker by the name of Abhijaat. He will know how to find the circus."

Tariq stared at his friend Jack as his breath grew short and his pupils changed. A small smile came across Jack's face as he went in and out of consciousness.

"Tariq, Aji says 'hello.' He says 'you've done well, but there is still much to accomplish.'"

Jack shuddered and coughed as life continued to drain out of his body. He looked at Tariq and smiled.

"Do not mourn my death; my true purpose was to protect you and the boys. Be bold in life and true to yourselves and to one another."

Tariq stared at Jack. He wanted to ask him how he knew Aji. He wanted to ask so many questions.

Then Jack went silent.

"Jack! Jack!" Tariq yelled, shaking his friend's body.

But Jack did not move.

In the distance, Tariq heard Aseem yelling.

"Tariq!"

Tariq glanced over and saw Fez and Aseem swimming towards him. Soon, they were next to him and Tariq helped them up to the basket.

"How is Jack?" Fez asked.

"I don't know. He was talking a minute ago, but now he doesn't say anything."

Fez put his fingers to Jack's neck to feel his carotid artery.

"He barely has a pulse."

"What do we do?" Aseem asked.

Fez looked at Jack as he lay unconscious, blood spilling out of him onto the basket.

"Help me pull the piece of wood out of him," Fez instructed.

Aseem and Tariq turned Jack's body over so that the fat end of the stick was pointing upward. Then, holding him down, Fez yanked the stick out in one quick motion.

Jack moaned and then went quiet.

Fez threw the bloody stick in the water, and Jack's skin appeared more and more pale. Fez frantically tried to stop the bleeding, but it was no use.

"I don't know what to do, Tariq," Fez said, sensing the futility of their situation.

The basket was still sideways and taking on water. They were surrounded by tangled ropes and material from the balloon.

Fez felt Jack's carotid artery once again.

"No pulse," he said.

Three times Tariq tried to revive him and three times Jack's body didn't move so much as an inch.

He stared down at his friend and watched as life left Jack's body. Only an empty shell remained.

Finally, after fifteen minutes, Tariq relented and said what everyone was thinking.

"We have to let him go," he whispered.

Fez and Aseem looked at Tariq, and they knew he was right.

"I don't know what to do, Tariq. We have to get this basket upright or we'll sink," Fez exclaimed softly.

Slowly, Tariq pushed Jack's body off of the basket and out to sea. Closing his eyes, he said a prayer that Zijuan had taught him and watched as Jack's body floated away from them.

It took twenty minutes, and a lot of effort, to right the basket so that the bottom was level with the sea. To make the craft a bit more seaworthy, they quickly covered the entire interior with material they had ripped from the balloon envelope. Then, they created a roof with more envelope material.

They had no food or water. But they did have a knife, some rope, and enough sail material to make some fishing nets.

Without water, they would be dead in a matter of days. Food they could do without, but water was a necessity.

Fez calculated they were perhaps thirty or forty miles from any piece of land and probably a great deal farther. The Mediterranean was an expansive sea and it was doubtful they would come upon a ship.

They needed a miracle.

The boys said little as they worked, and when they finished, all three stood up, their hands on the sides of the basket, and stared out at the open sea.

Nothing but miles and miles of ocean surrounded them and they could see absolutely nothing but water in every direction.

That night, they stared up at the stars as the basket bobbed up and down to the rhythmic current of the sea. Although the basket floated, water still seeped through, so they took turns bailing with a scoop they'd made out of Jack's hat. Tariq enjoyed bailing with the hat, as it reminded him of his friend, and it took his mind off their situation.

Early next morning, as the sun rose, something bumped into the side of the basket.

All three stood up, uncovered the tarp from the basket, and looked to see what was bumping against them.

To their horror, a giant dorsal fin cut through the water only five feet away. Below the surface, they saw an outline of a huge shark gliding through the water.

"Sharks," Fez said softly.

The boys continued to watch the shark as it circled them and occasionally bumped into the basket. After an hour, they forgot about it, covered up the basket, and returned to the shade of the interior.

They stayed there through the day as the sun baked overhead and the shark continued to circle and bump against the basket. Their arms grew tired from all of the bailing.

"I'm trying not to think about water—my tongue is like sandpaper," Aseem said softly.

Tariq felt the dryness of his own tongue. His thirst was unimaginable. He still had a headache and felt dizzy, but he tried to keep his focus on bailing. He couldn't get the image of Jack's dead eyes out of his mind. He couldn't sleep because all he dreamt of were the balloon crash and the final moments with Jack.

"I wonder what happened at the battle?" he asked, wanting to discuss anything but his thirst.

"I hope we won," Aseem replied quietly.

Neither boy had much energy for conversation. Although their shock was subsiding, the hunger in their stomachs and their terrible thirst drained what was left of their energy.

Through the night, they continued to bail, and still the shark circled them.

The next morning, the sun came up on the ocean and the shark continued to circle and bump the basket.

The sun weighed down on them unmercifully, and all three eventually found themselves sleeping in the basket, under cover, in the middle of the day. It was just too hot outside. The inside provided shade, but it was still very humid and hot under the cover. They all panted with thirst. Everyone was dizzy, and they would soon become delirious. The basket started to fill with water, and the boys were soon up to their waists in salt water.

They knew if they didn't get some fresh water soon, they would die.

They lasted through that day and night, but by the next morning, they were so weak they could barely stand. And still, they felt the shark bump against the basket.

Tariq slipped in and out of consciousness. At one point, he thought he felt himself float up in the air above the basket, only to be quickly brought back down—as if he were dying, but something was still tethering him to the earth.

He could barely keep his eyes open. He felt the ocean under his body, and it felt calm. Yet he inexplicably stood up and poked his head out of the basket—he suddenly couldn't remember where he was. Looking out over the horizon, life seemed so peaceful at that moment. All he could hear were the sounds of the sails flapping against the ocean water.

His eyes fluttered as he drifted in and out of consciousness. In his delirium, he thought he saw his friend Aji in the distance. He reached out and stretched his hand to touch his friend.

"Aji…" he whispered.

His body, completely limp, slipped over the edge of the basket and fell into the water. Even the chill of the sea couldn't bring him back from the brink of death.

Off in the distance, he barely saw it.

A dorsal fin!

The shark was heading straight for him. It circled and swerved beneath him and moved like a flash through the water.

Tariq's face bobbed in and out of the water. As the shark approached, Tariq could see its black eyes, devoid of all emotion. It was so enormous—maybe thirteen feet long—and it was moving so fast. In a flash, Tariq saw the shark open its mouth, its razor-sharp teeth heading straight for his neck.

He swore he saw his friend Aji holding onto the dorsal fin of the shark—as if the shark were pulling him through the water.

Then, everything went black.

Adventures continue in:

Thieves of the Black Sea

"Look you Cahusac; it's sick and tired I am of your perpetual whining and complaining when things are not as smooth as a convent dining table. If ye wanted things smooth and easy, ye shouldn't have taken to the sea, and ye should never ha' sailed with me, for with me things are never smooth and easy."

—Captain Peter Blood
Taken from a passage of Captain Blood
By Rafael Sabatini

ABOUT THE AUTHOR

The idea to write the *Red Hand Adventures* first came to Joe O'Neill while he was on safari in Sri Lanka. As he was driving along in an old jeep, under a full moon casting silhouettes of wild elephants against the jungle wall, the image of a rebel orphan in old Morocco popped into his head. While he wishes he could take full credit for coming up with the idea, it was, in reality, a story that was already out there, waiting to be told.

Joe O'Neill is the CEO and founder of Waquis Global, which has given him the opportunity for world travel and the experience of many different cultures.

JOIN THE RED HAND!

The Red Hand isn't just about reading books,
but also having a sense of adventure,
being curious about the world—where we've been,
and how we've gotten here.

It's about giving back to those less fortunate and
having a sense of justice in our everyday lives.

At Red Hand we are constantly holding writing contests;
trivia contests; sponsoring sports teams
(such as soccer and others);
teaching new adventure skills, and much, much more.

As a member of The Red Hand, you'll be privy to new books
and other cool stuff before their release to the general public.

To join The Red Hand, please go to
www.RedHandAdventures.com

CONGRATULATIONS TO THE RED HAND BRAVERY CONTEST WINNER!

As a strategy to promote young and aspiring writers, we at Red Hand Adventures hold monthly writing contests (and also periodically art, photography, and poetry contests). To launch author Joe O'Neill's second book, *Wrath of the Caid*, we held a contest on the concept of bravery. We promised these young writers that the winner would have his or her story included as part of the release of Joe's third book, *Legends of the Rif*.

Rebekah Hess, a sixth grader at Parkway Elementary in Ephrata, Washington, was our well-deserved winner.

Out of dozens of entries, we chose Rebekah's story because it had a great plot, was clever (try to find the references to *Hogan's Heroes*), and took place during World War Two (we always encourage young people to study history).

Visit our website at **www.redhandadventures.com** to learn more about our contests and to read more amazing stories submitted by our young readers.

BRAVERY

By Rebekah Hess
Parkway Elementary School
Ephrata, Washington

It all started when the Nazis came to Denmark. They spoke very poor Danish and couldn't care less about our families. I remember it all clearly. We (my family and I) had gone to my uncle's for a week.

"Ready???" Mama called. We took the express to the seashore where it stopped at a small village a couple miles from my Uncle Ryker's house.

"I wonder if he will be back yet?" inquired Kirsten, my sister.

"Soon he will be back I believe." Mama answered.

The house was unlocked as usual and Uncle Ryker had finally put a new coat of paint on it. Instead of being a white-yellow it was a happy cheery yellow like a sunflower.

"I shall make dinner soon, will you help me Lise?" Mama asked me.

"Sure what are we going to make?"

"Rye bread, mashed potatoes, and pork. Please wash the potatoes they look awfully dirty."

I set off peeling potatoes and washing. I wondered what my father was doing right then. He stayed home to not draw suspicions.

"I'm home," yelled Uncle Ryker. "Mmm what smells so good?"

"Rye bread," Kirsten proclaimed.

"How many did you take?" Mama asked, meaning how many Jews did he take to Sweden.

"Three families of four so that makes twelve."

"Did you use the powder for the baby rash?"

"Yes I did, it worked wonderful."

There was a powder I wasn't supposed to know about, that if you sprinkle just a little bit in someone's eyes, it made them blind. Uncle Ryker used it to blind the search dogs for a while, so they couldn't see. I once had watched it and the dog ran straight into the wall.

"Tomorrow I will need you to guide some families to my boat by the silk-road." The silk-road was a term used to describe a hidden path which led from the house to my Uncle's boat.

Even though he did own a boat, he employed a captain to steer it. His name was Captain Hogan. Both of them were part of a resistance group which helped Jews get across to Sweden. Captain Hogan escaped having to join the Nazis by becoming a captain. His former boss became a colonel and didn't appreciate Hogan leaving. Colonel Clink now patrolled the docks because of him. Watching to make sure Hogan didn't mess up.

The next morning when I awoke, Mama had already left and Kirsten was still sleeping. Uncle Ryker was preparing the hiding spot for the Jews to come. When I stepped out the door I saw a small package and realized it was the powder that makes the dogs go blind. I knew I had to think fast. The powder resembled sugar. I put it in a basket with some cream and herbs. If anyone asked, I was bringing tea to my uncle because he was going on a long voyage.

I set off down the path which led toward the sea. It was scary without Mama. You couldn't see the sky because of all the trees. There was a bend coming up, and I heard someone coming and froze in my tracks. The hair on the back of my neck stood as I wondered if this was the last of Lise Elizabeth Tenmark. Around the corner the person came, but instead of wearing a green uniform and black shiny boots, I saw a dress and a young girl a couple of years older than me step around the bend.

"Oh, hello Lise. Where are you going?" It was Sarah Ferris who had moved from the USA a couple of years ago.

"Hello, I'm going to my uncle's boat. Have a good day."

"You too."

With that we set off on our opposite ways. After a while I came to a lovely meadow which I recognized and stopped and said a quick hello to Schultz the horse. As I rounded the bend I realized I was back in the deep undergrowth. I also knew I was almost there. As I was about to turn yet another bend in the path I heard heavy foot falls of soldiers.

"Where are you going little girl?" a rough voice asked.

"To give my uncle his tea, cream, and sugar for his long voyage," I answered innocently.

"Let me see the basket."

With that, the older of the two soldiers grabbed by basket. I was terrified.

"Very well, I'll see you on your way."

As quickly as they showed up, the soldiers left. I relaxed and kept going. I finally spotted the ocean, and there was my uncle's boat. Its name was Willow Tree because my uncle's late wife's name had been Willa.

"Uncle Ryker, Uncle Ryker! I have some sugar for you. You forgot your tea and cream as well."

"Thank you ever so much! We would not have made it without these," he said with a chuckle.

On the way back to the house I decided to take the road with more people to blend into. As I was walking, another soldier stopped me. This time I had pretended to be an empty-headed girl.

"Where are you going?" asked a sharp German voice.

As I started to cry I said "Home to help my mama who was laying in bed sick, please let me go!" I had wailed.

"I see you're not carrying any medicine with you, why not?"

I had to think fast!

"I went to my papa and he had no money. Neither did my mama. You see we have no money for medicine," I wailed harder.

"Alright, scat and I don't want to see you again."

With that I left as quickly as possible. Two encounters with soldiers in one day! *"That was horrifying,"* I thought on my way.

Then I saw a group of people crowding around my uncle's house! As I ran toward his house a woman cried out, "Oh that poor man!"

As I drew closer I had heard everyone talking about my poor Great Uncle Maks. I remembered every story Mama had told me about her family and I was positively sure there was not a Great Uncle Maks.

By then I had found my uncle and asked him what was going on.

"In order to get the Jews across, we had to cause a distraction. We pretended that my uncle died. The casket is full of bricks."

"Ryker, time to remove the casket, my cousin Peter called.

A couple of days later my family went home. We kept hearing from Uncle Ryker and his son Peter until they passed away. They had helped many Jews escape across to Sweden. Happily they both died of old age. I now live in the house by the sea. It is still yellow also. The war started when I was eleven and it ended when I was seventeen. I will always remember those nasty German soldiers and their dogs. I will also remember the people in resistance and their bravery. Lights out!

(The End)

BRAVERY: What bravery means to me is that you are going out of your way to help someone else. It often happens in dangerous situations. Bravery also happens a lot when you don't know everything. Without bravery, this world would be in pieces. Life would be horrible! That's why bravery is important.